MISTER
LULLABY

Also available by J. H. Markert

The Nightmare Man

Writing as James Markert

The Strange Case of Isaac Crawley
Midnight at the Tuscany Hotel
What Blooms from Dust
All Things Bright and Strange
The Angels' Share
A White Wind Blew

MISTER
LULLABY

A NOVEL

J. H. MARKERT

CROOKED
LANE

NEW YORK

Copyright © 2023 by James Markert

Published in the United States by Crooked Lane Books, an imprint of The Quick Brown Fox & Company LLC.

Crooked Lane Books and its logo are trademarks of The Quick Brown Fox & Company LLC.

Library of Congress Catalog-in-Publication data available upon request.

ISBN (hardcover): 978-1-63910-547-2
ISBN (special edition paperback): 978-1-63910-802-2
ISBN (trade paperback): 978-1-63910-881-7
ISBN (ebook): 978-1-63910-548-9

Cover design by Heather VenHuizen

Printed in the United States.

www.crookedlanebooks.com

Crooked Lane Books
34 West 27th St., 10th Floor
New York, NY 10001

First Edition: November 2023

10 9 8 7 6 5 4 3 2 1

Lalaland:
a euphoric mental state detached from the harsher realities of life

Lullaby:
a song or folk poem meant to help a child fall asleep

Mare:
in Germanic folklore, a malicious creature that sits on people's chests while they sleep, causing nightmares

THE MOST PECULIAR *thing about Happy Jack's murder wasn't that we never found his legs, but rather that he was somehow still smiling when we entered the train tunnel and stumbled upon his torso.*

1

Beth

Now

DEPUTY SHERIFF BETH Gardner had only been on the job for two weeks when Simple Simon walked inside the station with a chainsaw.

Although her boss, Sheriff Grover Meeks, had told her days before that Simon had named his chainsaw *The Ripper*, Beth didn't know he'd gone as far as writing it with a black Sharpie on blue painter's tape on the chainsaw's handle. What caught her most off guard, other than how his massive, broad-shouldered frame filled up the sunlit doorway, was the fact that he'd spelled it correctly.

Beth stood from her desk when Simon took his second step into the room.

"Stop right there, Simon."

He halted as if he was in the middle of a game of freeze tag.

Simon was no monster. Just slow-brained and odd, a thirty-something orphan who'd been wreaking havoc on Harrod's Reach's acres of forestry since he was old enough to hold a chainsaw.

The Ripper's blade looked mucked up with wood chips and tree sap and Lord knew what else.

No blood, at least, thought Beth, as she took a cautious step forward.

Like most folks who lived in the woods around Harrod's Lake, Simon entered the Reach's Historic District when necessary, but to her knowledge he'd never entered the Sheriff's Department on his own. Sheriff Meeks had brought him in numerous times for felling the wrong neighbor's trees or cutting those on government property, never keeping him for more than a couple of hours, but this, thought Beth, was unnatural. And as much as Sheriff Meeks had taught her to stay calm when greeted by the unnatural, her heart let loose like a flutter of birds scattered by gunshot.

"What can we do for you, Simon?"

It was a warm fall day, easily eighty degrees outside, and Simon was dressed in saggy jeans and checkered flannel. She could smell his body odor from ten feet away. His brown hair was unruly, as was his beard, which seemed sleep-matted on the left side. Simon raised his right arm, and in his hand was a sheet of white copy machine paper.

"What do you have there?" asked Beth.

Simon nodded, his way of saying: *Just look. Take it.* He could talk— Beth had heard him more than once over the years, that muffled grumble so many in town liked to imitate, like Billy Bob Thornton in the movie *Sling Blade*—but he preferred not to, especially in a crowd.

Simon's best form of communication was with pictures, and the man had some talent. Whether God-given or developed out of necessity, Beth didn't know, but she could tell, even from the distance that separated them now, that what he'd drawn on this page was heavily detailed, and the ink took up most of the paper.

Beth stepped closer, took it from his big-knuckled hand, and after another glance at The Ripper's soiled chainsaw blade to make sure there were no human remnants, she focused on the drawing, realizing immediately that something was badly wrong in Harrod's Reach.

Simon had sketched two fully clothed bodies in the woods, both on their backs, one a man, the other a woman. The old train tunnel loomed in the background. From the paper she couldn't tell which side of the tunnel Simon had drawn—the north or south entrance—but the two bodies left nothing to question.

They were dead.

Side by side and holding hands, but dead. And apparently brutally murdered.

"You find these bodies, Simon?" she asked. He nodded, kept his gaze on his scuffed brown boots, the laces on the left one untied and wet. No telling what he'd tracked through to get here. "Did you touch them, Simon? The bodies?"

Simon shook his head, chewed on a fingernail. She looked at the picture again.

Amid the trees and deadfall, a man lay on his back, his severed head resting on his stomach like a volleyball, held there by his carefully positioned right hand. His left hand was extended out toward the woman beside him, clutching hers.

And the woman . . .

Beth looked up. "That a horseshoe? Simon?"

Simon kept his gaze toward the floor, nodded, and then grumble-spoke for the first time since entering, "Yes, ma'am."

2

Gideon

Now

GIDEON DUPREE DIDN'T feel like a hero.

So upon his return to Harrod's Reach, after over three years blowing desert dust from his nostrils and now limping home like a wounded dog, he didn't want a hero's welcome.

He'd told his mother as much when he'd phoned from overseas weeks ago, alerting her to his early discharge from the Army. An honorable discharge with a Purple Heart. He'd accepted the award graciously, shook the hands that needed to be shaken, made his final salutes to the brass who'd put up with him day to day, and then stuffed his life since the day after he turned eighteen into the same camouflaged deployment duffel they'd given him on day one.

The Purple Heart he'd stored in a plastic baggie, along with the bullet that nearly severed his right leg a month ago during the raid in Nangarhar. The same bullet he'd considered placing on the pretty airline attendant's counter after arriving at LaGuardia and telling her that was his real ticket home. But Gideon just thanked her and moved on, which was more his nature.

Stumbling through life hoping nobody would recognize his place in it.

Gideon had called his mother from the airport to let her know he'd landed, and that he'd Uber home. He should have known something was up when Maxine Dupree insisted on calling the Uber herself. *So that I can pay for it*, she'd told him. Before ending the call, he'd made the mistake of asking how Sully was doing. She'd said fine, but with enough hesitation to make him wonder if his now eight-year-old brother wasn't *fine*. Maxine then said softly to be careful. And then, *You've heard about the murders?*

No, Mom, what murders?

At the tunnel . . . the walls . . .

The walls? Mom, what about the walls?

Just be careful, Gideon.

He thought about the tunnel the entire ride from the airport. The train tunnel around which everything in this old railway town revolved, the place where his little brother had nearly lost his life. Gideon remembered giving the tunnel the middle finger after watching the final brick go in three years prior, closing that horrific stone-and-moss hole on either end of One-Side Mountain in the days before his deployment.

The Uber driver had *not* dropped him home, casually pulling into St. Michael's empty parking lot instead of the tree-lined driveway of his youth. Same one he and Sully used to skid across on their bikes, cleaving ridges in the gravel with their tires. The Uber driver glanced in the rearview and apologized. "She said no matter what to drop you here."

Gideon eyed the gymnasium doors. Knew it was full inside, even though the parking lot was empty. Harrod's Reach was a walking town, laid out in a grid of squares and gardens and courtyards many said resembled those in the more popular city of Savannah, Georgia. He said to the driver, "You can't be bribed?"

"No, sir. And thank you for your service."

Gideon swung his bad leg out of the car and gripped the heavy duffel.

The driver reached over the seat, helped push the bag along. "She said you're a hero. Purple Heart and everything."

Gideon kindly told him not to believe everything he heard, thanked him, and closed the car door. He stood for a moment, contemplating the walk home, limping a mile with that bag, and decided a little time inside the gym wouldn't kill him.

Heroes don't turn tail and run.

Father Fred's fat dog Max barked from the rectory shadows. Candlelight flickered through the church's stained-glass windows. The brick school looked smaller than he remembered, as did the gym, as did the freshly painted four-square box next to the courtyard and the bases on the kickball field. All of it made him think of skinned knees and recess, dress codes and made-up confessions. Sister Mary Pat snorting and asking *Who's the funny guy* whenever they'd cut up in the lunch line. Not really Gideon, because he never cut up, but he always seemed to be sidled up next to those kids who did.

Heroes don't hesitate.

Beth was probably in there. Jax, too.

His dad and mom, Archibald and Maxine Dupree, waiting for the Prodigal Son to return.

Gideon opened the gym door and limped into the eerily quiet dark. Somebody sneezed. Somebody giggled. Somebody shushed them, right before the lights clicked on and everyone yelled *Surprise!*

Gideon yanked out his SIG Sauer P320, pointing it at the first person he saw.

3

Beth

Now

BETH THOUGHT THE surprise party for Gideon was a bad idea when Maxine Dupree hinted at it two weeks ago, and she thought it was a bad idea now, clustered with ninety percent of the town inside St. Michael's stuffy gymnasium, awaiting Gideon's arrival.

Beth had hinted back at Gideon's mother that she didn't know if Gideon would like such a thing, but how do you say no to a mother who hasn't seen her oldest son in three years?

Gideon didn't like surprises.

Growing up, he could hardly tolerate loud noises. During middle school, he'd jump every time Father Fred's dog barked. He'd flinch every time the church bell chimed. Every Fourth of July he'd watched the fireworks from *inside* the Smite House by himself, while his little brother Sully, as a toddler, was out there with their father, Archie, not only enjoying the sizzles and pops of the fireworks but wanting to light them.

Such opposites, those two. So, no, Beth didn't think the surprise party was smart. No matter if Gideon was twenty-one now and apparently coming home with a Purple Heart.

Everyone had hushed when the lights clicked off inside the gym. That was the cue that Gideon's Uber driver had entered Harrod's Reach proper, which was what the locals liked to call it when anyone turned onto Guthrie Street from the highway.

Beth held her two-year-old son, Brody, on her hip. As soon as the lights went off, he started playing with the deputy badge she'd pinned to her off-duty clothes. Like her boss, Sheriff Grover Meeks, she was always on duty. True, she was only a few weeks into the job, and some said that adrenaline and passion would fade over time, but Beth didn't think so.

Not when you were born to do what you were doing. Born to wear a badge.

Brody said, "It's dark."

"Yes, it is."

"Why?"

"Because we're about to surprise Gideon when he gets here."

"Who's Gideon?"

"He's a friend from childhood."

"What's he look like?"

A big nerd, thought Beth. "You'll find out in a minute."

"Daddy said he's your twin."

"Daddy makes jokes, And you're terrible at whispering," she told Brody, and a few locals around them laughed. "But we do share a birthday," Beth whispered back. "Gideon and I were born the same night. Lived right down the street from one another most our lives."

"But is he really your twin?"

"No," she said. "Enough with the questions."

Brody fondled her badge. He didn't like the dark. He slept with two night-lights.

Beth broke surprise-party protocol and removed her phone from her back pocket. The light from the screen appeased Brody for the moment. "I promise I'll turn it off when I hear the door open," she whispered to whoever was standing around her.

Some woman said, "It's no bother, Beth. You do what you need to do."

She'd always been respected around town, but the respect had increased tenfold once she'd been sworn in. This surprise party was one thing, but gathering most of the town inside one building only two days after having discovered two mysterious dead bodies outside the tunnel? That she really didn't like, especially so soon after the bricks had collapsed at the tunnel. But the bodies . . . she'd been able to think of little else since she and Sheriff Meeks had located them, roughly an hour after Simple Simon had arrived inside the station with the picture he'd drawn of both bodies, exactly how they'd found them.

Beth turned her back away from people and scrolled her phone. She'd been looking for newspaper articles all day. Googling for hours, hoping to find something to help what had happened down by the tunnel make sense.

Brody made a move for the phone, but Beth was ready for it. "Wait, babe, Mommy's working." Beth reread what she'd skimmed earlier. With what little they had to go on with the two bodies—no identification, and probably not from Harrod's Reach—Beth had hunted for similar MOs. And while she'd yet to find anything that resembled the beheading of the male victim, the article she'd just found on her phone dated two months ago from Charleston, South Carolina, strongly aligned with the little they had on the female victim: evidence of rape, strangulation, blunt force trauma to head and face, and a bloody horseshoe left at the scene. In this case, the horseshoe—the weapon used for the blunt-force trauma—had been left atop the victim's chest.

"Bingo," Beth said softly.

Brody reached for the phone. "Bingo."

"Almost done."

Beth stopped on a headline that read: *The Strangler's Latest Victim Survives, but in Coma!* And in smaller print: *Fights for Her Life in Local Hospital.* She got far enough to see the survivor's name, Maddy Boyle, twenty-two, and that she was a senior at the College of Charleston, double majoring in English and creative writing, when someone in the gym whisper-shouted, "He's coming."

Beth shut off her phone and pocketed it.

The gym hushed with anticipation, which Beth still thought weird, seeing as how so many in town still snickered about Gideon and blamed him for his little brother Sully's accident. Now here they were preparing to celebrate his return.

Hypocrisy at its finest, thought Beth, the town itself so eager to gather and drink that they had no problem overlooking it all.

"Where's Daddy?" Brody asked.

"He's with Sully," said Beth.

The gym door opened; moonlight shone through double doors.

Gideon walked in.

The lights flipped on. Everyone shouted *Surprise!*

When Gideon pulled a gun, Beth had no choice but to pull hers.

4

Doc

Now

THE NEWLY POSTED sign outside the tunnel said: *DANGER! KEEP OUT!*

Dr. Travers Bigsby ignored it. Just as he had last night and the night before, when he'd gone on similar journeys through the woods, down the ravine, and into the overgrown channel where trains once held sway like kings over Harrod's Reach. A gully, one might think, if viewed from above, forged by locomotives from a bygone era, now green and lush and overgrown with grass and weeds and saplings and moisture.

Doc Bigsby shone the flashlight beam across the yards of rubble separating him from the tunnel's black-hole entrance. The air inside the tunnel smelled like rot, like what was in there had been bottled up for too long, and was in need of airing out. The stench hit like a wall from no less than thirty yards away.

But this was where he wanted to be. *Needed* to be, as he explained to his wife, Jane, who was currently at the surprise party where all those hypocrites were due to celebrate the same boy they'd shunned until his departure three years ago.

But good for you, Gideon Dupree, stick it to them.

Doc eyed the tunnel.

The tunnel that never should have been bricked up in the first place. Plugged by mortared bricks on both ends like corks in a wine bottle. Even though the tragedy with Sully Dupree had made him briefly waver in his opinions on the tunnel, Travers had been one of only a few in town *against* bricking it up. For two decades he'd argued every year the notion came up in front of the city council. Ultimately, he'd lost. What happened to Sully in the tunnel, a town favorite if there ever was one, had been the last straw. The bricks had gone up before Gideon was deployed, sealing it up like a damn time capsule.

The walls lasted three years before collapsing. The north wall, two weeks ago, during the minor earthquake that shook the Reach and all the bordering towns around it for three to four seconds. And just as Travers predicted, the south wall soon followed, toppling four nights ago at 12:45 in the morning. Doc had only returned from the tunnel an hour before it collapsed. He'd been there listening, his stethoscope pressed up to the bricks as if searching for a heartbeat on the other side of that wall.

It was the wind he was listening for, in a sense—the *tunnel's* heartbeat.

Once that north end crumbled, the inside of that tunnel *had* started beating again. The crumbled bricks on the far end made navigating not only dangerous but damn near impossible. Chimp Deavers and his fireman had tried on day one, and had gotten close to the top when the bricks below them started shifting. Made the decision to let the bricks settle before trying again.

Doc knew it was only a matter of time before the south entrance came down, especially with how the wind was swooping down the gully and into the gaping wound in that north-wall entrance, pushing like a thousand hands of pressure on the inside of the south wall. That's why the south wall had ultimately crumbled outward, *away* from the tunnel, like a giant had kicked it from the inside. It's also why Jane had been so cross with him, holding his stethoscope up to that wall, sometimes taking his lunches down there, listening—*for what?* the townsfolk whispered behind his back. *For the heartbeat*, he'd tell no one but himself. Jane feared the wall was going to fall *on* him, and it damn near did, missing him by an hour.

And here he was back at it, his third night in a row. He'd made some headway on that north side, clearing away bricks from inside the tunnel, one wheelbarrow at a time. For some reason a clogged tunnel seemed worse than a completely blocked one, so he was determined to chip away. To get it back to the way it was.

Travers aimed his flashlight beam over the rubble and started over the fallen bricks. He'd left his wheelbarrow and lanterns and shovels in there last night, doubting anyone would be daring enough to take them.

Unlike Doc, most in town abided by the warning sign.

Most still feared the tunnel.

Especially after what was found in the woods no more than twenty paces from the crumbled north entrance two nights ago by Simon Bowles, who everyone in town called Simple Simon. In Doc's mind, although Simon was mentally slow, there was nothing simple about him, and Doc still claimed his emergence into the world to be the most unusual delivery he'd ever performed. But the two mutilated bodies, according to the *Harrod's Reach Gazette*, had been found two feet apart, presumably dumped there, which to Doc meant they'd been killed elsewhere. All other details of the two murders had been hushed so quickly by the Sheriff's Department that ninety percent of the article had been speculation.

Doc promised Deputy Sheriff Beth he'd steer clear of that taped-off crime scene. It was outside the north end anyway, and he was coming in through the south.

Mist hovered through the hazy flashlight beam. Fog swirled in tendrils from the cracks and crevices made by the fallen bricks, as if something smoldered underneath the rubble, hissing like fumaroles. Mist and morning dew. The bricks glistened with it.

He took care where he stepped. The bricks began to level out and his pace quickened. So did his heartbeat. And the breeze.

Inside the tunnel, the temperature dropped, like it always had, not plummeting but just enough to conjure chill bumps and crystallize breath. Nights were always cooler in Harrod's Reach, cooler than every town that bordered it. Some said it was the constant breeze swirling over the dips and hollows of so much forest. The morning mist over Harrod's Lake, pushed out as fog by the weeping willows that surrounded it. Most, though—Doc included—knew it was the old train tunnel acting like an open-air freezer.

Like entering a cave.

History seeped in. Every water-drip echo from the ceiling came down in a plop of lore, an echo of legend.

Doc grinned. You were either afraid of the tunnel or you were consumed by it.

And age didn't matter. Just ask Sully Dupree. *His* infatuation with the tunnel had nearly killed him.

Many had fainted inside the tunnel. Kids ran through on dares, swearing this and that about what was felt and smelled and seen inside the belly of it, long enough for three school buses end-to-end, tall enough for screams to echo. And don't get the locals started on all the murders over the century and half of its existence—the missing body parts, the missing *bodies*. The old train tunnel ushered in air as if *that* had been its purpose—a giant lichen and moss, limestone breezeway—and not the railway Colonel Harrod Guthrie had envisioned the instant he'd stumbled upon it back in the winter of 1865, laying train track no less than two months later, calling it a bona fide railway town three months after that.

What made a railway town a railway town?

Train tracks and brothels, the joke went.

Not much of a joke, Doc thought.

Especially now that the once-thriving rail line was extinct. No train had gone through that tunnel since the disaster of 1923, when those railcars had come from Luxitoni like bats out of hell, derailing on the hug of One-Side Mountain, in the pitch black of that tunnel, killing every one of the thirty-three passengers on board. All they found of one man was his shoes, with both feet still in them. The bodies, they'd buried at White Wall Cemetery. The engine, which was said to smolder for six days no matter how much water they sprayed on that charred skeletal heap, stayed on that track like roadkill for weeks, months, and finally years, before it was eventually plucked clean by townsfolk and tourists eager for keepsakes. The rest of that abandoned, damaged train grew into the ground, or, as some would tell it, the ground grew up into *it*—that patch of track where the engine and railcars once rested like ancient monoliths was now nothing but weeds and brambles and saplings matured into trees. The track itself was gone for miles on either side of the tunnel's openings, the last vestiges plucked and peeled from the ground by the 1950s. Every Harrod's Reach resident had remnants somewhere in their home, garage, storefront, restaurant, or bar—plates and switches, ballasts and joint-bars, fasteners, welds, and fish plates—resting on mantels like works of art, relics from lost times. Sleepers nailed above porches and front doors for good luck. Sleepers refinished and stained and forged into coffee tables and rocking chairs and tree houses and benches. Sleepers placed into the ground as sidewalks and uneven courtyards.

Doc filled the first wheelbarrow, pushed it out the south entrance, dumped it into the grass on the upslope of the gully, and went in for more.

He heard a skittering around his feet, looked down, and saw a dried white leaf the length of a corncob and the width of a splayed-out hand, pushed in by the wind. He stopped it with his boot, held it up to the lantern light.

"I'll be damned." *Same as the others.* He stored it in his satchel. He'd take it home to examine it more closely under the microscope. Pin it on the wall next to the others he'd found over the decades. Not just the leaves—which made no earthly sense being as white and red-veined as they were—but the oddly colored frog he'd found dead, the squirrel that wasn't a squirrel (also dead), the weird seashell he'd found two days prior mixed in with all the dust from the brick rubble, even though Harrod's Reach was as far away from an ocean as a town can get.

Twenty minutes later, engulfed in sweat, Doc reloaded the wheelbarrow for the fourth time, and upon stacking that last brick, heard a rustling noise coming from the bricks at the fallen north wall. With each load removed over the past three nights, the entrance had grown larger, more open to the winds, to the sounds of the woods on either end.

None of those sounds had made him jumpy.

This one did.

He heard footsteps behind him, turned toward them, saw nothing but disturbed brick dust in the haze of the three lanterns he'd hung.

One of the lanterns went out.

More footsteps. This time from the shadows.

He gripped the shovel like a weapon. "Who's there?"

"Doc," said a young boy's voice, followed by a flash of light, and the slow whooping sound a windmill blade might make on a downturn.

Doc Bigsby stepped toward the voice. "Sully?" *This can't be possible.* "Sully Dupree? Is that you?"

It just can't . . .

But somehow it was, and the voice said, "Run."

5

Theodore

Before

TEDDY LOMAX ENTERED the lobby of the rural Kansas hospital much like he'd done the night before when he'd cased the place out—with a strut so self-assured it might one day be the detail to break him.

But not today.

Too much to do and too little time to do it, said the voice he liked to think belonged to his daddy. Voice so deeply rooted into his bone marrow it liked to make his entire ribcage thrum.

Unlike the night before, when he'd strolled through the automatic double doors with a trimmed beard, wearing a pink golf shirt, khaki shorts, and blue loafers—like he was casually visiting a loved one—he now wore the gray-blue uniform of the hospital's janitor, and his face was freshly shaved. The body of the janitor the uniform belonged to was in the woods behind the hospital's parking lot.

Collateral damage, Mother, Teddy had thought last night as he'd wiped blood off the knife blade and covered the corpse with leaves and deadfall. Smiling at how easy it had been. Nodding to this nurse and that orderly, both probably wondering when the new janitor had started, the new janitor—if they'd only looked close enough—who wore the same name as the old, threaded into the shirt's front left pocket in red letters.

Travis Beam.

Mother would have crossed herself and said *God rest that man's soul, Theodore*, and Teddy—never fucking Theodore, not anymore—would have laughed it off because God was fake juice and Mother was crazy as a loon.

Either way, killing Travis Beam had given him a boost of adrenaline that had lasted all through the night and into the morning, and remained with him still. Like a truckload of caffeine coursing through his veins. Because as much as you don't like it, Mother, this car runs on hurt. This car runs on pain and my tank has no limit.

The beard he'd shaved out of necessity. When it was grown out, Teddy had a round patch of white hair the size of a golf ball in the black hairs of his left cheek. Mother thought it was just another sign he'd been marked, and then she'd go pray on it, begging him to shave, and sometimes, depending on his mood, he would. The spot in his beard was distinguishing, yes, and an immediate talking point for the ladies he'd pick up at bars, but way too noticeable on a mission where he was trying *not* to be noticed.

Teddy smiled, flashing his pearly whites as he moved past the cute redheaded young woman at the front desk—different than the eye candy who'd smiled at him last night—this one's eyes following him just as that one had, though, all the way until he disappeared around the corner and into the main hallway, where he ducked inside the janitor's slop sink closet and came out with a mop bucket on wheels. Nobody noticing the name on his shirt because they were too busy noticing *him*. Six foot three and well muscled. Head full of wavy black hair with no sign of thinning or premature gray. Skin tanned to near bronze. Face sculpted, cheeks dimpled when he smiled. Blue eyes very few women had been able to resist throughout his twenty-seven years on earth. Had he the time and notion, he felt certain he could have picked up the redhead at the front desk. By the looks of the naked ring finger, this one was single.

Not that it mattered. If he wanted her, he'd have her. If there was one truth in this world, it was that Teddy Lomax now knew his place in it, and he always got his way.

It hadn't always been that way, but it was that way now, and had been ever since he'd laid Chuck Toomer out with a right jab to the nose in the spring of his eighth grade year and first felt the surge of tingle and static across his scalp as soon as he'd done it, only to feel it even more profoundly when he'd noticed the blood on Toomer's lips and the fear in the boy's eyes. The first evidence his car ran on pain. First of too many to count, as it would turn out, and Toomer, whose bloody nose looked all kinds of bright red, never called him Rudolph again.

None of them did.

Teddy used that memory as extra fuel and eyed room 188 at the end of the hall, where Beverly Madrich currently resided. She'd been a vegetable for three weeks now. A true, bona fide dead-head. A tow-truck driver named Butch Clee was currently behind bars for putting her there, driving drunk when he ran a red light and T-boned her into the next county. Butch was no doubt praying Beverly Madrich would soon wake up from her coma and breathe on her own. Maybe even walk and talk and get his charges changed from attempted manslaughter to something less likely to put him away for life.

Sorry, Butch, thought Teddy, as he wheeled the mop bucket down the hallway.

Teddy checked to make sure the coast was clear and entered Beverly Madrich's room, bucket in tow, and there she was, nearly dead on a bed that seemed to swallow her shriveling body, hooked up to machines by tubes and wires and IVs and sounds that made Teddy want to hit her. A month ago, she'd been a hotshot lawyer, rising up the ranks of a law firm toward future partnership.

So said the newspapers. So said the voice on the other end of that damn light blue seashell he'd found in his mother's underwear drawer months ago. What he had at first thought was some kind of vibrator, which would have been something considering how much of a nun-like prude his mother was. But that's also how come he'd known it was special, *because* it had been so out of place, hidden next to her granny panties and tube socks. He'd felt the electric current from it as soon as he lifted it from the drawer. Like it had the ability to be alive, or maybe once had been, this light blue seashell the size of a softball. It only made sense to hold it up to his ear, figuring, if he was lucky, to get a hint of ocean in there. That he got, but for that fucking thing to act like a phone line and talk to him? Not only that, but for the voice—THE voice—on the other end of it, telling him to pay attention because he had an important job to do, to finish his whiskey and get a pen and start writing down the names that needed to be written down.

Now *that* had nearly been too much to process.

The list had started with thirty-seven names, all dead-heads like Beverly Madrich.

Teddy had struck a match and burned the list in the bathroom sink soon after writing it down, because that's what spies in spy movies did, and also because he had a mind like a vault. Still knew every name, in order, and even added to it whenever the seashell called to him, not so much a ring like a phone might make but a distinct enough whistle for him to imagine it was one.

To this day he was amazed the voice had known he'd been drinking whiskey on the night of that first call, but hey, the voice was never wrong.

You get that, Mother? The voice is real. I'm not sick. I'm not marked. I'm not hearing things. Not seeing things. Not schizophrenic.

And don't fucking call me Theodore.

Teddy sighed, stared down at Beverly Madrich's pathetic form atop those sheets and knew it wouldn't take much to finish her off. Never took much to finish off any of the dead-heads. He'd been Dr. Lomax in Tennessee and New Mexico and Nevada. Nurse Lomax in Mississippi and Georgia and up north in Vermont and Michigan. Orderly Lomax in Kentucky and Virginia. And for those at-home hospice dead-heads, he'd run the gauntlet from nurse Lomax to plumber Lomax to last rites priest Father Lomax.

Anything to get him in.

And now, here in Nowhere, Kansas—just as in Montana and one of the Dakotas—he was Janitor Lomax.

He told Beverly to close her eyes. When she didn't even acknowledge his presence in the room, he whispered, "Enough is enough, Beverly," and closed them for her.

Five minutes later, about the same time the hospital nurses were realizing Beverly Madrich had breathed her last breath, Teddy drove down a country road toward the highway, thumbing the steering wheel in beat to Janis Joplin's "Me and Bobby McGee," heading north toward Iowa in a car he'd stolen three days ago in Arkansas, cruising toward the next name on his list, a teenage boy in a two-month coma after taking a hard-hit baseball off the left temple.

So said the newspapers.

So said the voice.

Teddy eyed the seashell on the otherwise empty passenger's seat.

Out on the road, he knew he couldn't take the chance of it wind-whistling at him and him not being home to answer it, especially now that Mother was useless and immobile.

He laughed as he drove, grinned as he listened to the music.

Imagined his mother asking, *What's so funny, Theodore?*

Him saying, *Nothing*, but deep down knowing the stars must be aligned, that next dead-head boy's name being Bobby McFee.

He sang along with Janis, but instead sang, "Me and Bobby McFee."

Not exact, he thought with a playful punch to the steering wheel.

But just close enough.

6

Gideon

Now

GIDEON DIDN'T KNOW how he'd react upon entering St. Michael's gym, but he hadn't foreseen dropping his duffel inside the doors of his alma mater and pulling his gun like he'd entered the O.K. Corral.

The crowded gym warped into a void of slow-motion words and soundless screams. Gideon's finger shook on the trigger. Mayor Truffant froze like a deer in headlights, dropped his cup of beer in an explosion of foam across the hardwood, and jutted his hands up like it was a robbery.

Father Fred, at the concessions, placed his cup of red wine on the counter, crossed himself, and took a hesitant step forward.

"Gideon, no!" His mother's voice, somewhere in the crowd.

Father Fred's eyes were red. Three sheets to the wind and on his way to four.

Lower your goddamn weapon, soldier. Gideon blinked, hard. *Or pull the fucking trigger. You're a cowardly piece of dog shit, Dupree.*

"Gideon, lower the weapon." Maxine Dupree entered his line of sight.

He glanced at his mother—when did she start wearing lipstick and tight jeans?—but kept his focus on Father Fred, who seemed prepared to take one for the team.

Just like Bobby Swain had done in Kandahar, right before the US-made land mine, left over from the mujahedin fighters in the 1980s, scattered him ten different ways.

The crowd in the middle of the gym rustled outward toward the basketball court's sidelines, creating a path to the far goal, the rim festooned with purple and gold balloons, to where Beth Gardner had just passed a curly-haired toddler from her slender hip to Justine Baker.

Beth approached, her Glock 22 poised on him. She crossed the half-court circle, the crowd parting like she was Moses and they were the Red Sea. Her sheriff's badge loomed large on her blue button-down, half tucked into sleek black jeans. "Gideon," Beth said, ten paces away now. "Put the gun down."

"So you're a sheriff now," said Gideon. *Skipped college and went right to it, just like you said you would.*

"Deputy." She corrected him, easing closer. "Lower the gun."

Gideon said, "You always said you'd make deputy before twenty-five."

"I did."

"And here you are."

"Here I am," she said, calmly. "Lower the gun."

His mind willed his arms to relax but something kept them rigid. *Pull the trigger, Dupree. You either kill or be killed, soldier.* He lowered his arms slowly, like they were on a crank instead of a swivel.

"There you go." Beth's voice cut like a scythe through whatever confused moment had seized him. He saw the ring on her finger. She'd married Jax.

Beth lowered her weapon.

Their eyes remained locked on one another. Hers still blue as a noonday sky, still able to tear him up in an azure blink. She seemed as confused now as he was, this sudden turn of events, but in the way she watched him, the subtle nod and glance to the surrounding crowd, he knew she'd have his back in whatever way he needed to get himself out of this. And when it was clear he'd thought of nothing, she put on a fake smile and shouted, "Surprise!"

Gideon, still shaking, grinned awkwardly at the crowd, caught on, and said, "Surprise." But it had no life to it. He'd never been able to pull off *funny*. Never had the chops. Never been able to be anyone other than Gideon Dupree, the boy born when the big storm knocked the power out all over Harrod's Reach, the boy born with a cleft palate on the same night Beth Gardner was born to cherubic perfection.

Gideon's "*Surprise*" settled like a stone tossed in quicksand.

Nervous laughter permeated the crowd, followed by a slow ripple effect of relief. And then Mayor Truffant guffawed. Gideon unzipped his duffel, slid the gun inside with his carefully folded clothes, and stood surveying the crowd that was either still staring or unable to look at him.

He imagined the first hug he'd get would be from his mother, but it was Mayor Truffant drunkenly corralling him in a sideways hug, squeezing Gideon's shoulder, like he was testing his muscles to see if the Army had, indeed, toughened him up.

"You got us good, Gideon!" Mayor Truffant looked at Beth. "You two got us good!"

Like that had been Gideon's intent, to turn the surprise on *them*. Except it wasn't. He'd come back changed, all right. Unhinged and unpredictable.

He may have left the war, but the war hadn't left him.

Beth holstered her 22, turned, and walked away, back to the toddler she'd passed off before she'd come at him.

Somebody handed Gideon a beer and he wasted no time downing it.

"Oh, Gideon." His mother came out of nowhere. Hugged him tight. He felt uneasy at first, but then wrapped his arms around her, full bear. He could have hugged his mother all day.

"Welcome home, dear," she said. "I missed you so much." Her breath smelled like gin. She hadn't been a drinker before he'd left. She pulled away. He saw worry in her eyes. She hadn't been fooled by his stunt, and by the way half the gym looked at him, they hadn't either. Like the war had only made things worse.

"I missed you too, Mom."

"Welcome home, son."

Gideon turned toward his father, who held his hand out for a shake, but still, after three years gone, appeared unable to look at him. His grip was firm. He pumped it twice, let go, and started away until his wife's gaze stopped him.

"Oh, come on, Archie," Maxine said under her breath, smiling for any onlookers, eyes staring daggers at her husband.

Archie had the chops. He laughed, like the joke was on anyone but him, and then hugged his oldest son with gusto and flair before forcing himself to look into his eyes just long enough to say, "I missed you, son, welcome home."

Somebody in the crowd boisterously said, "Hear, hear," like some hatchet had been buried.

Gideon watched his mother, who smiled. Archie looked down, and then away. Maxine was even prettier with age, but something about it rang untrue, like beneath it all lay the misery that had urged Gideon gone in the first place. And his father, usually put together and looking every bit the college history professor he was, appeared to have given up. Hairline receding, what was left of it uncombed. At least twenty pounds heavier and smelling of bourbon. When had he started drinking? With his diabetes? Shoulders that used to be broad and strong, now concealed under the doughy weight he'd gained while Gideon was gone.

Gideon had put on thirty pounds of muscle, and he wondered if Beth had seen that. Gone were the glasses, the soft nerdy edges, and pale skin. The faint scar on the left side of his upper lip no longer seemed a mark of deformity. On the surface, at least, the Army had hardened him into a man. That's why his mother had organized the welcome home party. Proof that the meek might one day inherit the earth.

And then Gideon said it: "How's Sully?"

That was Archie's cue to walk away. No hatchet had been buried. Archie Dupree still blamed Gideon for what happened to his youngest son, the good son, the one who came along more than a dozen years after Gideon, who everyone in town considered a gift from God.

Maxine watched Archie disappear into the crowd; she smiled at Gideon. "Sully's fine."

"Fine?"

"Still the same," she said. She gripped his arms, looked him up and down. He thought for a second she'd gotten taller, but then realized she had on heels, red and high and totally unlike the woman he'd known before he'd left. "Look at you, Gideon. A strong man now. Where did my boy go?"

Part of him is still in the tunnel, Mom. The other part . . . Pull the trigger, Dupree. Soldiers might leave the war, but the war . . .

"Does it hurt?" she asked.

It took a second to register. The wound. The reason for the Purple Heart stashed right next to the bullet inside his duffel. His ticket home. "No. Maybe a little."

"I saw you limping on the way in."

Giddy-Up Gideon.

"I'm fine," he said, scanning the crowd for Beth. "Where is he?"

"Who?"

"Sully?"

"He's home."

"Alone?"

"No." She seemed hurt by the notion. "Of course not. Someone's always with him." She squeezed his arm again and moved on. It was her job to make sure everyone felt entertained.

Slowly, after more alcohol was consumed, the party ratcheted up.

Kids zipped in and out of the throng like they did during a Lenten fish fry. A group of teens, on their way outside, stole glances toward Gideon before disappearing out the back of the gym toward the football field. Seemed like yesterday it was him being left out of *that* crowd. Not left out, but not exactly welcomed either. Invite him so they'd have someone to pick on. *Jax. Carson Knox. Blake Kline.*

Festival noises brought him back to the moment.

In the far corner of the gym, a wooden wheel spun. Townsfolk placed quarters on numbers to win a stuffed animal or candy jar. They'd even brought out the summer picnic cake booth and the frog pond for the little kids. On the opposite side, Father Fred had changed into swim trunks and was climbing up into the dunking booth. Douglas Downs's REM cover band was playing "Losing My Religion" and people had started to dance. Gideon shook hands, went through the motions. Through it all, he sensed desperation, like the town couldn't wait to celebrate *something*, and his arrival home happened to be their excuse. Because there sure hadn't been any rush to gather when he'd left. Which was why, despite the laughter and cheers he now saw—all now geared toward *him*, the one they'd scorned before—it rang fake.

Forced, like his father's embrace.

The longer the night went on, the more Beth seemed to avoid him.

Four beers in and having just been handed his fifth by some dude he should have remembered but didn't, Gideon started to relax. And Beth, moments ago, when they'd caught each other staring, actually smiled at him. Hand in hand with her little one, and just as the band was starting into "It's the End of the World As We Know It," she'd begun to make her way over to him. But before Beth reached him, just as Maxine Dupree was shouting over the music that she was about to cut the cake, Doc Bigsby's wife, Jane, collapsed in the middle of the gym floor.

Beth and Gideon were the first to reach her.

"She passed out," Beth said. She asked for ice, and Billy Claxton hurried to get it. And a wet towel, which Tammy Liebert rushed off to get.

"Bleeding, Mommy." Beth's toddler pointed.

Jane Bigsby's head was bleeding just above her right temple from the knock against the basketball court. Mrs. Bigsby's cell phone rested on the floor, pinned to the court by her bent left arm, the screen quickly fading to black. She must have checked it before fainting. Gideon tapped the screen just before it went to black, refreshing it to a text. It was from her husband.

Doc's text read simply: *help*

"The tunnel," Beth said without hesitating.

"What about the tunnel?" asked Gideon.

With a wet towel now on her head, Mrs. Bigsby was starting to come to. She moaned, "The tunnel. He's in . . . the tunnel."

Beth pulled out her own phone and called Sheriff Meeks, told him that Doc needed help.

Sheriff Meeks's voice crackled over the line: "The tunnel? Goddamn it, what's he doing down there?"

"Just go," Beth pleaded. "I'm on my way."

Gideon had tried dialing the doctor's number from Mrs. Bigsby's phone. Six rings, and then voice mail. "No answer."

Beth asked Justine Baker to take Brody home. Her son now had a name.

Gideon glanced at Brody and found him staring. Gideon flashed a smile and the boy returned it. Justine Baker grabbed Brody up.

Beth started for the doors.

Gideon followed. "How is he in the tunnel?"

"The walls came down, Gideon." Beth glanced over her shoulder. "Last week. The north entrance first, and then a few days later the south."

He wanted to know more, but a ringing phone halted him. The gym had quieted enough to hear it clearly—his father's ringtone, an old car horn jingle. Gideon turned toward it, saw his father standing only a few paces behind where Maxine still cradled Mrs. Bigsby's head in the middle of the gym.

Gideon took a step toward his father.

"Mr. Dupree," said the panicked voice on the other end. "It's Jax."

"Yes," said Archie. "Jax . . . Is it Sully? Is something wrong?"

Jax? What was Sully doing with Jax McBride?

"No . . . Nothing wrong." Jax sounded like he was crying. "Sully . . . he just woke up, sir."

7

Beth

Now

As a recently sworn-in officer of the law, Beth had been given permission by Maxine Dupree to drive her patrol car to the party.

She'd parked it behind the dumpster, so Gideon wouldn't see it upon his arrival, and was glad she had it now. Before leaving the gym, she'd grabbed her friend and off-duty nurse, Natalie Logsdon, who'd been in the bathroom when Mrs. Bigsby went down, and now wanted to check on her. Beth steered her toward the doors instead.

Deputy Lumpkin, who everyone in town called Lump, had been drunk before Gideon arrived, and was sleeping one off on a chair next to the dunking booth. With the Sheriff's Department short on staff after recent budget cuts, Natalie would have to be her impromptu help. The two of them had slipped out of the gym when Archie Dupree's phone had gone off, and now sped down Guthrie. Jax called, but she let it go to voice mail. Sheriff Meeks hadn't responded to her calls, so at the moment, *that* was more pressing than Jax asking her to bring him home some food from the party.

All Sheriff Meeks did was work, especially since his wife passed away from ovarian cancer four years ago, and once said he'd be on call 25/7 if the Lord could squeeze in that extra hour. Either he was already on his way to the tunnel or something else had gone wrong. All Beth could think about as she drove was Simple Simon walking into the station with that sketch of the two murdered bodies he'd found outside the tunnel—bodies, once she and Sheriff Meeks had finally located them in person, so bloody and covered in blowflies that even her boss had gotten sick in the grass— and she prayed she wasn't about to find a third.

Natalie rolled down the passenger's window and welcomed the cold wind in her face, her long black hair flapping like a tattered kite.

"I feel like we're Bonnie and Bonnie," Natalie said. "Me and you."

"Except we aren't criminals running from the law."

"That's right. We *are* the law."

"No, *I'm* the law."

Natalie scoffed. "And I'm the sidekick?"

"No, you're the drunk nurse," said Beth. "I should have left you at the gym with Lump."

"Lump's got issues."

"We *all* got issues."

Natalie chugged a bottled water she'd snatched from the concessions before they left. She'd just finished her fourth glass of pinot before Mrs. Bigsby went down, and wanted to sober up before they hit the ravine. Navigating that wooded slope was tough enough sober, would be down-right dangerous fully intoxicated.

"You gonna be okay?" Beth asked as she sped down the Reach's main drag, north toward the gully and the old train tunnel. "You can stay in the car if you need to."

"And let you go in there alone?" Natalie finished the water. "I'll be fine in a minute." She popped a stick of minty gum in her mouth, like fresh breath was going to help Doc, and then stuck her head back out the win-dow, into the wind like a dog might.

Aside from those who either worked or resided in the hospital, the shut-ins, or the dozens of out-of-townies Mickey French had hired to reno-vate the historic Beehive Hotel, most everyone else in town had been inside the gym, which meant the streets were vacant.

Eerily so, Beth thought, knuckles bone white on the steering wheel.

Beth hadn't known how the town would respond to Maxine Dupree's party. Maybe a fourth of the town would come, she'd guessed. Half, if the town overachieved. Who could have guessed most the town would crowd inside that gym to celebrate the return of a young man many still blamed for what happened to Sully? In hindsight, maybe Beth should have predicted it, especially with how everyone had become so anxious now that the tunnel was open again. And that had only been enhanced by the two bodies recently found outside the tunnel. The town, not knowing the macabre details like Beth and Sheriff Meeks did, assumed the tunnel killings had begun again, but Beth didn't think so. She knew the bodies had been dumped there, not killed *at* the tunnel, like all the other so-called tunnel killings throughout Harrod's Reach's sordid history, and Sheriff Meeks had agreed. What she'd also concluded, but had yet to discuss with her boss, was that she believed that the two victims had been murdered by two different people—despite the fact the corpses had been holding hands. The woman, quite possibly, by the Horseshoe Rapist who'd been plying his trade way east of here.

Regardless, Beth thought as she drove, stealing periodic glances at her rapidly sobering friend in the neighboring seat, *the town is afraid*.

And it's only natural to want to gather together when afraid.

She looked at her friend and suppressed a laugh. There were parts of Natalie she envied, parts she didn't. Maybe Beth needed to let her hair down and have some fun, like Natalie had been begging her to for years. But she didn't drink, ever.

Maybe she could have used one now. Her heart beat too fast. The tall canopy of tree limbs overhung the road like a tunnel of its own. White Wall Cemetery on the right. Harrod's Reach Park to the left. Mallard Street on the left, halfway up the Duprees' historic home, known around town as the Smite House. Higher up on Mallard, the historic Beehive Hotel, where hammering echoed, renovations ongoing even now.

All of it grew small in her rearview.

The cold air Natalie was letting into the open window shook the car.

Natalie reeled her face back inside, settled against the headrest, and closed her eyes. They were only two miles from the ravine and One-Side Mountain. Natalie's eyes popped open when they hit the Historic District and the bumpy part of Guthrie Street, the ten-block ribbon of old-timey cobbles, and Natalie did somehow look refreshed as they neared their destination.

"Have a nice nap?"

Natalie yawned. "How long was I out?"

"Ten seconds."

Natalie rolled up her window, tied her long hair into a topknot—ready to roll.

All the other roads jutted off Guthrie in perfect angles and grids and manicured, tree-dotted squares. Fuzzy streetlamps and fancy wrought-iron benches. Trees soared like redwoods. Beth turned onto DuPont, and then another quick right onto Malloy, which began the two-hundred-yard track of sharp curves downward to the gully, to where the train tracks used to be before trees had swallowed them up.

Sometimes the best way to deal with the tunnel was to go down like it was no big deal when they all knew it was. Before she pulled her car to a stop at the small clearing of grass and weeds overlooking the ravine, where Sheriff Meeks's patrol car was parked with the light bar flashing, sending smears of red and blue pulses out across the darkness of the tree-lined gully, Beth had hoped she could do just that. But all she could muster as she and Natalie got out of the car was, "Which one am I?" When Natalie looked at her, Beth said, "Bonnie or Bonnie?"

Natalie smiled. "Bonnie, for sure."

Beth shined a flashlight as they started down the slope.

In the distance, an ambulance sounded, grew louder, closer, and by the time they'd navigated the dew-covered downslope to where the ground bottomed out below in a sea of weeds and brambles and tall grass, the ambulance arrived up above. The siren shut off, but the lights still flashed in strobes of red and white across the foliage-draped cliffs.

Beth focused on her flashlight beam, her careful footsteps, Natalie two paces ahead and moving like she'd been down here more recently than she'd like to have admitted.

Natalie moved a stray branch out of her path, looked over her shoulder, held it for a moment so it wouldn't fling back into Beth's face. She went quiet as they emerged in view of the fallen wall at the tunnel's southern entrance. Nobody really knew where that part of the ravine got its name—One-Side Mountain—because if you searched hard enough, you'd find a second side. And the mountain-like outcropping through which the tunnel had been forged sure as shit had a second side to it, which was where Simple Simon had found the bodies.

Lantern glow flickered deep inside the tunnel.

Flashlight beams shone behind them—the medics had made it. About twenty yards before the tunnel's arched opening, Natalie and Beth glanced at each other as they continued over the rubble, to where the bricks gave way to dust and grass and hard pack right at the opening. They stepped inside, felt the temperature drop, the sensation of entering a cave. Breezes blew, upturning dust and the stench of sealed-up grime. Water dripped from a ceiling too dark to see without shining a light up there, which Beth wasn't about to do. Natalie mostly kept her eyes down. They were both aware of the story of Charlie Ponsetter, from back in the 1970s, who shined his light up there one night and swore he saw Leonard Stewart, the town barber, scaling the stones of the ceiling. Charlie was heavy into booze and pot, prone to making shit up, but *something* he'd seen inside the tunnel that night had turned his hair white out of fright. *Something* had left him more than a few cards short of a full deck for the next eight years, before he ended his life hanging from the oak tree in his stepmother's front yard back in the autumn of '82.

Lenny Stewart was questioned about it plenty in the years that followed. He'd chuckle it off. At the time, Lenny the Blade, as his loyal male customers liked to call him because of the close shaves he'd give after haircuts, was in his late fifties and fat. He wasn't scaling any ceilings, let alone the grimy one in that long, cold tunnel. But nobody was laughing ten years later, when Lenny the Blade died of a heart attack, right when he was shaving Henry Calcutta's right cheek. And nobody was laughing when Lenny the Blade's oldest son, Joey the Blade—he was a barber, too—read his father's will, which stated that Lenny believed he'd been possessed inside the tunnel by something called a Melino. Joey looked that up to find it was some underworld nymph *thing* from Greek mythology that manifested in weird forms and brought about nightmares and insanity, which fit the bill for Lenny.

But the will also said that he'd left a gift for the town of Harrod's Reach in a cellar beneath his barn. Joey had found it first, and spent two days drinking scotch, wrangling whether to call the police, knowing what he'd found in that cellar would change the town's opinion of his father. Eventually, he'd made the call. Detective Harrington, who'd been right in the thick of investigating the resurgence of murders in and around that tunnel—one of the tunnel's many decades of *Golden Years*—carried out from the cellar of Lenny the Blade's barn the bones of no less than two dozen dogs and over fifty jars of blood he must have siphoned from them. Blood, once they'd read through his journals and diary, that Lenny the Blade liked to drink from martini glasses on the rocking chair of his front porch whenever the moon was full—he truly believed he'd been possessed. The family had cremated Lenny's body, scattering his ashes, just like he'd wished, over the ravine Beth and Natalie had just passed through, and inside the tunnel they'd just entered.

Legend said you could still hear Lenny the Blade crawling along the tunnel's ceiling at night. And if you shined your light up at just the right time, and your eyes locked with his cold, dead ones, your hair would turn white like Charlie Ponsetter's had done in the summer of '76.

Beth held the flashlight in one hand and her gun in the other.

Lantern light flickered ahead, but no shadows moved in the hazy glow of it, no silhouettes cast large on the walls.

"Sheriff?" Beth's voice echoed. "Doctor Bigsby?"

Water dripped from the ceiling, rippled in puddles.

"You hear that?" Natalie asked, giving Beth an *I don't like this* look over her shoulder.

It was a chainsaw, not roaring like it was about to bite into a tree trunk, but purring. At rest, like distant thunder.

Beth caught up to her. She knew Doc had been ignoring the warning sign and clearing out rubble from the fallen walls. But why would he need a chainsaw? They walked side by side, now halfway through the tunnel, and after ten more yards Beth's pace quickened toward the lantern glow.

The chainsaw purred louder now.

"Sheriff?"

Sheriff Meeks was on his knees, his back to them, facing the open north entrance Doc had been working on. He'd made an impressive dent in the rubble; trees gave way to a dark sky and full moon. Even on his knees, Sheriff Meeks loomed large. But he wavered, slumped to his left, and lay unmoving on the ground. The Stetson he'd been wearing for the past thirty years spun away from his head. Breeze turned the hat clockwise, one tic and then another, and then it too lay still.

"Grover!" Beth hurried to her boss. The chainsaw purred a few feet away, fresh blood dripping from the blade, bits of clothing and flesh stuck on the jagged metal teeth. Blood pumped from a wound in Grover's abdomen.

Beth screamed for help.

Natalie doubled over, hands on knees, facing the shadows. From behind them, flashlight beams approached, found the walls, settled on them.

First responders from the ambulance.

Beth screamed for them to hurry, and then held Grover's wrist for a pulse. Faint, but there. Grover's eyes, set deep into the sculpted features of his walnut-colored skin, found her own. She placed her hands on his white-stubbled cheeks. "Grover, can you hear me? Who did this?"

The Ripper purred on the tunnel's floor, growling like a rabid animal. But where was Simon? Had he duped them both by drawing that sketch days ago? Had they too easily cast aside his possible role in those murders because of his feeble mind?

Simple Simon, the town called him. One of those big teddy-bear boys who'd physically grown into a man by his thirteenth birthday. He was thirty-two now, and mentally still back there, *way the fuck back there*, Grover had said of Simon just last week, days before the north wall had crumbled, and exhausted after bringing Simon out of the woods yet again, this time after chainsawing his initials into yet another tree. *SS* he'd carved into the bark, for Simple Simon, instead of *SB*, for Simon Bowles, which had prompted Sheriff Meeks to swallow a finger of Jameson, wipe his mouth, and say to Beth, "There goes the question of whether or not he knows."

"Knows what?" Beth had asked, eyeing the half-empty bottle of Jameson that Grover pulled out from his bottom desk drawer whenever the days began to wear on him. He'd pour two, offer Beth one he knew she'd decline, and then down both.

"What we call him behind his back."

Come to think of it, Simon hadn't been at Gideon's surprise party.

Natalie bent over and emptied her stomach. Shadows darkened her up to the knees. Natalie wiped her mouth, pointed a trembling finger at the rubble, closer to the wisps of lantern glow. To the trail of blood marked by dozens of large boot prints, all of which could have been the size of Simple Simon's feet, and then finally to what was left of Doc Bigsby.

To the severed arm still somehow holding the cell phone he'd used to text his wife.

And next to it, a set of antlers.

CHAPTER

8

Theodore

Before

THEODORE LOMAX DIDN'T start believing in God until he was fully convinced of the Devil.

He didn't know if it had warmed Mother's heart when he'd admitted it on that Sunday leaving church—that he believed in her beloved God—but it had spread a smile so wide across her face that she'd treated him to a cheeseburger and fries at Krispy's on the drive home.

She'd asked across the diner's table, still with that smile, what had changed his mind, and with his mouth full of juicy burger he mumbled, "The Devil."

Almost said *Mr. Lullaby*, but stopped short of it, fearing his explanation, at age thirteen, would do *that voice* no justice. Her smile melted away in an ooze, though, at that one word, Devil, and then her face puckered with rage when he added, "I just figured if there was one there'd be the other. You know? What's it matter which one I believed in first?"

She placed her napkin like a tent atop her half-eaten chicken sandwich and left him sitting in Krispy's Diner to finish his burger alone. She didn't say it, but he could tell that time alone should be spent repenting.

He took his time, too, finishing every French fry crumb in the greasy basket, every bun seed that had fallen on the table from his burger, knowing the drive home would be no fun thing. She didn't speak the entire ride or at home, but left her nicest red leather Bible atop the bed she made for him every morning, with a note that said: *Theodore, start reading before it's too late.*

He didn't open the Bible that night. Instead, he placed it on his bedside table and used it as a coaster for the tall glass of chocolate milk he'd sneaked into the bedroom. After locking his door, he began thumbing through the *Playboy* magazine he kept hidden in between his mattress and box spring. Three minutes later, after carefully choosing his *Playboy* model of the night—this one a lithe brunette wearing Air Jordans and nothing else—Teddy Lomax lowered his shorts, squirted some hand lotion into his palm, and got to work. As soon as he finished, he wiped his hands off on his bedsheets and chugged his glass of milk, thinking of the note still tucked inside the Bible.

He laughed. For one, he wasn't Theodore anymore. And two, it was *already* too late.

That toothpaste had been squeezed out of the tube long ago, and there was no way of getting it back in. Just ask the skunk he'd shot with the BB gun two months ago. It was buried out in the woods behind the backyard, right next to the raccoon and squirrel he'd buried in the days before that. And what he'd done to the deer last week? That pain he'd caused? Talk about fuel—he'd gotten out the *Playboy* magazine twice that night, woke up with the fuel still coursing through him like that tsunami wave he'd recently read about. One that rolled over that town in Indonesia like a heard of buffalo over prairie grass.

Now that's the type of shit I like to read about, Mother. Disasters. Tornados. Earthquakes. Floods. That's the gas that fills my tank.

One good thing about having a memory like a Rolodex, Teddy Lomax thought now as he drove through the hills and farms of Lexington, Kentucky, fresh off the euthanizing of that teenage boy, Bobby McFee, was that he could vividly draw on them at any time. Conjuring up the memory of Mother's face after seeing the ring stain from his chocolate milk glass on the cover of her favorite Bible the next morning gave him a jolt of laughter as he drove, a burst of wake-me-up no amount of coffee or Mountain Dew or Jolt ever could.

And while he had told his mother at age thirteen that he'd started believing in God by default, he'd *always* believed in signs, and to this day held them sacred, even up there with how strongly he believed in the voice. So when he peered through his windshield and spotted the lone sun ray through the hole of slate gray sky to his left, he immediately turned onto a country road to follow it.

Any skepticism went away as soon as the seashell beside him started sounding off, that whistle of wind he for months now had equated to a telephone ring. He picked up the seashell and put it to his ear and said, "Lomax here."

"Follow it to the end," said the deep voice Teddy thought sure now belonged to his long-lost daddy. Or maybe Mr. Lullaby himself. The voice said, "Make the stops, Teddy."

The voice hung up before Teddy could ask what was meant by it, so he placed the seashell back on the passenger's seat like it was breakable and returned both hands to the wheel.

Make the stops? What the fuck did that even mean? *Trust the process, Teddy. Trust the process.* The voice isn't real, Theodore. It's all in your mind, he imagined his mother saying.

Shut up, Mother. I've got work to do.

The orders he'd been given until now had been clear. Take out all the dead-heads on the list, and he was doing that with gusto, ticking off one name at least every other day, depending on the travel and prep required. But make the stops? First thing first, Teddy. Follow it. And he did—that lone ray of sunlight, shining down on a two-story farmhouse in the middle of nowhere. He came to a stop outside the white picket fence surrounding the property, and that's when the yellow school bus caught his eye. Parked to the side of the house with a sign—a real, physical sign—stuck in the ground next to it.

Son of a bitch was for sale. Not the house. The bus.

Teddy had always wanted one, so this was possibly too good to be true. *Make the stops, Teddy.*

"Because that's what school buses do," he said to himself, stepping out of the car seat with the warm fuzzies coursing through his chest and arms and groin before settling inside his skull like a warm nap.

That's how he knew this was right.

He knocked on the front door of the house and waited. His dark beard was already growing in, so he turned slightly to one side to hide the white patch coming in on his left cheek.

Twenty minutes later, cruising east on I-64, Teddy Lomax sat behind the enormous wheel of the fifteen-year-old school bus, reveling in how much higher he was than the cars he passed.

First thing he'd do when he got home would be to paint it.

Red. Not bright red; more like the color of rust. Dried blood.

And then he'd wheel Mother to the window to show her.

Maybe put Lomax Travel in big white letters on the sides. Maybe nothing at all.

The old man he'd bought it from hadn't cared what he'd do with it. He was just happy to get rid of it, and had been willing to take the seven hundred dollars in his wallet plus the stolen car he'd come in as a trade.

Teddy had a moment's thought to kill the man and take the bus for free, but after so recently ending Bobby McFee's life back in Iowa, the thought had held no flair for him.

It would have packed little punch.

His tank was still full and near to overflowing after killing *that* deadhead, who'd damn near woken up when he injected him. At least that's what it had seemed like, the fucker's eyes had gotten so big and wide.

After payment was made and the keys to the bus were handed over, the guy said, "Anything you want out of it?"

"Out of what?" Teddy had said.

"The car."

"Oh," said Teddy. "Sure. Thanks."

Damn.

He'd almost forgotten the seashell.

CHAPTER

9

Gideon

Now

EVERYONE IN HARROD's Reach had a piece of the old railroad. Gideon had always kept a rusted railway spike next to his bed. He'd found it when he was twelve. Archie, after he'd put on his glasses to analyze it through puffs of pipe smoke, told his oldest son it was a cut spike, or crampon. Said he could keep it, but to watch out for the rust.

Gideon knew it wasn't rust. His mom, Maxine, said it was too dangerous next to his bed, inches from his pillow, but relented when Gideon told her it was for good luck. The truth was, the railway spike reminded him of Beth.

Sheriff Beth now. Deputy sheriff, rather, as she'd been so quick to correct him back at the gym, eternally modest. Scared of nothing but attention. Pretty as anyone in town, but genuinely pissed off when anyone told her so; she went out of her way to do the beautification equivalent of dumbing herself down. No makeup. No dresses. Hair always up in a tousled bun or ponytail.

As Gideon followed the herd out the gym doors and down the moonlit street, many words crossed his mind—*insane, stupid, asinine*—that no one would have a car in case of emergency. He settled on surreal. The sound of so many footfalls heading in the same place with *no one* saying a word.

The crowd streamlined like a silent mob toward what they all—even the Duprees, who'd lived there for over two decades—called the Smite House, the old home of the town's first mayor, Lucius Smite.

Jane Bigsby passing out in the middle of the gym floor had excited the citizens of Harrod's Reach; but since the phone call from Jax moments ago, everybody was numb. Walking that mile down Guthrie like zombies.

If Jax wasn't lying to Archie—and why would he about something so serious?—Gideon's younger brother, Sully, had woken up from his coma for the first time in the more than three years since the accident. And on the very day Gideon returned home from overseas. With the way the crowd stole glances at Gideon as they walked toward the Dupree's family home, they all realized that too.

Footfalls whisked in rhythm.

Streetlamps buzzed as if their marching column was adding charge to the current. Most moved down the middle of the road, although now their column was starting to fray toward the sidewalks, as if some of the younger and more mobile couldn't wait to get there.

Gideon was right there with them, limping as quickly as he could.

Heroes don't limp, Gideon.

Two blocks, three blocks, and then four.

And then, after five blocks of walking, as if some unheard signal had suddenly given them permission, Archie started running. Maxine removed her high heels and followed in her husband's wake, her bare feet clapping almost comically off the cold pavement and eerily still, quiet air, high-heeled pumps dangling from her right hand as she ran. She gave Gideon a glance over her right shoulder, as if to encourage him.

Giddy-up, Gideon.

Jax's voice from the past. Of all people, what was *he* doing watching Sully?

Gideon hustled along with the throng, those who could running and jogging now, quickly gaining ground down Mallard Street toward the Smite House, the tree-canopied driveway visible a hundred yards in the distance. From the 120-year-old refurbished Victorian, two porch lights glowed among the trees and foliage like a pair of illuminated eyes.

Thoughts of Sully quickened his pace. He caught up to his parents.

At the high end of the street, the old Beehive Hotel loomed like an abandoned castle overlooking the town, except the hotel didn't appear to be abandoned any longer. Despite the night's festivities, work was being done to that century-old hotel. Scaffolding covered part of the stone and brick façade. Hammering sounded in the distance. An electric saw churned.

Archie was out of breath while Maxine seemed like this brisk walk was a warm-up for something else.

As they neared their driveway, Gideon asked, "Somebody buy the hotel?"

"Ask your mother," said Archie.

Maxine scoffed, rolled her eyes, but didn't answer.

He left it at that. He fought the stabbing pain in his leg, now real as the bullet in his bag that had caused it. As much as he claimed he didn't care fuck-all what the people around him thought, he did.

Always had. And at this moment, he couldn't appear slow or hobbled. Because the Army *had* changed him. He charged. His limp-run turned into a sprint, past his parents, thinking *Where was Beth? What had happened down by the tunnel?*

Beth had been with him when he'd found that railway spike a decade ago, that offset head of metal staring at him like a dirty eyeball from the clod of mud on the far side of the tunnel she and Jax had dared him to run through, knowing good and well how terrified he was of it. And how he ran like a lopsided goof. He'd done it, of course. For Beth. Only to find them cracking up after he'd passed through that cold, dank dark, hand on his chest and pale as a sheet, the two of them following right behind his every panicked step, Jax shouting *Giddy-up, Gideon* so loud it echoed off the tunnel's arched, stone ceiling like a nightmare. Heart hammering so fast his chest hurt. Him seeing his breath in there while it was still summer in the Reach, humid as all get out. Sunlight so bright on each end of that weird tunnel that he'd been struck dizzy by the sudden exit. So yeah, he'd taken that glare shining off the dull head of that railway spike as a sign. But digging it from the weeds and dirt and holding it up to Jax's throat while he was still in mid-guffaw, Jax freezing the way he'd done—in mid "Giddy-up, Gideon"—was enough of a payback for him. Nicking his neck skin with that rusted spike and watching Jax frantically swipe at the blood trickling toward the neckline of his favorite white cotton T-shirt, the one with the hooked bass as big as a football helmet—*Gone fish'n!*—was just icing on the cake. And although that part had been an accident, it was the first time in all the years Gideon had known Beth that she'd looked at him with admiration. That flash of a smile she'd given him right before Jax regained his focus, when she'd warned him with her eyes, *You better run,* all of it had warmed Gideon's heart and boosted him for weeks thereafter. In the days that followed, that smile—his one burst of bravery he could still vividly remember—in one of many futile attempts to become who he wasn't *because* of Beth Gardner, he'd shed his glasses in favor of contacts, cut his hair short, and even begun to rip off push-ups every morning before breakfast. Three weeks passed before Beth, one day at lunch, said something about him looking different, never saying anything about his glasses, or lack thereof. On some days he not only blended into the wall, he might as well have *been* the wall. Despite the fact that those contact lenses cost money they didn't have—all their money went into the never-ending renovation of the Smite House—his father had found a way to fork it over, hoping they'd make his older son look just a little less nerdy and maybe even more put-together, like his little brother Sully, who, even by the age of four, had already firmly established himself in town as someone with whom to reckon. Someone who mattered. To his father's chagrin, Gideon returned to wearing glasses the next day, and what little bit of sand he'd gained on the afternoon he'd drawn Jax's blood with that railway spike quickly hid itself again in the pages of his books and comics and board games he sometimes played against himself.

Heroes don't blend in. They don't crawl into hidey-holes to disappear.

Gideon continued toward home, the pain from his wound burning like molten lava down his leg. *Faster, soldier. Faster.* They'd blacktopped over the gravel driveway while he'd been gone. Smooth pavement now instead of the loose pebbles Sully used to terrorize with his bike. The three-story brick and stone Victorian loomed large as he neared it, the fancy ornamentation and large windows, the rounded turrets and gabled rooftops. A ladder stood slanted against the house's façade, stretching up toward a second-story window Archie must have been working on until the party stopped him.

Some things never changed.

The rest of Harrod's Reach had the decency to stop at the wrought-iron fence surrounding their yard to await any news, allowing Gideon and his parents to navigate the final forty yards to the wrap-around veranda alone, as a family. At the end of the driveway, parked in the shadows of their carport, was a white SUV marked with the lettering of the Harrod's Reach Fire Department.

While Gideon still had no idea what he wanted to do with his life, Jax and Beth had settled on theirs by third grade, and when asked each year at school, their answers never wavered. Beth would be sheriff one day, and Jax would be a fireman. And here they were, not only having already accomplished their goals, but apparently married in the process, with a kid.

At the veranda, Gideon stepped over a toolbox, wood scraps, and a handsaw his father had left on the sidewalk, and bounded up the second set of porch steps. He flung open the screen door, hurried through the foyer, past the curved central stairwell, into the front parlor, the kitchen, and entered another hallway, where it appeared the bathroom was being reconstructed. Gideon passed his father's study, rounded the curve past his mother's sunroom, and then heard crying coming from the back parlor, where they'd set up Sully's bed after he'd been moved from the hospital after the accident.

"Solomon," Archie shouted, right on Gideon's heels, nudging him aside. Archie had never called his younger son by his nickname, Sully.

Gideon let his mother and father pass, and then followed toward the back parlor. During his childhood the back parlor had been a second dining room for large gatherings, but by the time he'd gone to war it had been turned into Sully's glorified hospital room, complete with a fancy mechanical bed and computer monitors and constantly beeping machines. The sucking, hissing sounds of the oxygen and feeding tubes keeping him alive. Gideon heard it, the sensory overload of memory mixing with the here and now, and stopped at the door.

The sound of those beeping machines made him nauseous. For three and a half years now, his little brother had been virtually unresponsive. Doctors had thrown out words like *coma* and *vegetative state*. But what Gideon had not been able to take was the sight and sound of the nasogastric tube delivering that eight hundred calories of liquid to his brother's stomach day in and day out. Watching his little brother get thinner. Hearing his parents fret over how they were going to afford to keep him alive. Watching that picture of perfect health turn into something unrecognizable, so skeletal and weak, when Sully had always been the strong one. Watching his parents clip his fingernails, change his diapers, and brush his teeth. The catheters filling up with fluid. The trickling water from sponge baths chased Gideon all over the house, no matter what room he went into to hide, no matter how many pillows he squashed to his ears to blot out the squeezed drips from that saturated sponge into the bedside bucket. Watching them wash and cut his hair, turn him this way and that to stave off the bedsores, the therapy to keep his muscles from total atrophy. They encouraged Gideon to help, his father's accusing eyes sometimes demanded it, but he couldn't.

So he'd run, literally and figuratively.

Quit stalling, soldier! Enter the goddamn premises!

His mother was screaming.

His father shouted, "Nooooo!"

Gideon stepped into the parlor.

Jax, all six foot muscled four of him, stood in his fireman uniform, cradling Sully's limp, emaciated body in his arms like a baby. *What was Sully doing out of bed?* Tears wet Jax's cheeks. *He's not moving.*

The tall window behind them was open. Breeze ruffled the thin curtains.

Jax faced the three of them, and with a deadpan look in his eyes—a look of fear Gideon had never seen from him before—said, "I went to the bathroom. There . . . there was . . . someone in the room. He woke up. I swear to God, Mr. Dupree. He woke up."

Then why did he look so dead now?

CHAPTER

10

Maddy

Before

MADDY BOYLE WAS torn.
    Between what? She didn't know; she'd only recently begun to understand her place on the other side when she'd felt the tug to go back to the white room.

The white stone-walled grotto and her life before she'd entered it.

Thinking of it now made her mind fuzzy and her eyeballs hurt, and already she couldn't remember, which meant the *here* was already fading to the *there*. Made her wonder if it was even real at all. That fucked-up place with all the fucked-up things in it.

And the others? She'd miss them. She felt sure of that.

She could remember her name now. That was something tangible from her past, her previous life as Maddy Boyle. Born Madeline Louise Boyle, Charleston, South Caroline, in the year . . . the year still evaded her.

She remembered very little else, except that something bad had put her here. No, that's not right. Not here exactly; first, she'd gone to the white room. The bright, sunlit grotto with the pocked limestone walls, scarred with the stark green lichen and ivy that meandered and climbed, with dark doors the shape of fingernails, like Hobbit doors, but tall enough to walk through without ducking. More like open-aired corridors than doors, now she thought of it. She'd never really opened a door. She'd just—after her time was up in the white-walled grotto—gone in. Stood up like her name had just been called at the doctor's office.

Come back she did. And now she was coming back *out*.

Out of her hallucinations and back *into* the limestone grotto waiting room, where, like before, others waited nervous and confused like she'd once been. Trying to understand things like she'd once done, much like she was trying to do all over again now, because the walk back from *there* had been an arduous one.

Like wading through knee-deep water.

She entered the grotto, shielded her eyes from the brightness.

The others shielded their eyes too. One had a bullet hole in the center of his forehead, another in the gut, his shirt stained with a rose bloom of blood around the wound. A woman in a chair didn't seem wounded at all, as she stared at all those dark corridors punched into the grotto's ivy-covered walls. A little girl seemingly taking a nap on the grotto's floor had the worst head wound across her right ear that Maddy had ever seen.

Over there, in that place, Maddy had seen plenty of things that walked and lived and breathed that never should have, things that had no place anywhere outside the imagination. The place where the grass was a buttery yellow, where the wet-paint color of everything—the trees, the mountains, the rivers and roads—was just off enough to think it was all a mistake, like a painting a kid might have done when they didn't quite know yet how everything should really be.

Something that could only come from dreams and nightmares.

Limp, drippy images that made her think of Salvador Dalí.

See, Dad, I'm cultured.

Maddy willed her tired, heavy legs to move. Like she had to relearn how to walk. The slowness of her gait made her think of the rivers of molten lava that ran like scars all over the rugged terrain of that place, that constant flow of heat, the rising tendrils of smoke coming from the twists and turns of it, slowly churning and coiling under bridges, rolling through woodlands and prairies in meandering ribbons of glowing, red and black char.

Someone in the white room yelled, "Don't touch me."

Another woman, her skin blue as if she'd recently drowned, flexed her hand, cupped it like she was holding an invisible one, saying in hushed whispers, "Yes, I can feel your hand."

Even though Maddy saw no hand.

The light grew brighter. The grotto pulsed with it.

Maddy Boyle stood in the middle of the room.

"Maddy? Can you hear me?"

"Yes," she said to no one, to everyone.

"Squeeze my hand if you can hear me."

Maddy flexed her right hand, and somebody started crying.

Somebody—a man's voice: "She's coming out."

Maddy could *now* remember going in. That tunnel of light growing larger until it had consumed her.

Her head throbbed. She closed her eyes to the brightening light. Felt someone gripping her hand. Running fingers through her hair. Machines beeping. Her name being whispered. Her hand touched, squeezed. *Quit touching me.* It was coming back to her.

She'd been attacked. A blow to the head had knocked her out.

"Maddy? Can you hear me?" *Yes, I can hear you.*

During the sponge baths, the nurse wondered if she could hear her humming, and yes, she could. It was terrible, that humming. Off tune and wrong. But this wasn't the nurse.

"She's coming to!" Her father.

"Praise the Lord." Her mother.

Her parents. They wouldn't shut the fuck up, whispering fake words of remorse, wishing they'd done better, wishing they'd been there for her, wishing they'd given her more support. Maybe she wouldn't have been doing what she'd been doing if they'd done this and that?

If only she'd come back to them, they'd make things right.

Wet lips against the top of her right hand. Her forehead.

I'm coming back, but it's not to make things right. Not for you, Mom. And not for you, Dad. I'm coming back because I have a job to do.

And now I'm torn.

Torn because *both* places are bad. But at least *there*, where the ocean tides moved *away* from the shore, she'd been *somebody*.

Older than what she felt like now, but somebody for sure.

"Maddy!"

Yeah, I'm coming.

"She's opening her eyes," her father said.

Charleston, South Carolina. Born the year of Y2K. It's coming back to me.

I'm twenty-two years old. I was attacked. Brutally attacked. I fit the profile for all his victims.

I'd been scared for weeks, just like all the women like me had been scared. And when I say like me, I mean brunette, twenties, and what the newspapers called "pretty" and "petite."

Oh, and a stripper. Yes, Dad, a stripper.

So I carried pepper spray.

I was strangled, and nearly raped, but I fought back. And I'm strong, so I was able to spring loose. I hit him with the spray. He dropped to one knee and cried out like a boy. The goodness in me made me hesitate, to see if I'd killed him. But he was only stunned. He caught me. His weight on top of me. My face against the concrete, two bloody teeth out and bouncing on the Battery's walkway. The smell of body odor and mint. His garbled whisper in my ear. He called me a bitch—oh my God, that voice; like I imagined Owen Meany's might be in that John Irving book (yes, I'm a stripper who reads, Mom)—and he hit me in the back of the head with something hard, what the detectives trying for months to catch him believed to be a horseshoe.

Some of the newspapers had begun calling him the Horseshoe Rapist.

So stupid, Maddy had thought of the sensationalized headlines in the weeks before her attack. He doesn't rape *with* the horseshoe, so that nickname wasn't right. He'd hit me with the horseshoe—that much I can confirm now—and then he'd thrown me over the Battery wall and into the harbor, where I was found, unconscious, two hours later.

But he never got at me.

No one has ever gotten you, Maddy Boyle.

The pepper spray had panicked him. I'd broken him from his routine. All serial killers have routines.

I'm an English major. No, a double major. The other, creative writing.

The Charleston Strangler nearly killed me. The Horseshoe Rapist, but he didn't.

He never got that far—he didn't *get* me.

Not like that rat orderly sort of got at me in the hospital two days later, with his hand under the bedsheet when nobody was looking, when by then everyone had assumed I couldn't feel or see anything. Right before I'd completely entered Lalaland.

That's what they'd called it.

I take my clothes off and dance—to pay my way through college, Dad. Because you and Mom wouldn't. But that oftentimes makes men feel like they have the right to touch me. And they don't. You fucking don't, Jerry-the-Orderly.

"Maddy?" *Who's touching my hand?* "Can you hear me?"

My dad, before the attack, had not been able to look at me, not since he'd learned what I was doing at night to make money. He'd assumed the worst.

He'd never cried over me then.

So why was he crying over me now?

CHAPTER

11

Beth

Now

A s much as Beth wanted to accompany Natalie and the ambulances back to the hospital, she knew her presence there would not be helpful.

"Let the medical field do their job, Beth," Natalie had said inside the tunnel, her hands gripping both of Beth's arms at the elbows, fingers squeezing into her flesh to make her point, sober now that the crime scene had shocked her. "And you do yours."

Beth had nodded, clearly shaken by seeing her boss's gutted body. Grover Meeks was not only her boss, but her mentor, and for the past dozen years, her only father figure. He'd insisted on day one, when she was eleven and he'd first walked her into his home as her new guardian, that she call him by his first name. Had Harrod's Reach not already been aware of how close they were, there might have been whispers about a recently orphaned teenage white girl now living with a black couple old enough to be her grandparents, but were actually her godparents.

Everyone knew Grover and Beth's biological father, who'd been dying of colon cancer for two years, had been family friends for decades, and that Beth's mother died tragically in a car wreck when she was six. Some said the cancer struck her father's heart right there in the church, until it festered and slowly spread out all over the rest of his body as rotted heartache.

Beth had held Grover's hand during her mother's funeral because her father had been too broken to do it. She looked up at him for comfort. His gold sheriff's badge glowed that day, made her want to be like Grover. To do what he did. To put away bad guys and drunkards like the one who'd killed her mother in the car wreck.

A week after the funeral, on a playdate, she'd stared at the scar on Gideon's upper lip. Grover told her he'd had surgery when he was little and it was fixed now, and to not stare at it. But she couldn't help it. She'd known Gideon as long as she'd known anyone. They'd been born the same night, during one of the more violent storms to ever come upon the Reach. Their births had been talked about for weeks. Jax said she was only friends with Giddy-Up because they were forced to be. Like they were a weird set of twins born to two different couples. Beth told Jax to shut up, but it wasn't too far from the truth. The newspapers back then had done a story on them. Their parents had known each other, and had a few times in passing joked about who would give birth first, but they weren't yet the friends they would become after their children were born nearly simultaneously the night of the storm.

"Beth?"

Beth blinked away the reverie and stared at Natalie. "Go on. I'll be fine." Natalie's coworkers had already taken both men out of the tunnel on stretchers.

"I'll text you." Natalie turned toward the tunnel's southern exit and ran to catch up to the medics and the stretchers. Both men were still alive, but barely. Grover with a chainsaw wound through his gut. She'd taken pictures of every blood mark and footprint and fingerprint. The set of antlers that had looked real at first, but was made from branches and sticks crudely fastened together with tightly woven twine.

And Christ . . . Doc . . . his arm had been severed near the shoulder, the hand still holding his phone. His right leg had been severed at the knee and was still missing. Unlike Grover, whose wound was chainsaw-messy, Doc's two wounds had seemed to be almost cauterized.

Beth pulled out her gun, stood atop the north wall's brick rubble, stepped into the opening Doc had made wider, and entered the northern woods. She bypassed the crime-scene tape from the bodies found two days ago, following her flashlight beam, and forged a path through the trees. Simon's cabin was a half mile northeast, a mile if she followed the real path toward Harrod's Lake. Jax once told her the willows overhanging the lake were really weeping, that the tears that dripped from them created the steam so often seen skimming the water's surface, the morning mist floating through the woods.

She checked her phone as she walked. Jax had called six times. She ducked under overhanging limbs, stepped over a trickling creek, and continued toward the true path that was fifty yards in front of her. She knew she should call Deputy Lumpkin for backup, but even if Lump had awakened from his passing out at the party, he'd be useless to her out here. She let Jax's voice mails play on speaker as she navigated the forest.

Beth, bring me a plate of whatevs when you leave. Tell Giddy-Up I said hi. Chicken tenders if they got'm. If Mrs. Deats baked her brownies, grab some. Fucking love those things.

Beep.

Beth, call me, I think there's someone outside . . .

Beep.

Beth, it's me, I don't know where you are, but call me back . . .

Beep.

Beth, what the fuck? Somebody just tried to break into the house. Not ours, here with . . . Jesus . . . The message ended.

Beep.

Beth forged on, oblivious to the branches hitting her arms and face as she listened to Jax's voice: *He's awake, Beth, he's fucking sitting up in bed, he's talking . . . Here, listen . . .* Beth stopped cold as she heard Sully Dupree's voice clear as day: *Run, Doc. Run!* Beth's hand shook so violently she nearly dropped the phone. Sully's voice continued, softer now, more channeled to a certain purpose: *Kathy Locks. Madeline Boyle. Reggie Gathers. Clinton Booth, Amy Shimp, Lauren Betts, Steven Farnsley . . .*

What? Who are these people? Madeline Boyle? Why did that name sound familiar?

Jax's voice again, with Sully reciting mostly names in the background: *You see . . . he's just calling out names, Beth. I don't know what to do . . . Call me, goddamn it . . .*

"Write them down," Beth shouted into the woods. "Write them down, Jax."

Beep.

Beth, he's out again. I don't know what's going on. I can't tell if he's breathing . . . Jesus . . . Where are you . . . ?

The messages ended as she broke through the woods toward the foot-path to Simon's cabin bordering the lake. The shortcut had saved her at least five minutes, but had left her with scratches on her face and arms. She tried calling Jax, but her phone had no service, out near the tunnel and the lake. She followed her flashlight beam through the turns of the dirt path. Moonlight blinked through the tree canopies above. Swirls of fog slithered around her ankles and dissipated like cigar smoke.

Something moved in the woods to her left, then from the shadows to the right.

She turned her brisk walk into a trot toward Simple Simon's cottage, a small cabin with a centered front door flanked by two four-paned windows on either side. She'd been out to Harrod's Lake plenty as a teen and a handful of times as an adult, and although she'd seen the cottage she'd never paid it much attention. But she wasn't expecting to see what Simon had done to the dozens of trees all around it. He wasn't just using The Ripper to saw down trees, but to carve sculptures.

And he was good. Damn good. In terms of art, he was an imaginative genius. It seemed that every tree trunk within a thirty-foot radius had been made into a wooden tree sculpture, like an army of chainsaw-carved totems. Some stood four feet tall, others as tall as ten to fifteen feet. Each trunk had been turned into something sinister, strange totems of animals and gargoyles and monsters she scanned with the hazy beam of her flashlight.

It was common knowledge he could draw with the best of them, but to do this?

She closed in on the cabin. Firelight flickered through grimy windows.

The front door was open a crack.

Beth called Simon's name, waited a beat, and then nudged the door open with the flashlight. It felt like a furnace inside; a fire snapped in the hearth to her right. Upon closer inspection, a set of homemade antlers, reminiscent of the ones found inside the tunnel, burned in the flames, as if recently tossed in.

"Simon?"

A king-sized bed sat in the middle of the room. The bedsheets and covers were so rumpled she feared he might be hiding beneath them. She nudged them with her flashlight, and something skittered out from the folds.

Beth jumped back, pointed her gun at what appeared to be a rat at first, but wasn't.

Maybe a squirrel, she thought, desperately scanning for it again, trying to convince herself that what she'd just seen hadn't been fucking yellow. Or orange. Maybe it was the glow from the fireplace, but whatever she'd seen, the color of it had not been natural. Mounted on the wall above the headboard was another set of antlers, man-made as well but larger than the others.

She aimed her flashlight toward the wall opposite the fireplace. It was illuminated by two sconces and festooned with oddly colored animal pelts, mounted with nails. One from what might have been a deer. Another from a raccoon. Several squirrels and maybe a beaver. In between the pelts, Simon had drawn with chalk or white paint the same figure over and over, a tall, rail-thin monster with antlers. Sometimes he'd drawn it large, other times small, but the figures drawn numbered in the dozens.

The pelts and furs made no sense. The colors were wrong, all different hues of red and blue and green and orange.

He's painting them. He's catching them and painting them.

"Simon?"

Something moved on the bed again. The rodent she'd seen earlier jumped from the covers—it was sunflower yellow, for sure—and disappeared into the shadows, into a pile of clothes in the far corner of the room next to what she guessed was the bathroom.

That door was closed. Light shone through the uneven gap between the bottom of the door and the slanted floorboards. Steam slithered out like morning mist. She closed in on the door, heard running water, and then noticed tiny rivulets coming from beneath the door, finding grooves and whorls inside the floorboards to settle and puddle.

She knocked, jiggled the locked door. "Simon!" Again, no answer.

She kicked at the doorknob. The flimsy door splintered at the lock. A second kick broke it open. A steam cloud enveloped her as she stepped into the damp, humid bathroom. A gush of water splashed from the tub to her left, spilling across the tiles in a loud, clapping wave, soaking her boots and jeans to the ankles.

"Simon!"

The large man's body floated beneath the water's surface, fully clothed, his massive bare feet angled up from the water and braced against the tiled wall on either side of the faucet and knobs. His large, knuckled fingers clutched the side of the tub, not trying to pull himself out—holding himself in. His hair floated like seaweed from a head that seemed even bigger than normal, distorted by the water, brown eyes open and unblinking. Bubbles floated in torrents from Simon's nostrils and mouth, pockets of air exploding at the surface. She reached in, clutched his shirt at the buttons. Simon was twice her size, but when she grabbed his shirt and hoisted with all her strength he lifted upward. She pulled and yanked until Simple Simon slumped over the side of the tub.

He cried out, heaving, terrified.

Beth beat him on the back. Water escaped his lungs, his mouth. She backed away, gave him space. He draped a trouser-soaked leg atop the tub's siding and crawled from it, landing with an earthquake-like thump on the bathroom floor. He rolled to his back, coughing, beard soaked and bug-eyed.

"Simon . . ." She reached for her handcuffs. "Can you hear me?"

He stared hard at her, and then said, "Baa, baa . . ."

"What? Simon?"

"Black sheep," he sang, voice still gargled with water. "Have you any wool . . ."

That voice. "Simon, I need you to stand up and come with me."

"Yes, sir, yes sir. Three bags full . . ." He sat up, coughed out water, held his hands out in front of him to be cuffed, in complete cooperation. "One for the master, and one for the dame. And one for the little boy who lives down the lane . . ."

*M*OST IN TOWN *said they heard it right at midnight, that sound of an ocean tide coming in, a sound that made no earthly sense in the middle of a heavily forested town, and, to most who'd heard it, it lasted for a good ten minutes before fading; but I'd heard it briefly, and perhaps with more subtlety, earlier in the day, when I'd been down at the tunnel investigating the disappearance of Bret Jones, only to see a pink seagull fly out from the darkness.*

That shook me, for sure, but I wasn't mentally prepared for what was found down there at the south entrance the next morning.

Loretta Bevins, at the Gazette, may have caught me smiling in the photo as I held up that weird, bright orange fish, but it was forced.

Truth was, I was scared.

Terrified, even.

Still am.

CHAPTER

12

Theodore

Before

TEDDY KICKED HIMSELF.

He'd been kicking himself ever since he'd left the hospital in Charleston four hours ago. He'd spent three hours of it inside his newly painted bus, angry, contemplating where he could have gone wrong. He got so worked up at one point, it took the memories of a woman he'd had in Tampa three weeks prior to calm himself down. A curvy brunette who'd given him such a good night in the bedroom he'd considered, for the first time ever, coming back. Considered, perhaps, even becoming a one-woman man. For a while, reliving that night with her had worked in relieving his anger, but now that he was on hour four of kicking himself, of wondering what in the fuck to do, of waiting for that seashell beside him to give him a free answer or two, he realized where he'd gone wrong.

He'd spent too much time on the bus.

Finding and buying the bus had been in the cards, he was still convinced of that, but perhaps spending three full days painting it had been a bit excessive. He'd cleaned the bus, vacuumed, replaced five of the cushioned benches. He'd washed the windows, put on new wiper blades, and painted the exterior rust-red, not two coats but three, all while Mother had watched from where he'd parked her wheelchair at the living room window, finishing three days later, all because he'd decided, at the last second, and after hearing "Paint It Black" by the Rolling Stones, to paint the bus's red door black.

He'd taken *that* as a sign too, because music mattered. He'd been proud, damn near orgasmic, when he'd taken a step back to view in full the finished product, as majestic as these live oaks towering all around him. But the painting had put him days behind, and his anxiety had grown with every mile he'd sped south toward Charleston, eager to make up lost time, in a near panic to get to the next name on his ever-growing list of dead-heads.

Madeline Boyle. Maddy to her friends and family, a senior at the College of Charleston who moonlighted as an exotic dancer, and the latest victim of the yet-to-be-caught Charleston Strangler, also known as the Horseshoe Rapist. The horseshoe was his weapon of choice. So said the newspapers. So said the voice on the other end of that seashell.

Teddy smacked the oversized steering wheel with the padding of his hand until it hurt. Sometimes if he couldn't cause pain to others, causing it to himself gave him the necessary fuel, even if only temporarily, to plow onward.

Plus, a bruise could work as a visible reminder for him to never dillydally again.

He started the bus, holding the key in the forward position until the big engine growled to life. Teddy took to the low-country roads, and replayed the shock he felt when he'd entered Maddie Boyle's hospital room four hours ago as the pretend Dr. Lomax, only to find it full of family members crying and doctors and nurses flabbergasted and smiling, and Maddie Boyle herself, sitting up in bed and sipping from a straw.

When and how did that happen?

Him just knowing it had been during his last coat of paint on that bus. The unnecessary coat. And also that sometimes dead-heads just came back to life.

Life was funny that way. But did it have to happen to the next one on his list?

Teddy supposed he could stay in town and wait it out. Maybe sneak back into the hospital as Dr. Lomax again and smother her with a pillow. Of course, it was harder to kill the fully functional than a dead-head, but he'd done it in the past and could do it again. The bus was a problem. He had no doubt it would soon become useful, but it would only hinder as a getaway vehicle. Plus, Maddy Boyle would be watched and monitored for days, even after she returned home. Getting to her would not be easy.

And he didn't have time to be idle.

Not too many dead-heads woke up, so it had caught him off guard. Waiting around would only cause more problems. He had bigger fish to fry. It was more important to hit the road and get on with it than to wait around for some emaciated stripper.

You can't possibly win them all, Teddy.

Just win most.

Ten minutes later, with his mind starting to drift back toward that freak-in-the-bed brunette from Tampa—Brandy had been her name—recalling how knowingly her long, sky-blue fingernails had teased through his thick hair, not flinching or pulling back at all when her fingers traced over the two growths in there, smiling and chuckling even, groaning seductively like what she'd just felt within his hair she'd been *searching* for. Suddenly, her phone number came back to him, area code and all, and his heart began to pump with lust. Memory like a damn steel vault, he thought, eyes on the road, passing one live oak after the next, all that clinging Spanish moss glistening like magic crystals in the sunlight.

He thought of his childhood as he drove, and it infuriated him.

The awkwardness. The confusion. The numerous trips to the doctor. The tests and check-ups and experts. The ridicule over being different. Having an overbearing mother most thought crazy. A father he never knew yet whose voice he somehow distinctly remembered. The voice he'd heard in his head throughout childhood and adolescence and teenage years, and was only truly beginning to understand now as a man, when he'd become fully matured, fully bloomed.

The late bloomer mother always said he was.

That voice. *Mr. Lullaby.*

Teddy began to sing as he drove. "Hush, little baby, don't say a word. Mama's gonna buy you a mockingbird. And if that mockingbird won't sing, Mama's gonna buy you . . ."—he saw something on the road ahead—". . . a diamond ring . . ."

Not a thing, but a person. A man walking a hundred yards in the distance, first alongside the road, and then, at about fifty yards away now, walking down the center of it, toward him.

Like the man was trying to play chicken with the bus, what Teddy only now decided, in the exact moments when he'd made the choice to slow down and not steamroll the man, to call the Lullaby Express. The burly man didn't budge. He stood there in the middle of the road, long brown hair tousled down to the shoulders of his plain black tank top, beefy shoulders pinkened by the sun, camo trousers bunched at the ankles atop heavy, mud-crusted boots.

Teddy stopped the bus, let it idle, the grille ten paces from the man. The seashell wind-whistled beside him.

Teddy stared at it—the timing of that thing was uncanny. He let it whistle for a good thirty seconds before picking it up. "Lomax here," he said, keeping his eyes on the man through the windshield, half expecting *that* man's voice to be the one through the seashell. *Make the stops*, the deep, familiar voice said before going silent.

Teddy carefully placed the seashell on the dashboard, like if he tilted it too much one way water might come out, and sometimes he half expected it to. His hands shook. Not from nerves, he decided, but anxiety. Not a bad anxious, either, but the good kind. The best kind, in fact; so good he felt the tingle of static spread out as warmth across his scalp, a sensation so real it made it feel like his hair was growing.

Something was growing.

He swallowed hard, placed both hands on the wheel.

Finally, the man out on the road moved forward, two methodical steps closer to the bus before pausing again. Ten seconds later he walked the rest of the way, standing right outside the black door of the Lullaby Express.

Mother always told him to steer clear of strangers, especially if they were as odd-looking as this big hoss, but Teddy opened the door for the total stranger anyway. Maybe not total, thought Teddy, feeling an unexplainable connection as he sized the man up.

Up close, the man was more doughy than muscular. More socially awkward than not. Less of a threat than he had seemed out alone on the road.

"Where you heading?" asked Teddy, feeling the power of sitting high and looking down.

"I don't know." The man avoided eye contact. His hands were callused and dirty. He flexed and unflexed his fingers, like some nervous tic, and then said, "Wherever you're going."

Guess we'll know when we get there, the voice inside Teddy's head said.

Teddy jerked the man a nod, not even knowing for sure where he was going—other than tackling more names on his list, more dead-heads—and coaxed the man up and into the bus, thinking, *My first stop just might be Tampa.* "Watch your step," he said with a grin. "And welcome to the Lullaby Express."

Oh, how good that felt, saying it, like melted butter off his tongue.

The strange, large man paused as if something had just registered true, or perhaps in amusement, as the Lullaby Express would, he could tell already, be different than any other bus ride to ever precede it.

The man stepped onto the bus. It rocked slightly under his weight, each heavy step like a slow-motion event.

A butterfly entered the bus's open door and landed on the man's left shoulder like a pet. The man looked dead in the eyes, and paid it no attention. Teddy realized now that it was not a butterfly but a moth. A small, ashy moth, right out in the middle of the daylight. And then a second one flew in, but instead of landing on the man, it came to a rest on the Lullaby Express's dash, right next to the seashell, like it was fixing to crawl inside.

Teddy closed the door so no other moths would get in. The man flinched as the door shut behind him. Teddy said, "Sit where you like."

The man stared down the narrow lane between the seat rows, and headed slowly, almost wearily—like he hadn't slept in weeks—toward the rear of the bus, the three blood-crusted horseshoes attached to his waistline jangling like heavy wind chimes.

The moth stayed on the man's shoulder.

Teddy waited for him to pick his seat, the very last row on the right side of the bus.

"And if that billy goat won't pull," Teddy sang softly toward the moth watching him from the wide, recently Armor All'd dashboard. He put the bus in gear. "Mama's gonna buy you a cart and bull." He watched through his rearview mirror as the man settled in the last row and rested his head atop the seat back as if utterly exhausted. The man in the back of the bus closed his eyes as the bus picked up speed.

Teddy glanced in the rearview, smiled when he noticed the man snoring.

Kept smiling when he saw the dashboard moth had moved to his steering wheel. Teddy offered it his right index finger and the moth flew to it like a bird on a birdcage bar.

He remembered back to his childhood, to his adolescence, and said, "Hello, old friend."

13

Gideon

Now

S ULLY WAS ALIVE.
Once they'd all realized he was breathing, cradled as he was in Jax's outstretched arms, they'd all let out a collective sigh of relief. Maxine had carefully taken Sully's limp body from Jax's shaking arms.

Archie gasped, whimpered, and turned away, the heels of each hand pressed into his eye sockets so hard his eyeballs clicked. He stood suddenly, slapped the wall with an open hand, glanced toward Jax, or maybe Gideon, and stormed out of the room, yelling "Fuck!" so loud Maxine started crying all over again, even as she frantically hooked her comatose son back up to every tube and wire and device he must have ripped himself from upon waking up minutes ago.

Gideon heard his father in the kitchen, rooting around in the freezer. Ice clinked into an empty rocks glass, and then he heard the top of a bottle being twisted off.

"Mom," Gideon said quietly to his mother.

"He's doing what he needs to do, Gideon."

Jax said, "He came out . . . I promise he came out . . ."

Maxine crawled atop the bed with Sully and lay with him, stroking his hair, gently resting her head to his chest as if to track every beat of her son's heart.

Jax watched her. He watched Sully. Jax also seemed to be tracking Mr. Dupree's whereabouts in the kitchen, as if he could see through walls. He watched them all except for Gideon.

"What happened?" Gideon asked.

"He woke up."

"I got that much. You said there was someone in the room?"

Jax averted his eyes, which told Gideon some untruths were coming. While Beth was a straight shooter, Jax was a known liar, and terrible at it, and so he stammered, "I . . . I was in the bathroom."

Which told Gideon he wasn't, or at least hadn't been when Sully had come to.

"Did you flush?"

"What . . . what do you mean, did I flush?"

"I mean, when you heard my little brother wake up, did you immediately come running or did you take the time to flush?"

"The fuck does that matter?"

It doesn't, thought Gideon. It doesn't have anything to do with anything, but he knew that flustering someone was often crucial in getting to the root of the matter. If he was going to get Jax on his heels, it would be best to stun him from the get-go. By questioning him on something completely irrelevant. "Did you flush?"

Maxine stood from the bed. "Gideon, stop. What's this all—"

Jax stepped forward, arms folded across his chest. "Yeah, I flushed. And then I heard Sully and came running."

"Heard him how?"

"With my ears."

Maxine stepped in between the two of them. "What happened, Jax?"

"Sully . . . he . . . he woke up. I was down the hall." Jax pointed toward the kitchen.

"Bathroom's the other way," said Gideon.

Maxine said *stop* with her glare, and then urged Jax to go on.

"He was yelling *Run. Run.* Over and over again."

"That's it?" asked Gideon.

"Run." Jax closed his eyes, touched his temples, something Gideon knew he'd always done when he needed to get the hamster wheel running again. His eyes flashed back open. "Doctor Bigsby."

"What about him?" asked Maxine, gently touching Jax's powerful forearm in a way that made Gideon wonder exactly how close Beth and

Jax had gotten to the family since he'd been gone. Beth had always been a family friend, but not necessarily Jax, who Archie had always secretly ridiculed because he thought Jax's father was a Neanderthal, and apples, in his mind, *never* fell far from trees. But Beth and Jax were married now, thought Gideon. And with Jax's dad being who he was and both of Beth's biological parents dead, had Archie and Maxine taken on the role of grandparents for the two of them?

Jax said, "He was telling Dr. Bigsby to run."

That brought Gideon's mind back. "Beth is on her way to the tunnel now."

"Why?"

"Because Doc was in trouble."

"What kind of trouble?"

"I don't know." Gideon pointed toward the bed. "But somehow my little brother does. Or did. Enough so that he was telling him to run. Unless you made that—"

The punch came before Gideon could defend himself, or even duck, and it caught him straight in the nose, knocking him back into the wall, where he stumbled to the hardwood floor, seeing stars.

Maxine shrieked, knelt beside her oldest son, but Gideon waved her off.

"Oh dear." She seemed more upset at him than at Jax for throwing the punch.

Gideon leaned on his elbows, blinked moisture from his eyes.

Jax paced the room, clenching and unclenching his hands, back and forth past the tall open window he now pointed to. "He came in through here."

Gideon made it to his feet, kept a hand over his bloody nose. "It wasn't locked?"

"We open it sometimes, to let the fresh air in," said Maxine. "Sully likes it."

"And how in the hell do you know that, Mom?"

She turned on him and hissed. "He likes it!" *How dare you*, her eyes said.

And it was true, thought Gideon. *How dare he question any of it?* And now Mom was staring at his bloody nose. Maxine hurried from the room, Gideon assumed, to go get towels or ice, or who knows what. As much as it had hurt, the punch seemed to have calmed both him and Jax down. "Did you get a look at him? The man who came through the window?"

"Not a good one." Jax watched Sully on the bed, the sounds of the machines magnified by the sudden silence in the room. "He must have heard me coming."

"From the bathroom . . ."

"Yeah, from the fucking bathroom, Giddy-Up. And then he went back out the same window he came in."

"What was he wearing?"

"I don't know . . . like a . . . like khakis and a polo. Maybe it *was* Doc. That's why Sully called his name and said run."

"Doc's in the tunnel."

"Christ." Jax ran a hand over his buzz cut. "I know. I know. It doesn't make any sense." Jax pulled out his phone, checked it. "I've been trying to call Beth all night. She won't answer." He stopped pacing, snapped his fingers. "I left her a message. A bunch of them actually, one where I put the phone up to Sully when he was talking. There's your proof."

"I believe you," Gideon said.

"Doesn't sound like it."

"What was Sully saying?"

"I don't know," he said. "I mean . . . I do, but . . . I don't know why. It was so weird and I wasn't ready. But just . . . names. Random people." Jax hurried over to the bedside table and grabbed a newspaper, one of the crossword puzzles Archie would do while he sat with Sully. "I was so thrown, I missed the first five or six names he shouted, but he was yelling them out so urgently I hunted down a pen and that paper and started writing them."

Gideon held the newspaper, turned it, read the seven names written in the margins, jotted haphazardly atop, aside, and below the typeset print of the folded paper. "That was smart."

Jax laughed. "Thanks. Not a word I've ever heard much before."

"Did he start calling out these names before or after he told Doc to run?"

"After. I heard him yelling *run* when I was in the bathroom, and then coming down the hall. As soon as I entered the room, I saw whoever it was going out the window. He had dark hair, and . . ."

"And what?"

"Nothing."

"And what, Jax?"

"Antlers," he said. "Fucking antlers, okay?"

"Real?"

"Of course, they weren't real, Giddy-Up, what the fuck? It was like a Halloween thing or something."

"You're just remembering that detail now?"

"Things are coming back to me," he said. "I'm a little juiced right now if you haven't noticed. And save the interrogation bullshit for my *wife*. Mrs. *Sheriff*."

"*Deputy* sheriff."

"Yeah, might as well be full on. She lives, sleeps, eats, and breathes it. You should see her Murder Pit in the basement. All those murderers pinned to the wall. It's crazy the research she does. It's either the job or the kid, you know?"

"No, I don't know."

"Anyway, yes, she's my wife, Giddy-Up, so suck it."

Maxine returned with a wet towel, a bag of ice, and a palm full of Advil.

Gideon took the towel from her and left her holding the ice and pills. He blotted at the blood around his nose and mouth, quickly turning the towel red. Maxine said he should hold his head back and he said he would in a minute.

He wasn't done with Jax, although it seemed Jax was done with them. He brushed past Gideon toward the hallway.

"Where you going?" Gideon asked, still tasting blood on his tongue.

"To the tunnel."

Gideon followed him down the hall. "What did he say? After the names?"

"Nothing," said Jax, without turning around. "His voice kept getting weaker as he went, like whatever two-minute burst that was back there had taken a whole hell of a lot out of him. By the time he got to the last name, he was mumbling, and then he was out."

"Why were you holding him? Jax?"

Jax stopped and turned so quickly in the hallway Gideon almost ran into him. "Because he was sitting up in bed, Giddy-Up. He was scared. He looked like he couldn't even see. Had his arms out like he needed a hug. So I gave him one. Okay?"

Gideon nodded, like sure, fine. Unexpected from you, but okay.

"He clung to me. You'd think after being a vegetable for so long he wouldn't have any strength, but . . ." Jax choked up, first a hitch in his voice, and then his eyes pooled. "He clung to me. I didn't know what else to do. So I fucking hugged him."

Tears rolled down Jax's cheeks, and it froze Gideon like a deer in headlights. All he could muster was, "What next?"

"He whispered in my ear. Said . . . said something like, find them . . ."

Maxine had followed them from Sully's parlor. "Find who?"

Jax shook his head like he didn't know, but then said, "Those names. Those names he was saying. I don't get it, but that's what it's gotta be, right?"

"For something that doesn't make sense," said Gideon, "that might be the only thing that does. But Jax . . ."

"What?" Jax sounded annoyed.

"Did you unplug Sully from everything? When you hugged him?"

"No, the man did. Whoever he was . . ."

Gideon felt sick to his stomach. Maxine placed a trembling hand to her mouth, and then hurried back to see Sully. Gideon said to Jax, "Why would someone want him dead?"

Jax wiped his eyes, shook his head. "I don't know. I gotta go."

Gideon followed Jax as far as the kitchen, where Archie poured himself another two fingers of bourbon over ice that had yet to melt from the first glass.

Jax rounded the far side of the marble-topped island. "See you, Mr. Dupree."

Archie nodded, fighting his own emotions, unable to look at either one of them. His eyes were on the belt coiled like a snake atop the island, right next to the bowl of apples and oranges and bananas Dad was *supposed* to be eating.

Jax saw it too. He stopped, backtracked, and grabbed the belt before leaving.

But Jax was in uniform, his belt still laced around his waist. So whose belt had that been?

The front door closed.

Archie looked at Gideon. "What happened?"

At first Gideon thought, what happened to what? To Sully? But then he noticed his father eyeing the blood on his shirt, his swollen, bloody nose. "Oh, he hit me."

Archie downed his bourbon in one swallow. "You hit him back?"

Gideon's lack of a response was response enough, apparently, because Archie then left the room without another word.

14

Maddy

Before

M ADDY BOYLE WAS told by the doctors to ease back into things. With someone in her situation there was no distinct timetable. She'd been out for nearly eight days; the fact that she was speaking and able to move all her limbs was a miracle in itself.

Focus on eating, Maddy. On keeping food down, building back your strength.

"It's not a race, Madeline," her father had said on her second day home from the hospital, when he'd caught her in bed trying to do a sit-up but failing. Him patting her head like she was a puppy, and not the slut he'd called her in the weeks before her attack. *Yeah, Dad, I remember.* Little did he know he'd walked in on sit-up number ten, which had been her goal from the beginning, and not what he'd assumed was her first and unsuccessful attempt. She not only did ten the next day but managed to push out fifteen before collapsing back down to her pillow, exhausted, panting and sweating, but feeling good about her future.

And now, three weeks after her release, three and a half weeks from suddenly awakening from her coma—and now with two new fake teeth to replace the two her attacker had knocked out—she was up to walking three miles a morning, and able to rip through fifty pushups and fifty crunches without effort. And the more she became her old self, which was to say, driven, smart, self-assured, strong, and, according to her parents, hard-headed to a fault, the more her parents—especially her father—began to drift away. Drift *back* away, as she'd never been the favorite child; she had, in fact, been an accident. She didn't have time for second chances, which was what she assumed they'd been going for since they'd nearly lost her, acting the way they had that first week. Smiling and chatty and so constantly *there*. So physically present it had taken her only a day or two to snap at them to give her some space.

Before the attack it had been all about their southern, low-country social calendars and high-paying jobs—he CEO of a popular hardware store chain, she a lawyer who sued doctors for malpractice. Maddy's two older siblings, Mark and Theresa, were married to gorgeous people living cookie-cutter lives: they'd married within their own country club, spouses Mom and Dad had joking-not-jokingly set up with other families years in advance, so that they could promptly produce more little cookie-cutter kids.

Maddy was an aunt five times over. Her brother and sister married their high school sweethearts and they'd all attended the University of Alabama, where their parents had met, popular in their Greek fraternity and sorority back in the day. Not Madeline, five and six years younger than Mark and Tammy, respectively, and perpetually unattached. Or another way to put it, as her father had so often done, attached to *too* many, and none of their choosing. With her sandy-colored curls and pretty green eyes, she was considered beautiful, like her siblings—a real catch, as her father liked to say.

Any boy would be lucky to have you, Madeline.

But she didn't just want *any* boy. She wanted a man. Someone she could trust and talk to and maybe one day marry. And *have* her? What the fuck did that even mean? Like she even *needed* someone. She didn't, and that was the glory of it all to her. She didn't.

She'd been asked out numerous times by boys since middle school, and maybe a quarter of the time she'd say yes. Sometimes one date would lead to two or three, and once, in high school, with Jeffrey Lombard—who her parents had actually liked; he came from good stock—they'd gone out for three months, but even that had ended abruptly, when he'd slid his hand into her pants in the car after he'd bought her a fancy steak dinner, with the attitude that he deserved some kind of sexual repayment.

She'd slapped him, and that relationship ended on the spot.

Her fault, according to her parents, because Jeffrey was such a clean-cut young man. She'd had over a dozen boyfriends in her twenty-two years on earth, starting with holding Kenny Hockenslatta's hand in seventh grade to the asshole with the tattooed arm-sleeve she'd dated briefly, breaking up with *him* two days before her recent attack, only to have him—she remembered his name was Adrian when she saw him on the porch—unexpectedly ring their doorbell three days ago, with a bouquet of roses for her, in hopes of a speedy recovery.

She'd thanked him, gladly accepted the roses, and wished him a good day, not even asking him in for a drink, which was what her mother immediately told her she should have done, implying somehow that that was exactly why she was still single, still unmarried, still the perpetually unattached Madeline Boyle. Adrian would not have been someone her mother would have chosen out of a lineup for her—she abhorred tattoos—but Maddy could tell that over the years her mother had lowered her standards. Maddy knew her mother was tired of telling her friends, while drinking tea or gin or whatever the fuck they drank out around the pool in the evenings, that her youngest was still out there trying to find herself. Her mother's biggest fear, Maddy knew, was that after a time, most would start wondering what was possibly wrong with her. Madeline Boyle, the same girl who liked to run through the country club in shorts and a T-shirt and tennis shoes instead of dresses and blouses and cute little flats with bows, who cut up during cotillion, who quit tennis lessons and golf lessons in favor of reading books and writing poetry, who had even started writing a novel of her own until the Horseshoe Rapist had almost killed her out next to Charleston Harbor.

But seeing Adrian was what had begun her father's retreat away from her. Seeing Adrian and his tattoo sleeve had been an instant reminder of who, in his mind, she'd begun to pick up ever since she'd begun dancing.

Stripping. In his perfect mind, *trash*.

He'd found out about her secret profession through one of his country club friends who frequented the local strip joints, who said he could have sworn the tall glass of water he'd seen on stage that night, Trixie or Dixie, was Madeline. Her father confronted her the next morning and she'd admitted it, with the belligerent attitude they'd come to expect from her. Him saying how she'd always been a disappointment. Him getting even more pissed off when she said she'd been dancing for nearly two years. And it wasn't Trixie or

Dixie, it was Candy. Her blaming him. Blaming Mom. Him bringing up the full ride to Alabama she'd turned down. Him refusing to pay for the three-quarters tuition the College of Charleston had offered.

Him ultimately getting so worked up he called her a whore. Or was it a slut? Yes, it was a slut—spittle had spewed from his lips with how hard he'd said the T.

And it was that word that had fueled her recovery, because yes, Daddy, it *is* a race.

Not only to get out of the house, perhaps for good, but to do what she'd come back from Lalaland to do. Maddy zipped up her flowery Vera Bradley bag, slung it over her shoulder, and walked down to the kitchen, where her mother was fixing toast and her father was sipping coffee, both probably heading to work within the half hour.

Her father saw the packed bag over her shoulder. "Where you going?"

"I'm moving in with Adrian."

Her mother stopped buttering her toast. Her father sipped his coffee, stared out the window toward the pool and hot tub and pergola, but otherwise, other than a grunt, said nothing.

"I'm *joking.*"

Truthfully, she didn't know exactly where she was going. She had a destination, yes, Harrod's Reach, Nebraska, an old railway town that, according to the maps she'd pulled up on her phone, appeared to be right in the area where the northwesternmost tip of Kansas met both Nebraska and Colorado, what some called the Tristate Point, or the Three Corners, like Harrod's Reach was some kind of forested central hub connecting them all. Or she'd thought last night while studying the location, it could also be the absolute middle of the United States, if she was eyeballing it correctly. Like if the country had a navel, Harrod's Reach might be it.

When neither parent responded, she said, "If you want to know the truth, I'm leaving."

This got their attention.

Mom, toast in hand, waited for an explanation.

Dad placed his coffee mug down, leaned back in his chair, and folded his golf-tanned arms. He wore a smirk that said, *This ought to be good.*

In her mind it was. Not only good, but important in ways she couldn't yet explain. She remembered very little of what she'd seen in Lalaland while in her coma, but she assumed that was par for the course. Dreams were fleeting. She hoped it would come back to her, just as memories from her real life had come back to her over the past two weeks. But she told them where and explained it the best she could, and still they looked at her completely flabbergasted, speechless until her mother said, "Where again?"

"Harrod's Reach."

"Never heard of it," said her father.

"Doesn't make it less real."

Mom again, too shocked to be worried: "And who is . . . what?"

"Sully," Maddy said. "His name is Sully Dupree. First name is really Solomon. He's in a coma, like I was, but for three years now."

"And you're what?" said her father. "You're gonna save him or something?"

"I don't know exactly."

All I know is I have a message for him, she thought, although it was still cloudy what it meant. *One brain. Unify* . . . Maybe that wasn't it exactly, but give it time, Maddy, give it time.

"How old is he?" asked her father.

Maddy refocused. Back to Sully Dupree. "Six . . . Seven. Maybe eight."

Her father scoffed, then mumbled, "Little young, even for you, don't you think?"

Without pause, Maddy gave him the finger.

Her father stood from the table. "Get out."

"I'm going," said Maddy.

He stormed out of the kitchen.

Her mother was on the verge of tears. "Maddy, this is so out of the blue. It's nonsensical. Can you at least tell us why?"

"No, I can't." She touched her brow; Lalaland had come through as a shooting star trail of memories, and there were oceans over there that flowed backwards. Forests of mare trees. An island of bones. Every creature and beast under the sun. The days were short and the nights were long. Everything is backwards. Everything is wrong. She opened her eyes, cleared her head. "But it's something I have to do."

Her mother nodded, beckoned Maddy closer, and then hugged her hard and true.

Maddy returned it, awkwardly at first, before allowing herself to melt within her mother's arms, smelling her mother's perfume, the fresh shampoo scent in her hair, letting go before the sudden affection could begin to change her mind. For the moment it held her frozen, hammered home the fact that, yeah, she was scared too.

Maddy wiped her eyes, just like her mother was doing.

"You'll text?"

"Yes, I'll text."

Her mother rooted inside her purse, pulled out a torn piece of paper, and handed it to Maddy. "Read it."

Maddy forced herself to look at the two words written in black ink on it, in what appeared to be her mother's handwriting.

Sully Dupree.

Maddy looked up at her mother, who said, "That's why I'm not trying stop you. When you were coming out of your coma, you kept saying that name over and over. I felt I needed to write it down. And now I know why."

Maddy nodded. "Thank you. And I'll be fine."

"I'm sure you will. Only girl to survive the Charleston—"

"Don't," Maddy said. "I don't ever want to hear that name again. Not until he's caught." She started toward the door but stopped. "Tell Dad . . ."

"What, dear?"

"That . . . that I'm still a virgin."

"Oh, Maddy . . ."

"Tell him I was stripping to pay for a college he wouldn't pay for. And that I did it to spite him. And that I've broken up with so many boys over the years because I'm saving myself for the right one." She opened the door. "Tell him I'm not a slut."

Her mother chuckle-cried. "It's really none of his business either way."

Maddy shared a smile with her mother, their first in years, and then went on her way.

CHAPTER

15

Beth

Now

BETH WATCHED SIMON Bowles from her desk at the sheriff's office.
He seemed smaller now that he was on the other side of the bars of cell block A, one of four side-by-side cells left over from when it had been the Harrod's Reach Police Department, run for seven decades by the town icon, Detective James Harrington.

Simon sat slumped on the cell's cot with his big bare feet on the floor. At least he'd come willingly, having gone from attempting suicide in that tub to fearing for his life on the way back to the station. She'd watched him in the rearview just as she watched him now, twiddling his thumbs. Maybe it wasn't that he seemed smaller behind the bars, just simpler.

Adrenaline had fueled her through Simon's macabre cabin, but it had waned during her drive to the station, and now pure exhaustion gripped her. What to do with him? Where to even start? What to make of that thick photo album–like orange book he'd brought with him, the one with *Lalaland* written in black calligraphy letters on the cover.

And where the hell was Lump? He should have been here by now, off-duty or not.

"Simon says I didn't do it," he'd mumbled repeatedly in the car, until finally she'd told him he wasn't in trouble. A clear lie, but it had shut him up for the moment. Problem was, he was still shut up now when she wanted him to talk. *Simon says?* She wondered if that was something he used to play with his parents. *But what was your chainsaw doing at the tunnel?* It didn't mean he did it, but it was damning, for sure. He probably didn't know to even ask for a lawyer.

Her phone chimed with a text from Jax: *I'm home with Brody. Trying 2 put him 2 bed but he only wants u.*

Sorry, she texted. And then: *I'll be home soon as I can.* And then: *I'm going to the hospital.* And then: *as soon as I finish up here.*

Be careful, he texted.

I will.

Exhausted, she placed her phone face down on her desk. She could have fallen asleep where she sat, but time wouldn't allow it. On a fresh notebook page, she tallied what she'd seen at the cabin, starting with the carved totems outside. The antlers mounted to the wall. The antlers and the strange creature he'd drawn on the wall. All those oddly colored skins and furs. The thick, orange-covered homemade *Lalaland* book he'd insisted on bringing with him, the messy monstrosity of a book now resting on the pillow of his cell block cot. Beth had briefly flipped through it before letting him have it inside the cell. It was a book of his artwork, his portfolio. Every page full of colorful drawings, but all in strikingly vivid color and detail, of some imagined fantasy world.

Beth pinched her eyes closed for ten seconds and considered that her nap.

The door opened and Deputy Lumpkin walked in, disheveled but no longer drunk. The smell of coffee wafted from his thermos. He needed a shave and a haircut. Lump was too young, at forty, to be old school, but he resented her presence in the department, not only because she was a woman but because she was so well liked so quickly.

"Crazy night." Lump plopped down on his desk chair and swigged coffee from his thermos. He stared across the room at Simon. "He do it?"

"Don't know."

He still reeked of alcohol.

Beth stood from her desk and approached the cell block. She'd never known Simon to be violent, or even angry. He kept to himself. Fished Harrod's Lake daily, ate most of what he caught. Sometimes he hunted the woods. Went into town when he needed groceries. Nodded and smiled when people said hello, and then back to the cabin he'd go. Kids in town joked that he was an ogre and he'd eaten his parents, when, in reality, they'd both vanished one night fourteen years ago. Townsfolk said they'd run away and left their simple son to fend for himself, but Beth now knew that to be untrue. Grover had told her one evening two years ago that Simon's parents were two more victims of the tunnel. Two *unreported* victims, Grover had admitted to her, adding, *Beth, there have been as many unreported victims of that tunnel as ones reported over the past century.*

Why did they go unreported?

Because only Mrs. Bowles's left arm was found. And Mr. Bowles, only his left hand. We identified them by the rings on their fingers. And Mr. Bowles's watch was still on his wrist.

Like so many of the other victims of the tunnel, Beth wondered if their wounds too had been cauterized, like what she'd seen with Doc. Severed so rapidly and with such force that the wounds had seemingly clotted on contact. If it was a killer, like most in town thought, where were all the missing bodies? The missing body parts? And why were the bodies found so sporadically? Months and years and sometimes decades in between. The one-man theory had been debunked long ago, as the unexplainable crimes had been going on for well over a century now. At least as far back as the founding of the town, when Colonel Harrod Guthrie's niece, Connie Brine, went missing in the summer of 1865; it was that well-documented event that had started the legend of Connie Brine that still resonated today, as well as the game In-One-Out-One that kids started playing in the years after her disappearance.

In Beth's mind—and Grover's—it all added up to copycats. Evil minds piggybacking off the legends and lore for a quick moment of fame. Or something more sinister.

In his cell, Simon twiddled his thumbs, this way and that, staring at them.

"Simon," said Beth. "Simon? Did you go out to the tunnel tonight?"

He shook his head.

"Did someone steal your chainsaw? They steal a set of your . . . antlers?"

He nodded, reversed the direction of his twiddling thumbs, but didn't look up.

"You make those yourself? Those antlers?" When he gave no response, she asked, "Why do you paint the skins and furs on your wall?" He stopped twiddling his thumbs. She asked, "Why do you paint the skins? On the wall of your cottage. And that squirrel? Simon?"

He placed two massive hands over his ears like he didn't want to listen.

"Why are you catching animals and painting them?"

He shook his head no.

"What's that book there? *Lalaland*? Did you make that?"

He nodded, looked away.

Beth recalled Jax's near-panicked voice on the phone earlier, and how someone had sneaked in through the window and attempted to kidnap or kill Sully.

"Simon, did someone come into your cabin?"

He shrugged.

"How long have you been working on those totems?"

Lump asked, "What totems?"

"He carved an army of creatures in the trunks of the trees outside his cabin," she said to Lump, without turning to look at him. "Simon, those carvings? They're really good. How long—"

"Years." Simon spoke at last.

"Years, huh?" Where have I been, Beth thought, realizing that once things settled down maybe they should make a note of visiting the lake people more often.

Simon resumed twiddling his thumbs, watching them go this way and that.

"You hungry?" Beth asked. Simon nodded. She said over her shoulder to Lump, who had already started playing solitaire on his laptop. "You got anything to eat?"

That was like asking if the Pope was Catholic. Lump lived for food, most of it junk. But how he could act so casual and flippant with Grover fighting for his life down the road was beyond her. Lump opened a desk drawer and grabbed something, hoisted his fat ass out of the chair, and approached the cell block with a grin she couldn't quite read. And then Lump smacked her ass in passing.

He'd been eyeing her since she'd started her official training over a year ago, and truthfully, probably for years before that, as she'd been around the station most of her adolescent life. She was so stunned by his action that she turned and watched him walk, still grinning, toward Simon's cell, holding a pack of peanut butter crackers out to Simon like he was about to feed a zoo animal.

Beth thought, *I hope he rips your fucking arm off.*

Simon was waiting for Lump at the bars. His face had changed; Beth saw clear anger in Simon's eyes.

"Lump," Beth said as if to caution him.

But Lump kept going, dangling the crackers out toward the bars like a tease.

Quick as a snakebite, Simon reached between the bars and clutched Lump's wrist. He yanked forward, forcing Lump's face against the bars. The peanut butter crackers flew into the cell and slid across the floor.

"Simon," Beth shouted, pulling her gun.

Simon put his mouth right next to Lump's reddening face, right up next to the blood now pouring from Lump's nose, and hissed, "Simon. Says. No."

Beth aimed the gun directly at Simon. "Let him go, Simon. Right now."

Simon said it again, "Simon. Says. No."

He let go.

Lump staggered back, holding his nose, catching the blood flow as it dripped through his fingers. "Thon of a bitch . . ."

Simon had returned to his cot and was opening the pack of crackers.

Beth holstered her gun and said to Lump, "Let me see."

She used a bent index finger to tilt his chin up for a good look at his nose, careful not to let any of his blood touch her. "It's broken."

"Thon of a bitch," Lump said again.

"Lips busted up too." Beth gripped Lump's shoulders to keep him from going anywhere, and then plowed her knee into his groin.

He doubled over. "God damn!" He dropped to a knee. "Jesus wept, Beth . . ."

She knelt next to him, put her lips near his ear. "Don't ever touch me again." She said to Simon, "I'll be back soon." She said to Lump, "Call me if he starts talking."

Lump looked up with a smirk and said, "Sure."

She turned back toward Simon one last time. "Simon, what was that thing you drew on your wall? Looked like a man. With antlers?"

"Simon. Says. No," he said again, softer this time, and Beth couldn't tell if he was shooting down her question or just echoing what he'd said to Lump a few seconds ago. He lay back on his cot and the frame groaned. His heavy shoulders pressed against the iron headboard. He stretched his legs out, crossed them at the ankles.

Lump was on his feet now, retreating to his desk for some tissues. "Getting comfortable are you, Simple?" asked Lump.

Beth said, "Stop."

Comfortable, yes, she thought, but more like . . . protected now that he was contained. On his lap, he'd opened *Lalaland* and was flipping through it, each turn of the page like a palpable snap. He flipped forward, back again, stopped about midway through, and then began to read to himself: "Twinkle, twinkle little star . . ."

"The fuck is this?" asked Lump. Then to Beth: "This count as talking?"

She ignored him.

"How I wonder what you are . . . ," Simon went on.

Beth reminded Lump to call if he got to talking.

She closed the door behind her and stepped out into the cool night air, recalling how she'd recited that same lullaby to Brody last night.

Twinkle, twinkle little star . . .

And that now she didn't think she could ever bring herself to recite it again.

16

Gideon

Now

G IDEON STOOD AT the open doorway to the back parlor, watching his
mother sleep next to Sully, her snoring softly, Sully a culmination of
blips and beeps and sucking sounds.

He was dead tired himself, but felt guilty wanting to lie down, not
when he knew Beth was still out there trying to make sense of what all had
occurred over the past few hours. The past week, once you factored in the
tunnel's walls coming down.

He'd reached out earlier via text, asking how he could help, and she'd
told him: *by resting up*. A minute later she'd added: *I'll give you a job come
morning.*

Gideon's nose still throbbed from Jax's sucker punch.

He poured a shot of bourbon in the kitchen and downed it. The burn
spread across his chest. He poured another, knowing it could help as a
sleeping aid, and this one went down smoother. He walked the first floor
of the Smite House looking for his father. There was no sign of Archie
in any of the first-floor rooms, so Gideon walked up the curved stairwell
toward the second. Archie was a beloved history professor at the University of Nebraska, with tenure and just enough publishing credits to
keep him relevant. His expertise was the Roaring Twenties, through the

Great Depression, those years between the World Wars so many teachers glossed over. And while the Smite House had been built in the 1860s, he'd been renovating it for two decades now to match the pictures of what it had been in the 1920s, when the house—then owned by Lucius Smite's grandson, William, and his wife, Samantha—had been host to countless parties and nights full of jazz and dancing, not so much in competition with but an extension of the historic Beehive Hotel up the street. Archie took the history of the house so seriously he'd insisted they all call it the Smite House, as on the Historic Registry.

As Gideon navigated the second-floor bedrooms and bathrooms and library, he realized how much Archie had gotten done in his absence. Work to the hardwood floors and baseboards and crown molding. Painting and wallpaper and wall sconces. He was still a few years away from getting it exactly how he wanted it, but when money was limited, renovations crawled. Archie often told Gideon as a young boy, *sometimes it's preferable to be the tortoise over the hare.* True, Gideon thought now, but that's a tough pill to swallow if you lack the patience, which Archie so often did.

Gideon heard a chair scoot across hardwood above, and followed the noise to the third floor. Either Archie was up there, or the Smite House was haunted like so many in town believed, like he and Beth and Jax had pretended while they played as youngsters. William Smite, when the stock market crashed in 1929, had supposedly hung himself in one of these third-floor bedrooms. Archie had never denied that but had always refused to tell inside which room it had happened.

Gideon found Archie in one of the three third-floor bedrooms, sitting on a wooden chair in the dark, a glass of something in his right hand, staring out the dormer window toward the street. Toward the Beehive Hotel, Gideon assumed, and the dead look in his father's eyes saddened him. This bedroom had already been renovated. The bed was made up with sheets, a blanket, and pillows, and it didn't take much detective work to realize Archie had been sleeping up here. His furry slippers sat on the floor next to the bed. On the end table rested an alarm clock, his reading glasses, and a book on Al Capone. Across the room, on his desk, his laptop was open, although the keys and screen looked dust covered.

Made Gideon wonder how long it had been since his father had touched it.

Archie must have sensed Gideon in the doorway. He held up the glass in his right hand. "It's just orange juice. Blood sugar was dropping."

Orange juice was his go-to; if desperate, he'd down sugar tablets. Maxine had been on him for years to get the pump, but he was hardheaded and kept needles for his insulin. Fingerpicks to test his blood. Five injections a day to keep him regulated. Mostly he'd shoot it into his upper arm. Sometimes into his gut.

Gideon said, "You okay?"

"Yeah." Archie stared out the window.

When it was clear this was going nowhere fast, Gideon turned away. His father's voice stopped him. "This is the room," Archie said.

At first, Gideon didn't know what he was talking about, but when he saw the hint of a smile on his father's face, he knew he was finally admitting in which room William Smite had hung himself in 1929. "No shit?"

"No shit." Archie finished his orange juice, placed the empty glass on the windowsill, but didn't elaborate.

Gideon thought about how his parents used to dance in the kitchen to jazz music from the twenties, or oftentimes Sinatra. He doubted they danced anymore. He said, "Good night."

Archie nodded, and that was that. Gideon was nearly to the banister down the hallway when Archie said, "Welcome home."

*　*　*

Gideon found his second-floor childhood bedroom clean and dusted, the bed neatly made, and the air smelling of the cinnamon candle his mother must have lit earlier.

His Army duffel bag rested next to his bed. They'd exited the gym in such a hurry earlier that he'd left it behind. Someone must have returned it. He unzipped it. The gun was still inside. He removed the baggie that held his Purple Heart, and then the bag holding the bullet. He placed both on the desk, where he'd spent so many childhood hours reading and playing video games and watching movies on his computer. It wasn't the actual bullet that had traveled through the meat of his thigh inside that Afghanistan home, but, of course, nobody knew that but him.

And possibly Baxter. But Baxter had been as wide-eyed and shell-shocked as he had been, as they *all* had been, so there was no telling what was remembered after the dust settled and the room cleared of all that smoke.

Welcome home . . .

I'm no hero, Gideon thought, turning out the light. He slid underneath the bedcovers and closed his eyes. The house seemed more dysfunctional now than it had when he'd left. His time away had helped very little. Sully wasn't ever coming back.

His eyelids grew heavy from the bourbon.

He still felt like he should be out there hunting down whoever had tried to kill Sheriff Meeks and Doc Bigsby, but Beth had said she already had Simon in lockup.

He texted Beth: *How's it going?*

She responded a minute later: *At the hospital now. Doesn't look good.* And a few seconds later: *For either of them.*

Gideon sent: *Sorry and thanks*

For what

Having my back at the gym

What was that about anyway

Dunno

We'll talk tomorrow.

What's going on, beth?

Don't know yet. And then: *Get some sleep*

K goodnight

Goodnight

He waited five minutes before shutting off his phone. He closed his eyes, thinking back to the night before his deployment, replaying that evening like he had so many times overseas, coming to the same conclusion that it had all been a dream. But if that was the case, why could he still smell her hair, smell her arousal, smell the perfume on her neck . . .

Why had she not kissed him that night?

Because it wasn't real, Giddy-Up.

It had all been a dream.

He drifted off.

Thirty minutes later he awoke with a gasp, covered in sweat, the sounds of those two Afghan children screaming, tormenting his ears.

17

Beth

Now

ETH'S TWO-MILE RIDE to the hospital had been eerily quiet.
The entire town was in the middle of a collective gasp for air.
Creepy came to mind now, as Beth witnessed how silent the hospital was
as well. Nobody was talking. Everyone went about their business, fearing for the lives of two of Harrod's Reach's favorites. When Beth had
pulled into the hospital parking lot an hour ago, Father Fred had been
on the tail end of a heavily attended prayer service out by the garden, but
even that now had fallen to silence.

Most had gone home, which Beth couldn't bring herself to do yet.
Mayor Truffant sat in the second-floor waiting room, elbows on his knees,
looking as exhausted as she felt. She'd always thought Mayor Truffant
a goof, with his perpetual tan, toothy smile, and perfectly parted white
hair. His commercials and billboard campaigns were cheesy, but she
knew beneath all the fluff was some true heart, and seeing him outside
the operating room calmed her.

Grover was still in surgery. Doc was out of surgery, but in bad shape,
Mayor Truffant had said when Beth had taken the seat two down from his.
The mayor asked Beth, "Was it Simon?"

"I don't know," Beth said, thinking how fast word traveled. "I've got him in lockup, and he came willingly. I don't think so."

"I can't see him capable. Can you?"

"I'll pass judgment until I know more."

Mayor Truffant smiled. "You sound just like the sheriff."

"I'll take that as a compliment."

"Only way I know to give it," he said. "He's a tough man, Beth. Anybody can pull through that kind of damage, it's Grover. And he's not done yet."

"Hope you're right," she said. "And Mrs. Bigsby?"

"She's fine. Back with Doc now." She could feel him watching her, so she met his tired gaze. "You heard how they found him?"

"I'm the one who found him."

"Right . . . ," he said, scratching his head. "Whatever took off his left arm and right leg must have nicked his head too. Massive brain bleed. Natalie said they had to drain it."

"Not *who*ever? You said *what*ever took his left arm, not *who*ever . . ."

Mayor Truffant grunted, straightened his legs, and leaned back with his head against the wall. "Chalk up another victim of the tunnel," he said. "Least that's how I see it. Been living here long enough to be fully entrenched in the *what* club. No longer the *who*." He closed his eyes. "You talk to Gideon yet?"

"Was just texting with him."

Mayor Truffant opened one eye. "Surprise, right?"

"Surprise is right."

Jesus . . . She closed her eyes, leaned her head back against the wall, wondered what had really been going through Gideon's head when he'd entered the gym and pulled his gun. Panic. Fear. Him running away to the Army had solved absolutely nothing in terms of the guilt he carried over Sully's condition. All war had done was make him physically stronger, but beneath it all was still the same Gideon, scared of his own shadow.

"You heard about Sully?"

"Yeah," said Beth, eyes still closed.

"What do you make of it?"

"Dunno yet."

Beth was on the verge of drifting off when the mayor said, "Grover and me, we're not done yet, Beth." Beth rolled her head to the side, opened her eyes, watched Mayor Truffant start to doze off beside her. He grinned, as if reflecting on a memory only the two of them shared, and then finished his earlier thought. "War. The card game. It never ends, you know?"

"That's why I never play it," she said. "What war ever does?"

"Touché." That grin again. "We combined four decks. We pick it up every so often. Start where we left off. Play at the coffee shop, my house, his . . ."

"Same game?"

"Same game."

"Huh. I always assumed you all were playing something more sophisticated."

"Nah." He rubbed his eyes, looked away, perhaps so she wouldn't notice his tears.

She checked her phone. Lumpkin had deserved that knee to the balls, but she wondered if that was why he'd yet to text her back about the list of license plates she'd sent him twenty minutes ago. Before the hospital, she'd taken a quick drive through the Beehive Hotel's parking lot. Most of the men and women Mickey French had brought in for that renovation were not locals, and most, she'd heard, had been staying at the hotel while they worked. She'd written down eight license plates in all, and she'd sent a pic of the list to Lump, asking him to run them. Maybe one had a record of lopping off heads, of rape, of beating someone's face to pulp with a horseshoe. Grover always said to leave no stone unturned. Her phone chimed. Speak of the devil. It was Lump, finally, but *Ok* was all his text said.

She thought, at least he spelled it correctly, and texted back: *How's Simon?*

Sleeping

She shut her phone off, recalled Simon's massive bed in his cabin, like that was his respite, and sleeping was his profession . . . And *Lalaland*?

Mayor Truffant said, "Everything okay?"

"Yeah, it was just Lump."

"The Reach's finest."

She smiled. A minute later she rolled her head toward the mayor again. "How long's the game of war been going on between you two?"

He rolled his head back to her, eyes open now. "Since we were thirteen."

"No kidding?"

"Scout's honor."

"Didn't know you were a scout."

"I wasn't."

Beth reached her hand over the empty seats toward him. He gripped it. She squeezed, held it for a beat before letting go. "To not being done yet then."

Excerpt from Detective Harrington's notes
April 10, 2000
Harrod's Reach

*L*AST NIGHT'S STORM *was a doozy, for sure. One for the ages, even for Harrod's Reach.*

After a lightning strike near St. Michael at roughly 9 PM, at least three dozen bricks fell from the bell tower to the parking lot outside the rectory.

At 10:03 PM, strong winds took down the back side of Eddie Aidenbrook's barn, killing two of his horses, three goats, and thirteen of his chickens.

By 11:00 PM, Gary Tucker had gotten so angered over his Parkinson's he hammered a three-inch nail through the top of his left hand to keep it from trembling, pinning himself to the dining room table. Unable to wrench the nail free, he screamed for help, but due to the loudness of the thunder, his neighbors on either side didn't hear him until close to one in the morning. By the time the ambulance arrived, Gary was unconscious.

Around two in the morning, at the height of the storm, Chucky Pinrose, supposedly out of town on business, died of a heart attack while making love to his wife's best friend, Gloria Dansberry, who then, out of shame, overdosed on pain pills.

Somewhere between two and four in the morning, Rose Gitchner was murdered inside the train tunnel. According to a neighbor, she'd gone out looking for her missing tabby cat Trixie. Rose's body was found just inside the northern entrance, both arms cleanly severed at the elbows. Weapon still undetermined (see notes on previous cauterized-type wounds in and around the tunnel's north entrance). Rose bled out before anyone could hear her cries for help, despite my repeated warnings THE DAY BEFORE that nobody go in there until we find the man who'd tried to rape Julie McVain inside the tunnel the day before that.

Rose Gitchner's arms have still not been found.

At 2:45 AM the Harrod's Reach Fire Department was struck by lightning. The fire was put out within minutes, as the firemen didn't have far to go to get there.

At roughly 3:00 AM, Harrod's Reach welcomed by candlelight two new babies into the world. From all I can gather, the babies were born within seconds of each other. Due to the storm and subsequent loss of electricity, both families, unable to make it to the hospital, instead delivered inside their homes. Reports from three reliable neighbors claim two windows inside the cellar of the Smite House cracked just as Gideon Dupree was delivered, coinciding with a memorably loud clap of thunder. The boy, born with a cleft lip but otherwise healthy, was reported to have screamed so loudly upon his first intakes of air that the cellar door of the Smite House popped loose of a top hinge and threatened to slide down the stairs, where Professor Archibald Dupree had gone into insulin shock and passed out on the landing at the bottom of the steps.

Down the road, and fortunate enough to have Doc Bigsby on hand, Beth Gardner was born. She'd come out so perfectly, and with what Doc called "such utter silence," that he'd at first thought her stillborn, only for Beth to blink a few seconds later and stare at them all with a look that said (again in Doc's words) "what took you so damn long."

At roughly 5:00 AM, the memorable storm moved on.

18

Theodore

Before

TEDDY LOMAX WAS an attractive man.

He prided himself on many things, most of them superficial. With his sculpted face, azure eyes, and dimpled smile, he *was* an eye-catcher. What his mother had called a room-stealer. And when he grew out his beard, the white circular patch of hair centered in the dark of his cheek made him even more alluring. But what he took the most pride in was his wavy, mahogany-colored hair.

Even as an infant he'd had a thick patch of it, and all through his childhood and adolescence he'd always kept it long, although never unruly. There came a time, specifically when he'd begun to lust after the opposite sex, when his hair had become part of his vanity, but in truth, the hair was a godsend, and so Teddy kept it long out of necessity to hide the two strange growths on his head.

The two wood-textured, half-golf-ball–sized knobs atop his scalp, embedded into his skull since the day he was born, directly north of each ear. Two protuberances no doctor had ever been able to explain or rationalize.

Theodore would not be the first child born with an oddity or unex-plained deformity, but the doctors—and they'd seen many—were never able to hide their concern and confusion, no matter how wide they forced their smiles.

No matter how many times they said it wasn't cancer.

"Do they hurt?" each doctor would ask, taking pictures, measuring to see if they'd grown, rooting through his hair to find them, eyes growing monstrous behind the magnifying glasses they'd hold up to their intrigued faces.

Teddy would shake his head, and tell them no.

Except they *did* hurt sometimes. They'd hurt like little motherfuckers on some nights, especially during puberty. The protuberances themselves, according to the doctors and to Belinda, who'd checked them weekly to make sure *they* weren't growing, didn't seem to be any more raised from the skull than the day he was born. Perhaps they'd grown a little as his skull had grown, but even then, with all the hair, it was difficult to tell.

Difficult to tell indeed, thought Teddy, staring at himself now as a grown man in the mirror of a rest stop bathroom just west of Chattanooga, Tennessee. He'd parked the Lullaby Express in the tree shadows behind the visitors' center, so as not to draw any unwanted attention. He'd told his five passengers—no, he was up to six now, after picking up that odd man in Marietta, Georgia, who'd boarded the bus with an axe—to stay inside the bus. He couldn't have them strolling around, not here, and not yet, anyway, until Teddy figured some things out. Not until he had more answers. But it was clear all the passengers, when he'd found each of them along the way, seemed lost, which was why he understood that *this* was his calling.

The list was still important. Yes, he was still striking down dead-heads off his list, the latest in Salisbury, North Carolina, several hours ago—the poor kid had been comatose for only two days—but making the stops with the Lullaby Express now seemed to be the priority, and the voice in his head had yet to object.

But this stop was for him, and it had been urgent.

"Is it locked?" Teddy asked Brandy.

Brandy, from Tampa, sauntered seductively toward him from the closed bathroom door. "It's locked, baby."

Everything she did was seductive. He'd grown aroused this morning watching her brush her teeth and spit the minty foam into the grass alongside the highway outside Portsmouth, Virginia. And now. Tall red shoes click-clacking off the hard floor. Black miniskirt. Red halter top.

Tight stomach with the piercing—a tiny gold-colored dagger—at the navel. It had been two weeks since he'd driven the bus back down to Tampa on a whim to get her. She'd immediately dropped what she'd been doing when he'd knocked on her apartment door—she'd had red paint on her hands, possibly blood—saying *yes* before the question was even fully out of his mouth, her saying *fuck yes* once she saw his ride, never questioning him once when he'd told her it was called the *Lullaby Express*.

Like, of course that's what it's called. What else would it be called, baby? But that was Brandy. No bullshit, no questions, no judgment, carefree, go-with-the-fucking-flow Brandy.

That was what had lured him to her months ago, and the memories of her had reeled him back a second time. And now she was his. So much *his*, in fact, that perhaps he was now hers as well, like for the first time he was in a relationship where it was a two-way street.

Ever since, Teddy had been trying to figure out exactly what made this girl tick.

Well, he knew what mostly made her tick, and he felt a sudden stirring in his loins now just thinking of it, but first, the fucking bumps on his head needed to be analyzed.

Felt up. Whatever.

But right now. Without further delay. He couldn't have driven another mile without knowing. For the past four hours he'd felt them tingling. Or moving, shifting somehow. Like something was alive inside them. Like if they were indeed made of some kind of wood, they had fucking termites and they'd eaten their way into his skull. He'd been scratching at them for hours, and dare he say, dare he even think it, after feeling them both up . . .

No. They weren't fucking growing. They couldn't be. Not after a life lived learning how to hide them and disguise them and finally coming to grips with being cursed by them.

These . . . imperfections on an otherwise perfect . . .

Fuck!

Teddy gazed into the visitors' center mirror, fuming.

He braced his hands on the sink and watched Brandy approach. Her footsteps echoed. She had long curly brunette hair she'd pulled back into a twisted, coiling plait. Her eyes were as big and green as two ripe olives, her skin a tone he'd never been able to decipher, only that it was beautiful. Like what he imagined Cleopatra's skin might have looked like.

"What now?" Brandy turned him, placed a splayed hand on his chest, her fingernails painted black to match her skirt, with a small red dot in the middle of each fingernail to match her red halter top. This entire ensemble for her was not a one-off, but what she wore daily. He hadn't known this about her when he'd driven back to Florida to get her, that she'd been known for years now, in and around the Tampa area, as the Black Widow.

He'd asked, *Who calls you that?*

The newspapers. Adding, almost bashfully, *They tend to name the ones they can't catch.*

And why would they need to catch you?

She'd kissed his throat, then lightly bit into his neck skin and held it with her teeth, not long enough to draw blood but enough to leave a mark. *Because I do bad things. And I bite.*

Teddy removed her hand from his chest, faced the mirror above the row of sinks again.

Brandy stood behind him; with the stilettos, she was tall enough to rest her chin on his shoulder. Her breath smelled of the mints she constantly sucked on. "What's going on, Teddy?"

"I think they're growing."

She grinned, watched his eyes in the mirror, must have seen how serious he was, felt the tension in his shoulder through the underside of her chin, so she took a closer look. "Oh . . ."

He turned toward her. "Oh, what? Oh, fucking what?"

"I can see them."

He ran his fingers through his hair, touched them, and flinched. Goddamn it, he could feel them bigger too. She was only confirming what he'd known for hours. If he was being honest, the past few days, and maybe weeks, when he'd first felt them itch and tingle, felt the static in his ears when he slept at night, like something was being crumbled or crackled inside his brain, the nerve endings shifting and adjusting or some fucking uncomfortable thing.

"What do you mean you can see them?"

You know what she means, Teddy. You've known they were alive for years. The punch in the eighth grade flipped the switch. Hitting Chuck Toomer had turned them live. And ever since, with every bit of violence he'd committed, every bit of murder and every bit of mean, he'd felt them tingle with pleasure.

"I can see them, Teddy." She reached up, touched the tip of the right one. He stepped away, self-conscious for the first time since his childhood.

It hadn't hurt. Just that it made him feel exposed. Vulnerable. "The tops," she said, eyeing him in awe, like he imagined one might Michelangelo's *David* for the first time. "They're showing. Barely, but they're there."

"And you think this is funny?" He made a fist like he was going to hit her, not just hit her but punch her like he'd decked Chuck Toomer in the eighth grade, and for much the same reason. He bent over just enough to see the top of his head in the mirror. "They're fucking horns."

He punched the mirror, shattering the glass into the sink and onto the floor in dancing shards. Pain surged so quickly he saw stars. Pain ran through his knuckles, into his wrist, up his arm and into his chest, gripping his racing heart like a badly needed hug. Blood leaked from his knuckles. But the pain was what he'd needed. Exactly what the situation had called for, because how dare he feel sorry for himself. How dare you, he thought, preparing to punch the mirror again, what was left of it, just to top off his fuel tank.

But Brandy grabbed his arm before he could strike. She turned him toward her and aggressively pushed him against the wall. "Tell me about it." She stepped closer. "Tell me about it." She'd said it less aggressively this time, more like his mother might have before she'd really turned crazy. But mother was fake juice. Brandy was . . . she was something else entirely. She was becoming his Queen Bee. "Tell me about it, Teddy."

Just the way she said his name made him want to do her, and he could tell by the look in her eyes that she wanted it too. But even more, he knew exactly what she was talking about.

Tell me about it . . . That's why she didn't say *them*. Tell me about *them*. As in his . . . whatever the fuck they were. The things growing from his head. She'd said *it*, because she somehow knew the *it* was all still in there, growing like a seed. The *real* pain he'd felt from being born different. Him switching schools twice before the age of nine because kids had somehow seen them, or accidently bumped into him and felt them and kids are mean and he'd never met his father. Never *known* his father. Never *seen* his father. Never even known his father's name because Mother must have been a loose whore.

And he was born with fucking horns. Because of her. Because of him.

Brandy's face was inches from his own and he loved her. Aside from the voice he heard in his head at night, the same voice he heard through that seashell, he'd never loved anyone like he loved himself. But their eyes locked, and when they locked, they really engaged, like she was staring so deep into his eyes she could see his brain and synapses and nerves all feeding into those *things* on his skull. She undid his belt, slid her hand inside his jeans and gripped what had grown hard the instant his fist had shattered the mirror. She stroked him and he moaned, the pleasure resonating like a tuning fork thrum, building from his balls through his chest and up to his . . . *go ahead, Teddy, think it and say it and own those motherfuckers for what they are* . . . all the way to his horns.

He kissed her supple lips so hard their teeth clicked. The impact jolted fuel into them both, and if there was any question before, there wasn't now. They were doing this right here in the community restroom. The door was locked. They attacked each other like they were starved, ravenous. For dominance. He slid a hand underneath the bottom of her halter top and cupped her right breast. She bit at his earlobe and kissed him back. She unbuttoned his shirt with one hand, and with the other hand pushed down her skirt, her red underwear along with it. She took her hands off him long enough to slide them down the rest of the way. She placed his hands on her ass, turned them both around. He got the message. He lifted her up onto the sink. She undid his pants, forced them down, and with her eyes she beckoned him to tell her about it, the pain still festering inside him.

And he did. He entered her and he told her about it. He thrust and she clung to him and he told her about it. How he'd switched schools for the third time in the sixth grade, and just when he'd begun to grow into himself, to physically mature, to have friends, that's when it happened.

The lice.

He'd come home with lice and his mother had shaved his head. He'd teared up as he watched his hair feather down to the kitchen floor. She'd shaved him to the scalp with a buzz cut while she prayed to Jesus and he cried and she told him he could wear a hat and no one would see them. Him telling her, pleading, *Hats come off, Mother! Hats blow off in the wind. Hats aren't allowed in our weekly masses, Mother. Hats get pulled from the heads of kids by bullies, Mother.* When the other five kids in class struck itchy by the lice had mothers who went through their hair, strand by strand, with their fathers holding flashlights and removing the nits one by one with patience and not panic. *Not crying blubbery tears of panic, Mother!* But she shaved it off, regardless, and she told him he looked handsome. She carefully trimmed around the . . . the . . . them, because the lice, the little demons, were sent from the Devil and Theodore needed to be *completely* cleansed . . .

Still one with Brandy, Teddy lifted her from the sink, held her upright. His arms flexed from the slight weight of her. He felt like a king. A god. He held her and told her all about it. How his mother had gathered his clothes and blankets and towels and tossed them into the fireplace because that was the only way, Theodore. To burn them to ashes. Brandy kissed him and clung to him. Teddy gained fuel from the feel of her flesh in his hands. She whispered in his ear to tell her more and he did, all while she ran her fingers through his thick hair, not only touching his horns—three inches tall, at least, now—but stroking, and at one point hoisted herself up high enough under his grip to lick them, and that pleasure buckled his knees.

That sensation nearly made him drop her.

He widened his stance and held strong, even as she pulled, from somewhere—maybe she'd had it in her hand all along—a switchblade. She put the tip of it beneath his chin and they locked eyes again and she grinned. Like *I got you now.* And for some reason he wasn't surprised.

The Black Widow flashed her teeth. With one arm wrapped around him for support and one hand holding the sharp blade beneath his chin, like she was daring him to move, or she'd cut him, she forced the tip gently into his chin, puncturing it just enough to draw blood.

They panted, studied each other.

Someone knocked on the door and Brandy shouted for them to fuck off. She'd begun moving against him again, her hips in his hands, her breasts against his chest. And she'd nicked him. A tiny wet trail of blood ran down his throat. Was this why the newspapers called her the Black Widow? Because she lured men into her web and killed them with this knife? It was a game now, to see which one of them would blink first, to look away first, and even as he felt the blood trickle over the bulge of his Adam's apple, he broke into a laugh, and then she did too, and then he started up again, telling her all about it. How, despite the note Mother had written the principal asking permission for him to wear that hat, the teachers had looked at him funny. How it took Chuck Toomer all of two seconds to snatch that old timey flop hat off his head at recess. The few-second breathless pause of wonderment that followed, all the kids on the schoolyard staring at those two strange protuberances on his head, now so noticeable within the shaved buzz cut. How Chuck Toomer had laughed once, loudly—*Ha!*—a choked hiccup of fun right before he shouted, "Rudolph!" And oh how they laughed, Brandy. They laughed and they pointed, and they shouted, "Rudolph the Red-Nosed Reindeer and Rudolph with your nose so bright, won't you . . ."

Brandy tightened the grip on her knife. The thrill of being so close to death by her hand turned him on even more. Perhaps she felt it too; she'd begun to move more urgently on him as he held her, taking on more of the workload because this was a two-way street and they were partners, perhaps—dare he even think it—equals, and she was his Queen Bee. She panted in his ear. He squeezed her hips and told her all about it, how the ridicule lasted for two more years, even as his hair grew back, even when the growths were no longer visible—they all knew they were there—even as the girls had begun to *notice* him, laughing and snickering about him in different ways now, because by that time he was truly starting to bloom, to flower, just as Mother had promised, growing more handsome by the day, and Chuck Toomer and his pals didn't like this. So they ramped up their bullying, their name-calling, their pushing him in the hallway and throwing kickballs at his head and knocking his lunch tray out of his hands. Teddy talked faster as their pace increased, a perfect rhythm that had him about ready to burst.

There was only one Black Widow in the world, and she was his. And just as Brandy was coming down from her mountain, he was finishing his climb. Never had he felt such instant fuel. And Chuck Toomer—he whispered into Brandy's ear as he was about to explode—finally shouted out his last, *Hey, Rudolph!*

"Tell me what you did, baby."

Teddy felt the tip of her knife at his throat and he ejaculated into her. Which wasn't his custom. But he thought for the first time how good a father he would be. She laughed as he grunted and panted and he wondered if she could read his thoughts—because what kind of mother would she be, other than the best? He eased her down atop one of the sinks, and it held her weight. She rubbed his bare back. She ran her fingers through his hair. He flinched as she touched his horns—so sensitive now right after the act—and he finished telling her about it.

How he punched Chuck Toomer's fucking lights out.

How he broke the kid's nose and blood flew. How he stood over top of him and dared him to get up. Every kid on the schoolyard must have seen the look in his eyes and they never made fun of him again. They never again called him Rudolph. They never again asked him where was Dasher and Dancer, or Donner or Blitzen. They never again asked him directions to the North Pole. "Because on that day . . . ," he told Brandy as she lowered the knife from his neck, flicking her wrist in a one-snap motion that concealed the blade inside the handle. She jumped down from the sink and held his hands. "Because on that day I first felt the fuel. The buzz inside these horns. The pleasure from causing another one pain. From causing fear." He bent down, gently kissed her lips. "Because on that day, Brandy, I was born."

19

Beth

Now

AT THREE IN the morning, Beth awoke inside the hospital waiting room, alone and covered with a white blanket.

She checked her phone, folded the blanket, and placed it on the seat beside her.

"Hey, Sleeping Beauty," said Natalie's voice at the entrance to the waiting room. She looked exhausted. Natalie nodded toward the blanket. "Mayor Truffant's idea."

"When did he leave?"

"Thirty minutes ago." Natalie yawned. "I could sleep for days. Grover's out of surgery. Serious but stable. Lost a shit ton of blood. Had a line out the back door to donate, though."

"But they think he'll make it?"

"Too early to tell, but it's Grover. I like his odds just out of stubbornness."

"And Doc?"

"Little deeper down the hole." Natalie yawned again. "Unresponsive."

"You heading home?"

"For a couple of hours. You?"

"I guess I should. Although I've got Simple Simon locked up."

"He do it?"

"Something tells me no."

"Never known Simon to hurt a fly."

"I agree," Beth said, remembering though how aggressively Simon had forced Lump's face into the cell bars. "But at this point it'd be a mistake to let him go."

Natalie nodded toward the seat. "Take the blanket. We've got plenty."

Beth touched it. "Already losing its warmth."

"Leave the blanket then." Natalie forced a smile. "Careful out there, Beth."

"You too."

Beth read Natalie's eyes before she disappeared into the hallway: *Fearless doesn't mean indestructible.* Beth felt far from indestructible as she drove the three miles home, windows open to the cool night air to keep her awake. The tunnel itself was not visible from the town's historic district, but from that direction a brief flash illuminated the sky. It had been in her peripheral, but she assumed it was lightning, or maybe what Grover called heat lightning. She watched for another strike as she drove. None came, but seconds later, as she pulled into her driveway, she heard a rumble of distant thunder, giving credence to the flash she'd seen. She didn't think a storm had been forecast, but also knew how common pop-ups were in the area, and rarely lasted long.

She entered her house quietly, hoping not to wake Jax and Brody. With work pressing from every direction, she wasn't in the right mind frame to deal with either of them. She locked the front door behind her and headed directly for her office in the basement. Jax called it her Murder Pit. That had sparked an argument between them last week, as she'd fallen asleep down there twice; but the truth—and it hurt—was that he wasn't wrong, which was why she'd reacted so defensively and felt a pang of guilt now as she turned on the lights and surveyed the four walls of her basement office. Years of work that, if viewed without context, might have tagged her as mad. Obsessed, even. But as essential to her now as breathing, as one day she would gather it all into a book.

Her theory of cluster violence.

Her mother's abrupt death at the hands of a drunk driver had taught her anger at an early age, the true meaning of revenge, and how best to seek it. Although Doc Bigsby would say the minute she was born, she was the most intensely focused individual he'd ever encountered. He said it in jest, but not really. It had been Grover who'd helped her channel it. Not only channel it to something positive and goal-oriented like upholding the law and hunting down anyone who broke it, but to focus on Harrod's Reach and its history of what she would come to call "cluster violence," and eventually examples of the same type of contagious violent behaviors across the country. And, in recent years, across the globe.

It had started one Sunday after mass, while she was eating dinner with Grover and his wife, Patrice, and had brought up something she'd been researching for a freshman high school paper, about what many in Harrod's Reach had referred to as the tunnel's Golden Periods. Except, she told them in between bites of cheeseburger, what had happened during those Golden Periods was anything but golden. Because interesting and fascinating shouldn't equate to golden.

High activity, she'd told them, seemed more appropriate.

Grover had said she might be onto something, as he'd thought the same for years, as Detective James Harrington had before him. It was the townsfolk who'd called the more violent times golden. Grover had always gone more along the lines of *when it rains it pours*, so that had been the first thing Beth had ever written on what would become her project—*when it rains it pours*—and the first phrase she'd pinned to her basement wall after she and Jax bought the house in the weeks before their wedding. The first picture she'd tacked to the basement wall had been that of her mother, as a constant reminder of what she looked like and that bad shit happened to good people.

As a teen, she'd begun to dig into Harrod's Reach's past, and in particular, the history of the tunnel, going back to when it was founded by Colonel Harrod Guthrie in the winter of 1865. It didn't take long to notice the correlation between the years and decades the town referred to as Golden—or as she wrote, High Activity—and the higher rates of Harrod's Reach crime. And that wasn't limited to injuries and murders inside the tunnel, what many had for decades assumed was a serial killer fond of lopping off limbs. In the case of Happy Jack Kingston in the seventies, they found his body from the waist up but not his lower half.

After the mysterious "maimings," the most common term Beth found in the old newspapers to describe the attacks inside the tunnel, continued for longer than any normal human could live, whispers began to emerge that it wasn't a serial killer at all, or else the torch had been seamlessly passed to a copycat. Or—as even more began to believe in the past fifty years—that something supernatural existed inside that tunnel.

The tunnel had claimed, by Beth's latest tally, including the two muti-lated bodies found last week, fifty-three deaths, with thirty-three from the 1923 train derailment. There were fifteen serious injuries (fourteen result-ing in prosthetic arms, legs, or hands, and for Sully Dupree, a coma) and two strange disappearances (Connie Brine in 1865 and Bret Jones nearly a century later). Of those with serious injuries, not one, according to the newspapers Beth had scoured, could remember what had happened to them inside the tunnel, although a few claimed to see a flash of light, then blacked out. What Beth had found most fascinating, as she'd told Grover when she was seventeen, was that the periods surrounding those deaths and injuries *inside* the tunnel *all* coincided with a heightened number of crimes in *town*.

Murders. Rapes. Muggings. Robberies. Shootings. Domestic violence. The macabre.

Harrod's Reach saw upticks in all those during the so-called Golden Periods, periods of time that lasted, in some cases, as little as a few months (the disappearance of Connie Brine in 1865) to several years, and in the 1960s, a full decade, culminating with the disappearance of Bret Jones in the fall of 1968.

Not only a noticeable uptick in crimes, Beth had told Grover, showing examples from a meticulously researched paper she'd written, *but a big uptick in strange behavior from the citizens of Harrod's Reach*. It was bizarre enough behavior, Beth had pointed out, citing examples, to warrant visits from priests at the time, or ministers or psychiatrists and counselors. On several occasions a minister, Reverend Coleman Sharp (1980s) and two priests, Father John (1930s) and Father Tom (1960–70s), were convinced those people had been possessed by some kind of devil. Exorcisms were considered a total of seven different occasions but never sanctioned by the Church.

Beth felt a surge of adrenaline at being down here, and she couldn't wait to show Gideon. Not for praise or approval but because he'd helped her with quite a bit of the research early on, as teens, much done inside the Smite House, with Archie's help whenever they needed it.

She warmed day-old coffee in a microwave and sipped it as she sur-veyed the walls, covered with photos and newspaper articles and files and printouts on murders committed all over the country. A few more recent portions of the wall were devoted to murders worldwide, most recently a three-month cluster in Oslo, Norway. One of her five online forum friends, this one from New York—what Jax referred to playfully as her fellow online freaks—had brought that cluster to her attention two weeks ago. Before the current chaos in Harrod's Reach, Beth had planned to research whether Oslo had any abandoned train tunnels, coal tunnels, or cave systems near where the violence was occurring. The tunnel here had been the source for that inspiration, and she had over thirty matches on her walls to give credence to it.

A week ago, she shared her findings with Doc Bigsby, who not only stared wide-eyed and speechless at her years of work but said that he had some things at home he needed to show her. She hadn't gotten the chance to see what he was talking about, and perhaps now never would, but the way he'd said *needed* and not just wanted spoke volumes. It was clear they'd been on the same page. She'd been leery of showing anyone other than Grover and Jax before she was done with her book, but when the northern tunnel wall fell so suddenly, it had prompted her to confide in Doc.

But it was all hard evidence, as she'd tried to explain to Jax—whose only theory of the Harrod's Reach tunnel was that it was fucked up and haunted—that their tunnel wasn't the only one in the world with a history. Several jumped out at her as examples, among them the creek tunnels of Ocean Shore Railroad in California. The Buck Mountain Coal Co. Tunnel in Rockport, Pennsylvania. The vast cave systems in Crooked Tree, Kentucky. Grimms Bridge Tunnel in Ohio. Coal & Iron Tunnel #2 in Glady, West Virginia. The Florence & Cripple Creek Railroad in Colorado.

In a sense, with her fellow online freaks—her wide-reaching "team" this last year—her system of logging crime wasn't far from what the FBI had been doing for decades at Quantico, tracking and profiling and analyzing crime for patterns. Her system might be simple, but it had produced results.

And she trusted them.

No one more than a young woman around her age named Brianna Bookman, who was not only willing to help her at every turn—although they'd never met in person and had only had a few Zoom calls online—but was working on her own system of tracking criminals, mostly violent, all spawning from the decades of violent clusters inside her own small town of Crooked Tree.

Beth knew what time it was in Crooked Tree, but decided to reach out regardless. She fired off a short email about the Charleston Strangler

(Horseshoe Rapist) and explained, in strict confidence, how they'd found the body here in Harrod's Reach. She at least had a connection to go on and planned on emailing the detective in Charleston next, but what she needed from Brianna was any information—what they called *hits*—on anything resembling how the second unknown body, the one holding his own head, had been found.

Five minutes later she found an email address for Detective Phipps, the detective mentioned in the Charleston article about the most recent Horseshoe Rapist victim, Maddy Boyle, and sent a quick message about maybe having something here that resembled what was going on there. While she waited for responses from both, she warmed a second cup of coffee to help keep herself awake. By the time she took her first sip, her laptop chimed with an incoming email. It was the detective in Charleston, asking if she had a couple of minutes to talk. Evidently, he slept little as well.

Detective Phipps called thirty seconds later. He was professional and to the point, and by the tired tone of his voice, at his wits' end on any viable leads. "When was the body found?" he asked.

"Three days ago." She then explained in detail—as she'd written in the email—exactly how the female victim was found. "You there?" she asked after he'd gone silent.

"Yeah," he said, sounding like he was writing something.

"Does it sound similar?"

"Not just similar, Sheriff, but . . . exactly."

She'd written *Sheriff* instead of Deputy Sheriff in her email. Grover would have approved of her fudging the truth to get a needed seat at any table. "How long since the last victim in Charleston?"

"Over a month," he said. "With no leads."

"Plenty of time to travel across the country."

"Plenty of time to travel the world, Sheriff, but it doesn't mean he did," he said, adding. "Of course, it doesn't mean he didn't. We'd feared he'd gone underground here after nearly being exposed by his last victim."

"Which was . . ."

"Madeline Boyle," he said. "She was in a coma after the attack but made a recovery the doctors here are calling miraculous. She was my last good lead."

"Was?"

"Skipped town a few days ago."

"Where?"

"Didn't say, but she did give me a fairly solid description of the attacker."

"Can you share it?"

He did, and Beth, as she wrote it all down, realized no one she'd seen in Harrod's Reach of late, even the workers she'd seen at the Beehive, matched that description. Unless . . . no . . . Jesus, other than, perhaps, Simon Bowles? If anyone resembled that description—the size, the beard, the hair—it was Simon. But she couldn't believe it. And neither could Grover, so although they'd questioned Simon after he'd found the bodies in the woods, they'd never truly considered him a suspect. What suspect would take the time to draw those bodies?

She was hesitant to tell Detective Phipps about the second body, but felt he deserved the full truth about the crime scene. He went silent again, then said, "Well, that is weird, Sheriff, but . . . you said they were holding hands? The corpses?"

"Yes."

"That's where these cases would definitely begin to differ." For whatever reason this was the first time his southern low-country accent had struck her in the few minutes they'd been on the phone. Was it so farfetched to think a killer like that could uproot so completely? And once someone uprooted, what did the distance even matter? It was his turn to ask, "You still there?"

"Yeah, just thinking . . ."

"This is good, Sheriff. I'm gonna take a hard look, believe me, but with how swamped I am with another case, this one was placed on our back burner days ago. But please be in touch if something pops, and we'll hope to Christ it isn't another body."

"I'll keep you posted on my end," Beth said.

"I'll do the same. Stay safe. Sounds like some . . . weird times out your way."

Beth said "Will do," thanked him, and ended the call. She checked her email but saw no response yet from Brianna in Crooked Tree. Her coffee had gone cold while she'd been on the phone. It was five in the morning. The catnap she'd stolen in the hospital waiting room would not sustain her through another day like today, and now that she'd taken a moment to let some things settle into her mind, she realized how exhausted she was. A couple hours of sleep was necessary. She turned off the lights to her Murder Pit and headed upstairs to the main level of their ranch house. When she opened the door to Brody's room and saw his toddler bed empty, she remembered Jax had taken him back to his room.

Not their room, because they'd never had one together.

She passed the room she typically slept in—whenever she didn't fall asleep downstairs—and tiptoed into Jax's room further down the hall. She found Jax snoring on one side with Brody's tiny body asleep in the middle. She eyeballed enough room for herself on the other side of Brody and kicked off her shoes to lie there. She watched Brody lovingly as his closed eyelids moved in cadence to whatever circadian rhythms his mind had set. Was he dreaming? Tiny pushes of air escaped his little nose and open mouth. His chest rose and fell. The fingers on his left hand twitched. In fear of waking him up, she didn't ruffle his hair or kiss his forehead like she so badly wanted to.

She looked past him and found Jax's eyes open, watching her.

He grinned, mouthed the words, "You okay?"

She nodded.

"Good night then."

"Good night," she whispered, watching Jax's eyes close, and then looked out the window at the night.

Hoped she'd hear from Brianna by morning.

Noticed that it had never rained. Realized that that flash she'd seen earlier from the direction of the tunnel had indeed been an isolated event. The thunder sound, a one-off.

And that that might not bode well come morning.

20

Simon

Now

SIMON AWOKE WITH a gasp, and immediately sat up in bed.
What he thought was *his* bed, until he surveyed the dark surroundings and remembered he was in jail, and Lump was over there at his desk, asleep in a chair.

Good thing Lump had given him the crayons he'd asked for. They were resting on the floor where Lump had scooted them between the bars earlier. Must have meant there were no hard feelings, even though Simon was sure he'd broken Lump's face earlier. Or maybe Lump feared him, which was funny, because Simon would never hurt a fly.

Unless Simon said so.

Because you weren't supposed to touch a girl that way when a girl didn't want to be touched, especially Beth, so Lump had left him no choice.

Before his dream—which he knew now to be much more than a dream—left him to become memory dust, Simon picked up the crayons from the floor, opened his *Lalaland* book to a fresh, clean page, and started coloring what he'd just seen and done. He wished he could have gone back, because bad things were coming, but he knew it couldn't work like that.

But they needed him over there, now more than ever.

In a world full of fuzzy, that much now was clear.

CHAPTER

21

Gideon

Now

"YOU LOOK RESTED," Gideon said to his mother as he sat at the kitchen island.

Not only rested, Gideon thought as he smelled the steaming coffee Maxine put in front of him, but amazingly put together for someone who'd been so emotionally run through the wringer as she'd been last night with Sully.

"I was exhausted," she said, busying herself at the stove. Bacon sizzled, and scrambled eggs and biscuits, fresh from the oven, added to an already pleasant aroma. "I fell right asleep. Getting ready for that party last night . . ."

"You didn't need to do that, Mom."

"I wanted to, Gideon. You deserved it." She glanced over her shoulder. "Hungry?"

"Starving."

Maxine placed a heaping plate of food in front of him and he dug right in.

First thing Gideon had done on his way downstairs was to check in on Sully in the parlor. He hadn't expected to find his father sleeping in the recliner next to Sully's bed, when tradition had Archie awake with the sun. Not just sleeping, thought Gideon, as he'd watched his father from the doorway, but snoring like a bear, with a bottle of Old Sam bourbon on the end table, along with the Capone book Gideon had seen in the third-floor bedroom last night. At some point, his father had come down and passed out where he now sat sprawled in the chair, his clothes untucked and wrinkled.

Gideon sipped his coffee and tested the water. "Dad okay?" Thinking how the roles here had reversed since he'd been gone. Mom, even though she'd always been a cheery go-getter, once she got going, had never been a morning person like Dad, yet here she was, at seven in the morning, seemingly showered and made up and hair combed, in tight jeans he'd never seen before, with white sandals that highlighted her pink-painted toenails. Her butter yellow T-shirt said *The Beehive Is Alive*, whatever the hell that meant, right across her chest. But the shirt, which showed a plump bumblebee holding a rocks glass, was form-fitting enough to reveal how much weight she'd lost over the past three years.

"Dad okay?' he asked again.

"He's fine," she said with her back to him, jotting something down in a notebook she slid into a leather satchel full of other business-looking things. Last Gideon had heard, Maxine had retired from teaching middle school to become Sully's caretaker soon after Gideon had enlisted in the Army. But what she'd just been doing had looked a lot like paperwork, which brought his attention back to her T-shirt. The front of it made more sense now that he could see what was printed on the back: *Grand Opening*. Except right before the *O* in *Opening* there were two slanted letters in red, *Re*, like someone had at the last second edited it to say *Grand ReOpening*—how clever—followed by a date, *November 10*, still a month away. But apparently the historic Beehive Hotel, which had thrived in the late 1800s and early 1900s, and even more so during Prohibition, was about to open again.

The name of the drink on the front of his mother's shirt came back to him: the Honeybee, the hotel's signature drink back in the day, equal parts honey and sugar over crushed ice and filled to the top with whiskey, with enough room for the maraschino cherry. The Beehive had limped through the Depression, gained steam before, during, and after the Second World War, only to slowly founder through the fifties and much of the sixties, find a second life in the late sixties and seventies, before ultimately closing its doors in the winter of 1978.

Gideon knew all of this because his father had talked of the Beehive often.

Refinishing the Smite House had been his passion outside the college classroom, but the Beehive was his dream. *One of these days*, he'd tell them at dinner, *that hotel will be mine. I will restore it to its former glory.* At which Mom would scoff, pretending she was clearing her throat, and say something like, *More gravy, Archie?* Or *Can you pass me the potatoes, dear?* Anything to change the subject. But with their dinner table situated next to the bay window, the Beehive atop the hill at the end of their street was always in view from Archie's seat. They often saw him staring at it as he chewed, in lust almost, like Gideon often found himself staring at Beth when she'd begun to sprout curves.

It's good to have ambition, Maxine once told Gideon when he was a boy—after Archie had cursed and sworn from a second-floor bathroom, having accidently broken a pipe while laying a new tile floor that supposedly perfectly matched the one in 1925—*but like anything tangible, it needs to have a ceiling*. As educators, and especially after Sully's medical bills started arriving, the Smite House kept them monetarily strained and often stressed. But while his parents occasionally argued over money and reno projects, they rarely fought, at least not in front of the kids, but the tension over money was always there, biting at them like termites.

If the Beehive was about to reopen, who was behind it, if not his father? Who would take that on? Everyone in town knew of his dreams for that hotel, but by the looks of him, sleeping alone in that haunted bedroom upstairs, Gideon didn't think it likely he had anything to do with that massive reno.

But could Mom have had something to do with it? By the looks of her shirt, and the way his parents were *not* talking, perhaps she did?

Just as Gideon was starting to piece this all together, she turned so suddenly toward Gideon that he jerked on his stool and spilled a splash of coffee on the island. She grabbed a dish towel from the sink and wiped it up. Heroes weren't so jumpy. Heroes didn't open fire with kids in the room. Heroes didn't spill their coffee. And even though she smiled and seemed happy to do it, so quick to be a mother again, he saw the brief spark of disappointment in her eyes that he'd been so easily startled, because maybe it seemed he was still the same old Gideon. Jumpy and on edge and scared of his own shadow.

She leaned against the counter, folded her arms, smiled at him. Genuinely. She was truly glad he was home and right now that was enough. But damn if her fingernails weren't painted too, nothing showy, but a modest shade of red that, against the backdrop of her T-shirt, made Gideon think of ketchup and mustard.

But she kept staring and smiling, so eventually Gideon said, "What?"

"Can't a mother look at her son?"

He sipped his now tepid coffee. "I guess so. Just not sure I'm much to look at."

She grabbed his plate, filled it again. "You must have put on twenty pounds of muscle."

"Thirty."

"But who's counting, right?" She walked behind him and hugged him. She kissed the top of his head. "I'm so glad you're back. I prayed every day, Gideon. And here you are."

"And here I am." He finished his coffee and suddenly wanted to get up and go outside. The newness of Mom's enthusiasm was nice, but with the undercurrent of awkwardness he knew they both felt, he wondered how long it would last before things went back to how they'd been in the days before he'd gone. When Dad had stopped talking to him, and Mom . . . what she'd done had been, maybe not as obvious, but equally damaging, because she'd always been the one to smile and show compassion and ask questions like how his day went and what are you doing after school and what's Beth up to. Those questions went away after Sully's injury.

And as annoying to a teenager as those daily questions were, they hadn't been asked in jest, or just to fill air space, she'd genuinely cared. And while she'd outwardly shouted at Archie for blaming Gideon for what happened to Sully inside the tunnel, her silence after the tragedy hurt tenfold. No more daily questions, to him, had meant she'd stopped caring. And her praying had little to do with him coming home. That had been the bullet. And if they knew the truth of how the bullet had come to travel through his leg, they wouldn't be so quick to call him a hero.

"He shouldn't be drinking, Mom."

From where she stood behind the island, the Beehive Hotel was in view out the window, and he just knew she was staring at it, just as Archie had always stared at it. "No . . . no, he shouldn't be, Gideon," she said, looking at him again. This time he didn't spill his coffee. "How's your nose?"

"Fine." Although in truth it still throbbed. "I'll take those Advil now, though." She pulled the bottle from a counter drawer and shook three out into her palm. She glanced, as if to size him up, and then shook out a fourth. He downed them with the rest of his coffee. "And your shirt?"

She looked down at her chest. "Oh, this?" Like she hadn't known she was wearing it. "The Beehive is opening again."

"I get that much," he said. "But what's your part in it?"

"Who says I—"

"Mom, come on. You think you'd be flaunting that shirt around here?"

"I'm not flaunting."

He heard hammering even now from down the street and could only assume it was coming from the Beehive. "Then what gives?"

"You didn't used to be this persistent, Gideon."

"Well, you know . . . *killing* people does that."

He hadn't meant for it to come out so harshly. Hadn't meant for it to come out at all. What he'd done over there had meant to be buried the instant he'd boarded that plane home.

Maxine cleared his plate and rinsed it off in the sink. She wiped her hands on a dish towel and forced a smile, much like she'd done with him after Sully nearly died.

"Come here." Maxine rounded the island and motioned for him to follow.

Gideon followed her down the hallway and into the foyer toward the front door. She opened it, stepped out onto the sunlit veranda, and stood facing the end of the street, as construction carried on at the Beehive. Scaffolding had been erected along the three-story stone façade, where the final touches were being made to the ornate window frames and detailed cornices leading up to the steeply pitched roof. Birds flittered in and out of the colorful autumn trees that lined both sides of Mallard. Workers moved about the hotel like ants on an anthill.

Archie had taken the family there a decade ago, before Sully was born. The building had long been abandoned by then, but in every room shown to them by the realtor, Dad had seen potential. He'd seen history and charm and the glory years all folding back again. Mom had told him to close his mouth at one point during the tour of the grand bar inside the lobby. Archie had touched every dusty pillar and fluted column and commented on every floor, down to the woodworking of the baseboards and the down lay of the floorboards and tiles, all while Maxine tried to temper his enthusiasm and remind him with whispers and pats on the back that there was no way they could afford to take on this project with how in debt they were with the Smite House.

But the interest rates, honey . . . there's never gonna be a better time to buy.

And just imagine the money this place would bring in . . .

And she'd say, *Money from who, Archie? Nobody visits Harrod's Reach anymore.*

Which is exactly why we need this place to bring them back.

So, build it and they will come? She'd said it tongue-in-cheek, Gideon remembered clearly, but Archie had taken it as full-on seriousness.

And answered with a resounding, *YES! Build it and they will come.*

Dad never saw the eye roll Mom had given him after that, or maybe he had but didn't care, because—*This place!*—he kept saying, as happy about life as he'd ever seen him.

Gideon had listened around the corner of the living room that night as a fire crackled in the hearth and his parents discussed finances with the realtor, who seemed as convinced of the hotel's *good bones* as Dad was, all while Mom touched her forehead and sighed a lot and eventually poured them all a drink. Mickey the realtor, with his fine-looking Jeep Grand Cherokee parked outside, his yellow polo shirt, his nice slacks, shiny shoes, and full head of Ken-doll hair while Dad was trying to hold onto his with a combover that wasn't working.

He's just trying to make a sale, Gideon, as she would later tell her son. *That's what salesmen do.*

Mickey shook Dad's hand that night when he left the Smite House. Dad stood at the window watching until Mickey's taillights faded before turning around to face Mom, even though she'd already left the room. Gideon remembered that night as being one of the rare times his parents argued loud enough for him to hear, loud enough for Gideon to weep and attempt sleep with a pillow over his ears.

That next morning wasn't much different from this, thought Gideon, as he stood next to his mother and watched the workers hammering and sawing and painting at the Beehive. It had been just him and Mom at breakfast that morning after that argument years ago—Dad apparently having gone to his campus office to grade tests. Mom, still teary-eyed, smiled as coffee wafted into her face, smiled as if she'd won that battle, and said, "Sorry if we kept you up."

Gideon had shrugged, a tad disappointed because he'd secretly been on his dad's side, and by default, Mickey's as well. And now here they were with the Beehive a month away from a grand reopening and Mom was glowing in her yellow T and newfound body, reveling in the way she seemed to be getting younger while Dad looked fat and homeless.

And then she said, "You remember that realtor who wanted to sell the Beehive to us?"

Gideon said, "Yeah."

"Well, he bought it."

"When?"

"Two years ago." She slid her arm inside his for a sideways hug, like this news should make him happy or proud. "Been working on it ever since."

It *was* nice to see that place coming to life, even if it wasn't Archie Dupree doing it. But something felt off, so he said, "And you?"

"What about me?" She looked at her shirt again. "Oh, yes, well, he—"

"Mickey?"

"Yes, Mickey, he . . . hired me a year ago. Marketing. Social media. That type of thing."

"Why you?"

"You don't think I'm qualified?"

"Overqualified is more like it."

"We needed money. Plain and simple. Okay?" And maybe that had come out more harshly than she'd intended, because she immediately softened, sideways hugged him again. He sensed defensiveness, like maybe it wasn't really so plain and simple, and wondered if there might be more to it.

Mickey, Gideon remembered, had been a man with some charm.

She'd always been good at changing the subject, so she reverted back to what he'd blurted out earlier in the kitchen. "And you didn't kill anyone, Gideon. You can't look at it that way."

"You weren't there, Mom." *And yes, I did.* "So don't . . ." He disengaged, moved toward the veranda's steps.

"Where you going?"

"Down to the Beehive for a closer look."

He had turned that direction when someone screamed.

Like most sounds in the Reach, the wind carried it, made it sound like it had come from every direction at once, until on the second scream Gideon pinpointed it.

By the look on her face, Maxine did too.

"The tunnel," they said in unison.

And then a siren started blaring.

CHAPTER

22

Maddy

Before

CLARITY WAS A double-edged sword.

Maddy Boyle's mind and memory, for weeks now, had slowly been returning, bits and pieces from her childhood, and most recently her time in college before the attack. Despite what her parents had insisted, that she wait until next semester to go back, to not do too much too soon, she'd felt she was sound enough of mind to return to her fall classes at the College of Charleston right away. She was certainly physically ready, strong enough to run now—she'd done three miles this morning—but she'd feared the attention her walking into the classroom would bring. The stares, the questions she couldn't answer. Her awakening had been front page news for three days. *Charleston College Student Comes Back to Life!*

But school would be there when she returned.

When she'd left home, she hadn't been as confident in her mission as she'd pretended to be with her mother. She knew where she needed to go— Harrod's Reach, Nebraska. She knew who she needed to see—a young boy named Solomon Dupree. And she also knew he was a coma patient but had been under for much longer than she had. And that he was important over *there*. The rest had begun coming back to her within hours of leaving home, and the memories of both her previous life and Lalaland had come at her like a tsunami before she'd hit the South Carolina border. So hard and fast she'd had to pull over on the emergency lane gravel and vomit as semi trucks zoomed by. Waves of dizziness had forced her to take breaks at three different rest stops on the first day, until she'd ultimately decided to stop for a night on the north side of Atlanta to mentally regroup.

And that night, despite the intense urgency she felt to reach Harrod's Reach, had turned into three. She hadn't felt it was safe to drive, not with her mind fluttering so freely and without warning between reality and . . . and the memories of where she'd been, which was not only coming back in pieces during the day but as nightmares when she slept.

A Charleston detective named Phipps had called during her second day in Atlanta, leaving two messages, wanting to see what she remembered from that night at the Charleston Harbor. Even though there'd been no more reports of attacks in the area since *her* attack, they knew the Horseshoe Rapist was still out there. They needed her help bringing him in. They understood her reticence but would appreciate a few minutes of her time. Detective Phipps called again the next day, left another message. She would have loved to help, she'd told herself inside the hotel room, as she drank coffee and watched the world go by outside, but that motherfucker's face, thank the Lord, was still a blur to her.

Or at least it had been, until her third night in that hotel room, when the smell of his foul, rancid breath came back to her while she'd been watching the news and eating carryout Chinese. She'd eaten half of her shrimp fried rice when the stench hit her. Nausea sent her to bed early. That night she awoke sweating, having gone deep enough into sleep to bring back with her a nightmare. A nightmare where she'd been back in Lalaland, and that's when she'd fully started to understand about that place. That that was where everyone went briefly when they dreamed, when they had nightmares. They catch glimpses and then they wake up and mostly don't remember.

Because everyone has been to Lalaland, Maddy, Sully had told her in her first days there. *Only the strongest can stay. The rest of the world wakes up and goes about their days.*

But not you. You stayed for a time, and now you're back. Do what you need to do.

Along with a clear picture of her attacker's face, she'd awoken in the hotel room that night with another name on her lips.

Amy Shimp.

Throughout the day, four more names had come to her, and she'd written those down as well, but by then she'd already spent hours locating Amy Shimp, making phone calls and eliminating those she felt weren't *her* Amy, scrolling online before finally pinpointing a seven-year-old Amy Shimp in Tulsa, Oklahoma, who'd been comatose for two years. She'd been struck in the head by a foul ball during a Houston Astros baseball game, spending a month in intensive care in Houston before finally being transferred back home, prospects negative in terms of recovery.

Maddy checked out of the hotel that next morning and hit the road, no longer suffering the bouts of dizziness and nausea that had come along with what she now called her *memory dumps.* She could stop by and see Amy on the way to Harrod's Reach. After a few miles, she'd thought, *Quit kidding yourself. You don't mean to just see her. You mean to take her with you.* Not kidnap, thought Maddy as she sped west through Georgia, but convince the parents to let her go. At that point Maddy's nerves started shredding for different reasons, because how in the hell could she convince two grieving parents that their dead-head daughter needed to go on a sudden trip?

And dead-head? Where had that thought come from? It was heartless, and that wasn't her. Someone else called them that.

Dead-heads? Them . . . ? Because there's more.

Every name coming to you now, they're dead-heads, Maddy, and they need you. They need you to get them before . . . before *he* gets them . . .

A headache started behind her eyes, so she drove for the next few miles in quiet contemplation, no longer allowing herself to think of the big picture because the big picture right now was too big. Too much.

Do your best to not sound like a lunatic and get to Amy Shimp before *he* does.

On the road, she called Detective Phipps, and while he seemed pleased to hear from her, she kept it short and ended it abruptly when he suggested meeting in person. "He was tall," she told him over the phone. "Six foot four at least, and well over two hundred and fifty pounds." She wondered all over again how in the hell she'd fought him off. "His eyes were brown. Dead. Like there was no life in them. His face was doughy. His cheeks and neck were pockmarked, like he'd had bad acne as an adolescent. His hair was long. To the shoulders. Uncombed and greasy." The detective had asked if that was all. She said, "That horseshoe he left on me. That wasn't the only one on him. I know what you guys call that, like a calling card or something, but it wasn't the only one on him." Even now as she drove, she remembered the way the horseshoes at his waist had jangled and clanked together during their struggle. "You know how a janitor wears a bundle of keys off his belt. That's what the horseshoes made me think of. They just hung there, heavy and loud." She told the detective she had to go. She'd let him know if she remembered anything more, and no, it wasn't in her best interest to meet in person. Not right now.

She drove the next several hours thinking of a plan, pondering what to say to the Shimps, trying to conjure up the resolve she'd need to even broach *I need your daughter to come with me* . . .

The drive gave her ample time to think. Dreams might be fleeting, but this most recent memory dump from her time in Lalaland stayed like an ingrained image. The Lake of Fire. The Island of Bones. The Field of Black Roses. The Forest of Mare Trees and the three Backwards Oceans. Where pink birds soared large as condors, where monsters were as likely as the sunsets, and where everything dripped with vibrant, lurid color. What struck her odd now was that both Amy Shimp and Sully Dupree in Lalaland were young adults, while they were still children here. Sully and his 1920s-style Applejack hat. Blue eyes bright and bold and confident. Skin, sun-touched and darkened by whiskers, but not enough to hide the inch-long scars at his chin and right cheekbone. His black shirt unbuttoned down to the middle of his muscled chest, rolled up at the elbows, revealing strong, ropey arms. Her first moments in Lalaland, other than walking through the knee-high yellow grass, where purple snakes slithered through rich, moist soil and red spiders climbed up and down every distinct buttery-yellow blade, had nearly been the end for her. Which, Sully had told her, would have also spelled the end for her over here. She'd stumbled across a cluster of barbaric men sitting around a campfire, roasting meat on a spit—not animal meat, but a human arm being turned and charred and blackened. Beside the circle of men was a wheelbarrow full of body parts—arms, legs, feet, hands—with stray fingers on the ground, resting there like giant maggots. The noise of her retching alerted the men, and two came sprinting up the hill toward her, one with a sword and the other with an axe. When they were no more than ten feet away, as Maddy had stood too stunned to move, two gunshots echoed from behind her and both men dropped dead. The ones below stood from the fire and ran off, leaving their wheelbarrow of body parts behind.

She'd turned to find Sully behind her, handgun still smoking like they do in cartoons. He kicked one of the dead men with his scuffed brown boots and spoke in a deep, weathered voice. "We call them door-runners. They scavenge the doors for severed limbs that get lopped off when the doors breathe." He squinted against the intense sunlight. "Not all of us are good over here."

Maddy flexed her hands on the wheel as she drove, sure that she could still feel Sully's grip when, after saving her life over there, he'd shaken her hand, told her his name, and said in his deep, weathered voice, "Welcome to Lalaland." By the time she pulled into the Shimps' driveway in Tulsa and parked beside their modest ranch house, she had a carefully worded plan. But when she knocked on the door and waited, she grew nervous, because this was stupid, so irrationally senseless that her palms had begun to sweat. And by the time the door was opened by a woman way too old to be the mother, Tammy Shimp, Maddy panicked.

The woman stared. "Can I help you?"

Maddy said, "Is Amy there?" Which had not been her plan of attack.

"Is this a joke? Huh? A cruel prank? Or are you a reporter?"

A younger voice sounded from an adjacent room. "Who is it, Mom?"

That made sense, thought Maddy. This woman was her mother. Maddy's confidence grew. "Can I please talk to Tammy, Amy's mother?"

"I know who Tammy is. Who *you* are is the question."

"My name is Maddy Boyle, Mrs. Shimp."

"I'm not Shimp." The woman glanced toward another room. "And I wish she wasn't anymore either. Jeffrey's long gone."

"Um, this is awkward, but . . . Amy, she's . . . You see, I was . . . like her . . ."

Just then Tammy Shimp showed herself in the doorway, smaller than her mother, in height and in build, but on first impression, mighty. Tammy was pretty like Maddy had seen in the papers, but older now, like a mother whose child needed around the clock care, and Maddy wanted to tell her that she knew all about it. She knew what it was like on the other side.

That there was a link between Maddy and this woman's daughter she couldn't yet explain, only that it was as real as the sweat now gathering in her armpits. Tammy must have sensed the nerves; she placed a hand on her mother's shoulder to say without words *I got this, you can go*, and off her mother went, not pouting but certainly not trusting the stranger at the door.

Tammy removed an earpiece and small headphones and apologized that she'd been on a call, that she worked from home. She reached out her hand like she was eager for company.

That was what Maddy told herself, to make herself feel better. To prep herself for the weird *ask* she was about to throw out to this total stranger.

Only that her daughter Amy wasn't a stranger. And she was not a little girl where Maddy knew her. She shook Tammy Shimp's hand. "My name is Maddy Boyle. I'm a senior at the College of Charleston. Until three weeks ago I was . . ." Maddy trailed off when she saw how intently Tammy Shimp was watching her, and with pooling tears in her eyes.

"Maddy, I know who you are," Tammy said. "Please, come in."

23

Beth

Now

THEY NEEDED MORE bodies in uniform.

Beth had been on Grover about it for months. Another deputy, at least. Lump was useless and she was green. In his old-school way of doing anything, like a turtle out on a leisurely sunlit stroll across the forest, he'd say he'd look into it.

God love you, Beth thought, as she sped toward the tunnel for the second time in twelve hours, siren blaring, but I'm pretty pissed off right now.

Beth and Lump were basically it, the Sheriff's Department. Mrs. Downs, the last living relic from the old police department, handled all the processing and paperwork, but she was pushing seventy and forgetful. And their more experienced deputy, young talent named Matt Barnes, who'd been with Meeks for four years, up and left just over a year ago for a bigger job in Kansas.

And there was no blueprint for *this*. This madness.

They'd had no luck on the license plates Lump had run last night. Simon was still in his cell and she'd yet to have time to question him further. According to Lump, Simon had done nothing but sleep since Beth had left, and was still asleep now, snoring when Mrs. Downs had taken the call ten minutes ago from a hysterical Mrs. Dawson down at the tunnel.

The phone call had woken Beth up after only a couple of hours of sleep. She left Jax's bed as quietly as she'd climbed into it, both her husband and son still sleeping. She freshened up at the sink and left within five minutes of getting the call.

The flash of light she'd seen last night was at the forefront of her mind, what she'd thought to be a lightning strike, but now had her doubts.

She pulled her car to a skidding stop on the grass overlooking the gully. Before she opened the door, her phone chimed with an incoming email from Brianna Bookman, responding to her inquiry from last night. She opened the email as she got out of the car and could tell by the length of it that it was pertinent.

Three weeks ago a man in a Detroit, Michigan, suburb was found dead and beheaded on the back deck of his house . . . Beth looked away from the email long enough to navigate the downslope to the ravine, but once she hit level ground she continued reading . . . *with the severed head resting on his chest, the man's hands holding it in place.*

Hands, plural, Beth thought, which was *only* different than here because the body at the tunnel had one hand holding the hand of the other corpse, which strengthened her theory of two separate killers. Beth plowed on toward the looming tunnel. Sunlight glistened off weeds and saplings and stones wet with morning dew. Wisps of fog floated in front of her. Colorful leaves, still crisp from recently falling, kicked up with the breeze and spun cyclic in the air.

She finished skimming Brianna's message. *A week after the first beheading (these details were left out of the paper) another beheaded body, this a forty-year-old woman from another Detroit area suburb, was found by her husband on their living room floor, holding her head in her hands, eyes open and facing the door as he walked in from work. These details leaked and have only recently been connected to the first beheading the week prior* . . .

Beth pocketed the phone, pulled her gun, and hurried toward the tunnel's southern entrance, where Kelley Dawson, who ran Harrod's Reach's most popular fire-oven pizza joint, claimed to have seen a body. Some swore on crisp mornings they could hear the ghost roars of steam engines passing through the ravine; Beth heard birdsong, approaching sirens, and the thump of her own heartbeat. But what was Dawson doing down here? Too many residents still liked to do their morning runs through the woods, their morning hikes through the ravine, no matter how dangerous it was.

And now what?

The tunnel's entrance was visible forty yards ahead with a dozen people around it. Beth shouted, "Get back! Get back!"

They watched as Beth approached with her gun raised. Grover's voice sounded in her head. *They'll follow you, Beth. They'll listen.* This, after Beth, on her first day with the badge, questioned why the town would follow the orders of such a young, rookie deputy. A female in a male-dominated world. *Because you're a leader since the night of your birth.* She'd laughed, but he'd continued unabated. *Since the night of that storm, Beth, people here have looked at you in . . .*

Don't say it . . .

Awe, he'd said. *With respect. Sully garnered that same respect, Beth.*

I am not Sully Dupree.

Perhaps not, but you're cut from the same fearless cloth.

Beth carefully navigated the brick rubble from the collapsed southern wall, and saw what the people had surrounded.

A chair, occupied by what looked like a body, sat in the shadows of the tunnel's opening. Someone was crying. They averted their eyes. A few glanced but were quick to look away again. What the hell was sitting in that chair? It looked human, but at the same time not. It wasn't moving. Beth continued over the bricks, as she'd done last night under the cloak of darkness, but something about how this morning sunlight mixed with the wisps of fog and morning dew made this seem more surreal and fantastical.

Like something in the air was off and there was no way to pinpoint it.

That flash of light last night . . .

She glanced at the chair, knew right off it was too much to take in all at once.

Several of the bystanders cried out, talking in unison now that the law had arrived, some pointing at the chair while others pointed to the sky, where a large bird hovered twenty feet above the chair, its dark shadow the size of an albatross as it circled.

Beth glanced at the body in the chair, what appeared to be a woman with long blonde hair falling past the shoulders in ringlets. Something about the rich color made her think of corn silk, made her think it was not real, like a wig. But there was something wrong with the face as well. It looked clunky, like the skin had begun to peel off.

The bird swooped down toward the small group. They ducked, shielded their faces as the bird flew back toward the sky.

Justine Baker said, "Beth, what *is* that?"

Beth looked up toward the bird's flight for a true study of the thing. Until then, she'd only glimpsed it, squinting through sunlight, assuming it was a hawk, except this was the size of a vulture, or perhaps larger, like a condor. But it was the color that struck her—the bird was as blue as if it had flown through a waterfall of azure paint, and the image immediately brought Beth back to what she'd seen inside Simple Simon's cottage the night before, to those oddly colored pelts and skins on his wall.

Jane Bigsby, whose collapse on the gym floor last night had been the start of this never-ending nightmare, sat on the grassy incline with her face in her hands, sobbing.

What was she doing down here? Beth looked to Justine Baker, who was rubbing Jane's back in comfort, and said, "Doc?" She mouthed the words, *Did he die?*

Justine shook her head no.

Jane lowered her hands from her face and stared at the odd chair at the tunnel's mouth. "Something's happening, Beth. Something's coming through. Travers was convinced of it. There are some things at home you *need* to see."

The blue bird swooped down again, and they all ducked.

Beth aimed her gun at the bird, followed the flight path, until it retreated into the sky. She lowered her gun. A breeze blew a crisp, white leaf across the brick dust like a tumbleweed, and it snagged on Beth's left pant leg at the ankle. It was as large as a dinner plate, white with black and red veins.

"Look at the trees, Beth," Jane hissed. "He was so goddamn obsessed with this tunnel."

Justine Baker locked eyes with Beth and nodded toward the tunnel's southern entrance. For the first time, Beth saw what Jane Bigsby was seeing, what all of them had already seen, not just the strange bird soaring and the doll-like body on the chair, but what had happened all around the mouth of the tunnel's stone rim. The ivy and climbing vines that covered the stones, typically lush and green, had turned colors, with hues of pink and white and purple and gold dominating the tunnel's arch, coiled and intertwined as vines do, but more noticeable now with the different colors.

Beth heard movement behind her. The sirens had become background noise. The medics had arrived, along with Chimp Deavers, Jax's boss from the fire department, and Gideon beside him. The medics stopped in their tracks, stared in awe. Chimp stopped too, his eyes pinging back and forth from the bird's flight to the tunnel. "What . . . the fuck . . . is going on?"

Gideon moved toward where Beth stood. "The trees," said Gideon, like he too was ignoring what was in that chair. "Beth . . ."

Beth looked from the colorful vines edging the stones around the tunnel to the trees in the woods that bordered it. The leaves had turned white on at least a dozen trees, those closest to the opening, not as large as the leaf that had clung to Beth's leg before skittering, breeze-blown, down the ravine's gully, but similar in shape and texture.

Because the other one had come *from* the tunnel . . .

Carson Knox, the owner of Knox Plumbing, stepped from the cluster of people and pointed at Gideon. "It's him. Things all started when he came back to town."

Beth glared. "Shut up, Knox." She kept her focus on the smattering of white-leaved trees. The large blue bird circled low over the chair, the swooping wingspan strong enough to displace air.

Knox said, "Son of a bitch," and stepped back into a fighting stance.

Beth aimed her gun again, followed the flight of the bird, which was low enough to see oily black feathers within all that blue.

"Beth, look at the ground." Gideon pointed past the thing in the chair. "Just outside the tunnel . . . Are those shells?"

She allowed herself another glance at the thing in the chair as she followed Gideon's extended finger. Out from about fifteen feet from the tunnel's entrance, the brick dust and rubble on the ground appeared to have been pushed back, cleared away from the tunnel toward where they all now stood in the ravine, extending a good five feet from the body in the chair. And the only thing Beth could envision was an ocean tide, because that thumbnail patch of ground outside the tunnel now looked like a beach littered with what the tide had brought in. Black branches and rocks of every color. At least two dozen seashells, most of them light blue, were scattered about the ground, along with a dozen more fish that looked to be dead, with one in particular, over to the right, just in the grass, barely moving, slowly dying, and God damn if a few blades of that grass hadn't turned the color of wheat.

Chimp Deavers gave the chair a wide gap as he rounded toward the seashells on the ground behind it.

Beth said, "I wouldn't touch those, Chimp."

But he did, just like a kid needing to touch a candle flame to truly believe it was hot. He held one up to his ear and listened. "It's the ocean."

Raymond James called out, "There is no ocean in Harrod's Reach, Chimp."

Chimp dropped the seashell to the ground, moved closer to the tunnel's entrance, and gestured to the shells all around him. "Then how do you explain this, Ray?"

Carson Knox again pointed past Beth. "It's Gideon. I'm telling you, it's—"

"I said shut your fucking face, Knox." As soon as Beth took two cautious steps toward the chair, the bird swooped down, squawking, landed on the back of the chair, next to where the lifeless head lolled toward the left shoulder.

"Shoot it!" Jane Bigsby screamed from behind.

The bird's head rotated toward Beth as if daring her to, two beady eyes dark as coal and glistening wet, fresh from whatever hell it had just come.

Beth leveled the gun, said, "Fly away." She inched closer. "Fly away."

The massive bird dug its hooked gray beak into the curls of blonde hair and started pecking, as if hunting for food. Beth inched close enough to see that the hair wasn't real, but a wig with fake corkscrew curls, and when she got closer still, she realized the odd-looking skin wasn't skin at all. But as soon as the bird's beak went for that fake skin and came back with a small swatch of clothlike material and revealed a face behind it—the cheek of a face with whiskers, because it wasn't a woman—Beth fired.

The bullet plugged the bird dead center and sent it skidding, back-tumbling, beak-over-talons into the brick dust and dead fish and seashells. The wings still pulsed and fluttered; Beth couldn't take the screeching sounds coming from it so she shot it again, this time spinning the bird back into the shadows of the tunnel in a puff of blue feathers and bird guts.

"Mother fuck," Knox shouted, covering his ears.

Beth breathed heavily.

Another white leaf whisked out from the tunnel.

"Careful," Gideon said over her shoulder. And then, "Jesus," as he must have just noticed what she'd noticed. The taupe cloth over the body's face, not just resting there over the nose and cheekbones and jawline, but sewn with red thread into the skin. The stitching like that of a threaded baseball, running from where flesh met the hairline, in front of the ears, and down into the neckline below the chin. The mouth was a hatched line of red crisscrossed stitches. Brown coat buttons acted as the eyes.

Gideon stood next to her. "They made him into a doll . . ."

A female doll . . . Beth stepped to within a couple of feet of the chair. The body had been dressed in a paisley summer dress, the V-shaped neckline revealing a fat chest that had recently been shaved. Because dolls don't have hair. The corpse's calves were shaved as well, the chubby feet shoved into a pair of blue pumps.

Gideon moved around to the back of the chair to view the horror in full.

Carson Knox stood near the entrance to the tunnel, touching the colorful vines around the edge. Beth shouted, "Knox, stop! Don't touch it."

But he'd already plucked a footlong strand of vine and was analyzing it inches from his face. She didn't trust it, just like she didn't trust Chimp now lifting a second seashell despite her earlier warning not to. "Put those down," she ordered them, and then focused on the human doll in the chair. The chubby hands rested casually on each bent knee, obviously positioned there. But those hands, she recognized those hands. No . . . It hit her hard and fast. She'd seen those hands last night inside the hospital waiting room. No . . .

"Beth . . ." Gideon said, staring at something behind the chair.

Chimp Deavers nudged a dead orange fish with the toe of his boot, and then picked up a third seashell, this one larger than the other two in his hands, and a deeper shade of light blue.

Carson Knox plucked off another thread of pink and purple vine.

"Stop," Beth screamed. "Don't! Touch! Anything! This is a *crime* scene."

Deputy Lump finally arrived, and echoed her: "Don't touch nothing!"

"Beth . . ." Gideon watched her over the morbidly stitched human doll. "Look at this."

Beth made her way around the chair to where Gideon pointed. It didn't appear that anyone else had realized it was Mayor Truffant under that hideous disguise. A piece of printer paper had been stapled to the back of his neck, a handwritten note that took up the entire page. No, not a note, but a message for sure. Beth squatted down for an eye-level read:

I left my baby lying here,
Lying here, lying here
I left my baby lying there
To go and gather berries.

I found the wee brown otter's track
Otter's track, otter's track
I found the wee brown otter's track
But ne'er a trace o' my baby, O!

I found the track of the swan on the lake
Swan on the lake, swan on the lake
I found the track of the swan on the lake
But not the track of baby, O!

I found the trail of the mountain mist
Mountain mist, mountain mist
I found the trail of the mountain mist
But ne'er a trace of baby, O!

Beth nearly plucked the note from the body's neck but remembered her own orders. It was all evidence. "It's a lullaby," she said to Gideon.

"Not one I've ever heard."

"Me, either, but Jesus . . ."

"Beth, do you know who this is?"

"Yes." She watched the tunnel, as if waiting for something to suddenly come out of it. She called Chimp over. She'd noticed he'd dropped the seashells from his hands. When Chimp got close enough, out of everyone else's earshot, Beth said, "I need you to get all your men, Chimp. Block every street leading in and out of the Reach."

"Right now?"

"Yes, now. Do it last night. Do it yesterday. Blockade the roads. Nobody gets in or out."

"We're not officers of the law, Beth."

"Right now, we all are. Go on, but without too much commotion."

Chimp started off but stopped, nodded toward the chair. "You know who's under that?"

"I do," she said calmly, just for his ears. "It's Mayor Truffant."

Chimp tightened his jaw like he might explode. Chimp played poker with Mayor Truffant once a month at the parish rectory with Father Fred. "You sure?"

"I'm sure." Beth said, "But do your grieving in your car. Not here. Go on now. Act like you don't know."

Chimp hesitated at first, but then got a move on. A few others from the crowd followed him. Beth ordered everyone else gone, and then fired a shot into the air to reinforce it.

Knox gave her lip, eyed Gideon like he still believed him to be at fault, but moved along with the herd.

Beth watched them go, glad, despite all of Gideon's history of being chickenshit, that he hadn't gone with them.

Gideon said, "Beth, what's going on?"

"I don't know. But the two bodies found last week have yet to be identified. They're not *from* here." She stared at the chair. "But now they've gotten one of our own."

"They?"

"I don't think it's one person," Beth said. "Might even be looking at three now. And I think they're still here in the Reach." She faced the tunnel, the ground leading up to the dark entrance littered with things that had no earthly right being there.

But the way Mayor Truffant's body had been left *outside* the tunnel . . .

Gideon said, "What are you thinking?"

Beth eyed the note, the weird lullaby written on it, and then looked deep into the tunnel again. "That it's a sacrifice of some sort."

"For what?"

"I don't know."

Excerpt from Detective Harrington's notes
November 19, 1964
Harrod's Reach

L AST NIGHT *I arrested Anna Cruz Smith (36, married to Matthew Cruz Smith) for breaking and entering the property of Dawn Peterson (22, single). I also charged Anna Cruz with illegally inhabiting a home (for 6 days). After receiving a phone call from Dawn Peterson, who'd been hearing sounds in her house for those same six days Anna Cruz had been reported missing, I searched the premises. Dawn had been hearing footsteps and scratching coming from her attic for days. Sensing it was a raccoon, she did her best to ignore the sounds, hoping it would soon leave, which it apparently did after three days, only to then have scratching sounds begin under the floorboards of her living room. These sounds were off and on, according to Dawn Peterson, but on day six, and on little to no sleep for the past two, she called the police. After prying up a few of the floorboards in Dawn Peterson's living room, I found Dawn's neighbor, Anna Cruz Smith, on her back, wedged inside a small cubby between the floor joists. She'd managed to crawl into these tight confines from the ceiling of the basement storage room directly below. Having been there for days, with nothing more than a can of Diet Dr. Pepper and a snack bag of pretzels (not sure how she was able to drink from that position) Anna Cruz was freed from the floorboards, not of sound mind, and badly in need of nourishment. She is* now *convalescing inside the psych ward at Harrod's Reach Hospital until I can figure out what to do with her.*

What I could briefly procure from her incoherent ramblings, was that she truly believed she was something called a Kikimora, which I asked her to repeat and spell, and I later looked up in an encyclopedia. In Slavic mythology, a Kikimora is a female spirit that inhabits a house, causing disturbances and eventually sleep paralysis. They are rarely seen but can be heard under floorboards, in attics, or behind stoves. Anyone living in the same house as a kikimora will feel haunted, which Dawn Peterson most certainly did. When questioned on his wife's odd behavior of late, Matthew Cruz Smith said only that his wife was prone to sleepwalking (in his words she was a deep sleepwalker and it was not uncommon to find her on the front porch), and on the night before she'd entered Dawn Peterson's house, he'd found his wife walking inside the old train tunnel, at which point he directed her back home. According to Mr. Cruz Smith, she had never before ventured that far during one of her sleepwalking episodes.

Side note: The night Matthew Cruz Smith found his wife inside the train tunnel also coincided with Patricia Bell's report that she'd seen a flash of light that night from the tunnel's north entrance.

CHAPTER

24

Teddy

Before

I T WAS BRANDY'S idea to take a detour from *the list* and go see Teddy's mother in Virginia.

Teddy had warned her they had places to go and dead-heads to kill, but Brandy had been adamant. And with how deeply she'd gotten her claws into him, he couldn't say no. Good thing all her ideas had turned out to be good ones.

Everyone else on the Lullaby Express was afraid of her. Ever since that day in the rest area bathroom when she'd stroked his horns—five inches now and starting to sprout new branches—she'd insisted everyone on the bus call her the Black Widow.

One man who they'd picked up in Pennsylvania, a really twitchy fucker who was on the run he claimed for doing something bad, *real bad*, refused to call her that, and now he was no longer alive, his body dumped in rural Ohio, having bled out all over one of the Lullaby Express's seats after Brandy's knife entered his brain stem from the underside of his chin. Ever since that, everyone on the bus—up to twelve now—respectfully called her the Black Widow.

Teddy pulled the Lullaby Express to a stop outside his childhood home and said, "You sure you want to do this?"

Brandy stood up and yelled to the passengers, "Nobody gets off. You understand what I'm saying?" Some nodded, but others didn't. She said to Teddy, "Turn that shit down." He'd been playing lullabies on repeat over the speakers he'd put in; the lullabies seemed to calm a few of them when they got antsy. He turned it down; it had been playing the Haitian lullaby, "Dodo Titi," another ditty where the baby would come to harm if they didn't go to sleep.

Brandy repeated herself to the passengers and got all nods this time. Satisfied, she opened the door and said to Teddy, "Let's go."

Teddy stood from the driver's seat and his horns hit the ceiling. Bolts of pain shot down through his skull. He reached to the dashboard for the cowboy hat he'd been wearing to hide them, but Brandy said, "No. Leave it. Let her see you as you are."

Teddy left the hat on the dash, and thought *She ain't gonna see shit, she's practically a dead-head herself*, but followed Brandy to the front door. It was unlocked, which meant the old widow from next door, Mrs. Chastain, was here helping her eat. Once inside, they found Mrs. Chastain standing in the living room beside Belinda Lomax's hospital bed, but instead of her typical drugged-out gaze, Mother was sitting up on her own and seemed more alert than she had in a year or more.

Mother turned her head toward them, but after seeing his horns, her smile faded.

Mrs. Chastain gasped, stepped away. "Hello, Theodore." She spoke in pleasantries, but his horns had spooked her. Not only the horns, but perhaps what Brandy was wearing as well.

"Mother," said Teddy, and then to their neighbor, "Mrs. Chastain."

Brandy stared at Belinda Lomax just as his mother stared into her. Not so much in a bad way, thought Teddy, but more out of curiosity. And then the most shocking thing occurred: Mother reached out her hand toward Brandy and Brandy stepped closer and grasped it, lovingly, like they somehow understood each other, when Teddy had assumed that Brandy would have been the last woman on earth of whom Mother would have approved. But here they were, not only holding hands but smiling.

Brandy said to Mrs. Chastain, "You can go now."

Mrs. Chastain hesitated long enough for Mother to say, "Go on, Margaret." And then her eyes turned cold. Teddy saw hate flash through them, which he'd seen glimpses of before but never toward Mrs. Chastain. "I know you've been wearing my jewelry, Margaret. Wearing my *clothes*."

Mrs. Chastain paused but wouldn't look back toward her friend on the bed. Mother said, "I know you've been stealing cookies from my cookie jar." Something about the way Mother smiled made Teddy wonder if she was really talking about cookies. "But that's okay, Margaret," said Mother, grinning. "I used to have relations with Stan."

Mrs. Chastain closed her eyes like she might get sick, or maybe closing them could block out what Mother was saying about her dead husband

But Mother wasn't finished. "Every Monday and Friday morning," she said. "For years."

Jesus Christ, thought Teddy. Who *was* this woman?

Mrs. Chastain stormed out, but not before giving Teddy's horns one last look. The screen door slammed shut.

Belinda Lomax looked at Teddy. "I'm tired of fighting it, Theodore. So God damn tired."

Teddy stood speechless. Never had he heard his mother take her Lord's name in vain. This wasn't the mother who'd raised him. Wasn't the mother he'd expected Brandy to meet. Wasn't the mother who'd constantly gotten so under his skin he'd tried to kill her.

Tired of fighting what, he thought?

Mrs. Chastain started screaming outside.

Brandy let go of Mother's hand to look out the window. "Oh shit."

"What?" asked Teddy.

"The guy with the axe got off the bus." Brandy headed for the front door, hurried out, shouting, "Put her down!"

Teddy heard Mrs. Chastain screaming, and then she stopped. Brandy gasped loud enough for Teddy to hear her through the wall.

Teddy moved toward the window, pulled the curtains aside. Mrs. Chastain's body lay in the grass a few paces away from the bus. The big, beefy son of a bitch with the axe was stepping back onto the Lullaby Express, mission accomplished, blood dripping from the blade he liked to sharpen as they drove. The bus shook under his weight. Teddy didn't know his name, because the man didn't talk much. He'd been the third passenger Teddy had picked up, weeks ago in the Detroit area, and maybe this outburst had been brewing for some time. Brandy had warned that the man seemed to be getting fidgety and more anxious by the day. Like he badly needed to use that axe on *something*.

On *someone*.

Teddy looked back to Mrs. Chastain's body on the grass; the man had lopped her head clean off and placed it on her chest, eyes open and facing the road. Teddy should have been horrified, but the tingle inside his skull made him feel otherwise. From the tip of his horns on down to his toes he felt the thrum. Fuel coursed through his blood and bones and gave him a jolt.

Brandy turned toward him at the window and held out her hands like *What the fuck?*

Teddy thought, maybe we shouldn't have turned the lullabies down so low.

He gave Brandy a look that said *You handle it*, and then turned back toward his mother.

Belinda Lomax looked tired. She held a yellow paper out to Teddy. "Margaret got this out of the mail." Teddy grabbed the paper from his mother. She said, "Take me there."

Before he could read what was on the yellow paper—at first glance it looked like a flyer of some sort—Brandy came storming back inside.

Brandy had a temper and Teddy liked it.

Teddy told her, "Take her around back. Bury it."

"We're gonna burn it first," she said.

"Who's we?"

"Freddie. The dude with the black greasy hair and the lisp. Like Elmer Fudd. Sits two benches behind your driver's seat."

"Elmer Fudd doesn't have a lisp, he stutters," said Teddy. "You're thinking Sylvester. Although I think he does that on purpose."

"Whatever," said Brandy. "We picked him up in Kalamazoo. Right after you did that dead-head in Saginaw." She gestured toward the window. "He just walked off the bus and said his name was Firestarter Freddie." She scratched her head like she was annoyed with all of it. "And I said, 'Oh really?' And he said, 'Yeah, I start fires. That's what I do.' Except he said it with that lisp."

"Bring it in here," whispered Mother Lomax. "The body . . . Burn it all down" And Teddy thought, now we're talking, just let me get a few things from my room first.

He said to Brandy, "Tell Freddie to bring the body in here. Get that weirdo with the horseshoes to help carry it." Brandy rolled her eyes. He said, "It was your idea to come here." And that got her moving, albeit with major attitude and some bounce to her rump, barely concealed by that black miniskirt.

Finally, he looked at the yellow paper his mother had handed him, when she'd said *Take me here*. It was a flyer advertising the grand reopening of the historic Beehive Hotel in some place called Harrod's Reach, Nebraska.

At first, Teddy thought, *No way, no how, Mother*, but then the name Harrod's Reach struck him like a church bell.

Harrod's Reach was where he'd been heading to before this detour, where the most recent name on his list resided.

Some dead-head named Solomon Dupree. Goes by Sully.

CHAPTER

25

Gideon

Now

INSIDE THE HARROD'S Reach Sheriff's Department, Gideon stood side by side with the four others about to be deputized.

Next to him were Nurse Natalie, Fire Chief Chimp Deavers, Fireman Jax McBride, and Joseph Farrington, the editor of the *Harrod's Reach Gazette*. Now that word had spread about Mayor Truffant's murder, it was like a hornet's nest had been shaken and the residents were ready to sting.

Joe said there were more hoping to join.

Beth looked eerily calm as she paced before the four of them, churning out some deputizing words she must have just googled or was making up on the spot.

Gideon quivered when she put on his badge.

The night before he'd left town had been an unexpectedly memorable one. Beth had known Gideon had had a thing for her since he was a little boy. As young children, when she should have been too young to understand the transformation of his face because of his cleft upper lip— the surgeries and bandages he'd had to wear for weeks, until finally all that was left was the scar—she never pointed at it. Never made him feel small because of it. Like she knew underneath it all his face was healing.

Becoming something improved. During adolescence, Gideon's feelings for her painfully blossomed, as did his anxiety—the girls in middle school snickered about what it might feel like to kiss his lip, that scar—while Beth doubled down on beauty and perfection and a bravery Gideon could only pretend to know.

But Beth and Jax, by their teens, had become inseparable. Almost like they'd made a secret pact. Gideon and Beth had had their moments, just frequently enough to make Gideon think he might have a chance, but too often Giddy-Up Gideon was the third wheel. Which had made what she'd done the night before his deployment more jarring, slipping into his bedroom like she'd done, but even then, she hadn't kissed him.

Focus, Gideon. People are getting murdered. Focus on the badge now pinned to your shirt.

Beth looked over her shoulder at Simon, still asleep on his cot inside Cell #1, and thanked him for being the witness at their official swearing in. Simon had his shoes on the wrong feet.

Gideon wondered if he even counted as a witness since he was asleep, and technically under arrest. And what was that giant orange book tucked in his arms like a teddy bear? Thick with pages and loose papers, the size of a photo album Gideon's mother used to make before Sully went down. And what in the hell was *Lalaland*, which it said on the front cover?

Jax, Joseph, and Natalie funneled out the door to the sunlit street.

Gideon hung back because Beth did. She stood at Simon's cell and said, "I've half a mind to wake him up."

"He been sleeping this entire time?"

"Pretty much," she said. "Must sleep a lot at home too. Living room's practically all bed." She unlatched keys from her belt, unlocked Simon's cell door, and started inside toward where he slept. She said to Gideon, "You go on. Your post is on Mallard, right?"

"Yeah." But Gideon didn't budge. Didn't feel right leaving Beth inside here alone with this man.

"Always the gentlemen," she said in jest, but she didn't complain when Gideon stepped inside the cell with her. She bent down, nudged Simon's shoulder, once, twice, and then hard the third time, but he didn't so much as break stride with his snoring. "Simon." She nudged him again. "Simon," she called, louder this time, before making a play for the orange book in his arms.

"What are you doing?" asked Gideon.

"What's it look like?" The book's spine faced down toward the mattress, situated so that she was able to pry it open in the middle, just enough to see most of one page at a time. The one she stopped on was full of color, and featured a massive, creepy brown dog with sharp fangs and evil eyes. Below it, Simon had written: *Pesanta, Catalan Folklore, presence brings about nightmares.* Then she carefully flipped to another page. The two of them craned their necks to better see the page, which showed another beast, brown and black and gray, that looked like a hodgepodge animal. Below it he'd written: *The Baku, Japanese Folklore, the Dream-Eater.*

Gideon would have had to move Beth out of the way to see what had been written below that. "What's the rest say?"

Beth hunkered lower, her face inches from the page, and too close to Simon's body for comfort. "They eat nightmares. And if the nightmares they eat aren't bad enough, they'll eat your soul. Says here, God created all the animals, and the Baku is made up of all the spare pieces and parts." She started to turn another page, and the book shifted. Simon grunted, tugged it closer to his chest, and practically rolled over on it.

Gideon said, "What do you make of it?"

"Of him sleeping so much?"

"And the book?"

"I don't know." She checked her watch. "But we've got work to do."

Gideon took that as his cue to beat feet, and outside he saw Jax across the street in an animated discussion with another fireman, Rick Doogan. The two broke apart when Gideon saw them. Rick headed off toward his fire truck. Gideon felt Jax's eyes on him as he walked on, probably wondering why he'd spent that extra time inside with his wife. Gideon told himself to quit being paranoid, but had half a mind to ask Jax why he wasn't already at his post at the barricade crossing Guthrie Street.

Natalie was in charge of anything at the hospital. Joe Farrington had the beat at Jefferson and Taylor Streets. The good thing about Harrod's Reach being bordered on one side by the forest and lake, and on another by the tunnel and One-Side Mountain, was that there weren't many ways in and out of town. Gideon was quick to volunteer for the post at Mallard because of its proximity to the Beehive Hotel, so he could spy on the goings on there.

The town had grown quiet since Mayor Truffant was found earlier in the morning. Most had locked themselves inside their homes, their places of business. By the time Gideon made it to Mallard Street, he saw Beth's sheriff's cruiser idling next to the Smite House. She must have wasted no time after Gideon had left. Beth got out and ushered her two-year-old son Brody to the wrap-around front porch. Gideon's mom, still in her bright yellow Beehive Hotel T-shirt, greeted them at the front door. She and Beth exchanged words and Beth jogged back to her car.

What were they doing?

Maxine and Brody waved to Beth from the porch as she reversed the car and headed toward Mallard at the same time Gideon walked past the driveway. He continued up Mallard toward the Beehive Hotel.

Hammering echoed through the pines. White clouds hovered through a blue sky so pretty it was insane to think how ugly things were now beneath it. Gideon thought it was odd for his parents to be watching Brody. And he couldn't shake the feeling he'd had last night, that Jax's presence in the Smite House hadn't been a one-off. That he, Gideon, had been the visitor inside his own home and not his childhood nemesis.

And the tears. Gideon had never seen Jax cry. Beth claimed she'd seen it on the few occasions Jax, as a boy, had run away to her house after being beaten by his father, Tom. And another time as a teen, when Jax, in a panic, had knocked on Grover Meeks's door, looking for Beth and needing somewhere to hide, needing a place to lie low from his father for a while. They'd assumed Jax had meant hours, but "a while" meant days. Four, in fact, before Grover had convinced the boy to return home, where ultimately Jax got beat up again. After that, Grover had laced his boots, pinned on his badge, placed the trademark bowler hat on his head and had one foot out the door with his sidearm holstered before Jax grabbed the sheriff's arm to hold him back, pleaded with him to not make things worse. Grover agreed but swore if he ever saw another mark on that boy's body from that son of a bitch father of his, he was throwing Tom McBride behind bars and swallowing the key.

Everyone in town knew Tom McBride was not only a mean drunk who liked to put a hand to his wife and only son, but a bigot and a racist who'd been mumbling ever since Grover put on the star badge, *that uppity sheriff wouldn't last two weeks in Harrod's Reach.* Not only had the sheriff, to Tom McBride's chagrin, lasted two weeks, but his tenure now was best counted in decades, with Jax McBride—a bully in his own right—the first one in line to vote for him every time Grover came up for reelection.

Gideon strolled past the Beehive and imagined it suddenly imploding.

That renovation should belong to his father and not some upstart, out-of-town wannabe. Gideon recalled the realtor years ago sitting in their living room, making his sales pitch on the Beehive to Mom and Dad, how he'd thought it strange the realtor looked too young to be selling historic hotels.

And now *she* was working for *him*.

Gideon paced behind the barricades across Mallard Street. Harrod's Reach had seen its share of violence, but never anything like this. Violence begetting violence like it was contagious. Like what Beth had briefly explained to him right before the swearing in, her working theory of what she called cluster violence.

Bottom line: the tunnel was coming alive.

Gideon wondered what Sully would have thought about the tunnel right now, doing what it was doing . . . blooming? There was no other way for him to describe it. And here were the construction workers at the Beehive going about their business like someone hadn't just been stitched into a human doll two miles away.

From where Gideon patrolled, the back of the Beehive was visible. Hammering sounded. A worker sawed through boards in the back parking lot. A trio of painters strolled in, held the door as an electrician walked out. Perhaps their obliviousness made sense—they were out-of-town contractors with jobs to do—but to Gideon that alone made them the first people he'd talk to. Beth had enough on her plate, so as soon as his shift was over, he'd do just that, interrogate each worker and find out if any had a fetish for making dolls.

The hotel was looking good; he couldn't deny it. Not only had Mickey French taken over his father's idea, he was doing a bang-up job of it. Gideon had seen plenty of pictures of the Beehive from its golden days. When he blurred his vision and imagined it sepia or black and white, it could have been plucked right from the newspapers that had once made it famous. On one of the tours of the Beehive Archie had been given years ago, he'd found an old 1920s beige Applejack hat and Mickey had told him to keep it. He kept it and washed it and eventually Sully started wearing it. Gideon could envision his little brother now, walking inside the Beehive in that hat like he owned the place. He had walked all over town in that hat, like he owned the *town*. Now that hat, which Sully was clutching in his right hand when they'd found him in the tunnel that day, was hanging on the parlor wall above his bed.

Gideon felt sure Sully would have loved the hotel every bit as much as he'd loved wearing that hat.

The hotel's exterior courtyard had been given a proper facelift, with newly fashioned gazebos and stone walkways, fancy tables with umbrellas, trellises with climbing vines, and new wrought-iron fencing to surround it all. It was quaint. Lovely. He could see why his mother was so enamored.

A curtain moved in a third-floor room. At first Gideon wondered why someone would be up there a month from the grand reopening, but of course each room had to be readied too. Could have been a painter. Could have been someone hammering in a new baseboard or hanging the curtain itself. But Gideon couldn't shake the feeling he was being watched.

Quit being paranoid, soldier. But *someone* had snuck into their home last night and had attempted to abduct Sully. Someone had pulled the tube from his throat and unhooked him from the machines. It was hard *not* to be paranoid out here, to be untrusting of any strangers.

A cloud moved and the sun showed itself again, glistening off something in the woods beyond the courtyard and forcing Gideon to squint. He stepped aside so it didn't strike him directly. It was a mirror. A large side mirror from a red bus? Not bright red but more like the color of rust, or dried blood. It wasn't hidden in the woods but parked far enough back into the shadows to easily be missed.

Gideon made a mental note to check that out too.

Growing impatient, he started down the grassy slope toward the courtyard when a vehicle in the distance turned onto Mallard Street from the highway. Once it neared, he saw it was a minivan. A minute later it slowed, came to a stop outside the barricade, and honked repeatedly, like they were having an emergency.

Gideon hurried back up the slope toward the street, saw at least two people in the van, both women. The driver rolled down her window. She was dark-haired, thirties maybe, and looked tired with life. She said to Gideon, "Is something going on?"

Gideon didn't mean to laugh, but he was nervous. Because things never change. *Giddy-Up Gideon.* And to answer her question, there was a whole shit ton going on, but where to even start?

He said, "Sorry, I didn't mean to . . . We're in the middle of a . . ." He noticed the young woman in the passenger's seat and went tongue-tied. "Middle of . . . a lockdown," he stammered. The passenger was younger than the driver, lower twenties probably, and fit. And as soon as they locked eyes, he felt himself go red. *God damn it, soldier.* Gideon closed his eyes, fought that voice away, opened them. "There's . . . been a tragedy."

"This is Harrod's Reach, right?"

"Yes, ma'am," Gideon said to the passenger. "What brings you to town today?"

The passenger undid her seat belt, leaned over the center console. "This is going to sound strange, but . . ." And now it was her turn to feel tongue-tied. This was a new sensation for Gideon, being on the other end of uncomfortableness. She glanced toward the back seat, and for the first time Gideon noticed a third passenger. A young girl lay across the minivan's bench, covered in a blanket and hooked to portable machines. Gideon had to look away; the girl reminded him too much of Sully, both in age and condition. The passenger found her words, "We're here to find Solomon Dupree. Goes by Sully. He's eight years old . . . he's in—"

"I know Sully." Gideon felt blood rush from his face. He could see relief washing over both women. How far had they come to get here? "I'm his brother."

The passenger gestured toward the driver. "This is Tammy Shimp. That's her daughter Amy in the back. We have a . . . message for your brother. Could you take us to him? Please?"

"My brother . . . he's . . ."

"I know . . ." Obviously stressed over trying to explain the situation, she touched her forehead, closed her eyes for a second to regroup, and tried again. "I know his situation. A month ago, I was in a coma. It's not so much a verbal message, but . . . I . . . we . . . fuck! Sorry . . ."

"Don't be." Gideon had already begun moving one of the barricades.

"I don't even know where to begin."

"How about with your name," said Gideon, and it had come out as smoothly as melted butter, despite the strange circumstances, and it had made her smile.

"Maddy Boyle," she said, calmly.

"Gideon," he said. "Gideon Dupree." He nodded toward the Smite House in the distance "Follow me."

26

Maddy

Now

MADDY WAS RELIEVED now that she'd made it inside the town's perimeter.

She and Tammy waited in the van as Gideon hustled inside to talk to his parents. She hadn't tagged him as one to still be living at home, but then again, technically, so was she. She hadn't given thought to what Sully Dupree's home would look like, but she hadn't envisioned this Victorian monstrosity. Done up with all the bells and whistles of historical accuracy. It even had a name carved into a wooden sign in neat, calligraphy letters: *The Smite House*. Like the big hotel she'd glimpsed at the top of the road, the Beehive, this house had sophistication and charm all the way up from the columned veranda to the dormers and gables, the pitched roofs and flanking turrets.

Gideon exited the front door and hurried down the steps to the driveway.

She wondered what he'd done to cause that limp. Something about that scar above his lip made him immediately handsome. He carried himself with a weird bashful confidence she'd never seen before in a man, so she found herself wishing he'd look up more. Just before he reached her rolled-down window, the front door of the Smite House opened, and out came an attractive middle-aged woman in a bright yellow T-shirt and holding a toddler, who mimicked her wave.

Maddy awkwardly waved back, wondering what Gideon had told the woman she assumed was his mother to make her so welcoming, so quickly.

"Come on in," Gideon said with a smile.

"Really?"

"Yeah, do you like, need a wheelchair or something?"

"No, I don't think so . . . We carried her to the car."

Tammy Shimp was already out of the van and opening the hatch. Gideon opened the side door as Maddy hopped out and analyzed the best way to get the girl inside. Getting Amy and her essential equipment into the van with just the two of them had been a chore. At least Tammy's mother wasn't here pleading for them to rethink moving a comatose child across multiple states in a non-medical vehicle. To which Tammy had finally screamed at her mother, *Please shut up, this is my daughter.* And then: *You saw her in there! Don't tell me you didn't see her, Mom!*

Thinking of it now brought tears to Maddy's eyes all over again, enough for Gideon to put a hand on her shoulder and ask if everything was okay, and she nodded. Like maybe now that they were here things would start to be okay. But the way Amy's heart rate had instantly risen back in Tulsa when Maddy had entered their house and mentioned the name of Sully Dupree, had that not been something akin to a miracle? And then what happened next, when Maddy sat on the poor girl's bed and whispered Sully's name a second time, for that slight smile to emerge. That had been all Tammy Shimp had needed to see. She'd been quick to allow Maddy into her home because she'd seen the news on her phone: *College of Charleston Senior Suddenly Awakens from 8-Day Coma.* She'd read the article numerous times, she'd told Maddy, praying the same might eventually happen to her daughter. And now here they were, preparing to take her inside this stranger's home to see the boy in person.

Tammy looked pale, and was physically trembling. Maddy had warned her not to get her hopes up. That she didn't yet know what any of this meant. This might not work at all. But Tammy had wanted to do it anyway.

They'd come this far. What else was there to lose?

Gideon stood outside the open sliding door with his arms out. Together, Tammy and Maddy took Amy, still hooked up to the machines, and rested her carefully in Gideon's arms, at which point he proceeded toward the house like he was holding a loved one of his own.

He walked carefully up the porch steps.

Gideon's mother, still holding the toddler, opened the screen as wide as it would go, allowing Gideon to carry the child in sideways, with Maddy and Tammy in tow. The mother held a hand over her mouth like she might get emotional, but tears had already pooled in her eyes.

Gideon, once inside the extravagant foyer, said, "Coming through." And then entered a hallway to the right, where a man she assumed to be Gideon's father appeared, quickly picking up tools from the floor and placing them inside an adjacent room. He was sweating, wiping his brow, and looked at his son with confusion.

"Coming through," Gideon said again.

His father backpedaled as they approached, showing them the way past this room and that room, and then a beautiful, airy old farmhouse-style kitchen Maddy wanted to revisit once things got settled. The father looked over his shoulder, turned as the hallway turned. "This way," he said, eyes on Amy's body resting limply in Gideon's arms. "I'm Archibald Dupree," he said to the strangers. "Call me Archie. And who do we have here?"

Gideon answered. "This is Amy Shimp. Her mother Tammy and their friend Maddy Boyle. I explained it all to Mom. Just clear the way to Sully. I'll need somewhere to put her until we find another bed."

"Of course," said Archie, turning and hurrying forward now. "Of course. Just this way." He took them into a parlor with tall windows, a taller ceiling, and a hospital bed that seemed to swallow the little boy in the middle of it.

Gideon said, "Dad, move him over."

Archie rounded the bed and moved his son over as delicately as Gideon was handling Tammy's daughter. Gideon eased the little girl down on the bed, and Tammy followed right behind with the essentials. Archie was quick to clear off an end table and carry it around so that Tammy could place whatever devices she needed to on it. By then, Gideon's mother was inside the room with them with the toddler, who was pointing at the bed and saying, "Sully . . . That's Sully." And then, "Who she?"

Maddy laughed, but everyone's focus stayed on the two coma patients on the bed.

Tammy looked like she might throw up. Archie looked pale and on the verge of getting sick too. Gideon was the only one in the room who appeared calm. Because what now? What really had they been expecting? For both children to suddenly wake up and ask what was for dinner? The longer they stood there and watched and waited, the more it all seemed painfully futile and stupid. Like a big fucking waste of time.

Tammy had started crying like she knew it too.

But just as Mom Dupree, probably sensing things might soon turn south, had begun to take the toddler out of the room, Sully's right hand twitched.

Archie Dupree gasped. He covered his mouth when Sully's hand twitched a second time.

While everyone stood speechless, Gideon approached the bed. He leaned over his little brother's chest. "Sully, this is your brother, Gideon. There's someone in the bed beside you. Someone you might know?" He looked to Maddy and Tammy.

Maddy nodded to confirm, and even though she wasn't the girl's mother, she stepped toward the other side of the bed and hovered over Amy. "Amy, I know you know Sully's name. He's with you now. He's right beside you. If you can hear me . . ." She trailed off when Amy's left hand twitched, inches away from Sully's right.

Tammy Shimp said, "Oh my God."

Archie was recording it on his phone.

Maddy held out both hands for everyone to temper themselves. *Don't expect too much. Don't expect anything more than what was happening now.*

"Sully," said Gideon, looking over the bed toward Maddy, which she took as a prompt to then say Amy's name again.

"Amy, baby, we're right here," Maddy said. "Sully is right beside you."

Sully's hand twitched again, and then moved an inch toward Amy's extended fingers.

Mom Dupree behind Maddy said, "Holy shit."

Amy's hand responded to Sully's proximity again, scooting closer to his fingers. Sully's hand responded, this time prodding *her* fingers, gripping them until they held hands, palm to palm, and everyone inside the parlor was holding their breath.

Maddy and Gideon locked eyes over the bed. Like they didn't know what had just happened, but for now, job well done. The two comatose children on the bed, still dead to the world, kept alive by the tubes and machines they were connected to, held hands like they'd never let go, and God damn, Maddy thought, if they weren't both now slightly grinning.

Only then did she remember the connection between the two in Lalaland.

CHAPTER

27

Beth

Now

ETH HAD ALWAYS prided herself on being fearless.

It was a tag her parents had put on her early and often as a little girl, and the town had been quick to adopt. When Beth was two, when most children were afraid to get into the town pool, Beth got a running start and jumped in. At five, at an amusement park a town over in Crudup's Reach, she rode every roller-coaster, sat easily upon every ride. She was on a bike without training wheels at age four. Staying at home by herself for the first time at age seven. At eight, she and Gideon and Jax had been throwing a football around the lawn of her backyard, and a stray throw by Gideon sent the football to land in the neighboring yard, home to a Rottweiler Beth's dad had more than once threatened to shoot. Gideon and Jax shook their heads, each pointing for the other to jump the fence and get it, only to find that Beth had already done so and was casually approaching where the dog stood growling, watching her almost as ferociously as she was watching it.

And there was the tunnel, the infamous town landmark Beth had run through on a dare at age five. When kids ignored the family rules and played down there outside the south entrance, she was the first to run in to retrieve whatever ball or Frisbee was accidently tossed or kicked into the dark void. She'd first kissed Jax McBride inside the tunnel, knowing right then and there that she'd marry him but never really love him. Like Sully Dupree, years later, the tunnel had never scared her. The stories of it had never been a deterrent. In fact, more than not, she found herself drawn to it. If she was close, she felt the urgent need to go inside, even as an adult, which was why, even though Jax had begged her repeatedly to take someone with her, she was approaching the tunnel's south entrance alone, the second time this morning.

Mayor Truffant's body had been removed. The body, still with the dollish cloth material stitched into the mayor's face and the creepy lullaby attached to the back of his neck, was resting inside the hospital morgue, inside the third and final cadaver freezer they had, the first two occupied by the bodies found three days ago.

Those two bodies were the reason she'd returned to the tunnel.

She'd be neglecting her duty if she didn't go check more thoroughly the area where those bodies had been found. She and Grover had taken pictures. They'd taped off the perimeter, but now she questioned whether they'd gone wide and far enough. And the condition of the bodies had left them both so heartsick, it was possible they'd overlooked something. Now with the latest calling card left on Mayor Truffant, she was hoping for something to link the three murders.

Instead of walking around the tunnel to the crime scene, which was what Jax had begged her to do, she was fixing to walk right through it. Because she couldn't *not* walk through it, not after what had . . . had bloomed from it overnight. *You don't have to be so tough*, Jax had said. She'd laughed at her comeback to Jax, *It's not toughness if it comes naturally*. If it goes without thinking, it often meant barreling straight into a thing.

The chair Mayor Truffant's body had been fastened to had left four indentations in the brick dust. She'd put on gloves earlier to bag and tag samples of the fish and seashells that had been . . . *washed in with the tide?*

But what tide? What ocean? The only thing she could see on the far side of the tunnel was the fallen brick rubble and sunlit woods beyond.

What they hadn't bagged and tagged, they'd left on the ground at the tunnel's entrance, and it appeared the fish left behind, while still colorful, had begun to lose their sheen. As if they'd indeed been alive when they'd first washed in but had died and were slowly decaying. Unlike the seashells. Unlike the stark white leaves on the dozens of trees they now dotted.

Unlike the pink and purple and gold vines covering the stones around the
tunnel's arch.

Her phone showed no service. She'd missed a call from Gideon.

She turned her phone on video, navigated the patch of ground where
the dozens of seashells lay scattered, and entered the tunnel's south
entrance. The temperature change was instant, but it wasn't the typical
drop in temperature. Instead, it felt hotter, more humid. She kept the video
running and turned on her cell phone's light to help guide her through the
dark. She could see enough light on the north end to give her perspective.
The scattering of seashells and dead fish hadn't been limited to the ground
outside the tunnel—the inside was littered with them too. The breeze
brought with it a hint of the sea. For a few paces she closed her eyes as she
walked, and the sounds around her were magnified. The breeze whistled.
Water dripped from the ceiling. A bird cawed. Rodents and animals scur-
ried through the shadows. She opened her eyes, focused straight ahead. A
white leaf skittered across the ground, blew past her. It was the same tunnel, but something didn't feel right.

It shouldn't be hot in here. She should not be hearing ocean waves.

And even more distant, voices.

She walked on, filming. Her pace quickened near the halfway point
of the tunnel. Sunlight glared through the northern entrance, the right
lower portion still blighted by the mound of bricks blocking it, where Doc
Bigsby had been working with his wheelbarrow. If only she could question
him. If only she knew what had happened that night. What had he seen or
heard or felt before having his leg and arm severed?

Suddenly she saw the silhouette of a large deer standing atop the
mound of brick rubble, backlit by sunlight. A massive animal with a huge
set of antlers. The woods of Harrod's Reach were full of white-tailed deer,
but this was the largest she'd ever seen. It seemed to be watching her. She
slowly approached it. The deer got spooked and sprinted off.

Beth ran after it.

She searched for the sturdiest spots for footing atop the bricks, and
kept her eyes on the surrounding woods, hoping to catch a glimpse of the
massive deer again. And there it was, twenty yards to the right of the tunnel's entrance, as if waiting for her. Standing roughly where the first two
murdered bodies had been found by Simon Bowles, right in the center
of the taped-off crime scene perimeter. But that wasn't what had Beth's
heart in full gallop. The size of the deer, yes, and those antlers, yes, but the

color—the deer was black as tar, and the antlers were as red as fresh paint. It was a deer, but it wasn't. Beth did her best to hold her phone steady as she filmed it, and at the same time move closer, down from her view atop the fallen bricks and now eye level with the animal.

"Where do you come from?" she whispered.

The deer's head rotated toward her. The eyes were a stark white compared to the rest of it. It made a noise like a snort and took two steps toward her, the feet as large as horse hooves. It should have been too warm to see crystalized breath, but that's what came out when it snorted again. Like the warm *here* was cooler than the *there* this thing had come from, Beth thought—it wasn't of this earth. Even still, she slowly moved toward it, filming, now within twenty feet, fifteen, and then ten. The deer lowered his head, as if sniffing the forest floor, the area where those two bodies had forced the leaves flat days ago. Beth was close enough now to see swirls of orange within the red of those antlers, the tips sharp enough to impale.

Suddenly the deer's ears perked, and then it sprinted off toward Harrod's Lake.

All was quiet. Beth exhaled. Again, this animal reminded her of the colored animal skins on Simon's cabin wall. Maybe Simon hadn't been catching animals to paint them. Maybe he'd been hunting them down because they were different. Because they were wrong.

Maybe it was the world that had gone mad, and not Simon.

She stood on the ground the deer had just vacated and turned in a slow circle, analyzing the crushed leaves and flattened deadfall. She and Grover had gridded off the perimeter looking for evidence, finding nothing relevant before or after the two bodies had been moved, nothing to help make sense of why the bodies had been left there.

Three murdered bodies. Three different MOs and calling cards. Three different killers.

She started inside the crime scene tape and walked every square inch, visually combing the ground, kicking at the dry leaves.

After thirty minutes of finding nothing, she closed her eyes.

It was an exercise Grover had taught her soon after she'd moved in with them. *Because sometimes the inner eye sees things our real eyes can't. Our memory has eyes, Beth. Close your eyes and use your memory.*

Warm sunlight penetrated the canopy of boughs overhead. She smelled fall leaves, heard them skittering, breeze-blown, around her feet, just as she had on the day she and Grover had located the corpses. Corpses Simon had drawn in such detail. The woman, her face beaten beyond recognition by the horseshoe left in her hand. She'd been raped. All evidence pointed to it, the bruising and tears, the dried blood and semen, yet the murderer had taken the time to dress her. Because she hadn't been killed here. And the man next to her, the man whose hand had held her other one. The man who had been decapitated and was holding onto his own head had not been murdered here either.

And the same went for Mayor Truffant. But why? She kept her eyes closed, allowed her memory passage. The head in the man's hands. The eyes had still been open, staring at the woman beside him. Like, I see you. Like, I know who did this . . . No, thought Beth, that's not it. The eyes in that head, maybe they hadn't been left to stare at the dead woman beside him, but instead something off in the distance. Beth recalled the positioning of both bodies. She opened her eyes and started walking in that direction. She ducked under the crime scene tape and moved deeper into the woods. Ten yards. Twenty. Thirty. They'd been so consumed with the bodies that night they'd neglected to perimeter this far out. Forty yards.

And then a tree grabbed her attention.

It was tall and black, and canopied with limbs that were twisted, coiled, crooked, and bent. Unlike the trees around it, this one held no colorful leaves about to fall. In fact, it held no leaves at all, not because they'd already fallen, Beth mused, but more that it no longer grew them. But the tree seemed far from dead. Upon the bark, moths clung, hundreds of them in all colors, some stagnant, some with wings pulsing, while others moved in and around the grooved ridges of the bark, over each other, as if vying for space.

Space to drink, it looked like. Or to feed. Had this tree been here before? Of course it had, but the moths . . . the moths they would have noticed. Beth stepped close enough to hear their movement, like maggots squirming, like bees crawling in and out of a hive. She'd been in and around these woods her entire life and she'd never seen this tree before. Of course, she had, but it had never been like this.

She remembered her mother tucking her in every night. She used to tell stories. At first they were nice innocent stories, but you demanded more. You always demanded more because Beth Gardner was scared of nothing. One night your mother gave in. You knew she read those horror books and you wanted to read them too. It pleased you both to transition into the macabre. You bonded over those bedtime stories, and one night she told you all about the mares. How the mares at night, when you closed your eyes, crept into your house and into your bedroom and onto your chest and pressed down on you and whispered bad thoughts and gave you nightmares. You fell asleep hoping for one. Hoping for a mare ride, and when it didn't happen you still asked for more. And your mother gave it because she was cool and fun and knew that you could handle it. She told you how mares can tangle the hair of little sleeping girls and they awaken to matted, sticky plaits of marelocks. And the trees, Beth, do you want to know about the trees? If a mare touches a tree, do you know what happens? The branches become twisted and tangled as well. The bark darkens to black, and all the leaves fall off.

They call them mare pines, Beth. Mare trees. Crooked trees. And sometimes, if a mare has touched them enough, if the mare is strong enough, the moths will come to it and drink.

Have you seen one, Momma? A mare tree?

No, dear, I've never seen one. It's all stories. It's all make-believe, and it's late. You better get to bed . . . And tell your father, if he asks, that we read Green Eggs and Ham . . .

What if it's not make-believe?

But it is, dear, all for fun . . .

What if the make-believe exists? What if that's what we see when we dream . . .

Beth shook it away. Sometimes the inner eye didn't know when to *stop* seeing.

Through the moths on the tree she saw glimpses of what appeared to be yellow paper. She stepped closer, gently moved some of the moths from it. Some scattered. Some flew away and landed elsewhere on the tree. Some moved along with her hand as if bulldozed, like they'd been casually sleeping and brushed aside. And on the yellow paper nailed to the tree were words written in black ink:

> *Cover your eyes, Oh!*
> *The Oloro is coming. Oh!*
> *Go and hide. Oh!*
> *Should I open them?*
> *Open, open, open them!*
> *Open, open, open them!*
> *Whoever he finds will be killed. Oh!*

Beth ripped the yellow paper from the tree and blew off a gray moth that had come along for the ride. It was not a lullaby she'd ever heard before, but it was the connection she'd been *hoping* for. Another lullaby. Silly rhymes of make-believe spoken in pleasant sing-song voices to help children go to sleep at night, often hiding their true nature, their dark inner meanings.

Even "Rock-A-Bye Baby" has a sinister undertone.

The Oloro is coming . . .

Something is coming, Beth thought, turning the yellow paper over, reading what was on the other side.

A flyer advertising the grand reopening of the historic Beehive Hotel.

Excerpt from Detective Harrington's notes
December 13, 1929
Harrod's Reach

*F*IRST DAY ON *the job.*
    At roughly 9:00 PM, *Matthew Ordaine, senior partner in the law firm Ordaine, Fitzpatrick & Grimes, entered the Grand Lobby of the Beehive Hotel. At first, according to witnesses, no one paid him much attention. It wasn't until Matthew Ordaine, noticeably disheveled and smelling of body odor, bellied up to the bar, ordered an illegal Honeybee cocktail with whiskey and extra cherries, and plopped a muddy pair of wingtips on the counter, that the night began to get weird. Not only were these shoes covered in mud, blow-flies, and maggots, they still held the remnants of two severed human feet inside, what was left of them, rotten and decaying to the bone.*
    It wasn't until the Beehive waitress Jasmine Banner screamed and dropped her drink tray that the crowd began to hush and the band, who'd just started into "Bye Bye Blackbird," stop playing. Because of his gaunt, unshaven appearance, most assumed Mr. Ordaine drunk, a condition more common to his post-midnight departures from the Beehive Hotel each weekend, and not his typical entrance. Yet he'd sworn he hadn't imbibed a drop all night. He did, however, shout to everyone inside the stunned Beehive lobby that he was no longer Matthew Ordaine, attorney at law, but now well on his way to becoming a Wendigo.

I arrived soon thereafter, and although Matthew was boisterous, insisting his transformation was real, he left the Beehive willingly, and was utterly exhausted by the time I walked him into lockup. I have since researched said term, Wendigo, and learned the following: In some Native American folklore, it is believed that if one dreams of a Wendigo, this humanoid-like monstrous beast of the dreamworld, the body of the sleeper will become vulnerable to possession by the Wendigo's spirit. In a sense, making that spirit real. Once the possessed has consumed human flesh, the body will then begin the grotesque transformation in which Matthew Ordaine claims to currently find himself.

After a brief nap inside his cell, Matthew appeared more lucid and therefore more prepared to answer my questions, which makes what I'm about to write even more disheartening. When asked where he found those two severed feet (inside the shoes), Matthew Ordaine claimed they belonged to a street bum he'd killed earlier in the week. When asked who this bum was, Matthew claimed to not know. When asked what the bum looked like, Matthew could not recall that either, which leads me to believe he's not being completely truthful. Or has some sort of brain fatigue. When asked about the rest of this bum's body, Matthew, although hesitant, then claimed to have eaten it, adding, because that's what Wendigos do. When asked how he'd eaten the body, he said with a knife and fork. He then grinned, revoltingly, I might add, revealing teeth that looked stained enough for me to start believing he'd at least eaten something he shouldn't have. When asked about the bones, Matthew hesitated again, before saying he buried them in the backyard. When I took a lantern to Matthew Ordaine's backyard later that night, I saw no sign of any recent burial, as not one inch of his ground had been disturbed.

Under further interrogation, (and while Mr. Ordaine held strong to the belief that he'd been possessed by the Wendigo spirit) he did finally admit to finding the decayed feet and soiled shoes in the tall grass just outside the tunnel's northern entrance earlier in the evening. Like many of the locals had been doing now for months, he'd made his way down to the train tunnel with the idea in mind to take home a souvenir from the wreckage still remaining from the deadly derailment months ago. Mr. Ordaine also admits to feeling nauseous soon after entering the tunnel, even before stumbling upon the feet. He claims the Wendigo spirit entered him through the tunnel, during a ten-second bout of extreme dizziness.

My theory on Matthew Ordaine's sudden break from reality: extreme stress (lack of sleep) over the recent Hoskins trial, the highly publicized acquittal of whom he played a major part.

My theory on the found decayed, severed feet: No passenger survived the September train derailment inside that tunnel. Every passenger, although dead (and several disgustingly so) was not only accounted for but sent along to proper burials soon after identification; all save for one, whose name on the passenger list read Edward Ross, businessman, Iowa. *His body was never found. I believe the shoes (and subsequent feet) found by Matthew Ordaine belonged to the missing passenger, Edward Ross.*

Next project: Find the rest of him.

CHAPTER

28

Teddy

Before

Now that they'd finally arrived at the Beehive Hotel, Teddy was so serious about nobody getting off the Lullaby Express that he left Brandy behind on the bus to make sure.

His passengers could not be trusted, especially not in public. And with the last order he'd heard through the seashell sounding more urgent than any of the previous others—telling him to forgo the list for now, and put rubber to the road toward Harrod's Reach—Teddy couldn't afford any more hitches.

No more dead bodies to hide or clean up or burn. No more delays because of the uncivilized. *Just stay the fuck on the bus.*

Teddy was still trying to mentally process how readily, and with so much enthusiasm, that freak, Firestarter Freddie, had burned Teddy's childhood house to the ground. With their neighbor Mrs. Chastain's decapitated body resting all peaceful-like atop the kitchen table, holding her own head like that other freak from Detroit had insisted she do. But the luster in Firestarter Freddie's eyes had been something to behold. His passion for the project had been nothing short of extraordinary, and they'd had to physically move him back onto the bus as the insides of the house had started to burn. They couldn't have him standing in the yard and clapping when the fire trucks pulled in.

But while Teddy had driven most of the way across the country to Harrod's Reach, Brandy had driven the initial fifty miles after leaving the Lomax house behind. Belinda Lomax, resting in her wheelchair in the handicapped section behind the driver's seat, had shown so little emotion watching her house burn that Teddy, unnerved that he couldn't get any read on her current state of mind, had been hesitant to leave. And then for that stoic expression to turn to a grin so evil it made even *his* skin crawl; that was almost too much. He'd wheeled her up the ramp into the Lullaby Express and insisted it was time they go, so momentarily shaken he'd asked Brandy if she could handle the wheel.

Although it wasn't only his mother's demeanor that had him rattled. He hadn't expected seeing his childhood home going up in flames to tug at him like it had done. He loved his room, yes, and the large, wooded backyard, yes, he'd miss the peaceful solitude of that. But seeing the curtain in the living room go up in flames and Freddie smile so stupidly when the flame somehow jumped to the folded blanket on the back of the sofa, had reminded him too much of what his mother had done to that tree in the backyard woods when he was a boy. *That* tree. The one he'd found during an otherwise monotonous day of hiking and trailblazing, and for weeks had been sneaking off to read and relax and talk to the voice in his head. To imagine he was really seeing what he was seeing, all those moths—which he at first thought were butterflies—clinging and crawling atop the bark of that tree. It had mesmerized him. For weeks he'd visited that tree, until it got to the point where he considered those moths his friends, only to accidentally mention them one evening over dinner to his mother. And once she heard about it, that was that. He realized now that she'd never asked him where the tree was. She'd somehow known, and marched him right into the woods to it. The tree next to the tunnel, which was really a small, one-way, covered footbridge no more than six feet long, stretching over a creek that wasn't even there anymore, a creek that could have just as easily been stepped over back in its day. But this small footbridge out in the middle of the woods had never made any sense, not to them, not to any neighbors who'd ever lived near those ten acres of back-country Virginia woods before them.

His mother marched him out to the footbridge and found the tree immediately, covered in moths, some crawling, some flying away and landing again. And within the fluttering swarm were colorful vines of purple, pink, and gold, clinging to and around the entrance of that footbridge. And on the well-worn floorboard planks a large purple snake lay coiled, head facing the tree, as if waiting to strike.

Belinda Lomax hurried back to the house to grab her gas can and a book of matches, and doused both the tree and the footbridge and set them aflame, making Teddy watch as the wood snapped and burned, and the moths scattered in puffs of flame and smoke and hissing fury. Teddy had pleaded to Mother to stop, that the moths were hurt and screaming. But she stood there and made him watch, even as he cried and held his ears against the screaming moths.

That memory fueled him now as he approached the Beehive Hotel.

They'd arrived in the heavily forested town of Harrod's Reach under the disguise of nightfall, with virtually no one on the streets. Harrod's Reach was small and cozy and gridded by town squares. The Beehive, perched like a castle overlooking a kingdom, had not been hard to find. Still leery of any unwanted attention, Teddy had driven the Lullaby Express to the back lot, parking it off the pavement and in the shadows of the neighboring woods behind the hotel, so it wouldn't be easily seen, even in daylight.

Teddy had already decided if no one answered the hotel's front door, he'd spend the rest of the night on the bus. But after he pounded on one of the Beehive's two tall, wooden doors—one painted black, the other yellow—a lobby light turned on less than a minute later. Three houses down from the hotel, a living room light turned on and a dog barked, and in his mind Teddy urged the greasy-haired fucker he now spied through the hotel lobby window, hurrying toward the doors and tying a bathrobe, to hurry even more.

The guy looked through the window and his eyes grew big, surprised, Teddy thought, that the pounding had been on *his* hotel door. The guy mouthed, "We're closed."

Teddy said, "No, you're not."

This time the man shouted through the glass. "We don't open for three more weeks."

Teddy heard him but could also see some wheels turning behind those blue eyes, like perhaps this goon was expecting someone at some point, but wasn't sure Teddy was the guy. Maybe taking this tall hat off would help, let him see these horns. Even though they'd long progressed past horns, according to Brandy, and Teddy, if he was being truthful, knew they were full-out fucking antlers now. Teddy removed his hat so the man could see, as he was getting a strong feeling that he wasn't the only one on this earth getting messages. His mother had gotten that Beehive Hotel grand reopening flyer from halfway across the country for a reason.

After exposing the antlers, either the man would let him in, like he'd been expecting him, or would run instantly to call the cops, in which case things could get ugly.

The man didn't run. In fact, he smiled, which bummed Teddy out a little. Part of him had been craving a fight. Some bruises or cuts and some blood. His tank was running low after the trip, and he needed some fuel other than sex with Brandy, which couldn't, he knew, sustain him by itself.

The yellow front door opened. The guy beckoned Teddy inside and quickly closed the door behind them. Even with the lone light on above the entrance, the lobby was grand indeed. Tall and airy and spacious. According to the flyer, this was where the main party would be on opening night, with jubilant pomp and circumstance, with oysters and fancy hors d'oeuvres and signature cocktails from the original Beehive menu, all down to "the most minute historical detail." The hotel man—Teddy assumed he was the owner or manager—despite the unruly hair and five o'clock shadow, was well-built and handsome, and carried himself with a confidence Teddy respected.

But he wouldn't stop staring at Teddy's head, at Teddy's antlers, and so Teddy curled his hand into a fist and punched the man hard in the stomach, because even though he'd not been insecure for years, he didn't like being stared at. The punch doubled the man over. From there, Teddy raised a knee into the man's face, felt the nose crack against his kneecap, and blood squirted across the white-and-black checked tile floor. The man rolled onto his back and moaned, holding his nose as blood gushed. He blinked moisture from his eyes but didn't fight back. But with each moan and with each gush of blood from those busted nostrils, Teddy felt his fuel tank grow full.

"My nose," said the man on his back, although it came out more like *my nothe* due to the blood leaking over his busted lip and open mouth. The man's bathrobe had come undone, revealing his shriveled, flaccid prick. He was quick to move a hand to close the bathrobe and protect what was left of his dignity. Still on his back, and eyes blurred with tears, he said, "The fuck wath that for?"

He had a lisp now like Firestarter Freddie.

"I need rooms," said Teddy. "Nineteen of them to be exact."

"We're not open yet."

Teddy leaned over him. "I have a feeling you knew I was coming."

"I did," he said. "Thort of. Just not yet. You're early."

"Early birds get the worm," said Teddy. "So says Mother. Speaking of whom, make that twenty rooms."

The man swallowed heavily, choked on saliva and blood, but nodded that he got it. Teddy could tell he was staring at his antlers again, which in the past days had begun to sprout boughs like a reindeer. "Are they real?"

"Yes, they're fucking real." Teddy gripped the lapels of the man's bathrobe and helped him up from the floor, standing him upright so that Teddy could properly lower his head and aim for the man's sternum. It had not been something Teddy had done before, or for that matter had even imagined, using these things as weapons, but he suddenly felt the calling to do it. Teddy took two steps back for some room, for some momentum, and then charged, ramming the tips of his antlers into his chest, piercing flesh in at least three places before pulling free. The man staggered, shocked and feeling the new wounds in his chest, now bleeding through his bathrobe.

Not fatal wounds, for sure, thought Teddy, but ones that would scar, and he felt his fuel tank overflowing. He wished Brandy had been here to see it.

The man held out a hand toward Teddy, as if to keep him at bay. Like he didn't understand why he was being attacked after willingly allowing this stranger inside his hotel.

But I'm not a stranger, am I? You've heard of me before. You knew I was coming.

"Don't," pleaded the man, his voice sounding better as his busted lip-lisp left him. "I'll get you rooms. I'll kick out some workers if I need to. When do you need them?"

Teddy checked his watch, stepped closer. "Within the next five minutes."

"Don't, please . . ."

"I'm done hurting you," said Teddy. "But you needed to know who is boss, am I right?" The man nodded, frantically. "Because this is *my* hotel now," said Teddy. And the man nodded at that too. "Good, I'm glad we're in agreement." Teddy pulled the yellow flyer from his pocket and unfolded it. "This was sent to my mother's house. It had a profound effect on her. Why?"

"What's your mother's name?"

"Belinda Lomax," said Teddy. "Does the name ring a bell? And why did she get one?"

"I don't know. The name, yes, I remember sending it. But . . ."

"Do you hear voices?" asked Teddy. "No, check that, do you hear a certain voice?"

The man nodded, tried to plug the blood oozing from his wounds, but didn't seem to know which ones were the most important to contain.

Teddy was tired of watching him struggle. "One of my passengers. She calls herself the Nanny. Claims to have been a nurse. I'll have her attend to the wounds. Now answer my question."

"Yes."

"Yes what?"

"I hear a voice."

"Who does it belong to?"

"Mr. Lullaby," he said quickly. "He calls himself Mr. Lullaby."

"How does he contact you?"

The man scrambled for the pocket of his bathrobe and pulled from it a light blue seashell the size of a baseball. His blood-stained hand shook, holding it. It surprised Teddy none that the man always kept it on his person. Teddy didn't like to be away from his either, but this was interesting. So where were *this* guy's horns? This told Teddy a couple of things: one, this guy was just another spoke in the wheel, being used, and two, Teddy felt now more than ever that he was the wheel itself.

The man held the shell up to his ear for a listen, as if to prove a point, and then lowered his arm again. "I can hear him. Through here. Sometimes." He held up the shell. "I don't know how but . . . it started when I . . ."

"When you what?"

"Entered the tunnel," he said. "Two years ago."

"Is that when you decided to buy this place?"

"Yes," he said, wincing. "I'd had this hotel listed for years, trying to sell it. But that day, after leaving the tunnel, I heard a voice inside it. Maybe it was the wind. Or in my head. I don't know."

"What did the voice say?"

He chuckled, like an anxious reaction to the prospect of bleeding out on his hotel floor more than anything comical. "It said, yellow ball, right corner pocket. Yellow ball . . ."

"Right corner pocket," Teddy finished for him. "Interesting, then what?"

"I'd only left the Beehive twenty minutes prior. I recalled seeing the billiards room doors open, when I typically made sure they were closed. It's an ornate room."

"Can't wait to see it myself."

"It packs more of a punch to open the doors and allow the prospective buyers an entrance. Like they're being swooned. I returned to the Beehive, entered the billiards room, and right there on the table was a yellow ball and a cue stick. And inside the right corner pocket . . ." He held out the shell. "I found this."

"And that, as they say," said Teddy, "is fucking that?" The man nodded. Teddy stepped closer, held out his hand. The man flinched, probably thinking he was about to get hit again, or even gored. But instead, Teddy opened his hand for a shake, and said, "I don't mind the blood."

The man stepped closer, held out his bloody hand.

Teddy pumped it with a firm grip. "Teddy Lomax," he said. "Only my mother calls me Theodore." He surveyed the lobby, just a quick once-over before settling his eyes back on the hotel manager. "Love what you've done to the place."

The man said, "The name's Mickey. Mickey French." He grinned, ear to ear, like he'd just realized something monumental, like he'd been waiting his entire life to say his next words. "Welcome to the historic Beehive Hotel."

29

Gideon

Now

SOON AFTER SULLY Dupree gripped Amy Shimp's hand, the euphoria in the room was replaced by confused, anxious looks of *Okay, what now?*

Amy's mom, Tammy, started crying all over again. By then, Archie had left the room like a zombie to whatever part of the house he went when he needed to not be seen. Typically, it was where his current project was; they'd all learned long ago that when he was renovating, he wanted to be left alone. Way back when they'd first purchased the Smite House, he and Maxine did the work together. Then it became the job for the boys, after they were old enough to hand him whatever tool he required, to be his assistants. His little apprentices, he'd call them, although he gave them very little to do. Never once had he allowed Gideon to hammer a nail, although before Sully's accident he'd begun to trust his little brother with not only the hammer but the screwdriver, and one day Gideon had even spied him helping with the handsaw. After Sully's accident at the tunnel, Archie made it a habit to work alone.

Maddy comforted the woman with whom she'd driven into town. Her embrace with Tammy Shimp looked awkward, reminding Gideon that the two women didn't really know each other. Coma was their only bond. But that bond was why they were here, and the "what now" looks Gideon saw around the room had an easy answer.

· He started around the end of Sully's bed like his pants were on fire.

Maxine said, "Gideon, what's wrong?"

Gideon found what he needed on the end table beside the bed. He held up the newspaper. "The names Sully spoke last night. Jax wrote them down."

Maddy said, "He spoke?"

"We weren't here," Gideon said. "We were down the street."

"Gideon's welcome home party," Maxine added. "He'd been overseas." She smiled at Maddy, like she needed her to be impressed. "He was awarded a Purple Heart."

Maddy grinned, like it had worked.

Gideon shook the paper in his hand. "Jax was out of the room, heard some noise, and then a voice, and came running. Whoever it was escaped out the window. We don't know if he was trying to abduct Sully or kill him or what, but—"

"It was a he?"

"Yes."

"He had antlers," said Maxine.

"He was *wearing* antlers," Gideon corrected. "According to Jax. Like a Halloween costume or something." Gideon handed Maddy the newspaper. "But when Jax returned, Sully was sitting up in bed, shouting out names. Random names. Jax wrote most of them down."

"He has proof," Maxine said. "Jax . . . On his phone. He was leaving his wife a message at the time. He can play it for you."

"No, that's fine," said Maddy. "I believe you." She looked toward the bed, where Sully and Amy still held hands, both sleeping peacefully. "Right now, I'd believe just about anything." She looked at the names on the newspaper, turning it clockwise as she read, since Jax had written them so haphazardly, up and down, sideways, wherever he could find blank space.

Maddy bit her lower lip, closed her eyes.

Gideon felt something stir within him, because damn she was cute, but get it together. "Maddy, what is it? Do those names mean something?"

Maddy opened her eyes like she'd been hit with some newfound sense of clarity. "These names, they're not random at all. Ever since I came out of my coma, I've . . . I've had what I call memory dumps. Memories from my life, but . . . even more so from where I was during my coma."

"What do you mean, where you were?" asked Maxine.

Tammy Shimp perked up too. They all did. Because, perhaps, where Maddy *was* had something to do with where Sully and Amy were now.

"The names." Maddy pulled her own paper from her back pocket and unfolded it. "Tammy, before I picked you up, I stayed for three days in a hotel in Atlanta. I'd been having dizzy spells and wasn't confident I could safely drive."

"That's where you remembered Amy's name," Tammy said.

"Yes," said Maddy. "I remembered Sully's name early on. Amy's name came to me in Atlanta. But that wasn't it." She showed Gideon the paper. "I remembered these names as well. All of them cross-check the names your friend wrote on that newspaper. There's two more on the newspaper than what I have here, but all of mine are accounted for on yours."

"But what does it mean?" asked Tammy.

The question had been directed toward any or all of them, but Gideon settled on Maddy, who again had her eyes closed. He wondered if she might be having another *memory dump* right now. Or was she conjuring the strength to answer what Gideon had wanted answered since she'd said, *from where I was during my coma.*

"Maddy," Gideon said, prodding. "What is it?"

She opened her eyes, exhaled. "We need to contact these people."

"How?" asked Maxine. "We don't even know who they are, or where they live."

"They're all . . ." Maddy stopped, as if carefully thinking how best to explain. "They're coma patients. I'm sure of it. These names . . . they're familiar to me. I don't know how we reach them all, or how to even start, I just know that we need to get them here. Right now."

"Why?" Tammy asked.

"It's hard to explain . . . I still have holes." She gestured toward the bed. "Just know that when these two . . . on this bed, are unresponsive in *this* world . . ."

"This world?" said Maxine.

Maddy looked frustrated but continued her thought. "That they are *not* unresponsive over there. Their minds . . . They . . . Jesus . . . I'm sorry."

Maxine said, "Do you need to sit down, dear?"

"Maybe." She looked pale. Gideon grabbed a chair and helped her into it. Maddy stared at the bed. "*Their* minds are active. And they're doing more than you know over there."

"Over where?" Maxine asked.

"Later," Gideon said to his mother. And then to Maddy. "Tell us what you came here to tell us. Because I doubt it was just to watch my brother hold hands with that girl."

"The message . . ." She touched her temples like she was in pain or trying so hard to remember it hurt. "My message was to . . . the Seers, that's what we're called over there, but the Seers . . . they're arguing over how best to guard the doors . . ."

"Guard the doors?" Maxine asked. "From what?"

"Mom," Gideon said. "Not now."

Maddy continued: "We need to bring as many as we can here, together, to . . . to help unite them over there . . . And I think it has everything to do with the tunnel, here, at Harrod's Reach."

"But, dear," said Maxine. "Even if we find them. Even if we can track them down . . ."

"I don't know," Maddy said, looking at Tammy now. "How did I convince you?"

Tammy said, "By showing up at my door. By saying Sully's name and my daughter having a response to it." Her eyes grew wet. "By giving me hope."

"Then that's what we'll do," said Maddy.

"We'll give them hope," said Gideon.

"We're strangers," said Maxine. "And to all of them we'll be strangers even more. How do we convince them to come?"

"By showing them this," said Archie Dupree from the doorway.

They all turned toward Archie's voice. In his hand he held his cell phone, and on the screen played the video of Sully's hand moving toward Amy's, and then the two of them clutching hands. He too had tears in his eyes, and maybe, thought Gideon, a little hope in his heart. He smiled for the first time since Gideon's return home, and said again, with even more gusto this time: "We show them this."

CHAPTER

30

Beth

Now

O NCE BETH MADE it out of the ravine, her cell phone had service
again.

As she drove, she googled the lyrics of the weird lullaby she'd pulled
from the bark of the moth-covered tree down by the tunnel. This one was
a Nigerian lullaby called "Boju Boju," translated to the English written on
the back of the Beehive's yellow flyer. She pulled to the side of the road
long enough to read. The lullaby told children if they don't stay in bed
with their eyes closed, harm would come. In this case, a monster will eat
them. "Boju Boju" apparently meant some sort of mask, or as someone
else another link down mused, a version of the game peekaboo. The Oro
appeared to be in reference to the god Oro from the Yoruba religion. Until
the past twenty-four hours, she'd never paid attention to how dark lullabies
were. Parents might have for centuries sung them in sweet innocent voices
to get their babies to go to sleep, but how many really paid attention to the
lyrics and dark undertones?

Lullabies were full of monsters. Full of dark, disguised by beautiful
singsong rhythms. Or was it the sinister disguised by something beautiful?
Much like the colorful ivy now bordering the stone of the tunnel's southern entrance? The colorful moths on that tree down there. The colorful

seashells and stark white leaves. The yellow squirrel she'd seen running loose inside Simple Simon's cottage. The glimpses of the monsters she'd seen drawn inside Simon's *Lalaland* book. And as large and eerily foreboding as that black, antlered deer that had been outside the tunnel moments ago; it too had carried an aura of fantastical beauty.

Don't get lured into fool's gold, Beth. Another favorite saying from Sheriff Meeks. *Don't judge a book by its cover and don't always assume a smile means somebody is nice. There's evil out there, Beth, and it comes in all forms.*

Beth pulled back out onto the road and picked up speed toward town. The lyrics on the yellow flyer followed her. Just by reading them she couldn't tell exactly how those words might be sung, but she was doing her best to imagine it, and it made her skin crawl.

Three minutes later she turned onto Mallard Street and slowed outside the Smite House. There was a van she didn't recognize parked on the driveway. As mind-bending as the last hour had been down inside the ravine and tunnel, she felt a sudden need to see Brody. To hug him. He was right there, a hundred yards away, inside the Smite House with the Duprees. She could run in and get a quick fix. Squeeze him and smell his hair and at least make herself feel better for having dumped him again while she worked. Always working, according to Jax, even when she was home, downstairs in her Murder Pit.

She'd told him not to blow things out of proportion. But after that quick exchange of words that boiled down to her not spending enough time with her son—it burned how he'd stressed the word *her* son—she'd thought, yes, maybe Jax was right, it *was* a murder pit, and she always had been obsessed with what she'd collected down there. But to her it was essential. Beth thought better of it and cruised past the Smite House toward the Beehive at the top of Mallard. She would have only riled Brody up, to hug and run.

Brody is in good hands. He'll be there when your workday is done.

She pulled into the Beehive Hotel's front parking lot, mostly vacant except for a few construction vehicles. Before she got out of the car, a text came through from Jax saying men and women were coming to the fire station to volunteer in droves. He knew they couldn't all be deputized, but they were up to fifteen now, not only taking their turns at the barricades in and out of town but walking the streets and town squares, all eager to report the slightest unusual sighting or minor disturbance.

She sent back a quick *thanks* and then another, *keep me posted.*

Will do. Responded Jax. And then: *Love you.*

She did a double take at that, because it wasn't typical. He did love her, she knew, but not in the way a husband normally would a wife. This told her he was scared. Maybe for himself, maybe for her, probably for them both.

Scared for the town.

She thought about ghosting him, but then typed back: *Love you too.*

And she did. Jax had always been a dear friend, despite being a complete dick to Gideon his entire life, but that's what jealousy does, thought Beth. Early and often. Jealousy breeds contempt and Jax had always been full of both. If she didn't love him, she never would have agreed so early on in their lives to do what she was doing. To live under such a façade.

She grabbed the yellow flyer and got out of the car. Holding it now reminded her how long it had been pinned to that weird tree. It was damp and weather soiled, and stained by whatever ashy moth residue those things left behind. Beth started toward the hotel when she realized the barricades across Mallard Street had been moved and there was no one guarding this entrance into town. This was Gideon's beat.

She called him from the parking lot. Gideon sounding rushed when he answered. "Beth?"

"Gideon, where are you?"

"I'm home."

"You're supposed to—"

"I know, I'm sorry," he said. "I'll explain it when I can, but . . . where are you?"

"I'm getting ready to knock on the door to the Beehive."

"Why?"

"I'll explain *that* when I can," she said. "But what pulled you from your post?"

"Someone arrived," he said. "From Charleston. The other from Tulsa."

The van she'd seen in the driveway, Beth thought. "Go on."

"Maddy, she . . . she was a coma patient herself up until a few weeks ago."

"Wait, Maddy? Maddy who?"

"Maddy Boyle," he said.

"Jesus . . ." *From Charleston . . .*

"What? That name ring a bell?"

It does now, Beth thought, remembering the conversation she'd had in the middle of the night with the detective from Charleston. "Go on," she said.

"She brought with her another little girl," Gideon said. "She's in a coma as well, and . . . you're not going to believe this, Beth, but this little girl . . . her name is Amy Shimp."

"That one doesn't register."

"She's one of the names Jax wrote down last night when Sully started calling them out."

Amy Shimp? It was one of the names Jax had left on her voice mail.

"She's here," Gideon said. "Maddy brought her. And as soon as we placed her on the bed next to Sully, they . . ." He sounded like he'd just choked up and couldn't go on.

"They what, Gideon?"

"They held hands, Beth," he said in a gush. "Like they somehow know each other."

Beth saw a curtain move from a third-floor window at the Beehive. She said to Gideon, "I gotta go. We'll talk about this in a bit. Hug Brody for me."

"Yeah, okay. Sure."

"Gideon?"

"Yeah?"

She paused, lost her train of thought, if she'd ever had one. "Nothing. Be careful."

"You too," he said. "And Beth, there's a red bus parked in the woods behind that hotel."

Beth noticed his voice had fallen away to a hushed whisper. "What's wrong?"

"Nothing," he said. "Just that my mom walked back into the room. I didn't want her overhearing me talk about the hotel."

"Why?"

"I dunno, just can't figure out her part in it all. You ever see her with Mickey French?"

"The owner? Yes. But they're working together. She's running the—"

"Marketing campaign, yeah, I got that."

"Then what?"

"I dunno, maybe nothing. Just that I've been gone a while and she's . . . changed."

"We all have."

"Maybe so, but . . . I can't shake the feeling those two are more than just work partners, and Dad, he's like a zombie. Depressed isn't even the word for it."

The curtain in another window moved, this time from the second floor. "I gotta go. We'll discuss it later."

"Look for the red bus," Gideon said.

Beth ended the call, closed in on the hotel's curved, brick walkway and stopped at the double front doors, one yellow, the other black, just like it had been in the 1920s. She knocked on yellow, waited a minute, knocked again, this time on black. "Open up. Sheriff's office." She peered through a side window. "Mickey, I know you're in there." She saw Gideon's point about his mother. She was older than Mickey by ten years and the two could regularly be seen at the Dark Roast coffee shop having work meetings. Could there be more to it? She had lost weight. She had begun to dress younger, but that was nobody else's business.

Beth was about to knock again when she heard footsteps on the other side. The yellow door opened wide enough for Mickey to show his battered face. His nose was bandaged. His lip was busted. His left eye bruised.

"Mickey? What the hell happened?"

"Nothing," he said, looking past her, completely paranoid. "What do you want?"

"First, for you not to lie to me. Who beat the shit out of you?"

"N . . . nobody," he stammered. "I fell. Down the stairs. I was tired, working too late. You know? Trying to get this place ready and I'm running out of time, so . . ."

"Can I come in?"

"No. Not right now."

She held up the yellow flyer with the lullaby written on the back of it facing him. "This mean anything to you?"

"No, why would it?"

"It was written on your flyer?"

He hesitated, looked away. "So? Those were distributed all over town. Could have been anyone. Why are you *really* here?"

She folded the paper, slid it into her back pocket. Honestly, that *was* why she was here. Because of that flyer. But he was right. Anyone could have written it. "I saw someone in one of the rooms upstairs. Two, actually. One on the third floor and one on the second."

Mickey closed his eyes for a beat, opened them annoyed. "What'd they look like?"

"Just saw curtains move."

"We've been working on our air and heat system all day."

"That's not what I saw," she said. "I thought you weren't open yet."

"I'm not."

"Then who is upstairs in those rooms?"

"Workers. From out of town. They're staying here while the construction is ongoing. Everyone knows this."

"Mickey, we've had three murders—"

"I know about . . . the murders. Meeks questioned them two days ago."

"But I haven't," she said. "How about you open the door and let me in so we can figure out who all we can cross off our list."

He shook his head. "Sorry, not without a warrant."

"Seriously, Mickey? You gonna go there?"

"If I have to," he said. "Look, you give me a list of who all Meeks questioned, and then I'll give you a list of all who are currently employed working on this hotel. Anybody you need to see, then I'll send them to the station. I'll escort them myself. Fair?"

She sighed, annoyed, but said, "Fine."

"But nobody is getting inside this hotel until the grand opening."

"I said fine." Just when he looked relieved, she said, "You mind if I go take a look at that red bus behind your property?" He sighed, scratched his head. "Don't even say what bus, Mickey. I know it's back there." Really, she didn't. She hadn't seen it with her own eyes but trusted Gideon.

"Again," he said. "My property. You're gonna need a warrant, Beth."

She started down the hotel steps toward the walkway. "How about we shove the warrant up your ass, Mickey."

"That's professional."

"So is that bathrobe in the middle of the day," she said. "Is that silk?"

He closed the lapels. "Where you going?"

"Around back," she said. "To see the bus."

"I told you . . . not without a warrant. It's on my property."

She ignored him. It probably was. Unless it was far enough back into the trees *not* to be. He must have realized the same thing. He hurried down the steps after her, barefooted and rapidly tying his robe. She glanced over her shoulder at him. "What really happened to your face?"

"I told you . . ."

"You fell, right." She spotted the red school bus in the trees right away. Whoever had been driving it must have had a hell of a time getting it as far back into the tree line as they had, because it looked wedged in there. Desperately, almost. Like the bus had been there even before the trees had grown up around it.

Maybe at nighttime it was concealed in the shadows, but not during daylight. Of course, nobody had been looking for it, and work trucks and vans had been in and out of these front and back lots for over a year now. Other than the ribbon cutting when they broke ground on renovations, most the action at the Beehive had been ignored by the public. There was almost a *we'll believe it when we see it* vibe. Plus, most in town knew the Beehive had always been the dream of Archie Dupree, and not this out-of-town young upstart realtor who'd seemingly stolen it out from beneath Archie's feet.

"How's Maxine Dupree working out?" Beth asked Mickey on her way to the back of the lot toward the tree line.

"What? Fine? Why?"

"Just curious." Beth glanced toward the windows on the back side of the hotel, and damn if she didn't see another curtain move. "Somebody's watching me from inside that hotel, Mickey."

"Nobody is—"

"I want that list at the station within the hour. You got it?"

"Fine." He caught up to her. The slap of his bare feet on the asphalt made him appear even more pathetic. "But you're not getting on that bus."

"What bus?" She closed in on it, studied its positioning within the trees that hugged it. Expert driver, she thought, to get it nearly hidden like that.

"Warrant."

"These trees aren't your property, Mickey. Your property line ends at the pavement. It was a big sticking point when you bought this place, and we all know it."

He pointed to the front left tire, turned slightly toward them and touching the parking lot, the only part of the bus technically on the hotel's property. "See, the tire. Show me the warrant."

"How about I just not search that tire?" She'd already rounded the front of the bus, realizing how much time and attention had been put into painting this monstrosity. And the door, painted black? "How long has this bus been here, Mickey?"

"I don't know."

"If you tell me a week or more then we're gonna have some serious problems."

"I said I don't know."

"Suit yourself." She opened the door. A moth immediately flew out. She ducked aside, let it pass, and then stepped up into the bus. She instantly smelled ammonia, cleaning solvents. "Mickey?" she shouted, only to find him right on her heels. She pulled her gun, and that halted him for a beat. She said, "Somebody just clean this bus?"

"What?"

"Did the beating you took hurt your hearing? Did somebody clean this bus?"

"I don't know . . . it belongs to . . . one of the workers."

"Get me the—"

"I'll get you the list," he said so sharply she almost laughed. "Have you seen enough? It's a clean bus. Nothing special here."

Beth stared down the aisle and flanking benches. Nothing to see aside from the dozens of moths inside with them, some on the seat backs, others flying around like they were in a butterfly garden. Moths just like she'd seen smothering the bark of that tree down by the tunnel. She turned toward Mickey. "One of your workers, huh? Make sure he . . ."—she held up a finger—"or she, although I doubt a female would paint a bus this awful color, is the first person on that list."

"Fine."

"An hour, Mickey."

He nodded, stepped aside as she brushed past. She removed her phone, snapped off a couple of quick pictures of the moths on the seats, hoping to catch some in midflight. To Mickey, she said, "Smile."

He didn't.

She took a photo of him anyway. She stopped behind the driver's seat. Behind the massive steering wheel, a two-foot-long section of blue painter's tape had been stuck to the dashboard. In black Sharpie someone had written: *The Lullaby Express.*

She looked at Mickey again, "Make that thirty minutes. At the station."

He didn't fight it.

Her cell phone rang. Eyes still on Mickey, Beth answered the call.

"Beth, it's Natalie. Sheriff Meeks, he's . . . he's talking. He's asking for you."

31

Maddy

Now

MADDY DIDN'T WANT to let on how tired she was.

Maybe her parents had been right about one thing. Too much too soon. And the recent run of emotional events since leaving Charleston four days ago had only exacerbated things. Since her last memory dump inside the Atlanta hotel, she'd been going nonstop. She'd slept little. Eaten little. Hydrated little. Her body felt weak. And now, after running through half the list of coma patients, she was exhausted.

Turned out Archie was a wizard at tracking people, citing decades of experience researching as a history professor. Gideon had jokingly asked if he was a professional stalker. Archie hadn't laughed. Maddy got the vibe Gideon and his father were tolerating each other just because the situation called for cooperation—and Archie Dupree had delivered.

Maddy and Archie and Gideon had gathered around the kitchen island to work.

Archie researched the names, cross-referenced events, one depressing newspaper story after another, until he'd begun to compile and narrow down and pinpoint. One by one, with Archie's fingers click-clacking across the laptop he'd brought with him into the kitchen, he called out the cities and states and countries in which their subjects most likely lived. From cities all over the country. All over the world. One from Ireland. One from Spain. One from Mexico. Another from Italy. The rest were from right here in the States, although very few of them were within a hundred miles of Harrod's Reach, which prompted Maddy to say, "We've got our work cut out for us."

But their hunch had proven correct. They'd assumed the names were coma patients, and it turned out that every one of them was. Or had been. Out of the list of fourteen names they'd compiled, two had died suddenly in their hospital beds within the past month. One mother she'd spoken to believed someone had entered the Shreveport, Louisiana, hospital and killed her boy as he lay in bed, because he'd showed no signs of a decline. Maddy had taken that one and, politely as she could, offered condolences and eased out of the phone call, knowing nothing else to say but *I'm sorry, I'm so sorry . . .* But unless she had another memory dump, or unless Jax suddenly recalled the names he'd previously been unable to remember or write down, they were left with this list of twelve.

Eight if you left out the four from foreign countries.

And of those eight, Maddy had spoken to four, either family members or caregivers for their subjects. Gideon had spoken to three. The eighth, Helen Gathers, from Seattle, they were unable to get hold of.

She and Gideon had given the families their best pitch, with the video of Sully and Amy gripping hands being their main hook. Leaving out the urgency of why they needed these patients together—because truthfully, they didn't yet know—they stuck to the shock factor of not only their two subjects showing life, but Maddy herself fully coming out of her coma. And while six of the seven they'd contacted were emotionally moved by the video they'd seen of Sully and Amy, the calls were awkward, full of confusion and lack of trust. Not like the cathartic moment she'd had with Tammy and Amy Shimp inside their Tulsa home. But, as she'd told Gideon and Archie before they'd begun, *All we need is one.*

And the one they got. A fifteen-year-old girl named Lauren Betts from Springfield, Missouri, who'd been comatose for eight months after a car wreck on the way to a high school basketball game. Lauren's mom had been skeptical at first, even angered, until Gideon had sent the video. Mrs. Betts watched the video, started crying, and hung up without any response. Fearing he'd lost her, Gideon had been about to strike her name off the list when his cell phone rang, and it was her calling back, composed now, and asking for their address. They were gathering what they needed to transport their daughter so they could leave right away.

Gideon ended the call and hugged Maddy. Maybe this wasn't the right time to feel a charge from the touch of another human being, but it was there even after Gideon let go, and she hoped like hell she wasn't blushing.

"Hot damn." Archie Dupree closed his laptop with a pop and patted Gideon on the shoulder. "One out of fourteen isn't bad."

As odds went, Maddy thought, it was horrible, but with what they were asking of these strangers, one out of fourteen was a good start. And if one showed up and something else happened here to give credence to their cause, then they'd have more to double back and show the others some mounting evidence. Maddy wasn't about to say it now and break the sudden upbeat mood in the kitchen, but they needed more than three. She couldn't recall everything from when she'd been *there*—Lalaland, yes, that's what it had been called—but she knew enough to justify the feelings of anxiety and dread she'd carried since awakening from her coma a month ago.

This was real. It was bad. And something was coming.

Even though she'd yet to see this Harrod's Reach tunnel, she'd learned enough from Gideon over the past hour to know that whatever was coming through there was from Lalaland. Because that's what Lalaland was, the land of colorful deception, the land of wrong, the land of make-believe, the land where if you could think it, you could make it so, the land of Mr. . . .

Maddy went light-headed.

She braced herself against the island and tried to play it off like she was closing her eyes for a moment of rest. Right before she'd closed her eyes, she'd seen the warm look on Gideon's face when his father patted his shoulder. She could tell that simple show of physical affection was not commonplace, and perhaps not so simple. Like Gideon had been waiting years for that pat on the shoulder, and here she was breaking up the moment with a dizzy spell. Not a memory dump like she'd had in Atlanta, but something. Crumbs, residue, more names . . . Not names like the ones she'd written down in Atlanta, but names that were horrifying.

Mr. Dreams . . .

The Nightmare Man . . .

Right before blacking out, she verbalized the one that struck the most fear in her: "Mr. Lullaby . . ."

CHAPTER

32

Beth

Now

By the time Beth made it into the hospital, Grover's eyes had closed again.

"What happened?"

Natalie stood beside Grover's bed, touching his shoulder. "He was talking, Beth. They think he'll make it." She beckoned Beth closer, but seeing Grover like this, the unshaven white stubble on his chest-nut-colored skin, his chest bandaged from waist to neck, made Beth feel suddenly vulnerable. Like she might finally break down, and of all places, in public.

She stood bedside and grabbed Grover's limp right hand in both of hers.

Natalie looked across the bed at Beth. "It's Doc we need to worry about. It's not looking good."

Beth felt slight pressure on her grip, like Grover may have just squeezed her hand. She looked up to find Natalie watching how tenderly her thumb rubbed over his bony knuckles. Grover seemed like he'd aged ten years in the past twenty-four hours—near-death had a way of doing that to a person—but she hadn't expected him to look so skeletal.

"You look tired," Beth told Natalie.

"I *am* tired." Natalie looked down at Grover sleeping peacefully in his bed. "But this helps. You know he asked for you. First thing he did, he said, *Beth* . . ."

Beth's lower lip quivered. She looked away from Natalie. "Sorry."

"Don't apologize for being human, Beth."

Beth wiped her eyes, changed the subject. "I was at the Beehive when you called. There's something not right there. Something weird going on with Mickey."

"Something weird going on everywhere," said Natalie. "I know you aren't scared, but I am, Beth. I can't get what I saw down by the tunnel out of my head. That couldn't have been Mayor Truffant. A doll? I mean . . . who would do such a thing?"

"I don't know." But it reminded her she had work to do.

Natalie checked her phone. "Shit, it's Doc."

Beth followed Natalie down one main hall and into another, where a lot of noise and commotion sounded from Doc's room. One nurse hurried out while another ran in. Machines beeped. Inside, Jane Bigsby cried. Beth heard her first, and then once she got close enough, saw her standing bedside much like Beth had been doing moments ago with Grover, except Jane held a completely limp hand and her husband's face was ghostly pale, eyes and mouth open.

Beth had either just missed Doc's last breath or was witnessing it now.

Natalie slithered into the room, stood on the opposite side of the bed from Jane.

Jane looked at Natalie, and then at Beth in the open doorway, and said, "What did he mean? What he said, what did he mean?"

Natalie shook her head; she was crying now too. Doc Bigsby had delivered Natalie; he'd delivered half the town. "I wasn't in the room, Mrs. Bigsby. I didn't hear."

Jane looked at Beth.

Beth stepped inside. "What did he say?"

Jane looked shelled. "Something about the Island of Bones. Something about Simon . . ."

"Simon Bowles?"

She nodded. "Yes, Simple Simon . . ."

Beth moved closer to the bed, did her best to ignore Doc's emaciated corpse, mouth still open and eyes wide. "What else?"

"That he's coming . . ."
"Who's coming, Mrs. Bigsby?"
"Through the tunnel . . ."
"Who's coming?"
Jane Bigsby looked straight into Beth's eyes. "Mr. Lullaby."

Excerpt from Detective Harrington's notes
July 12, 1996
Harrod's Reach

I'M TOO OLD *to be navigating the ravine. Too old to be getting anywhere near that tunnel. But a job is a job and I suppose I'll do it until I die.*

On this sunny Sunday afternoon, I hadn't expected a call from one of the Reach's unlikeliest, Mr. and Mrs. Bowles, fearing their young son Simon (age 6) had run off. I got in my car right away and headed fast out toward Harrod's Lake, where the Bowles and a few other local oddities owned cottages around the waterline.

Gus and Deborah Bowles met me outside their cottage with tears in their eyes. In the rare times I saw the three of them walking through town, the two parents never seemed to show much affection to their little boy, Simon, who walked in their shadows like an afterthought. Many in town had begun to call the boy simple, due to his slow, befuddled nature, but it was clear as soon as I arrived that they loved him, and they truly feared him gone.

We first searched the lake, knocked on a few doors, but no one had seen Simon all morning, and it was already deep into the afternoon. Two hours into our search, which by that time had included a few locals who'd volunteered to help canvas the woods, we stumbled upon Simon's body just a few paces away from the tunnel's northern entrance. The boy was lying there on his side, motionless. I thought him dead for sure, because how long could a child sleep out here without waking up? But as I slowly approached, I noticed, beneath his head, the pillow Simon had brought with him. I noticed the blue blanket, covered by leaves and grime. The stuffed teddy bear nestled in the crook of his right arm. And finally, the subtle rise and fall of the chubby boy's chest. He wasn't dead, just asleep. Deeply asleep.

Once mom and dad Bowles got over the shock of seeing their son lying there, asleep, the realization hit them, and they exchanged looks of oh we should have known. They said their son often sleepwalked. That, of course, would have been the first thing I would have led with when the authorities arrived at my door, but it seemed to never have crossed their minds until I found him sleeping by the tunnel.

Not just sleeping, but something akin to hibernating, as the boy didn't even awaken when his father carried him back to their cottage at the lake. Out of curiosity, I waited around until he did wake up, an hour after his father deposited him back onto his bed. The longer I sat with the family, waiting, the more I realized through conversation, or mostly a lack thereof, that they were both, perhaps, a little simple too. But it turned out Simon was not only a heavy sleepwalker, but in fact slept most the day, every day. I'm making a note to check with Doc Bigsby whether this should be considered problematic for a boy that age. Was this too young to be depressed? Lethargic? Although both parents said when he was awake, he was usually full of energy and typically upbeat.

"Then what," I asked, "is wrong with him?"

"Nothing," Gus Bowles said. "Boy just likes to sleep."

"That ain't all of it." Deborah Bowles smirked. "The boy likes to dream."

"Where he goes . . ." Gus leaned forward like he didn't want anyone else to hear, even though there was no one else around to do the hearing. "He calls it Lalaland."

33

Teddy

Before

NOW THIS PLACE, Teddy thought as he breathed in the historic nuances of the Beehive's extravagant lobby, *I could get used to*. The fancy woodworking at the bar, the mahogany shelves, the countless liquor bottles, the plush stools. The checkered floor and bronze chandelier illuminating it. Tall wrought-iron tables for lounging. Fluted columns soared into the coffered ceiling. The main wall decorated with the words *The Beehive*, each letter the height of a grown man, each letter constructed of pieces pulled from the old rail line, from the wreckage of the derailed train.

So said Mickey. So said the old newspapers he'd shown Teddy before the personal tour, which he'd given them with an awful limp and hobble, voice muffled by his broken nose and puffy lips. The side walls were painted in murals, showing men and women in 1920s attire, singing and dancing, laughing and imbibing.

"Oh, yes, Mother." Teddy leaned down next to her ear as *she* took it all in from her wheelchair, more alive and lucid now that they'd arrived at the Beehive than he'd seen her in years. Since her accident. Since she'd fallen down the stairs and lay awkwardly crumpled at the basement landing. "I could get used to it here."

Sometimes he wondered if she remembered that it wasn't an accident at all. That he'd jumped at the opportunity that day inside the kitchen, her standing at the open basement doorway leading down, reaching for the light inside the stairwell so that she *wouldn't* fall, preparing to walk down those creaky stairs to get the green beans she'd canned earlier in the year. So that they could eat dinner together at their kitchen nook, just the two of them, holding hands over their plentiful bounty and praying words to her God and Savior. His hands had been covered in suds from the dishes she'd been on him all day to do, him a grown man and her the great nagging bitch. He'd heard the door to the basement open. He'd looked over his shoulder as he scrubbed a plate free of hardened gunk. He'd said, *Sure, Mother*, when she'd asked *How do green beans sound for dinner, Theodore?* It was her fault for taking too long fumbling for the light. It had given him time to take his hands out of the suds and cross the kitchen floor fast enough to not change his mind. He pushed her. Sent her reeling, arms pinwheeling almost comically. Sent her screaming and thumping down for a crash landing on the floor below, neck bent, arms and legs akimbo. Him looking down on her, hoping she was dead, and if not, hoping she would die soon, because *Don't fucking call me Theodore.*

And the two little growths atop his scalp—at that point still concealed by his hair—had thrummed with fuel-filling current, putting his mother in all that pain, watching her squirm down there on the landing, listening to her moan and wail.

But that was then. And here they were now. Her slowly coming back to the world of the living—of all things, due to a mailed flyer for the grand opening of a fancy hotel in the middle of a wooded Podunk railroad town—and he wondered if she remembered why she was in this wheelchair to begin with. If she remembered his footsteps coming behind her that sunny day, his hands pressed against her shoulder blades.

Did you really fuck our neighbor's husband? From the look in her eyes back home Teddy could see she had, and that she'd enjoyed it. That sinister grin warmed my heart, Mother. It made these antlers grow. Was the Christ-loving prude act all these years just that? An act?

As if she'd read his thoughts, Belinda spoke from her wheelchair. "I was here as a girl."

"In this hotel?"

"Yes," she said. "My grandfather was a musician. He toured the US. One summer he took me with him. I was eleven. He played three nights at the Beehive. I played hide-and-seek with the other children. I ran these halls, the stairwells. We were in and out of every room. We sneaked drinks from the bar." She closed her eyes, reminisced. "'Oh, Pretty Woman' . . . he sang it just like Roy Orbison in his prime. And the Mamas and the Papas. the Monkees. the Beach Boys, and the Box Tops and the Hollies. And the women. . . ." She opened her eyes and wagged a finger out toward Teddy like he was being reprimanded. "The women, Theodore, oh how they lusted after my grandfather. They swooned. Especially when he sang 'The Sound of Silence.' Simon and Garfunkel. He always ended with that song, and when the last chord drifted to silence you could hear a pin drop. Of course, as he told me after the first show, after his typical one drink, that women swooned after what they knew they couldn't have. You see, Theodore, my grandfather traveled without his loving wife, but he was eternally faithful. He would walk off the stage, part the crowd like Moses entering the Red Sea. He'd consume his one drink at the bar, and then lock himself in his room until morning."

Never had she mentioned anything that revealed she'd once been fun. That revealed she'd ever been anyone other than the religious fanatic he knew.

"Kneel down, son. Come closer," she said. He knelt in the open V of her parted legs, close enough for her to touch his antlers. Not seductively or with passion as Brandy would do, but out of analysis and awe. "I've always known you'd be special."

"Who is my father?"

She ignored his question, and instead stayed focused on his antlers, feeling them from tip to root. "There's a tunnel here, Theodore. I went in it that summer." Her hands slithered from his antlers; she folded them on her lap. "Grandfather didn't know. He slept late while on tour. It was a beautiful sunlit morning. I'd just been given a chocolate muffin from the kitchen. I ate it outside at a table, under a yellow awning with flowering hanging baskets, still dripping from having just been watered. Some of the local children I'd befriended invited me to go to the tunnel with them. So I went. One of the boys brought a basketball. Another brought a baseball. One of the girls brought a violin, and she played it right at the tunnel's entrance, Theodore, and the sound resonated across those woods like the tunnel itself was a microphone." She closed her eyes long enough to refuel. "There was a game they played called In-One-Out-One. Short for in one end and out the other. The children stand in a single file line on one end, and one at a time, each child would run through the tunnel. The first one through was to wait outside the other end for the next one. Silly game, I admit." She held up a crooked index finger. "Aside from the fact that the name of the game was *really* to avoid the monster inside that tunnel." She closed her eyes again, but only briefly. "I was the only one who did not win the game that day. I did not make it through."

"What happened, Mother?"

"I don't fully recall," she said. "I was in the middle of the line, and as my turn to run through the tunnel inched closer, my stomach filled with butterflies. The girl behind me gave me an encouraging nudge and whispered, 'There's not really a monster in there. It's all make-believe.' So I went in, walking at first, and then running. There never was a point where I lost track of the light coming from the other side, but the tunnel . . . it gave off a feeling of . . . endlessness. Of moving yet going nowhere. I reached what I assumed was the middle; it was so dark I couldn't see the walls or the ceiling. I slowed down at that point, and *that*, I fear, was my undoing, as more than one of the kids that day had warned me to keep running. To not stop for anything. But I stopped. I scanned the darkness. My heart was racing. My stomach started to turn. Dizziness, and then I blacked out. I was told the other children called out for me. They called and shouted until their echoes collided from either side, and eventually they ran for help.

"They found me unconscious, in the middle of the tunnel, thirty minutes after I'd gone in. It took that long for a couple of the kids to run and find help. The rest were too terrified to go in after me. It was a police detective who carried me out. Returned me back to the Beehive, where my grandfather, by that time, was at his wits' end, and I was slowly coming to."

Teddy positioned himself in front of her wheelchair again, his hands braced on the arms of it as he tried to come to grips with the sudden odd feeling of connectivity he was now experiencing with a mother he had for so long hated. "What happened inside that tunnel? Mother?"

Her eyes locked on his. "It was a succubus." An eerie grin morphed her face into something seductively macabre. Her eyes seemed to age in reverse. "And she's still inside me. She's *always* been inside me, ever since that day inside the tunnel."

His own grin mirrored hers, because *this* was the mother he was meant to have. He knew all about the succubus in medieval folklore. Female demons who appeared in dreams to seduce men. Repeated visits by a succubus could lead to insanity. Even death.

She said, "I returned from that road trip to Harrod's Reach a completely changed girl." She leaned forward, inches from his face, his antlers. "I *was* the succubus that entered me inside that tunnel. I slept with countless boys. Countless men, as I grew older."

"Who was my father?"

She smiled, like not yet, like this was all a game to her. "After you were born, Theodore, and I held you in my arms, I knew there was good left inside me. I forced myself to the Lord. I exorcised *myself*, because three of the local priests refused to do it. I did my best to keep you on the right path, but—"

"I am on the right path, Mother. Don't you see that now?"

"I do," she said, with what looked like regret in her eyes. "The right path for you. I could not, no matter how hard I tried, mask your nature, Theodore." She touched one of his antlers. "Somehow I knew your hair would one day be unable to hide your true self." She returned her hands to her lap. "I slipped occasionally throughout your childhood. I seduced men, and I repented hard."

"Who was my father?"

"Teddy!"

Teddy heard his name being called from somewhere in the lobby and had been so focused on his mother that he'd thought for a second it had resonated from her mind, because her mouth hadn't moved.

"Teddy!"

Closer, right behind him.

He followed his mother's gaze, turned to find Brandy standing next to the bar, panting and face-flushed from having rushed from an adjacent hallway to find him. "We have a problem." She pointed down the hallway, which was awash with light from the half dozen wall sconces running down the length of it. "Two of our *passengers* . . . Let's just say the hotel has two less workers than it did before our arrival," she said. "The crazy fucker with the horseshoes raped and killed the cleaning lady on the second floor. And the dude who lopped off your neighbor's head? He did it again. One of the painters. Third floor."

"Where are the bodies?"

"They're still where I found them," said Brandy. "But the rest of them are getting antsy. I just opened a door down the hall, because I heard some weird laughter coming from it. You know the man we picked up in Tennessee last week? The man who carried that weird doll with him onto the bus? He was in his room, hand-stitching a face, Teddy. With buttons for eyes. He looked at me and said . . ." She paused to swallow. "He said it was for his next doll. I'm telling you, they're getting antsy. What the other two did inspired them. Like they can't wait now to do what *they* do."

"Fascinating," said Belinda Lomax, still laughing and beginning to clap.

"Not now, Mother." Teddy paced the lobby, touching his antlers, thinking, thinking . . .

"Take them to the tunnel," his mother said.

"The tunnel? Why?"

"That's why we're here, Theodore. Is it not?"

The fuck if I know.

Until now, he didn't know why exactly they were here, other than that the voice had told him to, and the Beehive flyer had solidified it.

But maybe she was right?

Too many things were aligning and making sense now for her to be wrong.

Belinda Lomax said to both Brandy and Teddy, "Take the bodies to the tunnel, tonight. And leave them as sacrifices."

34

Maddy

Now

MADDY BOYLE SLEPT fitfully on the living room couch inside the Smite House, dreaming.

Below the steep cliffs of White Rock, lava smoldered throughout the Pits of Dundenny, flowing out in rivers of red char across the hills and valleys of Lalaland.

The voice of the Sandman sounded over her shoulder . . . *tick-tock, tick-tock, tick-tock goes the grandfather clock . . .*

Maddy felt him coming. Smelled him coming, pulling his canvas sack, heavy from the weight of so many eyeballs.

. . . *tick-tock, tick-tock . . .*

She glanced over her shoulder, then jumped into the air, plummeting down toward the Pits of Dundenny, before suddenly lifting with the wind, taking flight just as the Sandman stood at the cliff's edge.

. . . *They travel in packs . . .* Sully's voice now. *In Scandinavian folklore, the Sandman sprinkles magic dust into the eyes of children to induce sleep . . .*

Maddy flapped her arms, soared through blue skies, through low wisps of clouds that smelled like cotton candy but killed like poison. Passing through the wet mist, she kept her mouth closed, exiting into the clear, coasting above the shoreline, as Sully's voice played on.

. . . *in some more sinister versions, the Sandman steals the eyes of children who would* not *sleep* . . .

The beach sand below was the color of rich soil, thick grained and soft under foot, dimpling when knelt upon.

. . . *there are no waves to pack them down* . . .

So many seashells littered the brown shoreline. Seashells, every shade of blue, some small as diamonds while others were the size of coconuts.

. . . *they're placed there by the birds, and after they're plucked clean of the meat, they carry voices* . . .

As she flew over the ocean water, her shadow crinkled wide atop the churning whitecaps, the waves moving *away* from the shoreline, toward more cliffs of White Rock in the distance.

. . . *craggy and porous walls of ancient rock pocked with cave-like holes* . . . *many of the doors are still active* . . . *we're left to guard them* . . . *the Seers* . . .

She flapped her arms, changed course . . .

. . . *anything is possible in Lalaland* . . . no longer Sully's voice, but Amy now in her ear. *Leave real-world logic behind* . . .

. . . and coasted back to the shore, and then higher toward Four-Tree Bluff, where four massive black trees rested at the village's corners . . .

. . . *all there since the First Sleep* . . .

. . . Each tree five stories tall and full of large white leaves, veined in red. To the north and down below in a valley of wildflowers, dozens of fully antlered black deer sprinted as if in a herd, shifting like a bird flock toward the forest of gnarled, black, leafless trees to the east.

. . . *The mare trees* . . .

Mares aren't real . . . Nightmares aren't real . . .

. . . *the bulk of the mares in Lalaland live in the Mare Forest* . . . *they sneak into bedrooms and crawl upon chests* . . . *they press down and bring about nightmares* . . . *they turn into moths after the sleeper awakes* . . .

A forest, Maddy remembered, that had once been full of colorful leaves, but was now completely void of them.

. . . *leaves fall from trees touched by mares* . . . *The bark turns black* . . . *the limbs grow crooked and twisted* . . . *the moths come by the thousands to drink* . . .

And she flew . . . over the Bad Place, through the Land of Wrong, and across the Inside Out . . . over the Lake of Fire and the Frozen Land and back again . . .

. . . where yellow fields bloomed black roses with yellow eyes and purple stems . . .

. . . where red flowers bloomed bright as poppies and tall as goldenrods . . .

. . . where a heard of Wendigos taunted a flock of Batibats . . .

. . . where a young girl sprinted across the rocks at the Island of Bones, being chased by a monstrous Phobetor . . .

. . . *just a girl having a nightmare, Maddy . . . it'll pass . . . all in the imagination . . .*

. . . and the Baku charged from the woods to devour the Phobetor . . .

. . . *all in the head, Maddy . . .*

And the little girl disappeared; the nightmare ended . . .

. . . *But the imagination finds ways to become real. . . .*

Sully again.

. . . *Doc has known for years . . . that . . .*

". . . Sometimes they get through," Maddy screamed, sitting up on the Duprees' living room couch, gasping for air, eyes open, Lalaland fading like dreams do. "The monsters . . ."

Gideon hurried into the room, sat beside her.

She hugged him, rambling. "Cullcarney Pass . . . Kill Town . . ." All of it fading, making less and less sense as it went. "The Island of Never . . ."

Gideon shushed her, rubbed her back.

She spoke into his shoulder, softer now, "Peninsula of Shattered Dreams . . . we need more Elders . . . The Seers aren't strong enough . . ."

Gideon said, "Maddy, it's okay. You had a nightmare."

"We need more Elders," she said, wishing she could remember enough to understand. "Only the Elders can stop what's coming."

"What Elders?"

"I don't know," she said, gripping him, hard. "I don't know." She breathed against his chest. "But they're married."

"Who's married?" Gideon pulled away, just enough to lock eyes. "Who's married?"

"Your brother," she said. "And that girl in there."

"Amy?"

"Yes."

"They're kids," he said. "Maddy, they're kids."

"Over there, they're not."

35

Gideon

Now

Nᴇᴡs ᴏꜰ Dᴏᴄ's death spread like wildfire across Harrod's Reach. Phone calls, texts, word-of-mouth.

They knocked on doors, spoke to neighbors over fences.

By late afternoon, everyone in town had heard of his passing, and the mourning came heavy and hard. Maxine, now that Brody was down for a nap, cried in her bedroom with the door closed. Doc had delivered both of her babies. He'd been by their side during every moment of their post-accident hardships with Sully. Archie's first reaction was to pour himself a shot of bourbon, and Gideon had joined him. Tammy Shimp, he could tell, felt awkward with the sudden quiet now permeating the town. She hadn't known the doctor, but with how instantly the memory of him had infected every room inside the Smite House, she volunteered to return to the parlor while the rest of them dealt with the loss. Maddy, by then, had fully awakened on the couch, energized, from whatever nightmare had taken her an hour ago.

Archie, pale-faced as he tried *not* to cry, had eyed the bottle of Old Sam bourbon on the kitchen's island as if he was not only tempted to take another but *needed* it to cope. But after he and Gideon shared a look of disdain, Archie left the bottle and stepped out of the kitchen. A minute later, Gideon looked out into the hallway, where Archie stood outside a closed bedroom door, listening to his wife cry on the other side of it but not, apparently, confident enough to knock or just walk in to comfort her. Gideon withdrew to the kitchen. A few minutes later it was evident by the hammering from an upstairs bedroom that his father had chosen to bury himself in his latest renovation.

Maddy looked up toward the ceiling, to the hammering up there, and must have come to the same conclusion. She looked sad. She was a quick study, and Gideon wanted badly to know as much about her as she was rapidly learning about the Duprees. He was surprised that Brody, down the hall, hadn't awakened once Archie had started hammering. He looked at Maddy. She was no longer staring at the ceiling but right at him, biting her lip in a way that briefly distracted him from his grief.

"I'm sorry," she said.

"Yeah." He scratched his head, wondered why *he* wasn't crying. What he'd seen and done overseas had hardened him. Or maybe it was more of a numbing, but the truth was he'd learned nothing but how to bury things deeper until he didn't feel much at all. "Me too."

Maddy checked her phone, returned her gaze to him. "What now?"

They couldn't wait here, staying idle, until Lauren Betts and her parents arrived from Missouri. Gideon said to Maddy, "Can I ask you some questions?"

"Yeah, sure."

"Before you passed out earlier, you said, Mr. Lullaby . . . And something about *over there*? And all those things you were saying when I ran in . . . What were you trying to say?"

"I don't even know where to start. Or how."

"At the beginning?"

"How much time you got?" She pulled her cell phone from her jeans and started thumb-tapping, scrolling. Just when he thought she was blowing him off, she handed him her phone and said, "That was me."

Gideon looked at the screen, glanced, because he didn't want to read any more than what he'd seen from the headline. *Survivor of the Charleston Strangler Awakens from Three Week Coma.* And in smaller print right below it: *Charleston Native Madeline Boyle Expected to Make a Full Recovery.* He couldn't emotionally deal right now with any details of her attack, so he handed the phone back. "I'm sorry . . ."

"But that was me then, and here I am now," she said. "I'll do my best to explain the in between." She paused as more hammer blows sounded above them. "Where I was . . . when I was out. When I was in my coma, I was . . . my mind was somewhere else. It's hard to explain, just like it's hard to fully remember any dream or nightmare once we're out of it, but it was real. Even though it was in my mind, it was somewhere tangible. Vivid, like all nightmares and dreams when we're having them. You've dreamt, right? You've had nightmares?"

"It's rare that I don't," he said. *Shoot anything that fucking moves, soldiers.* Him opening fire. The little boy and his mother screaming. "I don't sleep much anymore."

"We all dream," Maddy said. "But where my mind was during those days in a coma, that's where, I think . . . that's where we *all* go at night when we dream, Gideon. When we have nightmares. But we always wake up. What we remember is fleeting. It disappears from the mind. Our imagination. But us coma patients, we stay. We're in it, and we're there for a reason."

"My brother is there right now? He and Amy . . . they're married? In his mind?"

"Not only *in* his mind, but his mind is *there*. And she's there too."

"Maddy? Maddy, look at me, please."

Her eyes were wet. "Yeah?"

"Are you saying you know my brother?"

"Yeah." She laughed, wiped a tear from her left eye. "We've met."

"I mean, before you arrived here today, did you know my brother?"

She stepped closer to him. "Yes. And can we assume now that everything I'm telling you is true? No bullshit?"

"Yes."

"Like I told you earlier. He's a man, Gideon. Over there, he's a man."

"In Lalaland?"

"Yes, Lalaland, and damn it, this is no joke."

"I believe you, Maddy, every word."

"Then stop questioning me," she said. "We age quickly there. They call us Seers."

"Seers?" *My brother is a Seer?* "And the Elders? Who are the Elders?"

She shook her head. "I don't know. Only that they need more of them. In Lalaland."

Gideon exhaled a deep breath, let it all sink in. "What does he look like? My brother?"

She laughed. "Ever seen the show *Justified*?"

"Yes."

"Raylan Givens," she said.

"No shit?"

"No shit."

Gideon nodded toward the parlor. "And the girl in there?"

Maddy looked up, but not at him. "She's beautiful. Somehow in Lala, we're all beautiful." She finally looked at him. "Say something."

"I don't know what to say."

"That you think I'm insane?"

"But I don't."

"Good." She uncapped the bourbon bottle, poured them both another shot. She tilted hers back first and he followed. It didn't burn as badly as the first shot, but the alcohol was starting to relax him. "And Mr. Lullaby?"

"Something *everyone* feared," she said. "He *is* the boogeyman. The monster under our bed. In our closets. He's all of it, Gideon. He *is* the night." She folded her arms, stared out the window at the encroaching dusk. "Funny how things come back, right? Our memory."

"You mentioned a couple of other names before you blacked out. Mr. Dreams? The Nightmare Man?"

She blinked. Her eyelashes were long and beautiful. "Every country in the world has their monsters," she said. "Every country has their lullabies, their legends and folklores. They all started the night of the First Sleep. Around a campfire one night, your brother told me this. The First Sleep. The Second Sleep. The Third Sleep . . . That's how they keep track of time. By the number of sleeps. Here, they say I was out for like eight days, but in Lala, I was on my seventy-fifth sleep. I'd . . . you're gonna think me nuts."

"Come on, at this point, Maddy, I'd believed anything."

"I'd started smoking," she said quickly. "Okay? I tried cigarettes once as a teenager, but about threw up. For whatever reason, over there, they prolong life. Yeah, like I said, the Land of Wrong. And there are fruit trees over there that'll kill you. But the First Sleep, maybe it's when the first people on earth closed their eyes for the night, who really knows? But that's what it is, that's when Mr. Lullaby was created. Or created himself. And as the sleeps went on, his imagination created others. Beasts. Demons. Creatures that terrify us all while we sleep. Two of his creations he called Mr. Dreams and the Nightmare Man. A set of entities that offset each other. One plants nightmares in the hollows of children and the other takes them away."

"The hollows?"

"Evidently all kids have them," she said. "And according to *that* legend, that's where the Nightmare Man plants them. In the hollows of children. That's where the seeds grow into nightmares. The mythical twin, Mr. Dreams, takes them away." She poured them both another shot of bourbon. She held it up and they clinked glasses. They downed them, winced in unison, and she went on. "At some point in the late eighteen hundreds, in Austria, these two mythical beings somehow made it through." She held up her hand to stop his question. "Their . . . spirits, or whatever, they found a way here. On *this* side. And they're still out there."

"How?"

"Inside real people, Gideon."

"What, like possession?"

"Something like it."

"And Mr. Lullaby?"

"Has been trying to do the same ever since," she said. "Or maybe worse."

"What could be worse?"

"I don't know," she said with aggression, and then softer. "I don't know. But I was sent back as a warning. They're fighting among themselves over there. They're disagreeing on how best to keep us protected. How best to guard those doors. That's why I was sent to unify them here." She touched her head at her temples, like she was battling a sudden pain or now, as they spoke, having more memories come to her. "That's what they do over there, Gideon. They might seem like vegetables over here, but in Lala, they're warriors, they're soldiers, and they live every waking minute trying to keep us safe."

"What, like Watchers on the Wall??"

She turned away from him. "Just stop. I shouldn't have come, this is crazy." He moved quickly around the island to her. She said, "Don't."

"I'm sorry," he said, pleading, like his old self. "But you have to admit that—"

"I know, it sounds fucked." She teared up again. "I admit that, but . . ."

He stopped a few feet away from her. "Come here." He opened his arms to her. They'd only met a few hours ago, and maybe it was asinine to think she would come to him for any form of comfort, but alcohol was coursing through him and probably her and whether she needed to be held or not, he did. His body hadn't stopped thrumming since he'd gotten the news that Doc had died. Doc Bigsby was like family. To many in town, he *was* Harrod's Reach, and even though Gideon hadn't seen him in three years, it did little to dampen the emotional blow turning his legs to jelly and his heart to concrete. When most in town had blamed Gideon for what happened to Sully, to the good son, Doc had taken up for him, even, to an extent, defending him to his own father, Archie, who, to this day, to this very fucking minute, upstairs hammering, still blamed him. So yeah, he needed a hug and Maddy Boyle gave it to him, slipping inside his arms right there in the kitchen of the Smite House, wrapping her arms around his waist and burying her face into his chest like she'd not only needed it herself but had somehow been there before.

In his arms. His embrace. She smelled his shirt. He rested his chin on her head and smelled her hair. He rubbed her back and felt her spine and shoulder blades, her heart beating, and he never wanted to let go. This was how he'd always imagined he'd one day hold Beth, but he knew that was never to be.

Maddy said, "What are you thinking right now?"

"That I want to know everything about you," he said. "Tell me something."

"Like what?" she asked, her ear against his chest.

"Something you think would turn me away."

She laughed, went silent. A few seconds later, she said, "I'm a stripper. Was . . . a stripper."

"Okay," he said. It wasn't what he expected to hear, and it didn't matter anyway. She could have told him she was an alien, and it wouldn't have mattered.

"And you?" she asked.

"I'm a coward."

She squeezed him tighter, said, "I don't think so."

Then you're the only one, he thought.

She pulled away just enough to look up at him. He'd always been self-conscious about the scar above his upper lip and knew that's what she was staring at. Every part of him wanted to kiss her. To see if she'd be put off by it, like he always feared Beth was.

Maddy's voice stole him from his reverie. "Thank you."

"For what?"

"For believing me," she said. "That was my worst fear coming here. That no one would believe me. But trust me when I say that our imaginations have no bounds. Some have bigger imaginations than others. But our thoughts all come from somewhere, right? Our imaginations? What if we're pulling them all from somewhere that's real," she said. "Because it is. And they're doing their best over there to keep it contained. But trust me, it isn't Mr. Lullaby they're scared of, because they don't fear for their own lives in Lala. They're fearless . . ."

Gideon closed his eyes.

She said, "What?"

"That's what everyone always said about Sully. That he was the most fearless boy they'd ever seen." And Beth, he thought. And Beth . . .

Maddy continued: "They're scared for *us*, Gideon, on this side. They're scared of what might happened if Mr. Lullaby gets through."

Gideon recalled what he'd seen at the tunnel this morning and knew that portions of Lalaland already had. He stared into her eyes.

"Your brother hugged me before he sent me back." She bit her lip again. "But you're better at it."

He was about to kiss her when Brody started crying down the hall.

She patted his chest. "I'll get him." She slithered away.

He watched her go. He should have been shocked by how easily she'd merged into the house and family here, like she belonged. Her footsteps trailed down the hallway. A few seconds later Brody stopped crying. Gideon's cell phone chimed with a text from Beth. *Meet me at Doc's house. I'm on the way there now.*

He responded: *B there soon.*

Maddy entered the kitchen with Brody in her arms. The boy looked foggy-eyed from having just woken up to Archie's hammering, but otherwise content.

The boy pointed, said, "Gideon."

Gideon smiled, and it was genuine, as he'd half-expected Jax to have taught him the name Giddy-Up.

Maddy walked Brody over. "Here, he wants you."

"What? No, he doesn't."

She handed him over anyway and Gideon had no choice but to grab him, awkwardly. She laughed, helped him reposition Brody. "Haven't you ever held a kid before?"

"I don't know," he said. "I guess."

Not since Sully was little.

Gideon looked at the boy, found Brody's face inches from his and curiously staring. His little finger touched the scar on Gideon's lip.

Gideon at first flinched away, before allowing the boy's finger to explore.

Maddy said, "He's got your nose."

Gideon said, "What? He's not mine, he's . . ."

"I know," she said. "But even so, he's got it."

CHAPTER

36

Beth

Now

BETH HAD SMILED when she'd shaken Maddy Boyle's hand a few minutes ago on the Bigsbys' front porch, and the smile had been genuine. Maddy had traveled across half the country to help them. It *was* nice to meet her, and Beth couldn't help but be in a bit of awe that this young woman was not only walking a month after awakening from her coma but fit as a fiddle and pretty as an ocean sunrise. Not just pretty, thought Beth, but intelligent and not at all afraid to voice her mind. But the truth was, Beth, before texting Gideon earlier, had walked up to the Smite House's front porch and was about to knock on the door when she'd seen the two of them through a window, embracing in the kitchen. And that's when it had struck her. Feelings of jealousy so foreign to her they had immediately made her teary-eyed, but what pissed her off most wasn't the jealousy, but the fact that she'd lost her shit.

She'd cried in the car all the way to the Bigsbys' house.

She was not one to cry. It was a running joke in Harrod's Reach that Beth had no feelings. She had compassion but had no clue how to show it. She'd loved her mother but cried very little when she was killed. And she'd cried even less when cancer took her father. She'd spent the better part of her life, like Sully before his accident, completely obsessed by that tunnel, so much so that at times nothing else mattered.

She didn't love Gideon like that. But something about seeing Gideon holding another woman like she'd always known he'd wanted to hold her, made her feel for the first time that she was missing out on something, that the life she'd chosen as an emotionless workaholic crutch for the town just might not be all she had in her. Like perhaps she could have been truly happy if she'd allowed herself to be.

But now she had to focus. Jane Bigsby had given her the keys to the house while she made the post-death arrangements for her husband at the hospital, and they had work to do. She sat straight in the hard-backed chair she'd pulled from out behind Doc's desk. "Where were we?"

"You okay?" Gideon stood so close to Maddy it was impossible not to think of them as attached.

"I'm fine," Beth said.

What Jane had so badly wanted someone to look at was her deceased husband's secret work, what Jane had called his obsession. It was clear she blamed *that* for his death. If not for *that*, he would still be alive. He would not have spent so much time inside *that* tunnel. He would not have been there *that* night.

Beth hadn't wanted to say it to Jane, but she, more than anyone in town, except for Detective Harrington when he'd been alive and Sully before he'd gone under, understood that obsession.

She'd long believed now that some in the Reach were born for it.

Beth stood from her chair and approached the shelves along the side wall and got to work. "She said it's all in here, these cabinets and drawers."

Maddy sidled up to Beth without any further prompting, while Gideon stood for a moment watching, perhaps unsure where to start.

Beth looked over her shoulder, said, "You waiting for a formal invite?"

Maddy laughed. Beth did too. They shared a glance, and their bond was instant. Every bit of jealousy Beth had toward Maddy, however brief, disappeared.

Gideon approached the cabinets and started going through them.

While she worked, Beth thought about how to ask Judge Paxton about a warrant for the Beehive. And after a quick phone call to the sheriff's station, she'd learned—along with the fact that Simple Simon was still sleeping on the cot inside his cell, and had been sleeping ninety percent of the day—that Mickey had yet to bring by the list of employees she'd demanded before leaving that weird, red school bus.

The Lullaby Express? Jane Bigsby, back at the hospital, had said that Doc, right before his passing, had warned them of a Mr. Lullaby.

Beth removed the files from the cabinets in bulk so that she could more easily spread them out on the floor across the room. Maddy joined her with stacks of her own.

As they worked, Gideon encouraged Maddy to fill Beth in on everything she'd just told him about Lalaland. Beth's reaction—or lack thereof—to Maddy's story had prompted Gideon at one point to say, "Beth, are you even listening?"

To which Beth said, "I've heard *every* word, Giddy-Up." And to Maddy, "Please, go on."

Truthfully, she believed every word, and it connected a lot of dots in Beth's mind. She had total belief in what was being said, and Beth assumed Maddy was astute enough to get that.

"We're on the same wavelength, Gideon," Maddy said. "Don't interrupt the process."

Beth looked over her shoulder at Gideon. "Exactly."

Gideon grinned at them both and resumed his work. It felt more natural, thought Beth, to gang up on Gideon, except in the past it had been Beth and Jax doing the ganging, but Maddy fit in like a long-lost sister. Gideon said, "Where's Jax?"

Beth said, "Down by the tunnel. He and Rick Doogan volunteered to watch over things, to alert me if anything . . ."

Maddy finished for her, "If anything else comes through?"

"Or if anybody shows up to deposit another body," she said, thinking, *another sacrifice*. Beth came across a manila folder full of medical documents. Two papers—one from a white note pad and the other from a yellow legal pad—were paper-clipped atop the folder, as if Doc Bigsby had pulled both for special reference. She scanned them, gave them the gist. Thirty years ago, a woman named Gabrielle (Gabby) Duvall, then a patient of Doc's, scheduled an appointment concerning her mental state of mind. "Per Doc's notes," Beth said, "the woman, age twenty-seven, was disheveled and smelling like it had been some time since she'd bathed. Completely out of character for her, he writes. She worked maintenance at the hospital. Overnight shift. But had been unable to work for the past two weeks due to severe anxiety and stress and was fired. She was distraught during this appointment, he writes—convinced, get this, that her body had been taken over by a spirit called the Alu. In quotes, here, Doc wrote Sumerian mythology." She looked up, made sure she had their attention. "It's in a different color ink, so I assume he did more research and then came back to these notes. But he wrote: 'The Alu is a vengeful spirit that terrorizes humans as they sleep, causing unconsciousness, nightmares, sleep paralysis, and in some cases . . . coma.'"

If she hadn't had their full attention before, she had it now. Both Gideon, across the room, and Maddy, beside her on the floor, stopped what they were doing.

Beth continued: "Says here she told Doc she'd been feeling increasingly strange since she and a coworker hiked down to the woods near the tunnel for a night of drinking. Says here, she told Doc that she'd been to hell and back, and was contemplating cutting off her lips, her mouth, and her ears . . ."

"Jesus," said Gideon.

Maddy placed her fingertips to her brow. "I know the Alu."

"How?" Beth asked.

"In Lalaland, I've seen them. Unlike most over there, they don't move in groups. They're loners. They stick to the woods, the shadows, and they come out most often during the sleeps."

Gideon said to Beth, "That's how they keep track of time. By the number of sleeps."

Beth finished reading Doc's notes on Gabby Duvall. "Prescribed sedatives and sent immediately to the psych ward, fearing self-harm, where she was admitted for observation. She sneaked out of the hospital a week later. Never heard from again. Presumably left town for good." Beth flipped Doc's page of notes up to reveal the second paper, this one handwritten like Doc's, but neatly scribed and written in paragraph form. "This is from Detective Harrington's journals." Her heart grew warm with excitement. She'd never known Harrington but had heard plenty about his storied career, dying in his late nineties, having watched over Harrod's Reach for the better part of eight decades. "Grover always said he kept extensive notes, daily, hinting one day he'd hoped to turn them into a book."

"Harrington?" Maddy asked.

"Yes."

Maddy grabbed a stack of yellow legal pads, at least a dozen of them full of writing and swollen with random pages and Post-it notes stuck throughout. "Just pulled these." She fanned through the top legal pad and handed the stack to Beth. "Says Detective Harrington right there, top left corner. Same handwriting."

"This is a gold mine." Beth hurried through the stack. "An entire career's worth of dailies."

Gideon faced them from the cabinets. "What's the one say? The one under Doc's note?"

Now that the lone yellow page had Beth's attention, she noticed more of them were connected to various files now scattered on the floor. Like maybe this wasn't the only loony Doc had ever seen in his office after going inside that tunnel. Another name jumped at her. Mickey French, from the Beehive. As with Gabby Duvall, Doc had written notes on this appointment with Mickey, from three years ago, which coincided with the time he'd abruptly purchased the Beehive Hotel. She saw the words: *sudden change in behavior, muddled thoughts, hearing voices* . . . And just knew that Mickey had probably been inside the tunnel too.

"Beth?"

She ignored Gideon and returned to Doc's notes on Mickey. Saw that Mickey had mentioned something to Doc about a blue seashell, and a voice coming out of it. A voice, Mickey said, told him to buy the Beehive Hotel. Doc had referred Mickey to the hospital's psych ward for a complete evaluation, fearing the beginning signs of schizophrenia. An evaluation Mickey must have either passed or faked his way through, because he purchased the Beehive soon thereafter. And now they were almost finished renovating, weeks away from reopening, and Beth knew there were people inside that building who shouldn't be there.

"Beth?"

She finally looked up at Gideon, who held in his hands a thick binder full of laminated pages. "What is that?"

He opened it toward the middle, showed her and Maddy. Even from her seat on the floor she could see a laminated photo of an animal Doc must have taken at some point. It looked like a fox, but it was orange. Unlike any color on an animal she'd ever seen before, other than what she'd witnessed inside Simon's cottage. "He wrote dates under it," Gideon said. "March fifteenth, nineteen ninety-eight. Spotted twenty yards outside the north entrance to the tunnel." He opened it to another page, and then another. "It's full of them. Different animals. Insects. Birds. Vines. Seashells."

"Bring it over," Beth said, suddenly overwhelmed, even before Maddy handed her another envelope she'd just grabbed, which was labeled *Theories and Findings*. And then below it: *Doctor Travers Bigsby (with Detective Harrington)*.

Doc Bigsby and Detective Harrington had been working on this together, perhaps, for decades before the detective's death.

Gideon said, "What does that say? Beth?"

Beth looked down, remembered the yellow page attached to Doc's file on Gabby Duvall.

She read it first to herself, and then aloud to them.

Excerpt from Detective Harrington's notes
November 2, 1993
Harrod's Reach

*S*HORTLY AFTER SUNDOWN, *my associate, Officer Grover Meeks, received a call at his desk about a disturbance down by the old train tunnel. Some local high schoolers had gone down there to drink and cut up. Kelly Bancroft, a sophomore at Harrod's High, was the first to hear noises coming from the woods just east of the tunnel's southern entrance. After being questioned, she claimed it sounded like a rabid dog growling. Alarmed, the group of teens prepared to leave. At this point a dark-haired woman, completely nude (who we now know to be one Gabrielle Duvall, recently fired from her maintenance position at the hospital) rushed from the bushes and chased after the fleeing teens. Gabrielle Duvall caught Kelly Bancroft, knocked her to the ground, and climbed atop her body. Although Ms. Duvall is slight in stature, Kelly Bancroft said it felt like she weighed as much as a car. She couldn't move. Couldn't breathe. Couldn't even scream for help. And in the few seconds it took for the rest of Kelly's friends to realize she'd been assaulted, Ms. Duvall managed to place her lips on those of Kelly Bancroft's and perform what Ms. Bancroft could only explain to myself and Officer Meeks as "an attempt to suck out her breath." Chase Denton and Clay Engels (two strong boys from the Harrod's High varsity football team who were with the group that night) together managed to remove Ms. Duvall from Kelly Bancroft's body. Both boys,* *under questioning, agreed that it had seemed like they were moving a stone, or a large-sized man, and not the petite frame of Gabby Duvall. Officer Meeks found Gabby Duvall two hours later hiding behind the bushes of St. Michael's rectory, still unclothed, and claiming to have been waiting for her next victim. Ms. Duvall was taken into custody shortly after 8:30 PM by Officer Meeks and myself, for what we both assumed to be drunk and disorderly (public intoxication), only for the Breathalyzer, taken both on the scene and later at the station, to show absolutely zero traces of alcohol in her system. We have since tested her blood for any traces of drugs but as of now she appears to be clean there too. While in lockup, she did not respond to me, but did open up to Officer Meeks, who wrote the following:*

> *"Ms. Gabrielle Duvall, after being possessed inside the tunnel days ago, believes she is now a Babylonian spirit called the Alu. After further questioning and some quick research, I've come to learn that within this mythology, the Alu can take the form of black dogs, and in some cases half human and half animal type beings. They lurk in dark places for their victims, with the intent to cause nightmares. Sometimes, just the very presence of an Alu could be enough to cause them. If that doesn't work, the Alu will physically assault the victim by climbing atop their bodies, pressing down on their chests, and in some extreme cases attempting to suck out the victim's breath while they sleep in order to induce nightmares. If an Alu enters your home, they can cause horrible nightmares, sleep paralysis, and in some cases, comas. Ms. Duvall personally warned me to never walk around at night. When asked why, she said that the Alu will certainly follow me home."*

I questioned Ms. Duvall later in the night, after she'd calmed down, and she said only that she wished to see Dr. Travers Bigsby.

CHAPTER

37

Teddy

Before

THE DEAD-HEAD LIST may have been put on hold for the more urgent need to take over the Beehive Hotel, but Teddy wasn't done with the list.

Especially after realizing the next dead-head lived no more than a hundred yards down the street from the hotel's front doors. The past few days had been full of waiting, and Teddy was sick of being idle.

As much as he liked that hotel, he didn't like being holed up in it. He'd been down to the tunnel each of the past two nights since they'd dumped those two bodies in the woods—the Sheriff's Department was still completely baffled by Brandy's brilliant idea to have the corpses holding hands—and he was planning on going again tonight, because there was something about that tunnel Teddy felt drawn to, and it had to do with more than just his mother's childhood story about it. Tonight's visit had been more out of necessity; one of their passengers got out, and Teddy had learned by now that when they did get out, they tended to migrate toward that tunnel. This passenger—one of only two females picked up by the Lullaby Express—was big-boned and tall. When asked for her name upon boarding the bus two weeks ago, the dark-haired woman had said, "I'm the Nanny." Not *a* nanny, but *the* Nanny, which Teddy had thought weird;

Brandy had just nodded like, to her, it made some sense. The woman hadn't said a word since. *But there's some wicked thoughts going on behind those eyes,* Brandy had said one night.

Teddy volunteered to go down and get her, and found the Nanny in the woods around the lake. He passed through the tunnel to get there, and enjoyed every second of that short blissful stroll before spotting that big, tall bitch at the lake's moonlit shoreline, silhouetted among the glistening weeping willows. What caught Teddy's attention was the cabin to her right, and the dozens of carved, statuesque totems all around it. Monsters and gargoyles and nymphs, and the next thing Teddy knew, the Nanny was standing next to him, studying them much like he was, perhaps even more curiously. And then she approached the cabin door.

"Hey," Teddy said. "What are you doing?"

She opened the door without knocking and walked inside. Teddy followed her. Found a king-size bed that took up most of the main room, and a giant man sleeping on it, snoring. Must be completely out, Teddy thought, to have not heard them walk in. On the floor by the bed's footboard was a set of homemade antlers. The Nanny grabbed them from the floor, positioned them on her head, stared at the shadow they made on the floor. A fire burned inside a stone hearth to the right. A yellow squirrel skittered across the floor and disappeared under the bed. Maybe Teddy would have been shocked if he hadn't seen similar things as a child in the woods behind his Virginia home. And likewise, with the colored animal pelts pinned to the wall to his left. They didn't belong to *this* world, he thought. Like he knew now that there *was* another world. Another side. He then recognized the sketches drawn on the wall in between and all around those hanging pelts, of a long, gangly creature with antlers, and suddenly he felt like he needed fresh air.

He said, "Come on," to the Nanny, who was lifting a chainsaw from the floor beside the bed. The blade was caked with sap and tree guts. He wondered if the big sleeping giant on the bed was the one who'd carved all those totems outside. When it was clear to Teddy that the Nanny wanted to take the chainsaw with her, he said "Fine."

The two of them slipped outside. Teddy saw that the chainsaw had the words *The Ripper* on the handle and wondered what damage that blade could do if the Nanny were to try it on something other than a tree. He led her back through the tunnel, and halfway through, she pulled the cord and the chainsaw rumbled. Teddy said, "Cut that off." She turned the chainsaw off without a word. He said, "Why do you call yourself the Nanny?"

She didn't answer until they reached the other end of the tunnel, but as soon as they stepped foot out the southern side, she said, "I watch the children."

"What children?"

"Any. All." He thought that was it, and then she added, "I make sure they toe the line."

"And if they don't?"

"Then the Nanny gets mean," she said. "And then violent."

Maybe he should take the chainsaw from her. But he didn't, and they walked in silence down the gully and up the ravine, and Teddy wondered how this was the same woman who'd known exactly what to do in cleaning up Mickey's face the other night, and in plugging those bleeding holes after Teddy had gored him with his horns. As they approached Mallard Street, he asked, "You also a nurse, by chance?"

"Used to be," she said. "Before I became the Nanny."

She didn't expand, and truth was he was tired of her weirdness. Tired of seeing that stupid-ass fake rack of antlers resting cockeyed on her head, when his were the real deal. Standing outside the mansion where Sully Dupree lived, he said to her, "You see that hotel down the street? The Beehive?" She nodded. He said, "Can I trust you to go straight there? I've got something I need to do. Can I?" She didn't respond. "I'll take that as a yes. Go on. Go."

He veered off into the woods surrounding the Duprees' house, the Smite House, according to the sign out front, and spent ten minutes casing the place. His typical dead-head killing process included a night of planning. But on this night, after feeling whatever surge he'd felt walking through that tunnel and back again, he craved it now. It seemed most of the town had gathered inside the gym at the church a few miles away, so there was no better time to strike than now. But he couldn't afford to get careless, so he took his time, checking all the windows, the best possible ways of escape, since he was on foot and didn't have far to go. After thirty minutes, he deduced the house had at least three people in it. Two fire trucks were parked in the driveway, but so far, Teddy had only seen one fireman, sitting with the boy Teddy needed to kill, in a tall room at the back of the house, where a window was open to the woods, with nothing more than sheer drapes to block his passage, and it was low enough to the ground to climb right in.

But, for now, he waited. A minute later, the voice of a second fireman sounded, and Teddy, from his spot outside the window, spied him entering the room. The two men met at the foot of the dead-head's bed and held hands. Teddy thought, what was this? A few seconds later the two firemen exited the room together, leaving the boy alone. He'd never get a better chance than this, so he waited to make sure they weren't immediately returning, parted the curtains, and quietly stepped inside the room. It wouldn't take much to kill the little fucker, so he got to it. He wasn't used to flying by the seat of his pants when dealing with the list, and he found the spontaneity thrilling. But when he approached the bed, the boy, this Sully Dupree, although his eyes stayed closed, started trembling. This wasn't normal. Most dead-heads stayed just like they were. The boy's movements gave him an impulse to flee, but he didn't. He couldn't. The boy was right there for the killing.

Teddy moved closer to the bedside and had in mind just to pull the boy's cords and run, but when his foot creaked over a dead spot in the floor, the boy's eyes flashed open. Teddy halted. The boy screamed. Well, as much as he could with that tube down his throat, but loud enough to alert the two men in the other room. When the kid sat up and tried pulling the tube from his throat, Teddy hurried back toward the window to exit. Teetering there in the frame, he heard the boy scream, "Run! Run, Doc. Run!" And while Teddy had no clue what the fuck the boy was yelling—and who and where was Doc?—he didn't wait around to find out. Because this was what happened when you went full throttle into something without a plan.

Outside the Smite House, where a flash of light lit the woods from the direction of the tunnel, Sully Dupree's voice chased Teddy as he fled the premises, and it sounded like the boy was reciting a list. Name after name after name, until Teddy made it to Mallard Street and could no longer hear the boy's strained voice—just the monotonous buzz of the streetlamps and the moths flicking against the light's clear dome. The street was still vacant because of the party, making the rest of the run up Mallard Street back to the Beehive uneventful.

Once he got there and locked himself in, he wondered if the Nanny ever made it home with that chainsaw.

Something told him she hadn't.

38

Gideon

Now

D OC BIGSBY HAD SO many theories about the tunnel that Gideon struggled to focus on just one.

His theories about time travel, second dimensions, and alternate worlds were so heavily detailed with scientific jargon and complex mathematics that the three of them were quick to cast those aside, not as impossibilities, but as over their heads. They were hunting for something more streamlined and tangible. After what Maddy had told them about her experiences in Lalaland, and after she'd seen some of the photos of the colorful vines and fish and seashells that had appeared around the tunnel's southern entrance overnight, Doc's theories on nightmares and dreams and sleep in general took them closer to where they wanted to be. And now, after they'd had time to read through much of Detective Harrington's notes—specifically those referencing strange occurrences in and around the tunnel, strange behaviors of so many locals over his time on the job after visiting the tunnel, and the dozen or more citizens (what he called *oddities*) he and Doc had discussed—it was clear that Lalaland, as Maddy described it, was somehow connected to that tunnel.

"Are we all in agreement on this?" Gideon asked Maddy and Beth as they stood exhausted inside Doc's home office, having spent the past two hours going through his files.

Beth said, "I don't think we can deal with it unless we believe it."

"Three murdered bodies were left outside the tunnel as sacrifices," Beth said. "I think whoever did it is hiding inside the Beehive. I'm waiting on a warrant."

Gideon said, "Screw the warrant." He found Beth grinning at him, tiredly. "What?"

"Just that you've changed, Giddy-Up."

"Whatever," Gideon said, eyeing the pile of files they'd deemed most relevant. He began to box them to take to the Smite House. Maddy had heard from the Bettses, and they were now less than two hours away from Harrod's Reach with their comatose daughter Lauren.

"Why do you call him Giddy-Up?" Maddy asked, amused.

"Because they're assholes," Gideon said.

"Because Gideon, when he was a kid," Beth said, "ran like a total goof. Like he had two left legs and didn't know which one to lead with." She grabbed Doc's binder of laminated pictures, of the *things* that had gotten through the tunnel. "There was a town near Charleston, in the 1920s." She seemed to be talking to Maddy.

And Maddy guessed at where she was going: "Bellhaven?"

"You know of it?"

"Every town has its legends." Maddy paused, then turned to face Beth.

Gideon watched both women. "What?"

Maddy said to Beth, "You don't think?"

"I do," she said.

"This have something to do with your Murder Room?" Gideon asked.

"Pit," Beth corrected. "Murder Pit. And yes."

Earlier Beth had explained her years of work on cluster violence, work Gideon knew she'd begun as a teenager, and he assumed this was where she was going with this. "Somebody care to fill me in, or are you two just gonna stare at each other?"

Maddy said, "According to legend . . ."

"More fact than legend," Beth said. "I have copies of some of the old newspapers."

"Wouldn't mind seeing those," said Maddy.

"I'll schedule the tour." Beth then said to Gideon, "The town of Bellhaven nearly ripped itself apart in 1920. It divided over religion, and completely turned on each other. It was on my radar because of the violence that occurred there, but if I'm remembering correctly now . . . the woods there . . ." She looked to Maddy.

Maddy said, "That's what us locals talk about the most. What happened to the woods that year. You either believed the stories or you didn't, but everything, every plant, tree, bush, or whatever, bloomed at the same time. And they tracked it all back to some weird chapel inside the woods. Like that's where all these blooms and colors sprouting throughout the forest were coming from. Like whatever was coming from that chapel was responsible for what was happening to the town." Maddy closed her eyes as if thinking hard on something.

Gideon asked, "Maddy, you okay?"

She opened her eyes, waved him off. "I'm fine, I just can't believe I didn't see that correlation until now. Especially after what I saw over there during my coma." Maddy broke the brief silence with a question for Beth: "Gideon told me about the mayor. Stitched up like a doll. But what about the other two bodies?"

Beth leaned back against the wall, folded her arms, is if wrangling with whether or not to reveal what she and Gideon knew.

Maddy must have seen the glance Gideon and Beth shared. Maddy said, "What is it? Why are—"

"One of the bodies was decapitated," Beth said quickly.

"And the other?" Maddy asked.

Beth answered again. "The other one was raped."

"And strangled," Gideon added.

Maddy's face went white. Gideon immediately moved toward her.

Beth finished what they both knew Maddy wanted to hear. "She was beaten to death with a horseshoe."

Before Gideon could corral her, Maddy slipped from Doc's office, hurried down a hallway, into the kitchen, and out the door to the deck. Gideon followed her into the backyard, where dusk was quickly approaching. Maddy paced, arms clutched against her stomach, and then doubled over near the bushes lining the garage to throw up. Gideon knelt beside her, held her hair back as she heaved until empty, crying. And who could blame her? Her assailant was quite possibly hiding in the town of Harrod's Reach. Most likely inside the Beehive.

"I'm going to kill him," Maddy said, wiping her mouth, leaning into Gideon's embrace. "If he's here, I'm going to find him and kill him."

Even as he attempted to calm her, Gideon felt rage burbling within him, thinking, *Not if I kill him first.* He looked up at Beth, who seemed preoccupied by something else inside the garage. "What is it?"

Beth said, "There's a light on." She stepped inside the open door. A second later she calmly said, "Gideon . . ."

He knew from experience that the calmer Beth's voice got the more urgent the situation, so he was quick to his feet, and Maddy stood with him. Inside the threshold of the open garage door, Gideon noticed Beth had her gun out. Her other hand she held out toward them, as if to keep them calm.

If it was a cat, it was the biggest one he'd ever seen, more the size of a German shepherd, but feline in its movements. It purred loudly and clawed at the second of what looked to be a series of four large freezers lining the garage's back wall. For now, it paid them no attention as it scratched at the second freezer with what looked like bird talons rather than claws. Its black, oily hair was long and, under the glow of the lone ceiling bulb, touched with swirls of purple and red. The paws, Gideon noticed, appeared more like knuckled human hands, and the head . . . *Jesus Christ . . . what was this thing? Those were ears of a human.*

Maddy's voice quivered next to him, "Pandafeche."

Beth stepped closer, aimed her gun.

"Shoot it, Beth," said Maddy in a low tone. "Now."

Gideon held an arm out to keep Maddy back.

"Shoot it," Maddy said again, with even more desperation.

And then the thing, what she'd called the Pandafeche, turned its head toward them, slowly, and instead of the feline face Gideon had expected, the features, although covered in thick black hair, resembled that of a human. It didn't just hiss, but grinned.

Maddy screamed this time, "SHOOT IT!"

Beth pulled the trigger. Nailed it on a back haunch. The thing blew back against the second freezer with a thump, and blood sprayed. Badly wounded, it made another attempt to come toward them, and Beth shot it again, this time exploding the head.

Maddy screamed, buried her face into Gideon's chest. He wrapped an arm around her, turned his head away as well, even as Beth calmly approached what she'd just slain.

Beth nudged it with her foot, and Gideon could tell it took some strength to do it. She gripped the handle atop the freezer lid the thing had been trying to open.

"Beth, careful . . . ," Gideon warned.

Maddy stepped away from him, inching closer to that dead thing.

Beth opened the freezer's lid. She gave the cool air a moment to disperse, and then reached inside. By then, Gideon was close enough to look for himself. She pulled out what looked to be a freezer bag, and inside it, a perfectly preserved, frozen frog, but instead of the typical greenish brown, this one was purple, and the size of a splayed-fingered hand. On the sealed freezer bag, in black ink, Doc had written: *December 11, 2018. 4:56 PM.* Could have been when he'd captured it, or killed it, or even when he'd locked it inside the freezer, but it was clear this was one of many.

Gideon stepped closer, felt the chill escaping into his face. The freezer was stacked high and deep with similar bags, some small, others larger. The next one showed a frozen yellow squirrel: *July 7, 2015. 12:01 AM.* And below that was maybe a mole, with fur as red as a ripe apple. One way to find out how long Doc had been collecting these was to go through every freezer, every bag, and catalogue them, but if Gideon knew Doc, he felt sure he would have kept a catalogue for reference.

A minute later, as Gideon was digging through the frozen carcasses in freezer two and Maddy was doing the same inside freezer number three, Beth, who must have been looking for the same thing, said, "Found it." She held up a brown, leather-bound logbook and fanned through it. "How old was Doc?"

Gideon said, "Sixty. Maybe sixty-one."

"Some of these dates go back to the mid-nineteen seventies," Beth said. "Which would have put Doc starting to collect them when he was an early teenager."

Gideon looked over his shoulder at the dead beast and said to Maddy. "What did you say that thing was?"

"Pandafeche," she said. "Italian folklore. They cause sleep paralysis and nightmares. But I've seen what they can do over there. They're vicious."

"How did something that big get through?" Gideon asked.

"I don't know," said Maddy. "We . . . over there, it was . . ." She grew frustrated, started again: "It has more to do with the imagination. And we tried to keep the . . . these imaginings, from coming through."

"Through the tunnel," Gideon said.

"Yes," she said. "And others like it. But that's what has been changing people's behavior. Sometimes, even though they fight like hell over there to keep it from happening, the spirits of these imagined things, these legends and folklores, get through." She pointed to all the frozen animals and reptiles inside the freezers. "But I can't explain this. These physical . . . I just can't."

Beth pulled out her phone. The open air from the freezers had already cooled the garage enough to see her crystalized breath. The sun had begun to set outside. "I saw this today. Down by the tunnel." She hit play on her phone, and a video showed the largest deer Gideon had ever seen, moving through the woods as Beth, he assumed, pursued it. But it was black and massive and . . . Beth said, "Take a good look at the antlers." They were red with swirls of orange, and sharp as knives at the tip. "It ran off," said Beth, pocketing the phone. "But it was even larger, as you can tell, than that." She pointed toward what Maddy had called the Pandafeche, which had already begun to invite flies.

Maddy said, "They're all over Lalaland, deer just like that one." She shook her head.

Gideon said, "What?"

"You were lucky, Beth," said Maddy. "That it wasn't hunting season. They'll gut you with those antlers. They travel by the dozens. They attack in herds. Hunting season . . . It's the opposite from hunting season here," Maddy said. "Over there, *they* are the hunters. It's the Land of Wrong. Somewhere, at some point, somebody dreamed those up enough for them to stick. They're all over Lalaland."

"And now we have one here," Gideon said. "At least one."

Beth said, "High activity."

"What are you talking about?" Gideon asked.

"I don't know yet," Beth said, although Gideon had a good idea she did. She flipped through Doc's logbook, his decades of inventory, scanning pages, scanning lines, before looking up. "But by the looks of what's in here, the things that tunnel is allowing through . . ."

Maddy finished for her: "They seem to be getting bigger."

CHAPTER

39

Harrod's Reach

Now

CARSON KNOX STARTED feeling funny soon after he'd returned from the tunnel.

Not funny ha-ha, but funny weird. The dizziness was real. The shaking in his limbs. The internal warning bells singing *You best do something about this and do it quick.* Except Carson had felt it in his right hand first. Was it even possible to feel dizzy in a hand? But sure as shit, that's what had happened, and within an hour of returning from the tunnel, within an hour of seeing Mayor Truffant murdered and done up like a doll on that chair, his right hand had gone dizzy, and then numb, and it didn't take a rocket scientist to figure out why.

Those damn vines he'd grabbed. He'd always thought Beth Gardner was a hot piece of ass, but her smarts intimidated him. Even as kids, her know-it-all nature had kept him on his heels. To combat that, he'd act tough around her. So, when she'd told him not to touch those colorful vines at the tunnel, her advice—a command was what it was—had encouraged him to do the opposite.

And now here he was, still dizzy, yes, but also sweating and feverish and sick to his stomach, his big breakfast and even bigger lunch coming out both ends for the past two hours. Now that the diarrhea and retching had subsided, he felt corn-shucked, and damn if those vines he'd kept in his pocket and fondled all the way home from the tunnel hadn't somehow taken root atop his skin and started growing up his arm. At first it had tickled, but the tickle didn't take long to turn into pain. What the fuck were these things, growing up his forearm, intertwining at the elbow, tightening around his bicep and shoulder and now spreading like a starfish across his bare chest? He turned to look at himself in the mirror, and damn it to hell, if the vines weren't showing purple and pink and gold and white across his back, and it was becoming increasingly harder to breathe. The vines were constricting him, suffocating him like a python would. Minutes later he felt a tingle down by his balls, and as much as he dreaded it he dropped his pants and underwear for a look, and holy shit, the vines had begun to reach down there too.

Reach, he thought, laughing, funny ha-ha, but that was the delirium talking now, because it felt like thirty pounds of pressure now squeezing his scrotum. He stood in front of the mirror and cried like a damn baby. Soon the crying turned into anger and finally rage, rage at Beth for thinking she could boss him, rage at himself for not listening, and finally rage at Giddy-Up Gideon for coming back into town. Carson left the bathroom, wheezing and wincing and stumbling through the hallway. He blinked through the encroaching blurriness and grabbed his shotgun from his bedroom. By the time he walked out his front door, naked, shotgun loaded, his body was completely covered by vine.

By the time he stepped out onto Guthrie and shot the first of his five victims—innocent little Joseph Farrington, the local journalist who'd only been deputized earlier in the day—a coiled threading of purple and pink and gold had started up into his left nostril.

By the time he made it down to the tunnel and caught his childhood pals Jax McBride and Rick Doogan holding hands as they stared into the tunnel, the vines had begun to enter his brain. He first shot Rick Doogan, because he was tired of keeping that secret. And by the time he said to the weeping Jax beside him *Don't watch* and blew his own head off just outside the southern entrance, just as the tunnel itself seemed to be whispering to him, the vines, in tangled clusters, had begun to blind him and show themselves again from his left ear.

*   *   *

Chimp Deavers had shit to do.

Not only as the Harrod's Reach fire chief, but as a newly deputized lawman. The town was under siege. The tunnel was coming to life and sprouting color? Bringing in ocean tides of shit, weird fish and seaweed and seashells that talked? What Beth had called blooming. He'd overheard her at the station say something about high activity, about the highest activity she'd ever seen, whatever that meant, but it was another Harrod's Reach Golden Period, for sure. One to eclipse what they'd seen in the 1960s, the 1920s, and even as far back to late 1800s and the legend of Connie Brine.

Yet Chimp couldn't bring himself to do anything other than listen to that damn seashell he'd brought back with him from the tunnel. Even as gunshots echoed outside, and the subsequent screaming followed, he stayed put in his recliner with the seashell to his ear, listening to the voices coming from somewhere, completely ignoring the texts coming through, the phone incessantly ringing.

He shut his phone off because it was too much of a distraction and placed the seashell back to his ear. Whenever one arm got tired holding it up, he'd switch to the other hand, the other ear, as it was evident by now the seashell worked on both. The ocean waves still sounded. The voices could still be heard, and this was even better than a TV show.

It was live like a radio.

"Isn't that right?" he asked his wife, Annie, who was squirming on the couch across the room, wide-eyed and currently hating him, with duct tape across her mouth to match the tape around her ankles and wrists. He just couldn't have her tossing the damn thing like she'd threatened to do, even going as far as trying to discreetly snatch it from his hand right in the middle of a good, far-off conversation between Sully—I mean what kind of coincidence is that?—and some woman named Amy Shimp, the two of them discussing some place called the Island of Bones and Four-Tree Bluff and some guy called Mr. Lullaby.

"I mean, you can't make this stuff up," Chimp said to his wife across the room. She stared at him with so much venom that he finally plopped the leg rest down from his recliner, marched across the living room, and flipped her to face the other way, toward the back cushions of the couch so that she wasn't facing him. She started flopping around like a fish out of water, and it reminded him of the fish he had resting on wax paper on the kitchen counter. The orange fish he'd picked up from outside the tunnel this morning and pocketed along with the shell.

Seashell to his ear, because at this point FOMO was real, he marched past his recliner and into the kitchen, where he got out a skillet and oil and turned the right front burner on to medium high. He didn't know until a few weeks ago, when Jax had jokingly brought it up during a meeting, what FOMO even meant—the Fear Of Missing Out—but that's what having this seashell had done to him. There wasn't always chatter on the other end of it, but when it happened, it was typically MWT. That's Must Watch Television, Jax, because two can play at this game. Chimp laughed now at how much FOMO sounded like what Jax really was, what he and Beth had been forever trying to hide from the town, that he couldn't believe how ironic it had been for Jax to have brought FOMO up in the first place.

His landline telephone started ringing across the kitchen.

It was Beth. He didn't answer it. Sometimes being the fire chief was taxing. And even though he'd only been deputized for a few hours now, he didn't much like that either.

While the oil heated in the skillet, he got a hammer from the garage and came back in and killed the landline phone with it. Next, he got out his cell phone, placed it on the table in the breakfast nook, and crushed that too. Something thumped in the other room. It gave him pause, but only briefly, after realizing it was probably Annie flopping herself onto the floor.

Like a fish.

He returned to the stove and saw that the oil was ready. The orange fish itself wasn't as brightly colored as it had been in the morning. He hoped it wasn't spoiled, but decided it still held enough color, and therefore enough intrigue, to cook up anyway. Because how often did he have a chance to cook up a catch like that? Some weird catfish had been reeled from Harrod's Lake over the years, but nothing like the majestic beauty of this thing.

Chimp placed it in the pan, eyes and skin and all, and watched it sizzle.

Flipping oil atop the fish with the spatula in one hand and holding the seashell to his ear with the other, Chimp realized the radio station had changed. His eyes grew wide when he heard somebody named Teddy making rough love to somebody named Brandy on the other end of that seashell. Chimp got so into the sounds of their love making, he was tempted to undo Annie in the other room and see what his chances were with her. Probably not good, all things considered. The sounds climaxed, and then abruptly stopped altogether on the other end of the seashell. The panting on the other end of the airwaves transitioned to words. *The show must go on*, Chimp thought, listening as he flipped oil over the bubbling fish. Listened to Teddy say something about things making sense. Brandy whispering, *How about another mare ride?*

Chimp thought, oh hell, yes, because that just sounded juicy.

So Chimp overcooked the fish in front of him. His mouth was watering. He should have thought it strange that the cooked fish smelled like Fruit Loops, and minutes later, all charred and blackened on that plate, that it had tasted like a well-done steak. But he ate it all anyway, contemplating, as he chewed, how many sheets of plywood and how many dozens of nails it might take to board up all his windows against whoever was out there right now knocking to get in. A minute later, feeling queasy and beginning to bleed from both ears, Chimp violently threw up what he'd just eaten, toppled from his chair, and died on the kitchen floor, the seashell inches from his desperate fingers, the voices on the other end of it laughing.

* * *

Simple Simon awoke like he always did.

Abruptly, and with a loud, air-stealing gasp of panic. The disorientation was typical, and depending on how deeply he'd gone under, rarely lasted long. The disappointment soon set in, not so much over still being locked inside the cell—truth was he welcomed the safe confines of it—but more so the disappointment of being back here, on *this* side, instead of over *there*, in Lalaland, where he preferred to be, where he'd learned at an early age he was most needed, where he was anything *but* simple.

Simon sat up on the cot and planted his bare feet on the floor. It had been daylight when he'd closed his eyes, and it was dark outside now, but he otherwise couldn't tell if he'd been down for one hour or twenty. The way he'd come up gasping, he had a feeling it had been a long one. A good, solid sleep with which he'd bring back plenty.

The sheriff's station was empty, and that was probably no good thing. Simon didn't mind being alone; in fact, he preferred it—with how vivid his imagination was and always had been, he was never really alone—but if there was nobody watching him *inside* the station, it meant bad things were probably happening on the *outside*. Hopefully the bad things weren't the result of Lalaland coming through already, before Simon could even have a chance to do what he was supposed to do. He'd spent his entire life getting acclimated, Sully had told him minutes ago, but first he needed to convince Beth to let him out of this cell. Sully, who was a strong man over there, said it was time.

Simon's time to shine.

In Lalaland, he knew exactly what acclimated meant. And also that in Lalaland there *were* no dummies. Simon surveyed the interior of the station—the lights had been left on. Simon retrieved his box of crayons and his book of *Lalaland*. Coloring right away was essential to him remembering. And therefore explaining.

Therefore was another smart word he'd brought back with him.

He opened his book of art, the book full of sleep memories he'd been drawing and coloring since he was old enough to hold a crayon or marker or colored pencil or paintbrush.

Colored pictures and renderings of *all* his Lalaland rememberings. From all the times he'd gone under for the deep sleep. From all the times he'd woken up with such a violent gasp. Starting the day Simon was born, when Doc Bigsby, counting in his head to forty-five before finally giving up and crying and declaring Simon Bowles stillborn and dead, until all of a sudden, he wasn't anymore.

Simon's eyes had popped open. And out came that gasp of air.

*   *   *

Jax ran.

Ran as fast and as far as he could until he absolutely had to stop on the incline of the ravine, panting and crying and thinking, Carson Knox, what did you do? *What did you do?* There was no way Doogan was dead. No way. It was just a nightmare, thought Jax, as he climbed the steep hill to where his fire truck rested on the bluff. It was just a nightmare, and that's why I ran. That's what you do in nightmares . . . you run. They can't end until you start running. So why was his heart still thudding? Why did he have Doogan's blood and brains all over his chest and face and in his hair?

Because it wasn't a nightmare, Jax McBride, you little fucking pussy.

Jax looked around for his dad, Tom McBride, who'd been hitting him and ridiculing him since he was a toddler. That man was unfortunately still alive, and still the World's Greatest Son of a Bitch. Jax got him a coffee mug his senior year of high school that said World's Greatest Dad. He'd borrowed Archie Dupree's paint one day when he and Giddy-Up and Beth were lounging around in the basement of the Smite House and marked out the word Dad. Instead, in white paint, with one of Archie's cherished detailing brushes, he painted the words Son of a Bitch. They got a kick out of it until Giddy-Up laughed and shook his head and Jax said, *What's so funny?* Giddy-Up never said, because he was always such a runt, but Beth sure did. Said that he'd never actually give him that coffee mug. And she was right. He never did. And here Jax was blubbering up the hill.

The man he loved had been murdered right before his eyes, his head exploded in a burst of blood and bone confetti. Carson Knox had pulled the trigger. Had to be, although as far as Jax could tell, he was naked as a jaybird and covered in those purple and white and pink and gold vines that had seemingly consumed his pal Carson, every inch of him, conforming to his figure like a body suit. When Rick Doogan had noticed the shotgun in Carson's hands, Jax had been more locked in on the vine clusters coming from the right eye and out his left ear, the coiled ropes wrapping around his neck so tight the muscles there were strained, and his eyes bulged. And how his voice had been so choked when he'd said, coming out of the shadows to surprise them, "What do we have here?"

Because Carson had no doubt seen Jax and Rick holding hands.

Innocently enough, at that point, because God knew he and Rick had done much more than that down here by the tunnel, and more often than Beth even thought. Right before Carson had shown himself, something had flickered inside that tunnel. A flash that caught both Jax and Rick's attention, and it was followed by a loud screech, like a bird call, and that's when Rick had grabbed his hand. Out of fear, even though Rick had always been the brave one. Slight of stature, yes, but mighty and quick to strike and never took any shit off anyone, even Jax's dad Tom, who still had no clue what had been going on under his nose now for over a decade. Which was when Jax, inside the tunnel, had come out to Beth. Happy and sad and scared all at once, wanting to be his own self but also knowing his dad would murder him if he ever knew. If he ever even suspected. That's why he'd always kept up that tough façade. That macho-man act of which Giddy-Up had always taken the brunt. If there was one thing Tom McBride hated, it was the queers and the gays, and everyone in town knew it. Which was why Jax had spent the first half of his life trying so hard *not* to be gay. Tried so hard *not* to be attracted to men. Until one day Beth had told Jax *That's just not how the universe worked. You are what you are, and your dad can go fuck himself sideways.* It was then they'd begun to make their plans. Beth, as a teen, had said she never wanted to be married. She wasn't cut out to be a wife. She wanted only to work. She wanted only to catch bad guys. She wanted only to find out what was on the other side of that tunnel. That's what turned her on. That's what got her wet, she jokingly told Jax years ago. She was attracted to men, yes, of course, but never wanted to be chained down to one.

"Then chain yourself to me," Jax had said that day in high school. "You do your thing and I'll do mine."

They shook on it, and years later, a few months after Giddy-Up went overseas, they made it official inside St. Michael's Catholic Church, with Father Fred presiding, Tom McBride done up in a tux and smiling like his boy done good. Rick Doogan done up in a tux as Jax's best man, and nobody was the wiser. And now Rick was dead, and his blood was all over Jax's shirt, because that sure as shit hadn't been a nightmare.

A nightmare would have ended by now.

He and Rick had gone down there to guard the tunnel. To make sure no other bodies were dumped near either entrance. This was serious times in the Reach, and Jax knew when and how to buckle down. He'd already had a close enough call the other night when Sully had woken up so suddenly and started screaming. Giddy-Up had been onto something, asking questions about the bathroom and did he flush, because the truth was he'd been in the kitchen with Rick up on the counter, slowly slipping the belt from the loops of Rick Doogan's uniform pants as a slow tease before unzipping his fly, when Sully had started screaming. Jax couldn't afford another close call like that. Rushing into the parlor of the Smite House and seeing that man with the antlers fleeing out the window had shaken him, but Giddy-Up's interrogation had shaken him more. Because he hadn't been in the bathroom at all, he'd been seconds away from . . . He couldn't even think of it right now. And of all places, where Maxine and Archie took their morning coffee. And as much as he'd hinted that the antlers on that man's head had been fake, Jax knew in his heart they were real. Sturdy like the racks his father would clutch after shooting a white-tail during deer season.

Jax made it up the incline to his truck, and as soon as he opened the door his phone started pinging with messages—most from Beth, the rest from a few of his fellow fireman. He'd missed a few calls while he'd been down by the tunnel. Bottom line: Carson Knox had gone on a shooting spree and the reporter, Joseph Farrington, was dead. So was Beth's good friend Justine Baker, and there was no telling how many more. Carson's body was inside the tunnel with his head blown off, and now Rick was dead. Jax read on. Fire Chief Chimp Deavers was dead. Found minutes ago on his kitchen floor, bleeding from his eyes and ears and mouth, his wife Annie tied up but still alive in the living room. He read that twice, one because he and Chimp went way back, and two, as second in command at the firehouse, it was go time now for Jax.

He steeled himself, because there was no time now to mourn.

Just before he got into his car, a vehicle approached, siren blaring, light-bar flashing. Jax shielded his eyes, knew who it was. The car skidded to a halt. The driver's side door opened, and Beth came out running. Jax opened his arms and welcomed Beth into his embrace.

"I heard he came toward the tunnel," she said. "I couldn't get hold of you."

"He's dead, Beth."

She gently pushed away from him, found his eyes. "Rick?"

Jax nodded, clenched his jaw to keep the tears from coming again. "Knox's dead too."

She didn't ask how, and he was glad for it, but she hugged him again, with all her strength this time, and it felt good to hold her body in his arms. He rested his chin atop her head and rubbed her back and told her things were gonna be okay, even though he doubted it. But he knew right then and there that the love of friendship could grow as deep as any other kind of love, and sometimes deeper.

Jax saw the silhouette of a large man in the back of Beth's patrol car. "Who's that?"

"Simon," she said, turning from Jax's arms to face her own car.

"What are you planning on doing with him?"

"Taking him with me."

"Where?"

"Smite House," she said. "There's something you need to see."

*　*　*

Maddy had been anticipating the arrival of the Bettses and their comatose little girl Lauren, from Iowa, all day, fearing they'd back out.

It was a big leap of faith for someone to agree to come here.

After what she'd witnessed inside Doc's office—a man she wished like hell she had gotten a chance to meet—and then later inside his garage, Maddy didn't think she'd have much left in the tank to properly welcome the Betts family, should they come. But when the Bettses pulled into the Duprees' driveway, Maddy had been the first out the door to greet them. And as soon as she saw Lauren Betts inside their van, she remembered her from Lalaland. Like Amy and Sully, this girl had been older over there. Not as old as Amy and Sully, who had been over there longer, but easily a teenager. The connection with the girl was instant, and Maddy wondered if the girl felt it too.

Here, the girl was a year older than both Amy Shimp and Sully, and while nothing as emotionally heart wrenching as the two of them holding hands had occurred, there had been a clear rise in heart rate from all three coma patients as soon as Lauren had been carried into the room by her parents. Enough to get both parents crying, enough to give them the feedback they'd needed to justify the long car trip they'd just made, on a hopeful, desperate whim, delivering their daughter to a house of strangers. Her emergence into the room had done *something*, and for now that was enough.

What they hadn't expected was the arrival, thirty minutes later, of Clare and Steven Farnsley. Steven was a twenty-five-year-old newlywed; he and Clare had been married for six days before he'd slipped from a waterfall and hit his head on a rock bed while hiking on their Jamaican honeymoon. He'd been comatose for just under a month. Maddy had called them earlier in the day, when they'd made all the calls, but the distraught wife, Clare, had hung up on them. Without calling back, without warning Gideon and Maddy that they were coming, Clare, after a good cry, had packed up her new husband and headed here from North Dakota.

Clare's knocking on the Smite House front door had been a surprise, but what had shocked Maddy and Gideon even more, after Archie had excitedly cleared any excess furniture from the parlor to make room for a third bed, was how the three comatose children had shown clear reactions to Steven Farnsley being wheeled into the room with them. Their heart rates had all gone up, just like with Lauren Betts's arrival, but there was also physical movement with all three of them. Their eyelids fluttered. Lauren's head had turned on her pillow, as if following Steven Farnsley's arrival into the room, which had nearly sent her mother into hysterics. And on Sully's bed—she and Gideon had both been watching intently—Amy Shimp squeezed *his* hand. And seconds later he'd squeezed back.

Clare Farnsley was a blubbering crying mess because of it all.

But it wasn't long after their shock had begun to settle into an anxious *What now*, when the gunshots had started outside, when Carson Knox had walked out of his house covered in Lalaland vines—what Maddy remembered were called *creepers* over there—and started shooting.

It wasn't until then, the instant Clare Farnsley had looked up and with true fear in her eyes asked, *What was that?* And Maddy had answered, not yet knowing exactly what it was but assuming that it was bad, that it was hunting season. Maddy then felt a surge of guilt and regret so strong she'd had to sit down before nausea physically took her to the floor.

Because what had they done? What had *she* done? She'd come to Harrod's Reach willingly, with a job and a message. As crazy as it had sounded, she'd done so out of desperation, not so much from this side, but desperation over there.

Because something *big* was coming. She'd heard the tales over there about Mr. Lullaby. The real fears of him finally making his play. About Lalaland not just making trial runs. Not just leaving crumbs. Not just poking fingers through holes to see how deep they went but hoping to come all the way fucking through this time.

Somewhere. Everywhere. All at once.

She didn't know. But desperate times called for desperate measures. So, if she'd lured these other three unknowing families into a town so upset by sudden violence and insanity, over the mere pretense of them *maybe* showing signs of life, she could live with her choices. If she'd talked these unsuspecting families right into the lion's den where killers roamed and the imagination was becoming real, right before their eyes, she'd done it out of desperation.

Even more, out of fear.

* * *

Grover heard gunshots and pressed the panic button beside his bed.

Nurse Natalie was inside the room within thirty seconds, looking exhausted. Overhearing chatter from two other nurses, he knew Natalie had yet to sleep since he'd been taken from the tunnel on a stretcher. And here she was, ready to go to battle again. "Sheriff?"

"I'm fine," he said, before she went into all-out panic mode. He wasn't fine, not yet. The stitching and post-surgery trauma still had him loopy and tired, and the regular doses of hydrocodone were helping to ease it all, but it felt like he'd been through ten different car wrecks. But he told her, "The show must go on."

Natalie sighed. "You can't ring me every time you want a Dr. Pepper."

"Can I have one yet?"

She yawned. "No."

"Jameson?"

"Maybe," she said. "It would probably burn through the stitches. What did you call me in here for?"

"Take me out of here," he said.

"No can do."

"I'm ordering you."

"You're not my boss."

"But I'm still the sheriff." This, at least, gave her pause. "And I heard gunshots."

She folded her arms, looked away, teary-eyed, and right then he knew he had her. He'd missed a lot in the past twenty-four hours and knew he was needed.

Grover said, "Beth is a godsend, Natalie, but she can't deal with this alone."

"You don't know the half of what's going on out there, Grover. It's a war zone."

"Then get me out of here."

"The tunnel . . . I don't even know what it's doing . . ."

"It's coming alive," Grover said. "Isn't it?"

She stared at him, blinked heavily. "How do you know?"

"Because me and Doc have been predicting something like this might happen now for decades. It's a wonder it's taken this long. How is Doc doing?"

She watched him; moisture filled her eyes. "Doc's dead."

Grover steeled himself and fought back tears of his own. "God damn it."

"And Mayor Truffant," she said. "He was left murdered this morning, out by the tunnel. Chimp Deavers was just found dead in his kitchen. They suspect he ate one of the fish that had washed in."

"One of the fish?"

"Yes," she said. "Several of them washed through. Along with some seashells . . ."

"Like what happened in the sixties," he said aloud.

"Carson Knox went on a shooting spree and killed four or five," Natalie said. "Joseph Farrington. Rick Doogan. Both dead. We think Knox went crazy after touching those vines."

"What vines?"

"Ones growing at the tunnel," she said.

"Where's Beth?"

"Smite House. *Everyone* is at the Smite House. Even people from out of town. Other coma patients . . ." She shook her head.

"What?"

"Sully . . . last night, during the party, about the same time you were heading to the tunnel, he woke up for a short time, he—"

"I heard him," Grover said. "I heard his voice, Natalie; except he was a man . . ." Natalie watched him sadly, as if he were delirious, but Grover knew what he heard, knew what he'd seen, that three- to four-second flash of that place. All that color. "There *is* another side."

"There's always been two sides, Grover. You're talking nonsense. You need to sleep."

He looked at her, lowered his voice to an octave that had always worked with Beth, grabbed her hand, and said, "Take me. To the Smite House. Please."

The tears came then. She laughed, wiped at them, said, "Might get me fired, but how can I say no to that?"

* * *

Inside the third-floor penthouse suite of the Beehive Hotel, Belinda Lomax told her son Theodore, "Sit down."

And he did, without question, having been summoned by Brandy at Mother Lomax's request, five minutes ago. Theodore pulled an antique wooden chair to where she lay on the bed, and sat, facing her, his eyes so focused they burrowed. Antlers large enough now that he'd had to duck upon entering the suite. Beard so fully grown that the white circular patch on his left cheek showed in full.

"That Brandy is a peach," Belinda said.

"Don't I know it."

It warmed her heart to see her son's sudden fondness for her. The *real* her. Well, the real her ever since she'd been pulled from the Harrod's Reach tunnel as a little girl—that girl was long gone and never coming back. "You don't know, do you? What she really is. Your Black Widow?"

"She's a killer of men. I know that much."

"But do you know *what* she is? Or even who she *was*?" He looked confused, so she added. "Brandy Lucado? Popular real estate agent in the Tampa area. Pretty face on billboards. Engaged to be married to her coworker, Roger Prentis. All *before* the mare got her . . ."

"What mare? What are you talking about?"

She adjusted herself on the bed so that she could better face him. "There's a family of doctors in a town called Crooked Tree. Inside an old mansion called Blackwood, they've learned how to trap nightmares inside books. Thousands of books, Theodore. Thousands of nightmares. And they've been doing this for over a hundred years. Trapping them.

"But sometimes they get out," she said. "Sometimes the books are opened and they get out. Similar to what happened to me inside the tunnel here, when I was a girl, they . . . they latch on. They go on mare rides. They become real. Imaginations come to life. They're out there by the thousands, and your Brandy, your Black Widow, is one of them."

Teddy leaned forward, as if eager for more.

"*She* is someone's nightmare, Theodore—a mare," said Belinda. "I confronted her. Once the mare latched on, and she'd begun . . . transitioning, her fiancé left her. She became the Black Widow, a nightmare made flesh. Except the nightmare had evolved, to what you see now. But once a mare rides you, they're on for good."

"Mother . . ."

"Yes?"

"What are you saying?"

"Your Lullaby Express . . . they're all mares. Someone's nightmare."

"I came to them," he said. "I made the stops. But why did I bring them *here*?"

"Because it pays to kill multiple birds with one stone," she said. "Because violence begets violence. Because *every* bee needs a hive, Theodore. Because once there's a rip, once things start to open, you need more hands to open it wider. And you didn't come to them, my son, *they* came to you. Like mosquitoes to pond water, they came to you . . ."

"Why?"

"Oh, Theodore." She stared at his antlers. "You know in Lalaland there are no mistakes." She adjusted herself on the bed. "You want to know about your father?" He nodded. She gazed at her boy, now a man set to become so much more—*she* hadn't been the only one touched by what was coming through that tunnel. This tunnel and others like it, like the small, covered footbridge in the Virginia backwoods at home, the one she'd burned to the ground when Theodore was a boy, along with the moth-covered mare tree he'd discovered next to it, all because she'd feared him learning that his father was a dream. A nightmare. An imagining. Truth was, his father could have been any one of a dozen men she'd slept with around that time, but she didn't think so. Even now, she could still clearly hear his deep, gravelly voice, smell his rotten breath, hear his whispered words—those lullabies with which he teased and taunted during the passionate throes. *I know what you are*, he'd hissed . . .

"I was walking through the woods like I did most mornings," she said. "I typically ended up at the footbridge, and I'd often walk through it. It sounds silly, but I pretended it was a rebirth every morning, to walk that bridge and come out the other side." Her eyes narrowed on him. "And I know you used to walk the footbridge at home, Theodore. I warned you against it, but I know you went through there just to spite me."

"I lived my life to spite you," he said.

She smiled. "That morning, at the footbridge, right on the floorboards, was a pile of acorns. They were not of this world . . . they were red as apples with orange tops. I knew right away not to touch therm. Not with my hands, at least, so I nudged them with my foot. They scattered like dice, but I knew something was afoot inside that bridge. I knew the feeling. I'd felt it before inside *this* tunnel, here, and I'd be lying if I said I wasn't drawn to it.

"The next morning, I came back. The acorns were gone, but strands of vines grew between the cracks of the floorboards. Laces of purple and pink, white, and gold . . . of *imagination*, Theodore. The air, it felt like someone was watching me. I heard footsteps in the leaves. And that's when I saw the first moth on that tree. But the next day, there were dozens."

"Moths?"

"Yes," she said. "And the leaves, even though it was the dead of summer, had begun to turn white, and then fall. I picked one up. It was brittle and delicate, and practically disintegrated in my fingers. In the thirty minutes I was in this tunnel here, as a girl, waiting to be rescued, I saw Lalaland, in all its magical beauty and grandeur." She leaned back against the headboard. "Oh, that day, how I wanted to go there and never come out, but *she* was already inside me. This *thing* from Lalaland, and she was stronger, and I was just a little girl. She wanted it more, you know. She wanted a taste of this side and there was nothing I could do to stop her. Nothing I could do but hold on for the ride, and here I am. But, Theodore, I digress . . ."

"The footbridge."

"Yes, the footbridge," she said. "For six nights I returned to it, only to find something new coming from it, *blooming* from it. Those vines. Leaves. Strange colored insects. Odd flowers with purple stems and black petals. Yellow grass that was spreading by the day."

"You were being watched?"

"Like whispers. I even felt it inside my home. On the sixth night of that week, I dreamt someone was in the bedroom with me. Touching me. Caressing me." She put a finger to her lips. "Shhh . . . shhh . . ."

"What?"

"That's what the voice did," she said. "It shushed me. It was all around me." She pointed to her temple. "But also, in here. Don't open your eyes, the voice said. *Shhhh . . . shhh . . .* and he started singing Brahms's Lullaby, 'The Cradle Song' . . . *Lullaby and good night . . .*" she sang softly. ". . . *with roses bed light. Creep into thy bed, there pillow thy head . . .*

"I woke up," Belinda said. "My windows were open. A breeze blew through the house like it had a mind of its own. I followed it. The back door was open. Brittle white leaves blew through. I stepped on one accidently, crushing it into dust. I followed my instincts into the woods and didn't stop until I reached the moonlit footbridge, where more of those black flowers had sprouted in the yellow grass. They were roses, black roses with purple stems. And inside the footbridge, a dusting of sand covered the floorboards. Not sand like from a beach but more like dry desert sand, and just enough of it to show footprints of what quite possibly had come through."

"Come though from where, Mother?" her son asked.

"From Lalaland, Theodore, because this tunnel here isn't the only door," she said. "But those weren't human footprints. More like hooves of a deer, except larger. But how these prints were distanced from one another, they made me think that whatever had come through had been upright, on two legs instead of four. And I heard the voice again in the woods, the *shhh . . . shhh . . .* and I knew it was real. I collapsed in the grass. The tree was visible, and by then every leaf had fallen. The bark had begun to turn black, and the moths, oh, Theodore, the moths, they were drinking by the thousands . . .

"And still, the wind, that voice, it shushed me, and then came the lullaby, a different one, but that voice was so hauntingly familiar that I gave in to it. In mind and body, I closed my eyes and gave in." She started to softly sing in recollection, "*Hush-a-bye, don't you cry. Go to sleep little baby. When you awake, you shall have all the pretty little horses.*" She stopped abruptly and stared at her son.

"Let them do what they need to do," she said, and could tell he knew exactly what she meant, that she was referring to the mares he'd brought on the Lullaby Express. "Open the doors and let them feast. Let them be the bait. The lighthouse in the fog." She leaned toward him. "Violence begets violence. Let them be the *pull* from here. And you put people there, in Lalaland, for the *push*."

He nodded, licked his lips, like he finally understood.

She relaxed back into her pillow, recalling the words that voice had whispered to her inside the footbridge that night as he entered her: "*Black and bays, dapples and grays, coach and six-a-little horses.*" She stopped abruptly and eyed her son. "And you do what *you* came here to do, what you came here to finish *becoming* . . ."

"I don't know what you mean . . ."

"Then take me back to that place, Theodore."

"How?"

"You *know* how," she hissed. "That voice in your head is real, Theodore."

"Mr. Lullaby . . ."

"Is you now," she said, letting the words settle. "Put the world to sleep, Theodore. Take me back to Lalaland."

CHAPTER

40

Teddy

Now

"SHHH . . . SHHH . . . SHHH . . . ," Teddy shushed his mother, who lay now with her eyes closed on the bed, hands folded, and fingers interlaced on her frail chest.

Teddy stood from his chair and put his lips next to her ear. "Hush-a-bye, don't you cry. Go to sleep, little baby. Hush-a-bye, don't you cry. Go to sleep, little baby."

He waited, listened to his mother's silent breathing. Never had he felt such power, such utter authority. The voice—his own voice—sounded inside his head . . . *the deep sleep* . . . That's what this was. That's what he'd just done to his mother. With his words alone, with his whispered lullaby, he'd sent his mother to Lalaland.

And something told him it could not be so easily *undone*. Because things were starting to make sense now. *Put the world to sleep, Teddy . . .*

"Mr. Lullaby," he said aloud, into the room, loving the sound of it.

. . . put them all to sleep . . .

He watched his mother's face from inches away.

. . . put enough of them over there . . .

The way her eyes barely moved behind closed lids.

. . . so that you can open all *the doors to here . . .*

The tiny intakes and out pushes of air at her nostrils.

. . . and then let all of Lalaland in . . .

All the age lines and wrinkles, the freckles and the pores and tiny little hairs.

. . . let it all start blooming . . .

Aside from the subtle rise and fall of her chest, she slept so deeply anyone else might have thought her dead.

The door to the suite opened. The click-clack of high-heeled shoes entered the room, approached him from behind. Teddy turned, faced Brandy. He opened his arms to her and said, "She told you?"

Brandy gazed up at him. "Yes."

"We need to open the hotel doors and let them all out."

She tiptoed, kissed his lips. "I already did."

Excerpt from Detective Harrington's notes
July 17, 1969
Harrod's Reach

*O*NE OF THESE *days I'm going to close the tunnel for good. Dynamite would do the trick to bring it all down upon itself, and maybe then I'll get a good night's sleep. But nothing troubles me more than pulling an out-of-towner out of the tunnel, especially a child. The locals know better. And the kids should have, but oh how that tunnel is a temptress, and if ifs and buts were coconuts, well, I don't know how the rest of it goes, but at roughly 10:30 this morning, I was called to yet another emergency inside the tunnel. Belinda Lomax, age 11 (and granddaughter to the talent singing last night at the Beehive), was invited by some local children to play down by the tunnel. During a game of In-One-Out-One (started in the late eighteen hundreds after the disappearance of Connie Brine, when, legend claims, in the fall of 1868, she ran in one side of the tunnel and never came out the other), Belinda Lomax entered the tunnel and didn't come back out the other side. The kids waited, and then, in a panic, hurried for help. Thirty minutes later, I found Belinda Lomax passed out in the middle of the tunnel. She awoke after I picked her up. I could tell how terrified she was by how hard she clung to my neck. She asked why I was crying. I told her it was because I found her. But in my head, I was thinking about the previous fall, in October of '68, when* kids claimed Bret Jones entered one end and never came out the other, and that he was never found. The little girl then said, "Did you see it?" I said, "See what, dear?" And she said, "That place. It's a painting." At which point I rested her head on my shoulder and told her I'd get her right back to her grandfather.

41

Beth

Now

BETH HAD BEEN present at too many parties at the Smite House to count, but she'd never witnessed anything like this.

The weird combination of locals and total strangers. The fear and anxiety, and now joy, so soon after Natalie had rolled Sheriff Meeks inside the living room to a burst of applause, which Grover was quick to wave away. Quick to accept Beth's hug, her tears on his cheek. Quick to pop another hydrocodone and immediately get to work. But no one seemed more out of place than Simple Simon, who'd been migrating from room to room since his arrival two hours ago, hugging the *Lalaland* book to his chest, avoiding the rest of the crowd.

The Beehive up the street may have been preparing to open, but the buzz was all here, inside the Smite House, and Archie, despite the madness going on *outside* the house, was smiling for the first time since Sully's accident. Welcoming and greeting and opening every renovated room he'd been working on for the past two decades. Roaming with his tools strapped around his waist, sagging like Han Solo's gun belt.

Natalie, after Beth ordered her to, took a badly needed nap on the living room couch. A newly stoked fire inside the hearth warmed the room. Brody was asleep on Beth's shoulder. She paced with him, hoping he'd be out enough to place down on a bed soon. Jax sat in a corner reading chair, still in shock after what had happened to Rick Doogan down at the tunnel. Firelight illuminated the left side of his face. His cheeks were wet. She left him alone to grieve and walked through the foyer, past the front entry staircase, and entered the dining room, where she found Maxine sitting alone in the dark.

"You okay?" Beth asked.

"Yeah, I think so," she said.

"Looks like someone lit a fire under Archie."

Maxine might have smiled; it was hard to tell in the dark. "This was what he always envisioned for this house. Well . . . not this, but . . ." Beth watched Maxine stare out the bay window. The hotel held her gaze. Maxine said, "I know what you're thinking."

"What am I thinking?"

Maxine nodded toward the window, toward the Beehive Hotel in the distance. "Same thing Gideon's been thinking since he came home and saw me. The hotel."

"It was just more noticeable to him," said Beth. "To me it was more gradual. I see you every day. I didn't notice. And it was none of my business, even if I had."

"Is it a crime to want to feel young again? Recapture youth? To try and feel just a little bit of happiness?"

Brody shifted against Beth's neck. She rubbed his back. "My arm's asleep."

Maxine held out her arms. "I'll take him. I know you're itching to get out there. And I know there's nothing I can say to keep you in."

Beth handed Brody off to Maxine; it was seamless, they'd made the transfer too often for it not to be, and Beth couldn't help but feel guilty for it. If only Maxine knew who she was really holding. Something in her glance told her maybe she did. "Maxine?"

"Yes?" she stroked Brody's back, kissed the top of his head.

"Why did you agree to work with him?" Beth asked. "With Mickey French. When you knew what it did to Archie when he bought it."

She sat silent for a moment, and then said, "Because we'd stopped dancing." A short laugh followed. "Because we'd stopped dancing. I know it sounds silly."

"No, it doesn't. I remember," Beth said, reminiscing; at night, after dinner, and sometimes during the cooking of it, how Archie would spontaneously turn on the music—typically Sinatra—and grab his wife's hand, and they'd dance. She'd smile and laugh, and he would gaze into her eyes like she was the most prized catch in the ocean. Beth had wondered if her own parents had ever done anything like this. "I spent a lot of time here as a little girl. I remember the two of you dancing. Envy, I suppose, is what I'd feel, watching the two of you."

Maxine stared up at the ceiling; Archie was up there now, in one of the rooms, getting it ready for someone to sleep in. "It was never more than one song," she said, returning her eyes to the window. "But it was enough." It had all come crashing down after Sully's accident. They'd not only stopped dancing, but they'd stopped communicating, stopped living, stopped being married, and perhaps that's what it all was to Maxine Dupree—all of those things, bundled into one word—dancing. "I thought maybe it would make him jealous. I thought it would help move him from his grief, somehow. I thought it would make him . . ."

"Want to dance?"

"Yes," she said. "But it only made him angry. It turned him inward, suspicious." She rubbed Brody's back; the boy snored lightly, his rosebud lips parted, head cocked to the side against her chest. "I got fit. I dressed younger. It was only natural, as coworkers, that I would spend more time with Mickey, and yes, I knew he was a salesman, of the cheesiest sort. And still is, but he has youthful energy . . . he . . ."

"He has charm," Beth said. "And the looks . . ."

"And the money to buy what we never did," Maxine was quick to add. "And when you came down to it, that was the dagger." She sighed. "I'm going to hell."

"You're not going to hell, Maxine."

She stared out the window. "I suppose hell has decided to come to us."

That got Beth back into work mode.

"Did you sleep with him?" asked Gideon from the kitchen's entrance to the dining room.

"Gideon . . . ," Maxine said, "How long have you been listening?"

"Long enough."

Beth said, "Gideon, not now."

"Then when?"

"It's none of our business," Beth said.

"Yes," said Maxine. "It is." She turned toward her son. "And *no*, I didn't."

"There we go," said Beth.

"Call it an emotional affair," Maxine said. "Maybe that's worse, but no, I didn't. It never crossed my mind. I love your father, Gideon. Maybe we're no longer *in* love, but I love him."

The room went silent. Something about having Gideon in the same room with them now, with Maxine holding her son—their son—made Beth anxious.

Gideon might have sensed what she was thinking. "What?"

"Nothing," Beth said. "Is everything okay in there?"

In there, Beth thought, Sully's bedroom, now the sudden living quarters for four.

"Yeah, they're fine. I mean, the same, I guess. Maddy's with them. And the parents."

Beth asked Maxine, "When was the last time you saw Mickey?"

"I don't know," she said. "More than a week I'd say. I was so busy with the party—"

"Have you seen his face? Somebody beat him up good. And he's acting strange," Beth said. "I think he's hiding people inside the hotel."

"Like who?"

"Whoever's out there killing . . . Do you have hotel keys?"

"I don't." She stood slowly from the table, careful not to jostle Brody. "I'm sorry." She kissed Brody's head. "But if that's what you think, just break down the goddamn doors."

Maxine Dupree never cursed, and Beth had never heard her say the Lord's name in vain, so the silence as she left the dining room was palpable. She stopped next to Gideon at the entryway to the kitchen and watched them both. "Perhaps it's time to tell him, Beth."

And then she walked out of the room, leaving Beth and Gideon alone.

Gideon said, "Tell me what?"

Beth faced the bay window, watched the street. "About Brody."

"What about Brody?"

"That he's definitely got your nose."

CHAPTER

42

Gideon

Now

GIDEON STOOD SPEECHLESS.
Of all things, thinking back to sixth grade sex-ed when Mrs. Masterson had told them it only took one time. Half the class had snickered, and she'd reiterated her point with another lecture on the anatomy diagrams she'd propped on the ledge of the chalkboard. Gideon hadn't laughed then, but something amid all the current chaos made him laugh now.

"What the hell's funny?" Beth asked, finally turning to face him from the bay window.

"Mrs. Masterson," he said.

She shook her head, smiled. "It only takes one time."

And then he went quiet again, because it was no longer funny. But never had—it only took one time—hit home more than now, because one time was all he'd ever done it. With Beth. With anyone. Overseas, when so many paid next to nothing for their whores, he'd stayed in. When so many soldiers frequented the bars on foreign land and later got lucky, he stayed in. Partially, because that just wasn't him, but also because none of them were Beth, and that night before his deployment had been so finely ingrained into him that he'd had no reason to hunt for another. His bedroom door opening, her sneaking in, putting a finger to her lips as she stepped out of her skirt and climbed atop his bed. Atop him. When he wanted to open his mouth and ask her what she was doing she put that finger to his lips. So after a while he stopped asking. He let her do what she'd come to do, and that much became clear to him very quickly. She'd winced and bit her lower lip when he entered her, like she was in pain after gently forcing her weight down atop him. And there was blood, which at first freaked him out and almost got him to talking, before she put that finger to his lips again to shush him. Whispered to him that it was normal for the first time. Because by then she'd settled into something and was moving atop him like he'd always dreamed she would. Except he'd dreamed she'd be bare breasted instead of fully clothed up top and would be calling his name instead of staying quiet and holding her eyes closed, which made it, even during the few seconds it took him to climax, more like a business transaction than anything passionate and arousing for her. She'd collapsed on him directly after, but only stayed that way for a moment before slithering off, putting her skirt back on, and sneaking back out of the room. The next day when they gave him his send-off, she hugged him and held him for an extra beat, long enough to whisper in his ear, "Be careful, Giddy-Up."

And he'd teared up right then and there, because he still smelled her from last night, because he'd skipped his shower just so he didn't have to wash her off of him.

And right now, he finally conjured the courage to say, "Why did you do it?"

"Because if I was ever going to have a kid, I wanted yours." She grinned at him. "And we both knew it . . ."

"It only takes once," he finished for her.

"Yes," she said. "Or I got lucky."

"And how do you know he's not Jax's?"

She laughed. "Because I know."

He moved behind her, touched her shoulder. "Why that night? Why the desperation before I left?"

She turned to him. "Honestly?"

"You've never given it any other way."

"You've always been afraid of your own shadow, Gideon," she said. "I really didn't think you'd make it back."

He stood next to her; they both watched the street, the lit-up Beehive at the top of it. "But would it have killed you to kiss me?"

Just when he thought she might answer, she shushed him, and then pointed out toward the streetlamp's fuzzy glow.

He followed her finger to the road, and immediately saw what she saw.

Not one massive black deer, but three, with full-sized racks of reddish-orange antlers.

43

Maddy

Now

BETH HAD WARNED everyone in the Smite House she was bringing Simon Bowles inside.

Maddy, at the time, had looked at Gideon. "Who's Simon?"

"That's who Beth had in lockup for suspicion of attempting to kill Sheriff Meeks with his chainsaw," Gideon had told her. "Otherwise, he's the town idiot."

Archie had overheard his son on his way to open the front door, preparing to personally escort Simon and Beth into the foyer. "He's no idiot," Archie had said. "Not even close."

"And it wasn't him," said Sheriff Meeks, wheeling himself into the foyer from an adjacent room. "It was a woman."

Gideon turned on him. "A woman?"

"Woman big as a man," he said, repositioning his trademark Stetson on his crop of gray hair, just as Archie opened the door.

In walked Beth, followed by Simon, who had to duck as he entered. Right away, Maddy knew she'd seen this hulk of a man before, the only man she'd ever seen bigger than her attacker back in Charleston. He had a thick, orange photo album–sized book hugged to his chest as he entered, clearly not liking the attention.

It was Sheriff Meeks who suggested everyone go about their business and give him some space. Maddy listened, but for the next hour found herself following Simon, and perhaps looking for an opportunity to talk to him. As the night went on, she became more convinced she'd seen him before, somehow, in Lalaland. And then it clicked. She found the boxes of files they'd brought back from Doc Bigsby's house on a table in the first-floor library and hunted through them for Detective Harrington's notes. Five minutes later she found the one she was looking for, detailing the day Simon, as a boy, had gone missing and was found later, sleeping out by the tunnel. At the end of Harrington's notes, which she read more thoroughly now, Simon's parents had spoken about his sleepwalking, and more importantly how often and how deeply their son slept. She found it: *Lalaland.* His parents said that's what Simon called it when he slept. He visited Lalaland.

She then searched the house for Simon, finding him alone in the second-floor library, pacing with his head down and hugging the orange *Lalaland* book to his chest.

She knocked on the open threshold before entering. He gave her a glance, but otherwise continued pacing. "Do you mind if I come in? Simon? That's your name, right?" He nodded. She entered, but kept her distance. "Lot of books," she said, not very good at small talk. "Do you like books?"

He nodded, squeezed his book closer to his chest.

"Do you mind looking at me, Simon? I won't hurt you." What a stupid thing to say, she thought. She was half his size. Yet he turned toward her, and even leveled his eyes on her, briefly, before looking back to his book. Maddy stepped closer. "I've seen you before."

He studied her, smiled. "You made it back."

His voice surprised her. One, because he spoke, and two, it was even deeper than she'd imagined. "Yes . . . I made it back."

"From Lalaland," he said.

She inched closer; she wanted to look at his book but played it cool. "Simon, can you . . . come and go, from Lalaland?"

He nodded. "Come and go. Come and go. Simon says. Deep sleep."

Maddy swallowed over the lump in her throat. A memory came back to her of Simon, over there, biting into the charred leg of a giant bird, chewing heartily, grease on his beard, shoulders covered in prized animal pelts like some king—this one the skin of a Wendigo, he'd told them, in much less broken speech—before he stood suddenly, dropped the bird leg, walked into the adjacent field of black roses, and disappeared before her eyes.

Because he'd woken up at that instant, she thought now. But it was clear she not only remembered him, but he'd recognized her. Sully had been important in Lalaland, and still was, and the same went for Amy, and the two new comatose arrivals inside the Smite House, but this man, she remembered now, had been like a king. He'd walked out of the ocean and entered their village at Four-Tree Bluff and immediately commanded respect, especially from Sully.

Because . . . because . . .

"Simon? Who are the Elders?"

Simon started to speak, but stopped, as if unsure how to explain what he might know.

Maddy stepped to within a few feet of him. His clothes smelled of body odor and tree sap. "Can I see your book? Your artwork?"

"Lalaland," he said. "Simon says. Lalaland." He opened it on one of the library tables.

Each page was bright with color, with expertly drawn and conceived renderings of what Maddy knew Lalaland to be. She turned each page and found her hands trembling with horrifying recognition. Every animal and creature of lore, every landmark and detail so vividly drawn. It was real. So real she felt like the book could at any moment reach out and pull her back in. Page after colorful page. She looked up, found him proudly watching her. "You drew all of this?"

He nodded. "From my sleeps."

She turned one page, and then the next, and the next, mesmerized with pangs of déjà vu and awe. She'd only been aware of the Seers, her fellow coma patients, but who were the Elders?

"Simon, are you an Elder?"

He shook his head, briefly looked troubled, and said, "Soon."

CHAPTER

44

Beth

Now

NOW THAT SHERIFF Meeks had his Stetson back on his head and another hydrocodone in his bloodstream, he was happy to hold down the fort at the Smite House while Beth and Gideon checked out the Beehive Hotel up the street.

"If I didn't know you better, I'd say be careful," Grover said to Beth at the front door.

She kissed the white stubble on Grover's cheek, said she'd try, and then walked with Gideon out toward where they'd seen the three black deer on Mallard Street. The deer had moved on, somewhere, but if there were three, there could be more.

"You armed?" she asked Gideon.

He showed her the handgun at his belt, the same one he'd nearly used inside the gym at his party. Gideon held it in his right hand as they closed in on the hotel. Sweat had broken out across his brow, and he was breathing heavily.

"You okay?" she asked.

He nodded, eyes trained on the hotel, the eerily quiet dark. But he didn't look okay. In the moonlight, he looked especially pale.

Footsteps sounded behind them. Beth looked over her shoulder to find Jax approaching with a shotgun in his hands. "I thought I told—"

"I'm fine," Jax said, catching up. "You're not going in there alone."

"She's not alone," Gideon said.

"Shut the fuck up, Giddy-Up." Jax pressed ahead of them toward the sidewalk leading up to the black and yellow double doors. "She might as well be."

Beth said, "Jax, you're still too—"

"Emotional?" he sprang on her. His cheeks were still wet from recent tears. "Too raw?"

Gideon said, "I heard about what—"

"I said shut the fuck up, right?"

"And I'm sorry," Gideon finished, almost defiantly. Beth thought that was maybe the end of it until Gideon said, "At least now I know who that belt belonged to."

Jax raised the shotgun, pointed it right at Gideon's chest. "The fuck you say?"

"Jax." Beth held her arm out. "Lower the goddamn gun."

Jax's arms shook. Tears welled. His jaw trembled. He listened to his wife and lowered the shotgun. What shocked Beth was that Gideon had his weapon raised and pointed right back at Jax, with no hesitation at all.

Beth moved on toward the hotel without another word, and assumed Gideon had finally lowered his gun, because both men were following her now. She started to knock on the yellow door before noticing it was slightly ajar.

Beth called out, "Mickey?" She gave it a second before nudging the door open wider and entering the grand lobby, which was fully lit up. Had there not been a blood-soaked body in the middle of the black-and-white checkered floor, she would have taken a moment to enjoy the historical ambience, the visual tiptoe back through time, because the lobby looked grand indeed, from the bar to the fancy tables and extravagant chandelier to the muraled walls and Beehive Hotel letters overlooking it all.

She approached the body. It was fully clothed in what looked like painters' attire, but resting there, oddly contorted, with a puddle of blood next to what was left of the face, which appeared to have been battered into the floor so many times it was hard to decipher exactly what parts of the face were left. No use checking for a pulse; the body wasn't moving.

But somebody was snoring.

Beth stepped around the slain body and followed the sound.

Gideon located it first, behind the bar, and said, "Over here."

They found Mickey on the floor behind the bar, but unlike the man in the middle of the lobby, Mickey wasn't bloody, or dead, but was instead in such a deep sleep that he didn't awaken even after Beth knelt and shook him. Not once, but three times, harder each time she put her hand to his shoulder. Mickey's face was busted up. No more so than she'd seen earlier in the day at the open door, but he was shirtless and his chest and abdomen were bandaged, with spots of blood over whatever wounds festered beneath.

Jax knelt beside Beth, shoved Mickey harder than Beth had, and shouted "Hey! Mickey!" But Mickey didn't so much as flinch.

"It's like he's hibernating," Gideon said.

Jax said, "What the fuck happened here, Beth?"

"I don't know." She stood, surveyed the lobby, didn't like how quiet it was. She knew there were more people here, possibly as many as could fit in that red bus parked out back, the Lullaby Express, as it said on the dash, but where were they now? She had a notion to split up, but thought better of it. Two hallways led east and west from the grand lobby, and they searched the east hallway first. While every door was closed, none were locked, and some knobs had yet to be installed. One by one they opened rooms on either side of the hallway, and either called out that they were occupied but clear, or completely empty and unoccupied. Most, Beth noted, appeared to have someone living in them.

And while the Beehive was ornate and fancy and three stories tall, it had never had an abundant number of rooms. But with each room checked, and with each room tallied, Beth's radar went deeper into focus. Because maybe that bus *had* been full of passengers. Full of whackos and murderers and misfits and they'd been living here right under their noses for how long? Days? A week or more? The west wing was much the same, as were both hallways on the second floor, where Beth had noted not only luggage and clothes strewn about, but in a couple of rooms things that made no sense. In room 218, atop the desk at the window, they'd found an impressive collection of matchbooks and lighters inside a shoebox. In room 204 overlooking the woods, they'd found the bed neatly made, but with a pile of hair left in the middle of it, next to a straight razor. Hair from a head, and smaller hair that could have come from someone's arms and legs, but enough to make Gideon almost gag when he saw it. On the floor next to the bed, next to a pile of male clothes, was a large bucket full of wet plaster, with drippings from it left all over the hardwood floor. On the third floor, in room 311, they'd found a cluster of horseshoes resting on the floor beside the bed, and more than one of them, Beth noticed, looked stained by blood.

At that point, Gideon started fuming. Started pacing the room like a moth caught in a lampshade. Mumbling, "He's here. He was here." And only then did Beth realize the depths to which Gideon had fallen for Maddy Boyle. Enough for Jax to put a hand on his shoulder and tell him, "Take it easy. We'll find him."

Inside the third-floor penthouse suite, they found a four-poster king-sized bed occupied by a woman who was borderline elderly. A wheelchair sat next to the bed. Like Mickey downstairs, this woman was asleep. Like Mickey, she didn't open her eyes or awaken no matter what they did to try and wake her.

"They're hibernating," Gideon said. "It's like someone put them in a coma."

Beth's cell phone started ringing. She pulled it from her pocket and saw it was Father Fred from St. Michael. "Father?"

"Beth, I don't know what's going on," Father Fred said, sounding desperate. "I just found Deacon Jim on a couch in the rectory. He's asleep. Passed out, or something, but I can't get him awake. He's completely unresponsive."

"Father, slow down."

"But that's not all, I'm in here with Kathy Clark, the sacristan, and she's asleep too, right on top one of the church pews. I can't wake her up . . ."

"Father, I don't know what's going on, but get out," Beth said, thinking whoever did this to Mickey and the woman here on the third floor of the Beehive, was possibly now inside the church. "Come to the Smite House. There's plenty of room there."

"The Smite House . . . why? Beth, what's going on?"

"I don't know yet, but we might need your help there."

She hung up, didn't have time for questions.

The power went off.

Gideon jumped, raised his gun, turned with it toward every noise in the room.

"Easy, Giddy-Up," said Jax, illuminating the room with a flashlight he'd had hanging from his belt. The woman on the bed slept on.

Beth looked out the window toward the street. Electricity still hummed through streetlamps and house windows, so the power had only been shut off at the Beehive. The three of them moved from the suite and into the only hallway they'd yet to check, and door by door—all were clear until Gideon opened one in the middle of the hallway and quietly said, "Hello. Hey . . . you there, turn around."

Beth approached the room slowly, as did Jax from the opposite direction with his flashlight. Gideon's gun was leveled, but both of his arms shook. He swallowed heavy and loud. Beth sidled next to Gideon, saw into the room, saw what he was seeing. Dozens of dolls rested on the bed. A man with close-cropped hair sat in a chair with his back to the door, sewing. It wasn't until Jax arrived with his light that Beth realized what it was atop the desk.

A body; a woman strewn across the top of it, legs dangling off one edge of the desk.

The man's head and shoulders blocked the view of her torso as he continued to pull thread.

Beth said, "Stand up. Stop what you're doing and stand up. Right now."

The man froze, right hand in the air, needle pinched between his thumb and index finger.

Gideon's arms trembled. Beth whispered to him to lower his gun because right now she didn't trust him. It was his party entrance into the gym all over again. But he didn't. He kept his gun leveled on the man no matter how violently his arms shook.

The man stood, slowly, giving Beth a glimpse of what he'd been sewing. Much like with Mayor Truffant at the tunnel, he was sewing a large swath of cloth to this woman's face, and without warning he turned toward them in an all-out sprint. The move caught Jax so off guard he dropped his flashlight as he raised his gun. The beam strobed across the room and the flashlight rolled, and the man continued toward them. From the hazy edges of the flashlight beam, Beth saw that his face was made up like a doll, stitched from the same type of cloth he was using on the woman, with buttons at his eyes.

Before Beth could pull the trigger, a shot rang out from directly beside her, from Gideon's gun. The human doll flung back, landed on the floor. Gideon screamed, fired a second time, plugging the man in the chest, and then a third, approaching the slain man, step by step, firing bullet after bullet until his gun clicked empty, until the man was a bloody, unmoving mess on the floor, until Gideon stood crying and Jax corralled him into a hug.

CHAPTER

45

Gideon

Now

As Beth nudged the dead man with her foot, Gideon stood trembling beside them, the gun hanging in his hand like a heavy dumbbell. "I froze," he said. "I froze."

"You didn't freeze, Gideon," said Beth.

Jax picked up his flashlight. "That was the exact opposite of freezing, Giddy-Up, you—"

"Don't call me Giddy-Up," he said. "Don't fucking call me Giddy-Up. And I froze. Over there. I froze and then I panicked."

"Overseas," Beth said to Jax. "He's talking about—"

"Yeah . . . overseas . . ."

"Well, you didn't panic here, bro," said Jax.

Gideon closed his eyes, saw gunshot flashes in the dark, heard children screaming. "I shot a kid. They weren't supposed to be in there. It was dark. I shot a kid." Beth grabbed his arm, walked with him back into the hallway. "Bullets . . . everywhere," Gideon said, legs trembling, heart still racing from having unloaded his weapon for the first time since that raid. The colonel's voice in his ear, *Well done, soldier, there's collateral damage in war, you either kill or be killed . . .* "I shot myself. I'm not a hero. I panicked. I shot through my own leg."

Instead of finishing the room-to-room search on the third floor, Beth, with the aid of Jax's flashlight, ushered Gideon down the stairwell to the first floor, with soft words of *come on*, and *let's get you out of here*. But when they entered the grand lobby, the front door was open again. They heard laughter to the right of the bar, and then a voice. "Shhh, he's sleeping." But with a lisp, so that sleeping came out *thleeping*.

Gideon disengaged from Beth's hand lock on his arm, tried to pinpoint where the voice had come from.

Jax pointed his flashlight behind the bar, said of Mickey, "He's still out."

Beth said, "Then who else is in here?"

"I am," came a hushed male voice in the shadows across the lobby.

Jax pointed his flashlight, saw nothing by the mural on the far wall.

Gideon pointed his gun again, realized he had no more bullets, but kept it aimed.

Beth said, "Show yourself."

The flick of a lighter sounded—like an old-timey Zippo—and briefly, a section of the grand lobby was illuminated enough to reveal a crouched figure in the dark. There and gone again, swallowed by the shadows. The figure laughed.

Jax's light hit that spot, but the man was gone.

"Who are you?" Gideon asked, following the shuffled movement.

"I'm Freddie," the voice said, closer to the door now. "Firestarter Freddie." Starter came out like *thtarter*. The laugh, and then, "I thtart fires. Thath what I do."

He flicked the lighter again, allowed it to glow for two seconds and then it went out.

Jax shined his light, finally caught the man, running, hunched over toward the front doors. Beth fired, missed. Plaster dust puffed from the wall. The man laughed again, and just as Jax froze him in his light, and as Gideon started a run to stop him, the front door flung open.

Backlit by moonlight, the silhouette of something monstrous filled the doorway. Firestarter Freddie slithered out the door just as the beast came in. But it wasn't a monster. It was a deer, ink-black like the three they'd seen out on Mallard Street earlier, except this one was large as an elk, with antlers to match the size. And as it craned its head to fit the rack of antlers through the doorway, Gideon saw crystallized breath jet out from the deer's nostrils, like an odd change in temperature only they could feel.

If what was coming through that tunnel was getting larger and larger, Gideon thought, what could possibly come next?

Its massive hooves clip-clopped over the lobby's checkered tile floor, cracking some of them under its weight. Jax hit it with the light, and through the haze of dust motes, the deer's red, oval eyes lit up. Its hair was thick and black and contracted, standing on end, like he'd seen white-tails do when showing aggression. The horns were a deep shade of red with orange swirls and looked luridly wet in the flashlight glow.

Gideon said, "That's blood."

Beth nodded in agreement and motioned them both toward the open door. The deer clip-clopped, aggressively prancing in a circle. It faked an attack and they all jumped back. "Go," Beth said. Gideon inched his way toward the door, but stopped, because he was tired of going. Tired of running. Tired of being Giddy-Up Gideon. "Gideon, go," she said again. But he didn't. Jax stayed put too, eyeing the deer, keeping his flashlight trained on it, as if daring it to come get him. Gideon recalled what Maddy had said about these deer, about how they hunted. And it sure looked like this one was in the middle of hunting season, because that *was* blood dripping down those sharp antlers. Beth said, "Jax, don't do anything stupid."

But Jax, Gideon noticed, suddenly looked dead in the eyes, like he was done with life, and it scared him. Jax said to the deer, "Come get it, you big Bambi motherfucker." Flashlight in one hand, gun in the other, Jax aimed both between the deer's eyes, and fired.

Gideon and Beth hunkered down, shielded their eyes.

The bullet hit the deer somewhere in the neck area, startling it, but only for a second or two because it then went into a head-lowered charge toward Jax, who fired now out of desperation, fired screaming out of rage and grief and missing because of it.

Gideon yelled, "Jax, no!"

Beth fired, once, twice, plugging the deer both times in the ribs, but the bullets were not enough to slow it down. The antlers drove into Jax's chest and neck with powerful ease and the deer kept plowing, not stopping until it had Jax pinned against the wall next to the bar, antlers so deep the deer had stuck itself to the wall, with Jax screaming, pinned.

Panicked, the deer pushed its antlers deeper into the wall. Jax looked to be screaming, but very little sound came out, like his lungs and windpipe had been punctured. He flailed at the antlers but had no way to wrestle himself free. Blood flew and Jax cried out in anguish. The deer pulled back, huffing, spitting, hooves pounding in a desperate attempt now to free itself.

Jax's flashlight had dropped to the floor, the beam rolled along with it, settled. Beth stepped in and out of the light, firing until empty, but the deer, although slowed by the wounds, still battled to undo itself from the wall, from Jax. Its hooves slipped and fought for footing atop the blood-soaked floor. Gideon approached.

Beth told him to stay back, but he kept going. Because fuck this thing.

"Gideon, what are you doing?"

He didn't know but stopped a few feet away from the struggling deer. Contemplating how best to wrestle the antlers from the wall and therefore free Jax from it, feinting like he was preparing to seamlessly enter a moving jump rope on the playground, waiting for the right time to make his move. He saw fear in Jax's eyes and didn't like it, so he jumped.

Beth yelled, "Gideon."

But Gideon barely heard her. He climbed atop the bloody, black deer from Lalaland, gripped the roots of those antlers, and held on. He pulled and wrenched and heaved back with all his strength, while the deer lost footing, stood upright again briefly, and then slipped, bucking Gideon like a bull. Gideon, with his hands blood-soaked, regripped and pulled, this time, with the deer's help, freeing it from the wall. Jax dropped to the floor, wheezing, choking up blood. Beth knelt beside him, pleaded for him not to die. But Gideon wasn't done with the deer, who was slowly dying but not yet gone. He regripped the antlers and plunged the deer's head into the floor, once, twice, and after a third time it finally stopped fighting. It spasmed on the tile floor of the Beehive, and Gideon, face covered with the deer's blood, stepped away to watch. Convinced it was no longer a threat, Gideon approached Beth and Jax, whose eyes were wide open with fright. Gideon feared he was dead until Jax blinked, long and slow.

Beth held her husband's hand and cried right along with him.

Gideon knelt on the other side, held Jax's other hand.

Jax's head lolled to the side. His eyes found Gideon's. Jax grinned, mouth bloody. "Hey . . . Giddy-Up."

Gideon choked out a sob, said, "Shut the fuck up, Jax."

"There ya . . . go," said Jax, skin pale at the edges of the flashlight glow. "Take care . . . of my boy."

Beth sobbed.

Gideon reached over and touched her shoulder. He squeezed Jax's hand. "I will."

"And tell my . . . dad . . ." He trailed off.

"I will," said Gideon.

Jax breathed his last breath, and it came with a smile.

Beth closed his eyes.

46

Teddy

Now

TEDDY, BY THE third random Harrod's Reach house, instead of barging in, found it more enthralling to knock before huffing and puffing and kicking the doors down.

And now this door hung by a hinge.

He entered the house, stepped atop the splinters of wood torn from the door's threshold, and heard someone crying in an adjacent room. Heard a father trying desperately to quiet whoever it was—a daughter? A wife? Either way, Teddy followed it down a hallway. *Shhh . . . Shhh . . .* Followed it into a dark room. *Shhh . . . Shhh . . .* Followed it into a closet and opened that door to find a family of four, hugging each other, hiding, because word spreads fast.

Mr. Lullaby was in town.

Teddy wasted no time, having already decided in the hallway which lullaby he would sing next, this one from Spain. He squatted down in front of the family, his antlers large enough to cast shadows, and put a finger to his lips. *Shhh . . .* "Sleep, little one. Sleep, my love . . ." *Shhh . . .* Immediately the family stopped crying, stopped panicking, and stared as if hypnotized by his voice, his words. "Or the Coco will come and take you. Away." The family stopped shivering, as looks of calmness washed over them. "Sleep, little one. Sleep, my love." *Shhh* . . . The family, one by one, began to close their eyes and nod off. "Or the Coco will come and eat you up."

CHAPTER

47

Beth

Now

STAY STRONG, BETH told herself as she walked down Mallard Street back to the Smite House. Stay strong. The town needs you.

She looked to her side, where Gideon walked with her, and thought, and so does Gideon, who'd yet to say a word since they'd closed Jax's eyes inside the Beehive Hotel, moments ago. Since he'd jumped on the back of that massive black deer and rammed its face into the tile floor. Since he'd opened fire on that human doll inside the third-floor room.

He was hardly even blinking. Just walked like a zombie beside her, the whites of his eyes stark against the blood smeared red on his face. He started to veer off, so Beth grabbed his arm and straightened his path again, the two of them walking down the center of the street like they were the only two left after the apocalypse.

And maybe that's what this was, the beginning of something bigger.

Or the end of something started long ago?

She surveyed each side of the road. Where did that freak go with the lighter? Firestarter Freddie? Had someone really brought a bus full of serial killers to Harrod's Reach? And Mickey French had welcomed them right into the hotel. And now he was out cold.

Like that other woman on the third floor.

Like . . .

A front door opened to her right and a woman ran out to her sidewalk, screaming, "My husband won't wake up!"

Beth shouted, "Go back inside, Mrs. Alderman. Please. Go back in and lock your door."

Two houses down on the left, Mr. Raglin ran from his front stoop toward them on the street. "Sheriff, my kids . . . They won't wake up. Justin and Jackson. Their window is open. Somebody came in."

Beth said, "Mr. Raglin, stay back. Go back in—"

"What happened to him?" Mr. Raglin pointed at Gideon.

"Go back inside and lock your door, Mr. Raglin, and that's an order."

Mrs. Alderman hurried inside but Mr. Raglin stood frozen, watching them pass.

"Look." Gideon pointed toward a streetlamp ahead, down closer to the Smite House.

"What the fuck is that?"

Someone screamed. It could have come from anywhere, but it sounded like it had originated from the direction of the tunnel.

Gideon said, "I smell smoke."

Together, they moved on, but both now watching the figure out on the street, standing frozen-still in the glow of the streetlamp. The figure was white from head to toe, not Caucasian white, but picket fence white. Paint white. Plaster cast white. And it was standing, posed, like an undressed retail store mannequin, facing them. Completely bald. And then she remembered the room inside the Beehive. The shaved hair. The bucket of white plaster or paint. Either way, the two of them moved onward, closing in on the Smite House but careful not to get too close to whatever this thing was.

Or thought it was.

The Mannequin, she thought, sidling next to Gideon.

The smell of smoke grew stronger, and just as she saw, through the trees, dark clouds of it billowing above a rooftop across the street, Mr. Buckhalter came running from his house, yelling, "Fire. Fire. My house is on fire."

And still, that mannequin didn't move.

Gideon protectively put an arm around Beth and ushered them another twenty yards closer to both the mannequin and the Smite House. Beth kept her eyes on the mannequin, still not convinced it hadn't been carried from a downtown store and placed there as a prank. But then the front door to the Smite House flung open and somebody ran out to the porch.

Gideon saw who it was first and yelled, "Maddy, stay inside. Go back. Stay *inside!*"

She either couldn't hear him or didn't listen because she kept running blindly into the dark night. "Gideon!"

"Maddy!" he yelled, and Maddy now caught his direction.

Beth hurried to keep up, and joined in, "Maddy, go back inside!"

"Gideon," Maddy cried, sprinting toward their location, close enough now for her to see Gideon's bloody face, and that made her scream louder. "Gideon!"

And they embraced.

Gideon told her it wasn't his blood, but Jax was dead and houses were burning and the town was falling asleep. Beth grabbed them both by the shirts and urged them back closer to shelter.

Maddy shouted toward both as they moved, "I talked to Simon. He knows more than you think. But the Seers, over there, they're in trouble, and . . ."

"And what, Maddy?" Beth asked as they moved across the neighboring yard beside the Smite House.

"The ones here," she said. "They're starting to move."

"Sully?"

"Yeah," she said, out of breath. "He's restless . . ."

Beth said, "Something's happening on the other side."

In Lalaland . . .

She picked up her pace, urged them on.

They were thirty yards from the house when the mannequin moved, and then started running their way.

CHAPTER

48

Maddy

Now

THE SPEED WITH which the mannequin bore down on them was uncanny.

But as it closed in to within a few yards, with the sharp dagger raised in its right hand, ready to strike, Maddy saw breasts, long lithe limbs, and a shaved mons pubis—the entire body coated in white—and realized, at the last second, it was a woman.

Maddy froze.

Up until her attack in Charleston, she'd never been one to freeze when confronted, but the PTSD was real, and she locked up as soon as she saw the whites of the mannequin's eyes, because in those eyes was the same utter lack of guilt or remorse she'd seen in the eyes of the man who'd nearly killed her on the Battery overlooking Charleston Harbor.

While Maddy froze, Gideon didn't, but he caught the knife on the downward arc and the blade plunged deep into the meat of his upper right arm.

He twisted away from the female mannequin, blade still stuck in his arm beneath the shoulder, and Maddy woke up. She charged, put her hands around the mannequin's neck and squeezed with all her strength. She pressed her thumbs into the mannequin's throat, and the bitch started choking. Because she *was* human. Maddy squeezed while the mannequin flailed at her, and she cried because she'd never truly allowed herself to grieve what had happened to her. She cried because she was far away from home and her daddy didn't love her and the world was ten different kinds of fucked and this place just took the goddamn cake.

Across the street, the house burned.

Something exploded in the distance.

The front door of the Smite House opened. A shotgun blast echoed loud and close. Birds scattered from trees.

The shotgun blast broke Maddy from whatever rage-filled stupor had overtaken her and she let go of the mannequin. This pathetic woman, painted completely in white, who suddenly looked as stunned and lost as they all were, stumbled backwards and fell to the grass.

On the porch, Archie Dupree stood at the railing, shotgun in hand. He said to the mannequin, "Get off my property."

Maddy thought, *Shoot her*, thinking Archie realized it was a woman, and that's why he didn't. They heard footsteps approaching from the dark shadows between the trees. Maddy saw a priest coming from the dark, a full satchel of something heavy cradled in his arms, and he froze as soon as he saw the mannequin, now back on her feet.

"Father Fred," said Archie, from the porch. "Don't move."

Father Fred stayed still, eyeing both the mannequin and the Smite House, which was where he was most likely heading. Tears streamed down his cheeks and he looked shell-shocked. His jaw shook as he spoke to any of them, all of them, "The bank is on fire, Archie. The diner is on fire. Half the historic district is burning." He said to Beth, "Deputy Lump . . . he's asleep back at the station. He's locked inside one of the cells snoring. I tried yelling, but he wouldn't wake up, Beth. *He wouldn't wake up!* Somebody is burning the town to the ground."

The mannequin smiled, whispered something Maddy thought sounded like *Firestarter Freddie*, and in that grin Maddy knew she was totally evil. Might not have always been, but she was now. The mannequin took a slow step toward Father Fred. He dropped the satchel, and it landed heavily in the yard. He lifted the cross from the chain around his neck, but the mannequin came at him.

A shot sounded from the porch. The mannequin went down. Above her right breast, red quickly spread across the white, painted flesh. She rolled, moaning and screaming, and the sound was ear-piercing. A second shot, this one to the back of the head, shut her up for good.

And Maddy almost threw up.

Sheriff Meeks stood beside Archie at the porch's railing, pistol raised, wincing as he held his abdomen with his free hand, his Stetson cockeyed on his head. "Get in the house, all of you."

Gideon, by then, had pulled the dagger from his arm, and it was bleeding freely down his sleeve. He was a mess from whatever had happened to them inside the hotel, and where blood didn't cover his face, Maddy saw pale skin turning paler. She ushered him toward the porch at the same time Beth helped the priest gather whatever bag he'd been carrying.

Maddy heard Beth say to the priest behind her, "What's in the bag, Father?"

Father Fred said, "Ammo."

49

Gideon

Now

EVERYONE IN THE Smite House, as soon as Gideon entered the foyer, wanted him to tend to the wound in his arm. His shirtsleeve was completely blood-soaked, and it was clear he was wobbling.

Maxine started crying as soon as she saw him, unaware that the blood on his face wasn't his, and she hugged him despite it all.

"I'm fine, Mom," he told her, although he felt nausea now coming in pulses and every room he entered was spinning. But he was determined to make it to the parlor to see Sully.

Gideon had already told Beth to go find Simon, and off she went upstairs.

Sheriff Meeks asked Archie if he had any plywood. Archie laughed and said, "I have enough in the basement to build a house."

"Then go get it," Grover said. "And start boarding up every first-floor window. I saw too many things moving out there and I think they're wanting to get in."

"At Sully?" Archie asked.

"No," Grover said. "I don't think so. It's Simon."

"Simon?"

"Go," Grover said to Archie, and off Archie went.

Gideon moved into the hallway, toward the back parlor, whispering, "Simon . . ." Someone grabbed his arm and helped guide him. It was Maddy. She knew where he wanted to go. What he wanted to see firsthand.

"I'll explain what I know in a minute," said Maddy, taking on much of his weight as he leaned on her. When Gideon entered the parlor, he rested against the doorway, and every coma patient's relative in the room looked up in fright. Tammy Shimp. Lauren Betts's parents. The wife of the man who'd come in hours ago . . . their names evaded him. Gideon ignored the looks. It was evident something had happened to the four coma patients. They were all now on Sully's large bed, all of them holding hands like links in a chain, all of them trembling like they were battling Parkinson's, mumbling under their breath, eyelids fluttering . . .

"What are they saying?" Gideon asked.

"I don't know," Maddy said. "But they've been doing this for an hour."

Tammy Shimp said, "Ten minutes ago, Sully sat up in bed. He yelled, 'We need help,' and then he went back down. Something's happening."

Simon . . .

Tammy Shimp looked at Maddy: "What's happening?"

Gideon stepped from the room, leaned on Maddy.

Natalie ran into the hallway from another room. "Beth said you were hurt." Her eyes went wide when she saw his bloody face and shirt. "Jesus."

"Nice bedside manner," Gideon said.

Natalie led them into the kitchen, where the lighting was better. She said to Maddy, "Get him up on the stool. Start taking his shirt off."

Outside the house, a siren blared.

Cold air hit Gideon's bare flesh and goose bumps spread in a flurry. Natalie's hands were warm on his chest. She said, "This is gonna burn."

He opened his eyes when the alcohol splashed atop his wound. "Fuck!" There Natalie was, pouring Old Sam bourbon right from the bottle, over the wound, and he was thinking deliriously, *Save some.* His head lolled.

Maddy held him upright on the stool, helped him rest his back against the island.

Natalie took gauze from a bag she'd brought with her and started folding it, he assumed to place over the wound, but she did one better and stuffed it *into* the deep cut instead, saying *sorry* and *had to be done* and *it'll help it clot,* and she looked like she was turning pale too. Gideon yelled out, "Fuck me!"

And Maddy might have whispered *maybe later* in his ear, just to calm him down, or maybe he'd imagined it, but his arm was now on fire like the rest of the town and his mom was holding Archie's diabetic sugar tablets out to him like he might be hungry. Natalie said *Good idea* and made him crunch a few of those tablets down and suddenly he thought maybe he might not die today. Where was his dad? And then he remembered he was carrying plywood up from the basement to cover all the windows. Hammering echoed throughout the house a few seconds later, as if on cue, and Gideon told Mom to give the rest of those sugar tablets to Dad, and to make sure he was watching his blood sugar, because he too often went low when he was deep into something. Natalie cleaned the wound with wet kitchen towels, tossing each to the floor as they became soiled with his blood, but five minutes later the cut didn't look as bad as it once had, especially as she started wrapping it with more gauze and tape, and now that the sugar tablets had kicked in the room was a little less spinny.

Gideon said to Natalie, "I'll take the bottle." She handed the Old Sam to him. He tilted the bourbon back for a deep swallow and welcomed the burn as it spread out across his chest. He said to Maddy, "What was that out there?"

"I don't know," she said.

"Jax is dead," he said.

Maddy said, "I know. I'm so sorry."

And Maxine Dupree started crying all over again. Gideon said, "Mom, please, go check on Dad." And she did. And then he looked at Maddy, found her watching him, teary-eyed, and for a second thought he might melt. She hugged him, hard, despite all that blood, and he briefly held her. "Help me upstairs," he said. "This deer blood is drying like plaster."

He didn't say it was Jax's blood he most wanted washed off.

50

Teddy

Now

MOTHER ALWAYS SAID seeing was believing.

And now that Teddy and Brandy had returned from the tunnel and had seen how much more color had come through in the past few hours—more vines and yellow prairie grass, more trees with white leaves, more seashells and fish brought in by another Lalaland tide—he believed now more than ever.

Lalaland was where all the dead-heads go.

And the dead-heads are no friends of mine.

"Unless *you* put them there, baby," Brandy had said on their walk back into town, a town now burning from every corner. Firestarter Freddie was as good as he'd advertised. There was so much smoke in the air that some of the streets looked impassable. Every minute somebody in Harrod's Reach screamed from somewhere, and the sound of all that mayhem and turmoil—all brought here by him—kept Teddy's wick lit. And Brandy was right. Brandy was always right. The dead-heads were no friends unless he put them there, and to his count now—yes, he'd started a brand-new list, Mother—he'd put twenty-seven of Harrod's Reach's finest, and some maybe not so fine, into Lalaland to do *his* bidding. To help open what the other dead-heads had for centuries now tried to keep closed, and it was working.

He and Brandy held hands as they walked down the middle of Guthrie, his antlers casting wicked-long shadows as moonlight lost dominance to the flames illuminating both sides of the road. Freddie never seemed to grow tired. It was like each fire fueled him, and that, thought Teddy, was something he could wrap his mind around.

A black deer sprinted across the street and disappeared into the woods to their left, near White Wall Cemetery, where Brandy, earlier, had noticed a few of their Lullaby Express passengers loitering, walking in between the tombstones and headstones and mausoleums as if confused, although not as large a number as the ones who'd migrated to the tunnel, and were down there now, completely taken in by it all, waiting—these living breathing nightmares—for Lalaland to completely come through.

Teddy led Brandy toward a row of three houses that weren't yet burning and entered the middle one with one swift kick to the door. He thought of Firestarter Freddie as he searched from room to room. How he'd told him too many people were gathering inside that place called the Smite House, and that that should be his next target.

Freddie's eyes had lit up with excitement.

Freddie, who apparently had been a middle school math teacher called Jeffrey Tungston, before a mare took him over.

And Teddy thought now he heard noises in a back bedroom.

Brandy must have heard them too, because she flung the door open, revealing a young couple clinging to each other on the bed as the town burned all around them. A bottle of pills rested empty between them on the bed, and Teddy thought, *Oh no you don't.*

Brandy licked her lips. Teddy could tell right away she wanted to do the young man with the knife she'd just pulled from her skirt, and Teddy thought, *Fine by me.* Although by the way their eyes were glazed and the fact they weren't trying to flee, it appeared they'd done a good job of putting *themselves* down. So he got to it.

He climbed atop the bed and put his face inches away from their faces, and as they looked, horrified, back at him, he sang, "The itsy-bitsy spider, climbed up the waterspout . . ."

Brandy said, "Good choice, baby." And plunged her knife under the man's chin.

Blood spurted across the bed.

". . . Down came the rain, and washed the spider out . . ."

51

Gideon

Now

GIDEON FOUND BETH with Simon in the second-floor library, the two of them standing at a table hunched over Simon's wide-open *Lalaland* book. Beth held up a finger when he stopped at the open doorway, a *give me a minute* gesture, because it appeared she and the giant were deep into something.

And then something hard and heavy thumped against the side of the house. Everyone jumped. Beth said, "Meet me in the kitchen in five minutes."

Gideon heard hammer blows as he descended the stairs. In the living room, he found Sheriff Meeks in his wheelchair, with Natalie rewrapping his bandages. One of his stitches had opened during his walk to the porch earlier with his gun.

Again, something smashed against the outside of the house.

"Birds," Natalie said, finishing up on Grover and helping him to lean back.

Sheriff Meeks offered Gideon one of his hydrocodone pills, but Gideon declined in favor of a clear head. The pain he would deal with. The hammering was coming from the other side of the house. Gideon passed through the kitchen, ducked into the hallway, and stopped at the parlor door, where his mother leaned in the doorway watching the coma patients, sipping from a glass of bourbon, face panicked, hands shaking.

"How's Sully?" Gideon asked.

Maxine said, "Same. Restless."

Gideon looked over her head into the room. Archie had boarded up those windows. Something smashed into the house outside the parlor and everyone in the room jumped, except the four on the beds. Lauren Betts's father about came out of his chair. Tammy Shimp started crying as she held her daughter's hand. "And Dad?"

She nodded toward the dining room. "Refusing to eat the candy bar I gave him. He's gonna go into insulin shock if he's not careful."

Gideon kissed the top of his mother's head and hurried down the hall to the dining room. Archie sat in a chair at the head of the table, slumped over, head in between his knees, blood sugar no doubt plummeting. It looked like he had one more window to board up.

"Need help?" Gideon asked.

"No," said Archie. He looked woozy and pale. The Twix bar rested unopened on the middle of the table. "I'm fine."

Gideon rounded the table. "You're not fine. What's your blood sugar?"

"I dunno . . ."

"Then check it, Dad. Jesus." Gideon rummaged through the drawer of the china cabinet, where Archie kept most of his diabetic equipment, close to where they most often ate. He pulled out the machine and testing strips and said, "Eat the candy bar."

"I'm—"

"Eat the goddamn candy bar," Gideon yelled. Archie looked up, but didn't reach for it, so Gideon opened it for him and held it out. "Don't make me shove it in there."

Archie's hands were trembling. He grabbed it, took a bite, and then another, closing his eyes as he chewed. Gideon found what he needed from the drawer, and while he'd never checked his father's blood, he'd seen it done enough to do it in his sleep. He pricked one of Archie's fingers and his father barely batted an eye. He squeezed a drop of blood out onto the strip and put it on the handheld machine and waited as Archie got the candy bar down, bite by bite.

Just then, something flew into the window, shattering one of the panes of glass. They both jumped. Natalie had mentioned birds a minute ago, and in his mind, he'd wondered what kind of birds would do that, but now he saw that this one was black and blue and big-beaked, and while not as large as the bird they'd seen Beth shoot out by the tunnel earlier in the morning, it resembled it. Enough for him to know where the thing had come from. And from the movement Gideon saw outside between the trees, they weren't alone.

A tall figure emerged from the shadows. A man with long hair and thick arms and broad shoulders. He made eye contact with Gideon and started slowly walking toward the house, toward the window with the broken glass, the final window that needed to be closed off by plywood. Archie's machine went off. His blood sugar read 83.

Gideon lifted the sheet of thick plywood learning against the table and held it up against the window. He had heard something jangling on the approaching man outside. *Please tell me those weren't horseshoes hanging from his waistline.* He knew they had been, but first things first. Right shoulder on fire, Gideon grabbed the hammer and a handful of nails from the table, holding several in his teeth. He moved the plywood, braced it in place with his body, yanked a nail from his lips and started hammering. Outside he heard heavy footsteps on the floorboards of their wraparound porch. He heard the horseshoes jangling against each other as he moved. Gideon hammered at the nail but the plywood slipped.

"Put your weight into the board," said Archie, slowly gaining life inside his chair. "You can hammer . . ."

"I got it." Gideon held the nail with his left hand and hammered with his right. One good hit plunged it halfway through, and then two more clean ones burrowed it the rest of the way in, and behind him Gideon heard his father say "Good job."

Even as that big bastard with the horseshoes paced the porch directly outside.

He hammered the two lower corners and more nails between for good measure. By the time he turned around, Archie had filled a needle with insulin and was sticking it into his gut. Archie took a big breath and let it out, and told Gideon, "Thank you."

Gideon nodded and was about to leave the room when something stopped him. The thing that had been poisoning him since the day his little brother went down to the tunnel and came out injured. The little brother who'd been born with the eyes of an angel. Who walked at six months. Who'd been potty trained by two years. Whose dimples when he smiled—and he was always smiling—got pinched by every woman who ever passed him. Who, by kindergarten, was already reading at a fifth-grade level. Who was sketching anatomically correct human beings instead of the stick figures every other child his age drew. Who turned heads, even at age four, when he entered the grocery store or church or gymnasium because it was, for whatever reason, impossible *not* to look at him. Who—and this was what it really came down to—like Beth, was afraid of absolutely nothing, especially that tunnel. Whose presence had always made Gideon wonder if maybe Sully wasn't meant to be born that same night as Beth instead of him, with his deformed lip and cautious nature. If maybe Sully were the one meant to be Beth's pretend twin. Like the two of them had been destined to do something together but his lack of whatever had made that impossible. And without any preamble, Gideon, with his back to his father, said, "It wasn't my fault. I told Sully the rules. I told him to stay in the goddamn house, Dad." He breathed heavily, felt his blood pressure rise as something thumped into the side of the house. "And all Mom wants is to dance!"

"Gideon . . ."

"We were playing hide-and-seek. The *only* rule was to stay in the house."

"Gideon, turn around."

He faced his father, who was standing now, shirt untucked from having pulled it out for the needle injection. "Sully was supposed to be hiding. I heard the front door open. I gave him a minute, thinking maybe he was hiding on the porch. But I remembered he'd been asking all day to go to the tunnel. To play In-One-Out-One. I went out. He wasn't on the porch, so I started toward the tunnel." Gideon wiped his eyes. "He was fast. He was little, but he was so damn fast, and I . . . I was Giddy-Up Gideon. As fast as I went, I couldn't catch him. Chased him all the way down the slope, into the gully. I hated that tunnel, and he knew that. But he'd been down there so often he could have navigated the ravine blindfolded, Dad. He wasn't only not scared of it, he was . . ."

"He was drawn to it, yes, I know . . . He always was."

"He stopped before going in the south entrance. Waited for me. I thought I was having a heart attack I was breathing so heavy. He waved. Yelled, *Hey, Gideon. Go to the other end. Go around. In-One-Out-One.* I told him no. I said, let's go back to the house. We're not supposed to be here. He said . . . he said . . ."

"Gideon, what?"

"He said, *Maybe you're not supposed to be here, but I am.* And then he said, *I think I can make it through, all the way through.*" Gideon could see his face now, could hear his confident little kid voice clear as day: *I think I can win the game, Gideon . . .* He felt chill bumps break out across his skin. "*Like Connie Brine. And Bret Jones.* That's what he said, Dad."

"Those two disappeared, Gideon." Archie took a step forward. "They were never seen or heard from again."

"I know. He said, *I got a story to tell.*"

Archie choked up. "He always had a story to tell. The imagination on that boy . . ."

"Dad, what was it?"

Archie gently tapped his forehead like he did when he was thinking. "I don't know yet."

"And then he ran in."

"And you ran in after him."

"Yeah," said Gideon. "Of course I did. And that's when the earthquake struck."

CHAPTER

52

Beth

Now

BETH GATHERED THEM all in the kitchen.
It was perfectly centered in the middle of the Smite House, with no direct window or wall or opening to the outside, where more and more it sounded like the house's exterior was being bombarded by something, by someone, but hopefully not yet breached.

Maddy stood silent at one end of the island.

Shit was hitting the fan over in Lalaland.

They were somehow being overwhelmed on the other side.

The four Seers inside the parlor, even in the past ten minutes, had become more noticeably restless. Their arms trembled. Their eyelids fluttered, and occasionally opened and closed. They mumbled indecipherable words. They tossed and turned, yet remained connected, holding hands in a chain that Beth, when she'd spied on them a moment ago, hoped was strong enough to hold off whatever else was coming. Because Simon had made it clear to her upstairs in the library that Mr. Lullaby, the figure he'd drawn all over the walls of his cabin, the figure he'd been trying to ward off with his own sets of fake antlers and his constant reciting of lullabies he'd written throughout the pages of his *Lalaland* book, had already come through. Or at least some form of him had.

"He's already here," Simon had hissed upstairs.

Their job, Beth explained to them all now in the kitchen—Gideon, Maddy, Grover, Maxine, Simon, and now Archie, who'd just come in running from his study—was to close the door to the *rest* of Lalaland.

Funny, she thought, how that didn't even draw skepticism, not from one of them. They all listened, rapt, eager to get going, even as another bird crashed into the boarded-up window in the parlor, smashing glass on the other side of it. Even as someone outside paced the porch, and had twice tried to enter the front door, jiggling the doorknob, before continuing to reconnoiter the house's rim, horseshoes jangling like heavy windchimes as he moved. Beth and Gideon knew he was there but had yet to tell Maddy.

Beth reiterated her theory on the tunnel's periods of high activity, pinpointing the three highest periods as the 1860s when Connie Brine disappeared, the 1960s when Bret Jones disappeared, and now, the highest period of activity yet. "We should have listened to Doc three years ago. We never should have closed that tunnel. We never should have bricked it up. In my opinion it only exacerbated it."

Archie held a pile of old newspapers he spread out across the kitchen island. Another bird thumped into a wall. Archie pointed to an article, and then two more. "Gideon reminded me of the earthquake three years ago, when Sully entered . . ." He closed his eyes for a beat to fight off his emotions. "When Sully entered the tunnel. It wasn't a long one. Two seconds, maybe three, more of a tremor than anything, but enough for rocks to shake loose from that ceiling. And we all know one hit Sully on the head, when he'd made it halfway through the tunnel." He looked at Gideon. "Tell them what you saw."

"A light," Gideon said. "Just a flash of light, lasted no more than a second. I assumed then . . . and all the way up until now, that it was me just getting light-headed, because I was seeing stars. Dizzy."

"But now we know it was more than that," said Beth. "From what Sully told you before running in, he thought he could make it. He somehow knew there was a chance."

Gideon nodded. "He thought he could win the game."

"In-One-Out-One," said Maxine, stone-faced.

"In one end," Archie said.

"And straight into Lalaland," said Simon, his words hushing them all, as they waited, eager for more. But he didn't give it; instead, he paced the kitchen, around the island and back again, staring down at the *Lalaland* book he hugged against his chest.

Beth watched Simon but said to Archie, "Back to the earthquakes."

Archie found the relevant articles again. "In eighteen sixty-eight, on the day Connie Brine disappeared, Harrod's Reach experienced a minor earthquake that brought down several stones around the northern entrance."

"And Bret Jones in ninety sixty-eight?" asked Gideon.

Archie referred to another article. "The same. Short earthquake. Some rubble from the inside toppled down to the tunnel floor."

Maxine said, "What is this about?"

Beth said, "Bret Jones and Connie Brine didn't just disappear from Harrod's Reach. They went in the tunnel and never came out." Beth took a second to collect herself. "Those earthquakes would not have occurred had they not entered the tunnel. At those exact times."

Natalie said, "You're saying they caused . . ."

"Yes," said Beth. "Their running through the tunnel *caused* those minor earthquakes."

"The severed limbs over the decades," Gideon said, thinking out loud.

"All during periods of medium to high activity," said Beth. "But every one of those . . . injuries at the tunnel, over the past century, where people lost arms or legs, and in Happy Jack's case in the seventies, his entire lower half, they'd all been unsuspecting. They just had the bad luck of walking through that northern entrance at the exact *wrong* time."

"Right when the doorways breathed," said Maddy, taking on the attention now. "That's what they call it over there. The doorways breathe. They let off steam like pressure. Like a teapot whistling, so things won't blow."

"And Connie Brine?" Sheriff Meeks asked from his wheelchair. "Bret Jones? Are you saying they went in when they did because they somehow knew?"

"Yes," said Beth. "They were unique. Like Sully was unique. Maybe Sully would have made it through too if part of the tunnel hadn't fallen on him."

"Would have been an Elder," said Simon. He stopped pacing to open his *Lalaland* book atop the island. "Sully . . ." He flipped to a page that showed Sully, now, over there, as a rugged twenty-something-year-old man. He pointed hard at the picture he'd drawn and said, "Sully. Lalaland."

Maxine covered her mouth and started crying. Maddy put an arm around her shoulders and hugged her. Maxine rested her head on Maddy's shoulder.

"Sully is what they call a Seer over there," Beth said. "As are the rest of them in the parlor. And Maddy, when she was in her coma. And anyone now in a coma . . ."

"Anywhere in the world," Maddy added.

"Yes," said Beth. "According to Simon, and his book, they're Seers."

"And the Elders?" asked Gideon.

Simon flipped a hunk of pages one way, and then back-turned two more pages, to one that showed a picture of Connie Brine at the same age she was when she disappeared, a teenager.

Beth said, "The Elders are stronger. But they're rare. While the Seers over there might number in the thousands, the Elders . . . Simon?"

"Thirty . . . two," he said. "Thirty-two."

"The Elders, they're not *only* over there in mind," Beth said. "But in body, having made it all the way through unscathed."

"With all their limbs attached," said Archie.

"Yes," said Beth. "Connie Brine. Bret Jones. Sully, I believe, tried. Simon's parents tried, thirteen years ago . . ."

"I thought they ran off?" Natalie asked. "They left Simon an orphan."

Sheriff Meeks rolled himself closer to the island. "They were unreported victims of the tunnel. Instead of losing limbs, their limbs were the only parts left. It made no earthly sense then, but it does now. Simon's mom . . . her left arm was found, from the forearm down. With his dad, only the left hand was found, with his watch still attached at the severed wrist. We identified them by their wedding rings. Now whether they knew something or they didn't, whether it was on purpose or a stroke of bad luck, but they nearly made it."

"Didn't last long," said Simon. "Blood . . . attracts. In Lalaland."

Maxine sat at the island and covered her face with her hands. "How is this . . ." She looked up, red-eyed. "It's insane. Am I right? It's insane!"

Maddy comforted her again. "It's real, Mrs. Dupree. I wish it wasn't, but it is."

Beth said, "Doc Bigsby, for decades, Maxine, was tracking . . . things . . . animals . . . small enough to somehow make it through to this side *from* Lalaland. He's collected them and kept them frozen inside his garage." She pulled out her phone. "We have pictures."

"I don't want to see them," said Maxine. Beth showed her anyway. Waited until she looked and swiped through five in a row until Maxine pushed the phone away and said, "Fine. So he's really over there. My Sully."

"And he's keeping us safe," Archie said to his wife. "Like Sully always said he'd do. We'd laugh it off every time he said it because he was just a little boy, but I don't think Sully ever was just a little boy. Not anymore."

"Whatever has been sneaking through that tunnel over the decades," Gideon said. "They're getting larger."

"And according to Simon"—Beth gestured toward Simon's orange book—"it's threatening to open all the way for good. You've seen what's come through already. Those vines. The leaves. The shells. The deer. I think that's only the beginning."

"Beth," said Natalie. "Why are we here? Right now. There's something trying to get inside the house as we speak. Why are—"

"Simon is number thirty-three," she said. "Thirty-three is an important number over there. They're waiting for him to come through. They've been waiting for him for years."

"Now," said Simon, "is the time."

Beth spoke for him. "Connie Brine was small. Bret Jones was small."

"They're all creatives," said Archie, as if something had just dawned on him. "They've all been blessed with vivid *imaginations*." He pointed to Simon's book—in a sense, his portfolio. "We all know of Simon's artistic ability. You told us about the sculptures he made of the trees around his cabin. Connie Brine. From the records, from what I remember reading while researching, she was a writer. Even as a teen, she'd written several full-length novels. And Bret Jones, he was an artist as well. But his talent was with comic books. Comic strips. And even Sully . . ."

Gideon said, "The kid could tell a story. Right off the top of his head. Without hesitation. It was uncanny . . ."

Beth let it all soak in; it all made sense. And as no one made a move to refute it, Beth finished her point. "According to Simon, most of the Elders over there are small. Yet still they made the earth move."

Gideon said, "You think Simon is large enough to bring down the entire tunnel."

"Hoping," said Beth.

"Then why has nothing happened before?" asked Maddy. "When Simon has been in the tunnel, why has nothing happened before?"

Beth welcomed all their gazes. "Because Simon has never *been* inside the tunnel."

Gideon said, "Bullshit."

Simon shook his head. "Never. Never been."

Beth recalled the story they'd read from Detective Harrington's notes, about finding Simon as a boy sleeping just *outside* the tunnel. She said, "We all are aware how much Simon sleeps. He's been waiting. His sleeps are deep. He's spent more time in Lalaland than any of us know. Call it getting acclimated, or whatever, but it's got to be now. And then we pray his passing through is big enough to bring that tunnel down."

"And if not?" Maxine asked.

Beth said. "Then we hope Father Fred brought enough ammo."

53

Maddy

Now

MADDY WASN'T THE first to smell smoke, but she *was* the first to see it coming out from below the basement door and spreading across the hallway floor of the Smite House like thick fog.

How long a fire had been burning in the basement, she didn't know, but she could tell by the heat coming from behind that closed door that they were beyond fire extinguishers. And with so many fires now burning across Harrod's Reach, calling would be futile.

But the plan they'd come up with in the kitchen would have to be altered, so she hurried to tell Natalie they'd now need two ambulances instead of one. One, to escort Simon and several of them to the tunnel, and now another one to drive the rest of them off the property before the entire Smite House went up in flames.

She found Gideon in the parlor with Sully and told him. While Gideon swore his dad would go down in flames with the house, Archie was the first he told. And Archie, to Maddy's surprise, after staring stoically for a moment at all the windows he'd just boarded up, didn't seem to panic. In fact, he looked as calm as she imagined he'd look delivering a lecture on Prohibition to one of his history classes.

Beth sprinted upstairs to retrieve Brody from his bed, and by the time she returned downstairs with him, the entire house was in flux, with Archie orchestrating their escape plan, all of them gathering in the living room to await the ambulance.

For over an hour they'd heard birds slamming into the house. They'd heard windows shattering. They'd heard people out there pretending to come in, pacing the porch. There were cold-blooded killers out there. They'd waited until every window was boarded up to set the house on fire, and now there were only two ways out of the house—the front door and the back—and Maddy feared they'd be pigs led to the slaughter in the woods, like rats blindly fleeing a burning ship.

Maddy found Beth holding Brody in the kitchen with Sheriff Meeks, who'd again gotten out of his chair to help organize every weapon and box of ammo they had.

Smoke had made its way into the kitchen.

The fire alarms were going off, which only made Brody cry louder, covering his ears as Beth tried to multitask and calm him down.

Gideon entered the kitchen. "They're preparing everyone in the parlor for transport. The ambulances are on their way."

Beth held Brody out toward Gideon. "Take your son." Sheriff Meeks looked across the kitchen island toward Beth. She said, "I'll explain later." Gideon grabbed the boy with reluctance but held him tight against his chest. "Go," Beth said. "Get him away from the smoke. And grab a gun." Gideon showed her the gun at his waistline and then ducked out into the hall. Maddy started to follow until Beth stopped her. "You ever shoot a gun?"

"No," Maddy said.

Beth handed her one. "Just in case."

Maddy was surprised by how heavy it felt in her hand and was afraid to put it anywhere else on her person, so she held it, aimed at the ground as she caught up to Gideon in the foyer, and hoped she wouldn't have to use it. By then, Archie had Sully and Amy on a cart on wheels parked next to the front door. In the adjoining room, Lauren Betts rested, cradled in the arms of her distraught father, the mother beside him holding the essentials they'd brought with them. To Maddy they looked shell-shocked. What had she lured them into? This was no way to go out, for anyone.

Next to Betts was the young couple who'd showed up unexpectedly. Steven rested in a wheelchair, head lolling, as his wife gently cradled it and wept.

Simon paced from the foyer to the living and back again, staring down at the floorboards as smoke entered from the kitchen. Something crashed into a boarded-up window from the front porch. Something popped and exploded below in the basement, and a gush of flame erupted upward from a floor vent, catching the curtains in the adjoining dining room.

Sirens blared outside.

Screams sounded across Harrod's Reach.

Maddy, thinking any minute now they might have to make the choice to deal with the flames and smoke or take their chances outside.

Sheriff Meeks wheeled himself into the foyer.

Beth followed behind him with two leather bags, one over each shoulder, and told them the order in which they would load into the ambulances. One ambulance would carry her, Maddy, Gideon, Natalie, and Simon to the tunnel. The second would carry the four coma patients and their loved ones, plus Grover Meeks, to the outskirts of town. Beth looked relieved that nobody argued.

Archie didn't try to play the hero and say he was staying with the house. Although, Maddy noticed, he was crying. Maybe it was the smoke, but she didn't think so. The house he'd put so much blood, sweat, and tears into for over two decades was going up in flames before his eyes. He paced much like Simon, until he stopped at the built-in bookshelves across the room and started fiddling with something. A second later, Frank Sinatra started singing "Fly Me to the Moon" from the stereo, which got everyone's attention. Enough to briefly distract them from the increasing smoke in the room and the madness outside.

Maddy about started crying when Archie walked across the room toward his wife in the foyer. Archie held out his hand to Maxine, and didn't need to speak for her to understand exactly what he intended to do.

Maddy thought of her own father, and how he was a prick. And then she thought about how Nero was probably a prick too, and supposedly fiddled while Rome burned. But this, as she watched Maxine take Archie's hand and follow him out to the middle of the living room in a warm embrace, was too much. This was what she imagined love should be. Messy and convoluted and silent and loud, but when shit hit the fan, when the house was on fire, you still danced.

Lovingly danced.

Archie held his wife and Maxine cried. He spun her in a circle and pulled her back again and with tears on his cheeks, he sang along with

Frank, the two of them flying to the moon as smoke gathered around their ankles and the ambulances finally arrived.

As Natalie had instructed, the ambulance drivers pulled all the way up to the front porch steps of the Smite House and backed in, side by side.

Beth, with her eyes on Archie and Maxine dancing in the living room, shouted, "It's go time."

As Beth opened the front door, Sheriff Meeks, in his wheelchair, readied his shotgun.

One driver opened the back doors of his ambulance from inside the vehicle, and he lived.

The second driver made the mistake of getting out of the vehicle to open his back doors, and he didn't.

One of the black deer Maddy had seen so prevalent throughout Lalaland came out of nowhere and was on the driver in a flash, head lowered and goring through flesh with those sharp, reddish-orange antlers, pinning him to the side of his own ambulance before he even knew what hit him.

Which at least gave Beth a few extra seconds of cover to open the ambulance doors and begin directing everyone into their respective vehicles. Sheriff Meeks, now on the veranda in his wheelchair, raised his shotgun toward the yard. A man in a business suit holding a machete and another figure with a clown face and carrying hedge clippers stepped into the clearing; Meeks fired, and they retreated back to the trees.

Maddy stepped cautiously out to the covered veranda and glanced to either side. Dead birds littered the floorboards from having crashed into the windows and the house's siding. More birds flew at them under the veranda's rooftop.

Maddy ducked as she helped Beth usher the rest of them into the ambulances. Sheriff Meeks fired another shot, and she saw a figure emerging from the woods falter and fall.

Gideon had already handed Brody off to his mother, and Maxine stepped into the ambulance, shielding her grandson's face. Archie emerged from the house with what looked like a small safe. As he joined his wife and grandson and Sully in the ambulance, he said, "The original house plans." He sat next to Maxine on the bench. "We can always rebuild."

She held out her free hand and he grabbed it.

Simon, instead of boarding, handed Gideon his *Lalaland* book and approached the panicked deer, whose antlers had pierced the side of the other ambulance. He was calming the beast down, petting it with one hand while attempting to wrench it free from the vehicle with the other, while the pinned driver's cries grew weaker, then silent.

While Simon wrestled with the deer, someone screamed from the ambulance carrying the coma patients. To Maddy, it had sounded like Sully.

One frantic word: "Hurry!"

Simon finally pulled the deer free, and the driver dropped to the grass in an unmoving heap. The deer huffed and cantered and backed away from the ambulance, as if stunned, before darting into darkness under the trees.

Gideon, hugging Simon's book, had migrated toward the second vehicle, where *something* was going on with the coma patients.

Beth shouted to Gideon, "Come on, get in." And then went around to take the dead driver's seat.

Sheriff Meeks now was firing his pistol at something else in the woods, not so much as a warning shot but with more of a dead aim. And then with Maddy's help, he boarded his ambulance.

Maddy, alone now on the veranda, heard horseshoes clanking together, and her blood froze. She would have been the last to board, but she didn't, even as Gideon beckoned her. Someone standing at the tree line twenty yards away from the porch caught her attention.

The size of him, yes, but even more so the horseshoes hanging at his waist, clunking together like heavy windchimes.

Watching her, before stepping back into the trees.

Maddy yelled for them to go on and closed the ambulance doors.

She ran into the woods after the man who'd tried to kill her back in Charleston.

54

Gideon

Now

G IDEON YELLED, "WAIT, Beth, wait!" By the end of the driveway, when it was clear Beth either wasn't listening or couldn't hear, he shouted, "Stop!" Beth brought the ambulance to a skidding halt on Mallard Street and looked over her shoulder. Gideon said, "Maddy's not here."

"What do you mean Maddy's not here?"

"She didn't get in," Gideon shouted. "She saw something in the woods. I think she went . . ." *Oh Christ*, he thought, recalling the man with the horseshoes he'd seen outside earlier.

"Went what? Gideon?"

He opened the back door and jumped out.

"Gideon!"

"Go," he shouted. "Go on. Get Simon to the tunnel. We'll meet you there. Go."

Beth hesitated only momentarily. "God damn it, Giddy-Up." He closed the door. She lurched the ambulance in gear and sped off.

Gideon ran in the direction he'd seen Maddy staring when she'd closed the ambulance doors. He entered the woods running, gun poised, recalling, as he ran, how Sully had yelled *Hurry!* from the other ambulance right before those doors had closed. Like they were over there holding a dam about to break. The door to Lalaland was about to burst open and there was little the Seers could do about it.

Gideon entered the woods. Birds swooped and another deer darted across the clearing behind him, but no matter where he looked through the surrounding trees now, the horizon was smoke filled and glowing from fire.

"Maddy!"

He slowed his pace, navigating over deadfall, using his cell phone flashlight, the trees more spread out than they were in the woods surrounding the tunnel. His eyes darted in every direction. He followed every sound. Something in the shadows moved. Sounded like an animal chewing.

Gideon froze when he saw something hanging from a tree twenty feet away. He pointed his light, approached it slowly. It wasn't some*thing* but some*one* in the tree, a male, gutted from neck to pubic bone, suspended in the air by ropes at both wrists, arms pulled back and fastened to two limbs behind him, feet crossed at the ankles and tied to the trunk by more rope. The man's open entrails had spilled out from the chest cavity and hung down in coils to the ground, where another one of those black deer feasted.

Gideon backed away but kept his light on the black deer, red antlers swirled with orange and glistening wet with someone's blood. It watched Gideon as it chewed. Watched Gideon as he slowly stepped away, walking, walking, afraid that it he ran the deer would give chase. After he put fifty yards between them, Gideon took off in a sprint, slowing when he reached the outskirts of the trees and a dirt road flanked on both sides by recently harvested cornfields. Smoke swirls lifted from the field to his right, and he smelled fire.

Ten yards ahead he saw a horseshoe resting in the dirt. He picked it up and started running down the dirt road. "Maddy!" Calling her name as he surveyed both sides. And then he saw something in the harvested field to his right, a silhouette of someone forty to fifty yards in the distance. He veered off in that direction with a fully loaded gun. "Maddy!" He saw an arm raise in the air, holding a horseshoe. Bringing it down. "Maddy!" He closed in, fearing her dead, bludgeoned to death. He aimed, but then realized it was Maddy holding the horseshoe, standing over a massive man lying on the ground, unmoving. Giving no resistance as Maddy brought the horseshoe down upon his face, again and again. Gideon winced at the dull sound it made, colliding with his skull. "Maddy, stop."

She looked over her shoulder toward him, crying. "Is he dead?"

Gideon approached. Saw the exit wound from a bullet in his chest. She must have chased him down, shot him in the back. His face was gone. Gideon said, "He's dead. Maddy, he's dead."

She dropped the horseshoe on the man's chest, said, "Good."

55

Beth

Now

THERE WAS TOO much smoke in the streets to speed.

Too many stunned, bloodied, and now homeless citizens of Harrod's Reach wandering aimlessly. Ripe for the picking, thought Beth as she drove the ambulance down Guthrie at thirty miles per hour. Afraid to go any faster. She'd almost hit too many people appearing out of nowhere from the smoke, moving like zombies, some of them burning.

Beside her in the passenger's seat, Sheriff Meeks took it all in. She'd never seen him this shell-shocked and emotionally gutted. His town was burning, and there was nothing he could do about it. He was supposed to be in the other ambulance, but he'd convinced that driver to drop him at the sheriff's station, which was where Beth found him when she'd detoured from the tunnel to run in and grab Simon's chainsaw.

She'd asked Simon what he needed before entering the tunnel, and he'd said, "The Ripper." The chainsaw rested now between his boots on the floor of the ambulance. Beth kept her eyes out for anything and everything that moved, but also for Gideon and Maddy. She knew Gideon couldn't leave Maddy out there alone. And Beth had refused to allow Sheriff Meeks, in his condition, to stay at the station and *go down with his ship*, as he'd put it.

She had Father Fred in back now as well, with Natalie and Simon, because he'd gotten off the ambulance with Grover, refusing to let him go alone. So many heroes, Beth thought, gaining speed as the smoke began to clear in the open land leading toward the ravine. She glanced in her rear-view and saw Father Fred next to Simon on the bench, hunched over and praying the rosary clamped in his hands.

Simon sat with his head down, hands folded, twiddling his thumbs, mumbling. Every so often Beth heard him say *Simon says*, as if he was playing a game. Number thirty-three, she thought as she closed in on the ravine.

Beside her, Grover pointed to their left. "Beth, look."

Beth followed his finger, saw two figures running through the dark. Closer toward them, she realized it was Gideon and Maddy, and they were sprinting.

Sprinting away from something, she noticed, from something running on all fours. Not a deer, but . . . something that resembled what she'd shot inside Doc Bigsby's garage, faster than she could have ever thought. Beth turned toward it, floored the gas, and steered the ambulance at an angle through a recently harvested cornfield as the thing gained on Gideon and Maddy. "Hold on," she told Grover, and he braced himself with his hands against the dash. "Hold on," she said to her passengers in the back. In the rearview she saw Simon reach out like a human seat belt across Father Fred's chest. Beth bore down on the beast and as soon as it passed into her head-light beams it froze. She tore through it going fifty miles per hour. The thing splattered onto her hood and across her windshield, splintering the glass. Beth brought the ambulance to a stop thirty yards later. She hurried around back, opened the doors, and shouted for Gideon and Maddy to get in.

This time they both boarded, and Beth was on the move two seconds after their doors closed, watching them both in her rearview, watching Maddy violently shake while Gideon held her, Beth thinking how proud she was of him. But also thinking how badly she now wanted to hold her son. Their son. Thinking how she may never see Brody again.

A minute later, Beth slowed the ambulance near the edge of the ravine, where they typically parked before walking down.

A light flashed from the direction of the tunnel. They all started to get out, but Beth said, "Wait."

Another black deer walked atop the hillside, as if prowling, a few yards away. And ten yards beyond the deer, a man stood holding a scythe or a machete, and looked eager to use it. If these deer were indeed hunting, why wasn't it attacking that man beside it?

"There's no telling what's down there," said Beth.

Sheriff Meeks started to roll down his window and point his shotgun out toward the deer, but stopped when Beth told him to. Both the deer and the man had begun to walk their way. Beth watched them with caution. "If we waste all of our ammo getting down there, we've got nothing left to defend us on the way back up."

"If we don't get Simon down there soon," Gideon said, "then it's not gonna matter."

Sheriff Meeks said, "What then, Beth?"

Beth nodded toward the tunnel, where another flash of light lit the sky. "The ravine levels out about fifty yards down."

"You wanna *drive* down into the ravine?" Sheriff Meeks asked.

"It's been done before," said Natalie. "Rick Doogan did it in high school. Tore his car up something awful but he made it."

Beth knew this because Jax had been in the car with Doogan, along with Carson Knox and Chimp Deavers. Beth slipped the ambulance in gear and started coasting parallel to the ravine. The deer moved out of the way, as did the man with the scythe, although as the ambulance passed, he ran the tip of the scythe alongside the vehicle, scratching it. The son of a bitch looked crazy; no doubt, thought Beth, one who'd ridden into town courtesy of the Lullaby Express.

Natalie said from the back seats, "You have to hit it at the right angle."

"And with enough speed," said Sheriff Meeks.

"But not too much," added Gideon.

Beth coasted along the bumpy terrain of grass and weeds overlooking the gully, saw someone else standing atop the ravine in the distance.

"Angle in soon," said Natalie. "Or it'll be way too steep."

Beth gripped the wheel with both hands and started the ambulance down the incline at an angle that, for a moment, made her think the vehicle might flip, but then it leveled slightly. She tapped the gas, hit a dip in the slope that made them all rise from their seats.

"Gas," Gideon said.

Smoke sifted out from under the hood in two places, and something rattled loose below.

Beth gunned the engine again. The ambulance tilted the opposite way from before, righted itself, hit another dip, but the bottom of the ravine was in view now. If she gave it enough gas, she'd have enough momentum to make it without stalling out on the thick brambles and saplings near the bottom of the slope.

"Hold on," she said, closing her eyes on impact, which was rough, but not as rough as she'd feared. When she opened her eyes, they were on somewhat level ground and still somehow moving clunkily along, lucky the airbags hadn't deployed. At least two of the tires had blown on the descent, and now something hissed below the hood, along with the smoke, but the tunnel was finally in view.

Grover clutched his stomach, winced in pain, and as much as she wanted to tell him *I told you so*, she felt better having him here. They passed through tall weeds and over small saplings where train tracks once lived, but now it was more akin to driving through a jungle. From what Beth could tell, the right headlight was out, so only the ambulance's left light illuminated the rest of their passage to the tunnel.

Up ahead, light flashed inside the tunnel.

"How close can we get?" Gideon asked from the back.

"I don't know," she said, slowing the ambulance fifty yards away from the southern entrance. The vehicle sputtered, died, and rolled to a stop well short of what she'd hoped, which wouldn't have been an issue had the southern entrance not looked like an apocalyptic dreamworld.

Moonlight revealed at least a dozen people standing outside the tunnel's entrance, many holding sharp weapons. One massive man held an axe. Another a scythe. One wore a business suit, but clutched a dagger. They all watched the hissing ambulance like it had just landed from outer space. Like it had interrupted whatever intense waiting they'd been doing.

Beth knew they'd all come into town on the red bus, staying inside the Beehive Hotel right under their noses.

Grover said, "Rip it off."

"Like a Band-Aid," Beth said, opening her driver's side door. She said to Grover, "Stay in here."

He nodded, didn't look like he had the energy to open his door even if he wanted to. But before she closed hers he said, "Beth?"

"Yeah?"

He smiled. "Told you they'd listen."

She closed her door, walked backwards alongside the ambulance to keep all those weirdos in view, and opened the back door. Simon was the first out, followed by Gideon and Maddy. Natalie was on her way when Beth told her to stay with Sheriff Meeks and Father Fred.

Beth said, "Sorry, Father. I think we're beyond praying right now."

Father Fred watched the tunnel. "Yeah, me too."

"You're all armed?" she asked the three of them.

They were.

She closed them in, walked with Gideon, Maddy, and Simon toward the tunnel, where another flash of light briefly illuminated the entrance. There and gone, but enough to reveal that more of Lalaland had come through. The people weren't the only ones standing and waiting. She'd seen glimpses of animals. A couple more deer. More seashells and fish had come through with another Lalaland tide. More trees had leaves that had turned white. Grass and weeds had turned yellow.

They had no time to waste. Beth led them toward the tunnel. The atmosphere was eerily quiet.

Simon moved up beside her but said to their group. "Don't look. Simon says, don't look."

And while some of the people and animals standing on either side of the gully may have pinched closer to them, none of them made a move to attack. Beth wondered if they'd had their fill of carnage and death for the moment. But then, she realized, their eyes weren't so much on their cluster closing in on the tunnel, but on Simon, who seemed to grab everyone's attention, including the animals, many of which had started growling and snarling but staying put as they moved toward the tunnel, now only twenty yards away.

Beth thinking, *It shouldn't be this easy.*

A purple snake, ten feet long at least, slithered across the path and disappeared into a thicket of yellow prairie grass. As they closed in, the crowd started to circle around behind them, blocking any passage out.

Simon said again, "Don't look."

The tunnel lit up again, and inside the flash of light at the entrance stood a tall man with a head full of antlers next to a woman in a black miniskirt and red halter top.

Simon unstrapped the chainsaw from his shoulder and started The Ripper purring. "Mr. Lullaby," said Simon.

The man with the antlers stepped out under the moonlight, and the woman along with him. She held a knife, while he appeared unarmed.

"Stay back," Simon told them. "And if he starts into his lullabies, cover your ears."

It was the longest sentence she'd ever heard Simon mutter. Beth thought back to the woman sleeping in the third-floor suite of the Beehive, Mickey down in the lobby, and then all the others across Harrod's Reach who'd somehow been put to sleep.

Simon distanced himself from their pack.

The man with the antlers gently guided the woman beside him off toward the side of the gully, and then approached Simon. He put a finger to his lips and went *shhh . . . shhh . . .* And then he started singing, "Sleep, sleep, sleep . . . Don't lie too close to the edge of the bed . . ."

Simon said, "Bayu bayushki Bayu . . ."

". . . Or little gray wolf will come," sang the man with the antlers.

"From Russia," said Simon. And then again, "Cover your ears. Now."

The man with the antlers slowly approached, the tunnel behind him acting like a microphone for his voice, and Beth had already begun to grow dizzy. She aimed the gun at the man with the antlers but couldn't hold her arm steady, as the man sang, ". . . And grab you by the flank."

Beth, gun still in hand, did as Simon said and covered her ears. As did Maddy and Gideon behind them. But the words seemed not to affect Simon, who continued his approach toward the man he'd called Mr. Lullaby, unfazed and unabated. What had Maddy said? That Simon had spent his entire life *here*, getting acclimated for *there*.

Because he was number thirty-three.

". . . Drag you into the woods," Mr, Lullaby sang. "Underneath the willow root . . ."

Gideon dropped to a knee, hands over both ears and pressing hard. Maddy dropped to her knees beside him, and then slumped to the ground, doing her best to keep both hands over her ears, and at the same time battling whatever sleep the man with the antlers was trying to force upon them. Beth wobbled next and then dropped to the ground, vision blurry. She pressed her hands over her ears. The lullaby also didn't seem to affect the people who'd gathered.

Light briefly illuminated the tunnel again.

Beth saw a glimpse of an ocean on the other side.

A pink bird flew through.

It went dark again.

Simon raised The Ripper and charged.

Mr. Lullaby lowered his head, pointed his antlers.

CHAPTER

56

Teddy

Now

INTERESTING, THOUGHT TEDDY, that his lullaby had done nothing to the big mountain of a man now charging at him with a chainsaw.

The same chainsaw, in fact, he'd allowed the Nanny to take from the cabin in the woods. And then it struck Teddy that this was the same man who'd been sleeping in the bed that night.

Teddy lowered his head and charged.

Braced for impact.

Felt the chainsaw blade churn through part of an antler at the same time his antlers punctured the man's chest.

57

The Tunnel

Now

THE SCREAM THAT came from the antlered man upon Simon's collision with him sent chills down Beth's spine, but the sensation worked as proof that she was still alive.

Still awake.

And therefore—like Gideon and Maddy getting to their feet beside her—still vulnerable.

She stood, weak-kneed, realizing the crowd had moved closer, mostly encircling them, as Simon wrestled with the antlered man at the tunnel's entrance. In the background, another flash came and went, but it was clear that the man's antlers had punctured Simon's chest and the chainsaw now rested on the ground, still purring.

The woman in the black skirt stepped closer, as if willing to help. Beth fired at her, clipped her arm. The woman spun, regained her balance, and the rest of the mares broke into action, enclosing them in a circle.

Beth and Maddy and Gideon stood with their backs to each other, aiming their weapons at the encroaching crowd of human mares and Lala-land beasts.

Simon placed his hands around Mr. Lullaby's neck and lifted him from the ground. Lifted him and carried him and slammed his body hard into the inside wall of the tunnel. Mr. Lullaby dropped, moaning, but struggled back to his feet.

By that time Simon, bleeding from his chest, had already grabbed The Ripper from the ground and had run into the tunnel.

On instinct, Beth went in after him.

*　*　*

"Nooooo!" Gideon yelled when he saw Beth enter the tunnel with Simon.

The ground started shaking.

Rocks fell from the southern entrance.

*　*　*

Maddy had no choice but to pull the trigger at the man running at her with an axe.

The bullet hit the man's forehead, killing him instantly.

The shaking ground knocked her down.

*　*　*

Beth thought, *Too late to turn back now.*

Behind her the entrance to the tunnel was collapsing.

She hurried to keep up with Simon, thinking, *Brody, I'm sorry.* Ahead, at the northern entrance, Lalaland flashed again. She saw blue sky above a purple horizon, ocean waves crashing against the craggy shore of an island, and then it was gone again, the fallen bricks of the northern entrance now back in view.

"The Island of Bones," said Simon, hurrying toward the other end of the tunnel.

Beth followed him as rocks fell from above.

As Simon closed in on the northern entrance, rocks began to fall from that opening too, and all Beth could think was the game In-One-Out-One.

And that she'd never lost.

*　*　*

The ground shook.

Rocks fell from the tunnel of One-Side Mountain. Blinding dust clouds broke out in roiling plumes as boulders collided with the ground, the southern entrance closed, and the mountain turned in on itself, collapsing before their eyes.

People screamed.

Animals fled.

Gideon fired at the crowd.

Back-to-back, Maddy did the same.

Just as the dust cloud began to engulf them, turning the air black, Gideon gripped Maddy's hand, and together they ran toward the ambulance.

* * *

Twenty yards away, Lalaland flashed and went, flashed and went, as large as a drive-in movie screen, and Simon never broke stride.

He picked up his pace, and Beth sprinted to keep up with him. As more of the northern entrance collapsed, Beth felt increasingly trapped.

She imagined being crushed.

She imagined her severed limbs joining those found over the hundred-plus years of the tunnel's reign.

She thought, as she jumped atop Simon's back, if he was number thirty-three, why shouldn't I be thirty-four?

Lalaland flashed.

Beth's face lit up with light.

And she couldn't help but smile as Simon ran into it.

* * *

Maddy and Gideon made it out of the heaviest smoke clouds, coughing and choking as they closed in on the ambulance, which rested in the gully much like he imagined the derailed train had a hundred years before, buried in the weeds and deadfall like a relic.

There was no way Beth was alive.

There was no way she and Simon had survived the mountain coming down atop them.

There was no way anyone could discover their bodies beneath the rubble.

A shotgun blast made them both duck.

Sheriff Meeks stood beside the ambulance, firing at things Gideon didn't know were fleeing all around them. Father Fred and Natalie hurried out to them, ushered them along the ravine, away from the chaos, as Sheriff Meeks, bleeding from his wounds, fired and reloaded.

They ran from the dark rolling clouds tunneling their way. Sheriff Meeks walked backwards, firing again and reloading, before finally turning and doing his best to run.

At the top of the ravine, after Gideon had helped everyone up the steep hillside, the second ambulance awaited, lightbar flashing. The driver had returned for them after taking the others to the next town over. Gideon's parents and brother were alive, Amy and the others too.

Gideon was the last one to get in the ambulance. Before closing the back door, he looked out toward where the tunnel had been, and something told him Beth was alive too.

Somewhere.

It was the only way to convince himself they could go, that they weren't leaving anyone behind. And he figured, born on the same night as they were, he'd feel it in his heart if Beth had died beneath that mountain.

Gideon closed the rear door, sat beside Maddy, and held her close as the ambulance sped through smoke and Harrod's Reach burned.

ACKNOWLEDGMENTS

W̲RITING A NOVEL is never dull, and while all novels have a beginning and an end, the paths traveled in between can certainly carry stories of their own. I started *Mr. Lullaby* a couple of years ago but stopped at fifty pages to finish writing *The Nightmare Man*, the first novel under my pen name, J. H. Markert. When I picked back up with *Mr. Lullaby*, it was with a new perspective on the overall narrative, and while all the characters are new, I was able to easily connect it to the world I'd created in *The Nightmare Man*, which pleased me on two fronts—I was able to give my readers somewhat of a sequel, yet at the same time create another stand-alone. And both novels now should give me many options for creating more from this world. For those readers hoping for the return of the storyline and characters from *The Nightmare Man*, it will, I promise, happen at some point! Halfway through writing this novel, I was asked to be a long-term substitute teacher for a dear friend battling cancer. It also happened to be for my daughter's eighth grade class, so I agreed to do it, and suddenly here I was teaching middle school history. Having been used to writing full time, this certainly created some challenges, as my writing time was limited. But alas, I got it done, leaning on the teachers and administration along the way, and wow, what a year that was! Thank you to everyone at St. Edward, and all my new teacher friends for pulling me through, as it was certainly a year I'll never forget.

For me, at least, thanking people at the end of a novel is the most stressful part of writing a novel, as I'll inevitably leave someone out, although certainly not on purpose! But thank you to Matt Martz, my publisher at Crooked Lane, and Sara J. Henry, my editor, for your expertise, constant support, and belief in my work. To Rebecca Nelson, Dulce Botello, Thai Fantauzzi Perez, Melissa Rechter, Madeline Rathle, Heather VenHuizen, and everyone at Crooked Lane Books—you're amazing! This cover— WOW! To my cousin and loyal reader Shawn Lockhart for being the first person to read an early version of *Mr. Lullaby*. To Gill Holland, for your constant support of my work. To my siblings and parents, where creativity always abounds, thank you! To my agent, Alice Speilburg, thank you for putting up with my craziness and my nonstop book ideas; you've single-handedly changed the course of my career and I can't thank you enough. To my wife, Tracy, I think I'm getting closer 😊; thank you for continuing to keep the faith, for being the breadwinner for twenty-four years, for being such a wonderful mother to our two children, aaaaaand I'm not sure you want to read this one! And thank you, dear reader, for making it this far, with hopes that you'll continue to read whatever comes next.

Continuously onward and upward!

J. H.

Read an excerpt from

SLEEP TIGHT

the next

NOVEL

by J. H. MARKERT

available Fall 2024 from
Crooked Lane Books

NEW YORK

Before

*T*HE BOY COLORED *so hard the black crayon snapped in half in his hand.*

This wasn't uncommon with that color.

The darkness he remembered around those eyes was thick, and only the right amount of pressure could reproduce that deep, dark black.

From his seat on the hardwood floor, he pulled another black crayon from the bucket beside him and resumed coloring, furiously, hurriedly—Mother was on her way up.

He'd done something bad, and she was mad.

And when she was mad, she got mean. But he couldn't remember what he'd done this time.

"Noah," his mother's shrill voice called from the stairwell outside his closed bedroom door. "Noah Nichols!"

Her footfalls made the steps groan.

Made his heart feel wrong, sick and swollen and thumpy.

He imagined her knee-length cotton skirt, thick like a curtain, swooshing upon each step, her big feet crammed into heavy shoes.

He pressed hard on the picture.

Had to get it dark.

Had to get it right.

Her voice grew closer outside the door. "Noah, I'm coming up. Someone's been a baddy. Someone's been a big baddy boy!"

He imagined the stairs splintering under her weight, her falling through into a dark, dusty hole, plunging into the basement where all the spiders slept, into the cellar with the snakes and guttersnipes, into the earth with the worms and the roots and the dinosaur bones, and he imagined her dying down there.

Decaying into dust.

Like motes.

He colored, hard, broke another black crayon. He tossed it aside with the others, content now that he'd finished the picture in time. Finished it enough.

"NOAH!" She was right outside the door.

What did he do?

You know what you did . . .

He blew crayon dust from the picture, scattering the black remnants through the air, through the dust motes already hovering next to the sun-touched window. The black slivers settled on the faded floorboards, blending with the dozens of other colors now staining the wood like a paint pallet, like he imagined a rainbow might if it suddenly blew apart into billions of miniscule pieces.

The doorknob rattled.

"Noah, unlock this door, right now! RIGHT NOW!"

He wasn't supposed to lock the door. She swore the next time he locked it Father would get out the belt. Not the one he wore, but the one he used as a weapon. The one with the globs of hardened glue in each of the holes.

But he didn't remember locking the door.

He looked down at the colored picture in his hands and it scared him.

It was signed in red crayon at the bottom right corner—Dean.

The doorknob shook like it might snap off. "Do you want the ark, Noah? Is that what you want?" He tried not to look at the closet door in the corner of the room, small like a hobbit door, looming as large as a tunnel now in his periphery.

The words painted carefully above it.

"Don't put me in the ark," he whispered to himself.

He stood, weak-kneed, and shuffled toward the wall, eyeing the expanse of drawings he'd tacked to it, all various versions of the eyes—they numbered in the dozens now—after his return from that scary house. The bedroom door shook, and his mother screamed about flood waters and the ark.

"NOAH!"

He grabbed a couple thumbtacks from the Tupperware bowl on the floor and pinned his picture to the wall with the rest of them, hanging there like a giant collage, all signed by names he didn't know.

Missing Teens Found in Twisted Tree
Month Long Hunt Ends in Tragedy

*Y*ESTERDAY AFTERNOON, SHORTLY *after 4 PM, the hunt for two missing teens, Grisham Graham and Jeremy Shakes, both seniors at Twisted Tree High School and stars of the football team, came to a sad and disturbing ending. After an anonymous letter was dropped on the steps of the Twisted Tree Police Department, hinting at the location of the missing teens, the bodies of both boys were found buried twenty yards from the abandoned Crawley Mansion, a popular Twisted Tree haunt for teenage dares, a stone's throw from the town's famous twisted trees. Both boys were found with similar head injuries, fatal blows from a blunt instrument, still undetermined. With the first reports of the two boys missing coinciding with the night of Jeff Pritchard's arrest four weeks ago, authorities are now investigating a suspected link between the two incidents, as the Crawley Mansion, the last place the boys were known to have been, is only a mile jaunt through the woods to Jeff's "House of Horrors." Grisham and Jeremy both had promising college careers . . .*

CHAPTER

1

THE PORCH LIGHT was on.

It was ten minutes before nine, and Julia was still awake; her small silhouette had been at the living room window and disappeared as soon as they'd pulled to a stop at the curb. Four fat raindrops plopped against the windshield, and then a steady drizzle fell from the night sky.

Tess Claiborne paused before getting out of her partner's idling, unmarked sedan.

"You okay?" Danny Gomes drummed the steering wheel with his thumbs, something he knew drove her crazy—not so much that he'd do it—but because he had no rhythm. No sense of tempo. No hint that it was even a particular tune. And for someone like Tess, born constantly needing to get to the bottom of things, his drumming was like fingernails on a chalkboard. But who was she to gripe? Her car had a dead battery she hadn't had time to mess with, and she was grateful for the lift.

She said, "Fine," and looked back at the now vacant window. Truthfully, she wasn't yet ready to face her own daughter, and she didn't like how pathetic that felt. If it hadn't been clear before the breakup with Justin, it was now—the *favorite* parent was the one kicked out and she was left to deal with the confusion.

And with Danny, sitting beside her, also being her husband's best friend, Justin was often the favored spouse, as well. Tess glanced at him.

He stopped drumming.

Rainwater cascaded down the windshield. She straightened her white blouse and fingered the shoulder holster that held her 9mm. "Turn the wipers on. Please."

He did. The water cleared. "Better?"

She nodded. "I'm giving him the papers tomorrow."

"What? Tess, really?"

"Yeah, Danny, really? You got a problem with that?"

"No, I mean . . . hell, I don't know. Maybe. Just seems kind of fast, you know? What about counseling? Eliza gave you that number, right?"

"What about minding your own business?"

"You brought it up."

"Somebody needed to."

Danny shifted in his seat to better face her. He had corn nut dust on his shirt from earlier, right above his belly, where he liked to wipe his hands after eating anything powdery. "What about your business is ours and ours is yours? We tell each other everything? The Four Horseman and all that shit?"

"We were joking," Tess said, remembering back to the night the four of them had said something along those lines, all of them drunk around the fire pit, Justin going as far as saying they should make a blood pact, like they were teenagers, Tess crumbling the wrapper of the Dum-Dum she'd just dunked into her Vodka tonic and plopped into her mouth and calling Justin an idiot, because it was just that way between them.

Thick as thieves. The two couples, always together.

And now it was all shit because of her husband.

God damn you, Justin.

She looked away from her partner, back to the house, the vacant window.

She couldn't tell who Danny was more pissed at, Justin for cheating or her for kicking him out. Which she'd had every right to do. Even Danny's wife, Eliza, a social worker who still somehow made time to properly raise their five kids, had admitted to that. Or maybe Danny was pissed off in general because their world had been disrupted.

Either way, the silence between them lately had only made their job as detectives in the Missoula Police Department more difficult and her partner's habits more alarmingly annoying, exacerbating the fact that Danny, a natural born goofball, flew by the seat of his pants while she was nuts and bolts and spreadsheets and nonstop serious.

Thunder vibrated in the east, a slow rumble. Tess grew uneasy. Her heartbeat quickened.

A storm was coming.

Danny scratched his thinning brown hair and exhaled like a puffer fish, something he did when he was resigned to certain things. He asked, "You going to be okay tonight?"

Tess nodded. "I'll be fine." Her phobia about storms, a problem since her teenage years, back when she'd gone by Tessa, was not *his* problem.

"What time is the thing, tonight?"

"Midnight. Eastern time."

"Hopefully it'll give your dad some peace."

"Yeah," she said, thinking of the execution that was to take place across the country in a few hours. "Hopefully." She watched the rain, opened the car door. "I'll see you in the morning." She closed the door, dodged Julia's pink bicycle in the middle of the sidewalk and hurried inside.

Tammy and Lincoln Bellings were neighbors who had become regular babysitters since she'd kicked Justin to the curb. They'd raised four children who were grown and out of the house, and relished the time with Julia. Tess entered the kitchen and found Tammy with her hands in the sink, suds to her elbows, Lincoln at the table playing checkers with Julia.

Tess said, "Look who's still awake."

Julia shot her mother an annoyed look, a staple for months now, since she turned nine, and more frequent since Justin's departure.

Lincoln moved a checker. "It's my fault. She suckered me into one more game." He moved a checker and collected the pieces he'd jumped. Julia frowned, studying the board like she was wondering how she could have missed that move. Lincoln said, "I charged your car battery."

"You didn't have to do that but thank you."

"We do for neighbors, Tess." He stood from the table, ruffled Julia's sandy hair and handed his wife her raincoat.

Tess watched Julia clean up the checkerboard.

Tammy touched Tess's arm, lowered her voice. "Hang in there. And call if you need anything." She lowered her voice. "I'll say a prayer for your father tonight."

"They're at the cabin," said Tess. "Figured they'd need their privacy."

Tess saw her neighbors out and locked the door behind them. When she returned to the kitchen, Julia had readied the checkerboard for another game.

"Not tonight, honey. It's already past your bedtime. It's a school night."

Julia stood, shoving the checkerboard to the floor, scattering the pieces. "*Daddy* would have let me." She ran from the room.

Tess called after her, but her daughter was already down the hall, slamming her bedroom door.

Thunder rumbled; Tess's heartbeat raced. She pulled a glass from the cabinet, filled it with two fingers of Old Sam on the rocks, and sipped until warmth slowed her heartbeat. She'd have Julia pick up the checkers in the morning. She sipped bourbon. The caramel note reminded her of Twisted Tree, her childhood hometown in Kentucky, where bourbon was not only a drink, but a lifestyle.

Deciding she didn't want to face an argument from her daughter in the morning, Tess began picking up the red-and-black checkers, plucking them piece by piece from the tile floor.

Until thunder sounded again, a fierce clap instead of a rumble.

Tess flinched, then, out of annoyance, kicked the remaining pieces across the floor and left the kitchen, thinking about how she and Eliza always had to be the disciplinarians while their husbands were the playmates. They loved their children just as much as their husbands, yet it was always Justin and Danny the kids ran to when they returned from work. How Justin, as soon as he'd walk in the door, would drop his briefcase in the foyer—his symbolic way of leaving his work at the door; something she'd never been able to do—and stand there like a statue with his arms out to either side. He called it the Panda Tree. Julia would come running from whatever room she'd be in and jump at him. Sometimes she'd cling to his chest like she was giving him a hug. Sometimes she'd land sideways and cling to him that way. But no matter what angle she'd jump from, she'd cling there like a panda on a tree and there they'd stand, frozen together, like she was attached by Velcro, until one of them would break character and start laughing.

Tess found herself at Julia's bedroom door, smiling at the memory. She nudged the door open and found her on the bed, pretending to sleep, her arm around her new doll she'd named Dolly. Tess left her alone, entered her own bedroom, tried to ignore the smell of Justin's cologne she'd sprayed nostalgically that morning. *Pathetically.* Somehow it still lingered, like the toughest memories tend to do. She tossed her purse to the floor, kicked off her flats, removed her holster, and locked her gun in the middle dresser drawer. She stripped down to her bra and panties, turned sideways to catch her profile in the vanity mirror. At thirty-three her figure was still athletic, toned. Eliza joked with her about it, her still having that body, when, after five kids, Eliza had grown a little heavier—curvier and more voluptuous, she'd say, adding that Danny, because he was such a good husband, had graciously gained weight right along with her. They'd joke about Tess and Justin still being fit because they only had one, hinting, like they always did, that they were well past due for another.

Hinting that one was easy, when it wasn't.

Tess would force a smile, but deep down it hurt every time it was mentioned because not having another came down to her. Not that she couldn't, but more so that she wouldn't, and it was well known between the four of them that Justin had wanted another child now for years.

Tess turned away from the mirror and did what she'd always done whenever the guilt crept in about never giving Justin that second or third child, she thought back to how difficult it had been with the first. The rigorous delivery. The problems she'd had breast feeding. The post partem depression weighing down on her like a bolder for nearly a year. The sleepless nights. The constant crying of a colicky baby.

Julia had been a difficult infant.

Danny and Eliza seemingly had gone through none of that, with any of their five, or if they had, never admitted to it.

Eliza, as Tess often told her, was just better at it.

At motherhood.

And this had all become more prominent in her mind since she'd forced Justin to leave.

Screaming at him two weeks ago because she couldn't, at that moment, stand to look at him. And now, here she was putting her shoulder-length brown hair into a bun and slipping on one of Justin's T-shirts, because old habits die hard.

And she was starting to miss him.

Rain tapped against the roof, spilled over gutters that needed cleaning. Her wedding ring rested on the dresser beside the manila envelope with the divorce papers.

Tomorrow's problem.

Lightning flashed outside the window. More thunder, louder this time. She finished her drink and put it down hard on the dresser, still annoyed at how Julia had stormed out of the kitchen earlier.

But it *was* a school night and she needed to get to bed.

With Justin not in the house, she wondered if she had what it took to play both roles, good cop and bad?

Her bedroom door creaked open.

Julia stood in the threshold with Dolly in one arm and her frayed pink blanket in the other. "Mommy, does the lightning come first or the thunder?"

Her baby blue eyes reminded her of Justin.

Daddy's little girl.

God damn him.

And now her daughter was inheriting her fears. The electricity went out. Tess remained calm, but it was a front. "Should I get the candles?"

Julia nodded. "I'll get the paper."

The walk-in closet perfectly buffered the storm noise.

It was dark except for their candle glow—Tess held a red candle while Julia used a yellow. Artwork took their minds off the thunder and lightning—a Justin idea from years ago. But it was the first time during a storm where it was just the two of them and Julia looked aware of it. But she tilted her candle toward the paper regardless. Yellow wax plopped on the page in front of her, adding to the shape that had already dried.

Julia stared at it cock-eyed. "Kind of looks like a flower." She looked at her mother's paper. A red blob smeared the middle of it. "Is that an elephant?"

"I guess it could be. That does look like a trunk." Tess added two more drops to form a leg, and then another to make the trunk longer.

Sometimes instead of dripping wax they'd draw pictures. Pictures to form words, sort of charades by drawing, another Justin idea that Julia favored. Tonight, they just dripped wax, but pictures they'd made in the last storm remained, the top one showing a Christmas tree and a cookie, with a plus sign in between. *Christmas cookie.* Very simple game, but Tess liked the wax better. With the wax she didn't have to think.

Julia leaned forward and tilted one drop of yellow into what could have been the head of Tess's red elephant. "There. Now it can see." She blew her candle out and rested on the floor, her hair fanned out like wild grass over her pillow. She closed her eyes as distant thunder rumbled. "You remember when Uncle Danny tried doing the Panda Tree with all five of them?"

Danny wasn't her uncle, just what she'd always called him. Neither Tess nor Justin had siblings, and Julia had wanted an uncle. In the dark, Tess said, "Yeah, I remember."

Tess thought Julia was done, but then her daughter said, "When's Daddy coming back home?"

A lump formed in Tess's throat. She'd rather talk about the storm. "I don't know."

Julia left it at that, and Tess was relieved.

A few minutes later, Julia snored softly.

Tess watched her daughter sleep, watched her skinny chest rise and fall with only a hint of sound. It made her heart swell.

She checked her phone; she'd forgotten to take it off vibrate earlier. Justin had sent a text ten minutes ago.

How U holding up? Candles are in the closet. So is the paper. Talk soon?

She didn't respond. She placed the phone face down against the floor and the closet went dark again. It was ten o'clock. She wondered how her parents were holding up at the cabin. She could see her father in his recliner listening to the radio, waiting for word that *it* had happened.

Midnight in Kentucky.

The execution.

"A N EYE FOR an eye," a woman in an anti-abortion shirt screamed outside the Kentucky State Penitentiary in Eddyville, where low clouds covered the prison grounds like a purple caul. "He deserves to die."

The lines had literally been drawn across the parking lot, hours ago with white paint, and now hundreds of death penalty protestors shouted across No-Man's Land at the supporters, all of them holding signs as riot police struggled to keep them at bay.

FRY FATHER SILENCE
KILLING IS NEVER RIGHT
ABOLISH CAPITAL PUNISHMENT

The most widely followed execution in United States history drew near. The state was minutes away from putting a man to death by electrocution. In seventeen years on the row, exhausting every appeal known to the courts along the way, Jeff Pritchard—a former parochial school janitor who had for years disguised himself as a priest to his victims, to lure and later kill what he considered the outcasts of society—had yet to say a word.

After his arrest, the newspapers had given him the name Father Pritchard, and when it was clear he'd gone silent, completely refusing to talk, they'd then dubbed him Father Silence, and Jeff had embraced that moniker with a smirk. He was not a priest and never had been, but the pictures from his arrest at Twisted Tree, wearing the stolen priestly clerics, had flashed all over the news channels and newspapers and internet and had become so engrained in the minds of the public that they'd taken it as fact.

News crews from every state crowded the woods around the prison, maneuvering to get as close as they could to the wrought-iron gates. Cameras flashed. Many held candles. Various religious sects shouted at one another over the morality of what was about to happen; others were irate over how long it had taken.

"Abolish capital punishment," screamed a suited man.

"Do it for the children!" shouted a woman in dreadlocks.

"Fry Father Silence!"

From every angle it was videoed—by phone, on tripod and iPad, the atmosphere dangerously close to riot.

But inside the prison walls, the execution process moved on.

And all was silent.

The warden followed four prison guards as they escorted Jeff Pritchard to the execution room at the end of No. 3 Cellhouse.

So far, all had gone as practiced.

On a humid night in May 1911, an eighteen-year-old boy named James Buckner had made history as the first electric chair victim in Kentucky. While awaiting his death, he was baptized, reborn, and spent his last hours reading the Bible.

Jeff Pritchard had participated in none of those now-common customs. He'd denied the chaplain, along with a last meal. Fellow death row inmates whispered goodbyes as he made the long walk. Jeff nodded in acknowledgement, but his eyes never wavered from the black door at the end of the hall.

The execution room that housed Old Sparky was sterile and cold, having not been used in over thirty years, as the state had transitioned from the electric chair to lethal injection in the late 1990s. But the new governor, Clinton Bullsworth, was an old school ball-buster cowboy who'd campaigned on finally putting Jeff Pritchard in the ground *hot.*

Bullsworth knew his execution history: lethal injection had the highest rate of botched executions, and he didn't want to take a chance with Jeff Pritchard, aka, Father Silence. Truth was—and there was evidence of the very words in a video gone viral on TikTok—that he wanted to see the man sizzle. Just weeks into office, papers were signed, the electric chair was recommissioned, and Old Sparky was set for a comeback.

Media watched from the adjoining room, through shatterproof class, as the guards helped Jeff into the chair. After the first strap was fastened, the warden faced the adjoining room, stoically. On the other side of the glass sat members of the victims' families. The executioner. Jeff's lawyer, Barrett Stevens. The sheriff, prison doctor, and chaplain. The only people to decline the invitation were the detectives who'd caught him nearly two decades ago.

Jeff avoided eye contact with the families, but nodded at his lawyer, then the governor, who took a step back from the glass inside the viewing area. The guards tightened straps around Jeff's arms and adjusted electrodes at his calves and wrists. In a handwritten note weeks ago, Jeff claimed he was a giver, not a taker, as Christ had been, and he was ready to die for his beliefs, although it was widely believed Jeff had formed a cult of followers who lived the *opposite* of Christ's teachings.

They pulled the thick leather belt across Jeff's chest and dropped the wired leather mask over his long silvery hair. Only his lips and nose showed through the holes.

The warden nodded and the guards left the room, faster than they'd practiced.

"Jeff Pritchard, can you hear me?" He nodded. "You have been judged by a jury of your peers, sentenced, and condemned to death by electrocution. If you have any last words before the electrocution is carried out, please state them now."

In his years on death row the man in the chair had never given the warden, police, counselors, or reporters a word. He'd turned down psychologists, NBC, ABC, CNN, Fox, and Barbara Walters.

But now his lips moved, and he whispered something the warden couldn't make out—but the guard standing nearby went pale. The warden glanced to the viewing room and then back to the chair, where Jeff sat peacefully.

The circular clock on the wall read midnight.

He signaled the executioner, then joined him in a side room. The first charge of 1500 volts started with a low whine and a loud snap as current surged into Jeff's body.

CHAPTER

3

AFTER THE STORM passed, Tess blew out their candles, opened the closet door, and lifted Julia from the carpeted floor.

She was almost to the hallway when Julia mumbled. "Sleep in your bed."

She hadn't posed it as a question, more of a statement. Justin always said children in the bed were the best forms of birth control, but he wasn't here, and Tess didn't feel like sleeping alone.

She tucked Julia in on Justin's side and watched her slip back into sleep. She'd told herself earlier in the day that she would not turn the television on tonight. Her father had said the same thing. He and her mother had escaped to the cabin in Lolo National Forest, to get away from the media swarm. It wasn't as bad as the days right after Jeff's arrest, but three weeks ago the local media had begun to call, requesting interviews and statements, and her father willingly obliged, until Mother put a stop to them and demanded they go out of town.

Enough is enough, Leland.

But Tess doubted that her father, a decorated former detective who had, along with his partner, Burt Lobell, been the ones who had arrested Jeff Pritchard, was passively sitting by. He was probably awake now watching CNN.

Just as they'd made a pact *not* to do. But Betsy always said Tess got her stubbornness honest, from Leland no doubt, and if they wanted to do something they did it. Tess grabbed the remote and turned on the television to see if the execution went off as planned.

A beautiful woman with a microphone spoke to a well-dressed man at the CNN studio.

"... *and finally, the controversy came to an end this morning after midnight when Jeff Pritchard was electrocuted in the State Prison in Eddyville, Kentucky. As one of the most mysterious serial killers ever to—*"

She turned the television off and dropped the remote on the bed. Her heart hammered and her blood pressure spiked. *Jeff Pritchard. Father Silence.* No matter what he was called, he was finally dead. *However deep they bury him won't be deep enough.*

She considered calling her dad. *Leave him alone. He's fine.* Probably drinking Old Sam just as she was. She sent him a text anyway:

Well, it's over. How are you and Mom doing?

She hit Send and waited, doubtful he'd text back—he wasn't a fan of texting. If he responded at all it would be a phone call. She put her nose to the rim of the rock glass, smelled caramel and vanilla notes that reminded her of home, and downed a healthy gulp of the bourbon to bury any memories trying to resurface.

Buried memories Justin, as a professional psychologist, had too often tried to *unbury* over their ten years of marriage, convinced it all stemmed from her childhood. A childhood that had been good, up until it wasn't. But she grew tired of his questions. She wasn't his fucking patient. She was his wife. And after a while felt like she wasn't even good at that.

Her phone rang.

She smiled, found her hand shaking slightly as she answered it. "Daddy."

"Tough detective still calling her old man Daddy?"

"He's finally dead."

"As a doornail," he said.

"How do you feel?"

"On the record?"

"Sure."

"Relieved."

"And off?"

"Relieved."

"You could have texted me that much."

"Then I wouldn't have gotten to hear your voice in the middle of the night, Sugar."

The quiver in his voice hadn't gone unnoticed. Try as he might, her father wasn't a good actor—he wore his emotions on his sleeve—and the phone did little to mask his unease.

He's hiding something.

"Mom in bed?"

"Drawing a bath. She has her way of relaxing." Ice clinked in a glass as he swallowed. "And I've got mine."

She did likewise and the sip went down smoother than the previous ones.

Now that she'd heard the ice in the glass, she realized her father sounded tipsy. But who could blame him on this night? "Have you heard from anyone?"

A pause. Another sip. "Burt called. Talked briefly. He's hiding too, at least for the night."

Together Burt and her father had led the charge into Jeff's house on the night of his arrest. He and Burt had talked regularly for several years after the move to Montana, but now only on occasion. At least they kept in touch. Tess knew that sometimes talking to his old partner made him sad, and she wished now that she hadn't asked. She had always thought that Burt had been hurt when his partner of so many years up and left suddenly and without warning, four weeks or so after Jeff Pritchard's arrest.

Tess had been a young teen, suddenly struggling to maintain friends when it had never been a problem. Her parents said the move was because of the attention they were getting, to get away from the circus, although by the time they'd made the move out west the media swarm had all but stopped. Not completely, but close enough that it shouldn't have mattered. The reporters were no longer hounding them; her father and Burt weren't on the news nightly. But they pulled up stakes, moving from a distilling town they'd always loved until so much evil got dug up and fears surfaced.

Tess felt it then as she did now—somehow they'd moved because of her.

That need to protect.

But from what? What had she done? Those were the memories now lost to her—the ones Justin knew were in there hiding—not everything during that time when Jeff Pritchard was arrested, but clearly enough to do damage.

I don't need to be fucking fixed, Justin, she'd once screamed at him, not able to admit to herself at the time that her anger was at least partly stemming from the fact that he wasn't wrong.

"River's high tonight," her father said, luring her back to the present.

The Pattee River snaked behind their cabin in Lolo. Her father liked to sit on the back porch and drink his morning coffee, black, and listen to the water move.

"You okay, Daddy?"

A long pause. "Nothing like they'd ever seen before. The execution." He took another drink. "That's what my insiders said. Took three cranks of voltage to send him back to hell."

Tess had a hard time remembering her father before that arrest—only that he had used to smile more—but Mom said what he'd seen in that house changed him for good. He'd begun to drink more and sleep less, and when he did manage to close his eyes, the nightmares would wake him up. That went on for years after, waning over time but never going away.

Mom said he'd had a nightmare last week.

Tess let him talk, because he rarely did.

"They said some of the people in the viewing room threw up. The governor turned pale as a sheet, and then the warden laid into him, and they argued right there in front of everyone. Should have never churned up Old Sparky again." *Another drink.* "And the smell. On the phone, my guy . . . he said he couldn't get over the smell. Thought he might never could."

Ice clinked in an empty glass again. Karen felt queasy. This conversation wasn't good for either of them. "How about we talk tomorrow? I'll bring Julia out to the cabin. Maybe a pizza from Tony's."

"I'd like that. So would your mother." He paused. "How's Justin?"

"Justin's Justin." She hoped he wouldn't ask for more because she wasn't prepared to give it. Justin and Leland had always gotten along—Justin got along with everyone—bonding from day one like frat brothers over sports, Leland the father figure Justin never had. Truth was, her father had been pissed when he'd heard what Justin had done, but not pissed *enough* for Tess's liking. He'd told her more than once to remember that she wasn't married to the job. That she spent too much time working and not enough with her family. Like his affair was somehow partly *her* fault.

Just when she was about to say goodnight, he said, "It was the best thing for all of us."

At first, she thought he was talking about Justin's affair—and his *it was one time and I was drunk and it meant nothing* argument—but realized he'd gone back to before. "What was?"

"Us moving out here."

He left it at that. Didn't explain why and she didn't ask. More fodder for tomorrow when the sun was out, and the bourbon bottle was topped.

"Love you, Daddy."

"Love you too, Sugar." She was about to hang up when his voice caught her. "Tessa?"

"Yes?"

Nothing.

He was wrangling, holding back something. *Stop trying to protect me.* She was about to end the call when he said, "He talked."

"What? Who talked?"

"Pritchard. He had a few last words."

She sat up in bed. "What did he say? Dad?"

"We'll . . . we'll talk about it tomorrow, Sugar. Goodnight."

He ended the call.

She finished her bourbon.

Didn't sleep all night.

4

Lisa Creighton slept with a shotgun next to her on the bed.

Hoped she wouldn't have to use it, but figured she might.

She'd refused to watch the news in the days building up to the execution of Jeff Pritchard. It all brought about too much anxiety.

Too much stress.

And too many in the small town of Twisted Tree already thought she was crazy, living in this house, after all that had been found in it seventeen years ago. Would have thought her crazier still, had it not been for the picture the newspapers had posted when she'd bought the place years ago. She was what many considered an attractive woman. In her forties, but already a widow. What the papers had called southern genteel, even though she'd always heard that term used to refer to a gentleman instead of a woman.

But if Jeff Pritchard was executed at midnight, as was reported through the grapevine, then it surprised her none that the first rock came through her living room window at 12:01. Followed soon by laughter and the sound of some other things that weren't so heavy colliding against the façade of her house.

Her house.

Not his anymore.

Damn kids.

They took off as soon as she opened her front door and fired a shot into the trees, speeding off on their four-wheelers and bikes, and a few of the faster ones on foot, their laughter trailing like gun smoke before dissipating altogether out near the main road.

Her front yard looking all a mess.

Eggs all over her porch. The walls. The door. One window shattered. The two dogwoods festooned with what looked like dozens of unraveled toilet paper rolls.

She waited for a beat to make sure they wouldn't come back, glad at least that the electrocution was finally over. Wondered if living in the house of a former serial killer would be easier now that the serial killer was dead.

She went inside, locked the door, and called the police.